Cathelina Duvert

The Box

a novel

The Box

Cathelina Duvert

Published by Cathelina Duvert, 2024.

THE BOX

First edition. July 2, 2024.

Copyright © 2024 Cathelina Duvert.

ISBN: 979-8990319509

Written by Cathelina Duvert.

For Manman and Daddy

Part 1
Life inside the Box

Chapter 1.

Thursday Morning, August 1, 2002

My mother didn't deserve the bouquet of flowers I bought her, but I placed them on her gravestone anyway. I hadn't visited her gravesite since her funeral just one year before. But that's all it was, a gravesite. My mother's spirit was not there.

The gray marble stone that had been chiseled to resemble a book had an image of a scale inscribed on it with my mother's name, Dolores Hill, largely and boldly etched beneath it. The words "Loving Wife and Mother" were also carved on the stone, just below her name, only those words were not as prominent. I questioned why those words were even considered for her headstone; nothing about it was true. Not in my experience, anyway. In fact, looking at the arrangement of the pink petunias and yellow marigolds that I had placed upon her grave, I could hear my mother's voice criticizing my choice.

Actually, it wasn't so much a choice as it was some imperceptible impulse to focus on those very flowers in the back of the flower shop that morning. For some reason, those were the ones that stood out to me the moment I questioned why I even bothered to buy flowers for a woman who criticized me and my choices my whole life. In my hurry, I had not questioned why those flowers were presented to me. As the florist arranged them together, he noted something about the unlikely brilliance the combination made.

Seeing them there now at her gravestone seemed wrong. In fact, it seemed wrong for me to even be there. Maybe I was there because I thought it was the right thing to do on the anniversary of her burial.

My watch beeped. 10:30. I sighed, knowing I had to meet my boyfriend Derek for lunch in Manhattan and I wasn't sure how the trains were running from Brooklyn. I looked at the flowers again. No, she did not deserve them.

With a strong desire to discard them on my way out of the cemetery, I picked them up from where I had placed them. I held them close to my chest before placing them back onto her gravestone. She did not deserve them but something inside me had compelled me to bring them for her so I trusted that instinct. There were still so many conflicting feelings about my mother that stormed inside of me. I wanted to understand her but that meant visiting with my father and my sister Nancy, both of whom I had not seen since my mother's funeral the year before. It was too much for me to think about so I opted to leave the cemetery. Instead, my focus was on how I was going to finally break up with Derek.

Chapter 2.

Thursday Afternoon, August 1, 2002

I sat across from Derek at a table set for two. He had on one of his tailor-made Italian suits. I wasn't familiar with many of them, but I always liked the way that particular one made him look. The dark blue, pin-stripe suit somehow elongated his already lean physique, making him appear taller than the six-foot man that he was. His suit jacket was hanging over the back of his chair, forcing me to notice the crispy white shirt that complemented his dark brown complexion. His small, fierce brown eyes stared at me impatiently. He knew why I had invited him to lunch during one of my busiest days at the office. As a successful publisher and founder of Jones Press, his own publishing company, I knew how valuable his time was also.

The restaurant was called Alimento Del Alma. Located on Thirty-Seventh Street, Alimento was almost always crowded during lunch hours. The food was delicious, the service was quick and the quaint Dominican style paintings and decor welcomed everyone into a true cultural experience. I knew I wouldn't have any lunch that day. Lunch was not my purpose for being there.

I spent a great amount of time working up the courage to tell Derek what I needed to and therefore had to be particularly careful with the words I chose to convey my decision. Derek had an uncanny way of making me doubt myself whenever it came to my feelings for him. As far as my work at the magazine was concerned, I was a powerhouse. But get me alone in the room with Derek, and I became a meek child who lost all ability to stand her ground when I felt this vulnerable.

"So, this is it, huh?" he said with a stalwart attitude that I found intimidating. He sat with one arm over the back of his chair and one leg crossed over the other. He was cool; even while he was being dumped, he was the coolest guy I knew. He was no different from the first day that I had met him five and a half years earlier at a black publishing conference in Chicago. I was twenty-three years old. My friend Glory and I had attended the conference together. Besides Derek being one of the keynote speakers, what first attracted me to him were his eloquence and confidence. I remembered how he walked through the conference auditorium with an air of quiet modesty as he greeted everyone with a firm handshake. I noticed him and the way he moved even before he approached Glory and me as we discussed a featured memoir that we had both recently read.

Yes, he was the same confident man who instead of cordially asking me out that first night, boldly suggested that we have dinner together. Sitting with him now, he had the curious ability to confuse me simply with the way he remained so self-assured. The more confident he seemed to be, the more I doubted myself.

I avoided his eyes. "I've- I've been thinking about this a lot..."

He stared at me with squinted eyes that made me feel uneasy. "This isn't over, Mia."

It was just like him to remain so confident, a trait which often left me feeling powerless.

He sighed as he looked down at his drink.

"Derek, it's not working," I said in a desperate attempt to convince myself once again. "We're too different; you know this. We're both always working. We barely even make time for each other." I paused. "We don't act like a normal couple! Things aren't going to change between us because we've been this way for years."

"But we haven't," he quickly responded. "Mia, our problems only started when you buried your mother a year ago. We weren't always this way."

"Our problems started before that. You just kept your eyes closed to it until it got worse when my mother died."

"I know you, Mia. This is your way of coping. You push the people you love away before realizing that you actually need them in your life."

I stared at him because his eyes never left mine. I couldn't allow him to confound my thoughts; I had to remind myself why I was there in the first place.

He continued. "I know that you're still dealing with your mother's death—"

"I'm not," I lied. "I'm just fine, Derek." I tried to maintain my emotional strength.

I could see that his cool demeanor was slowly melting. He looked at me with sympathetic eyes as he slumped his shoulders and reached to hold my hands. "You're not, Mia. Let me help you. You know I'm always here for you. All you have to do is say the word."

I slowly pulled my hand away in an attempt to maintain my composure. I needed to end it, but I felt myself backing down. I suddenly questioned why I was doing this.

"You must be the strongest person I know. But even strong people need time to break down. You haven't given yourself that time, Mia." He said it with so much confidence.

Derek was someone who could never be destroyed: someone who wasn't bamboozled by my inability to stick to a decision when it came to matters of the heart. I had to go before I changed my mind.

"That's not what this is about," I said, standing up to walk away.

Then, in a pleading tone, he said, "You are more like your mother than you want to be. The sooner you come to terms with that, the sooner you can work at being happy, cause you're not happy, Mia."

Now, why would he say something like that when he was trying to win me over? I looked down on him. "I have to get back to work, Derek. Thanks for understanding." Aware of the tightness in my chest, I wanted to leave before Derek could see that I was actually not okay.

"Alright." He lightly grabbed my arm as he stood up. I turned to look up at him. His cool disposition was as strong as ever. He was weakening my resolve. And there was nothing I could do to stop it.

"But once you walk out that door," he said, "you know you'll never see me again. Are you sure that's what you want? Are you ready for that?"

I hesitated. It was happening. I felt myself giving in. The finality of it. No, that wasn't what I really wanted. The tightness in my chest reminded me just why this was so challenging for me. I softened my attitude and sighed, avoiding the arrogance in his eyes.

"We can talk this weekend," I said.

I quickly stepped out of the restaurant with relief and found myself in the midst of an afternoon sidewalk traffic jam. I took in a deep breath as I walked, realizing that my heart had been pounding from my exchange with Derek. Walking down Fifth Avenue, I tried to block Derek from my mind.

I cursed under my breath each time someone bumped into me. I had gotten used to all the bumping and pushing, but I guess my interaction with Derek made me extra sensitive and compelled me to take notice.

When I first came to Manhattan to attend New York University only seven years before, it was frightening and intimidating. I felt as if the hordes of people who had as much right to be there as I did were deliberately trying to invade my space as I walked through the city's densely populated streets. I didn't think I'd become so comfortable with it so quickly, becoming a part of what made it so intimidating. Growing accustomed to its fast pace, its distinctive fashion trends, and its multicultural richness, I simply experienced a great sense of belonging.

But my sense of belonging to the city also included a need to blend in, to the point where I would pass unnoticed. Though attention at work was necessary to help others understand how important I was to the company, I wanted to live my life in Manhattan as an inconspicuous being. I was part of city life, just like everyone else in Manhattan, no more or less important than the next person. My work regarded me as significant; that was enough for me.

My rush through the city streets quickly transformed into a relaxed trip, now walking at a moderate stride as a result of the environment forcing me to live in the present. I took in the distinctive salty-sweet aroma of peanuts and cashews roasting in the cart usually positioned on the street corner, inviting passers-by to stop and gratify their sudden cravings. I slowed down to admire the imagination it took to create such fabulous window displays for the stores and boutiques carrying professional and casual clothing. Despite all the appetizing eateries that made up a large part of the community, I took notice of all the street vendors selling their own types of foods, forcing my way through the crowd of people who waited for the food cart that sold Halal meals.

Fresh Voices, The African American Magazine for the Arts, where I was the Executive Director, was housed on the seventeenth floor in the large office building on 23rd Street. My first days there as an Editorial Assistant were intimidating. There was so much to learn and I felt like an irrelevant nobody in a sea of notable decision makers who brilliantly put out content they impressively knew people were hungry for. My success at *Fresh Voices* could easily be attributed to Derek. I had just started working at the magazine when we first started dating. He had given me suggestions on how to increase my presence in the office, which later helped me move up from an unknown editorial assistant at *Fresh Voices* to one of their top research assistants. He listed ways that could help determine whether a particular event would be popular among which type of audience. Having a true talent in observing and identifying entertainment trends, Derek taught me how to be among the first to feature up-and-coming entertainment personalities for the magazine. Before long, I had moved up from Research Assistant to Editor's Assistant. I was soon promoted to Junior Editor and a few months later, I became one of the highly respected editors of the magazine before finally making a major leap to Executive Director—all within a span of six years. My sights were currently on the recently vacant position of editor in chief. I had a great track record with the company. Seeing how I had proved myself a worthy hire from the beginning, there was no way my boss Morgan Riley was *not* going to promote me.

Finally strolling into the building where I worked, I silently promised myself that my day would go on as if I were not still harboring the idea of breaking up with the man I had been with for the past five years.

But my mind failed to cooperate as I stood at the elevator bank amidst a crowd of other professionals waiting for their lift to their respective floors. A thought, a memory was imposed upon me: my first date with Derek Jones the very night we first met at the black publishing conference in Chicago.

We had both been amazed at the fact that we lived fairly close to one another in Manhattan. Always looking for a sign to inform my decisions, I had made up my mind that serendipity had pushed us together.

"Isn't that something?" I had said. "We live only a few blocks from each other and it took us coming out all the way to Chicago to finally meet."

It was his suggestion to meet for dinner that night and, after witnessing his presentation at the publishing conference, I felt like I'd be a fool not to agree. As one of the keynote speakers, he had stood at the podium earlier in the large auditorium, talking about how he started Jones Press from his parents' basement and how he grew that company with patience and drive into the successful publishing house that it was, filled with opportunities for up-and-coming writers and those new to the workforce. I wasn't sure if it was his determined spirit that captured my attention that evening or if it was his deep brown skin, his powerfully lean physique, and his six-foot stature that mesmerized me. My goal was to get to know the striking man and pick his brain.

I was suddenly thrown back into the present as people shoved their way past me to step into the elevator. I, too, made my way in as I pushed the memory from my thoughts. I couldn't allow myself to think about him or our conversation anymore. Thinking about him would only make me emotional and there was no room for any of that in an office where men looked for any reason to keep a woman down where they thought we belonged.

Stepping out of the elevator, I made my way through cubicles and groups of people conversing about the details of their work. I walked past my assistant's desk and gave a quick hello as I reached for the door to my office. I felt that my assistant was trying to get my attention but needing to be in a private space to gather my thoughts, I didn't stop to see what she wanted.

Upon opening the door and entering, I found my friend Glory Williams sitting at my desk, her left elbow propped on the chair's arm rest, reading a book that rested on her right leg, which was crossed over her left leg. She made herself quite comfortable and showed no shame for it. She flashed a smile at me in a way that reminded me of how she liked to use her beauty to her favor. She was actually quite stunning. Her big, brown eyes with perfectly shaped eyebrows and long lashes simply added to her beauty. However, her small round nose, high cheekbones, thick lips and her smooth skin the color of golden honey were actually her best physical attributes and she was very aware of that.

Glory and I had met when we both attended NYU in Manhattan. We both had been accepted into the master's in publishing program and thus found ourselves in many of the same classes. It took me over a year to warm up to her. I wasn't quite sure what it was about me that she liked so much. But she clung to me as good friends are inclined to and she grew on me. This was especially true after an incident in my dorm room. She interrupted a desperate moment in which I almost did something so utterly irrevocable.

It was something whose memory I was quite successful at blocking from my everyday thoughts.

Glory lifted her head from her book and smiled at me. She looked better every time I saw her. Men liked her thickness, and she used her voluptuous body to her advantage. Her dress suit ended just above her knees and the high-heeled slip-on shoes she wore looked so good with her outfit that even I became conscious of the simple white sleeveless blouse and dark blue dress pants I threw on. Her brown, wavy curls fell just at her shoulders and made her look more like a classy model than the vulgar, nonfiction literary agent that she was.

To the right of the doorway was a small beige couch on which I placed my bag. The sun shining through the window to the right was beaming down on the couch. Only a couple of feet from the door, two matching armchairs with fabric cushions were placed directly in front of my rather large and chaotic desk. I hadn't realized how messy I was with all of my papers, unopened mail, and a few past issues of the magazine strewn all over my desk. Even my desktop computer seemed to grow different color post-it notes all around the screen. The only thing that seemed to be in order was my bookcase that stood to the right of the desk. I populated it with books on writing journal articles, magazine publishing, how to write articles for the Internet—basically books that had helped me throughout my career.

"Okay..." I said warily as I sat on one of the chairs. "What are you doing here?"

She had been reading a book by the popular African American novelist Patrick Jerome, Derek's most successful author. His style of writing, which consisted of beautifully executed plots, characterization that was well thought out and an impressive attention to detail, always followed by shockingly tragic, yet very realistic endings had won him fame with his first novel a few years before. Glory was not a fiction reader; I assumed the only reason she even had the book in her hand was because she had recently met the author. She closed her book, fixing herself upright on the chair.

"Why the fuck don't you ever return my calls?" she blurted.

Glory's constant use of vulgarity took getting used to. I had to admit that I had my moments where certain obscene words seemed the best choice to express a particular feeling, but Glory simply could not function without the use of profanity.

"What are you talking about?"

"Tyrese *fucking* Black."

I smiled. "Okay. Who is he?"

"A *god*." She said it as if she were really serious. "Oh! You should see this man, Mia. What I would do to him! You don't understand. Sex just pours out of him." She closed her eyes and stretched her arms in a contemplative meditative pose. "He is the kind of man that could make you forget your own name if you stared long enough into his eyes..."

Whoa. Glory prided herself in always having the upper hand in any dealings with men, both professionally and romantically; to have her describe this Tyrese Black as a man who could make a woman lose herself was a very big deal.

"Ooh! You got yourself a new guy?"

"Ugh!" she groaned. "I wish!"

"Well, then, get to the point. Why would I care about this man?"

"Because he's a painter. And I know you guys are always looking for new talent and shit for your magazine. I think you'll like his work. You see the cover of this book? This is his work."

"Really?" I said, taking the book into my hands. "I always liked the covers of Patrick Jerome's books." The artwork was beautiful, the colors bright and vibrant. The artist somehow made his painting look like an actual photograph of a woman hiding her presence behind a wall from a man throwing blood-stained clothing into a large metal trash can. The look of rage on the woman's face was clearly visible as the man conveyed a look of deception and crookedness. "Hmmm... I wonder why Derek never mentioned him before. He must have met this guy if he does the art for all of Patrick Jerome's books."

"Derek is probably jealous. That's how fucking delicious this man is."

"Oh please. Derek? Jealous? And since when are you interested in the art of painting?"

"Oh, my goodness!" she exclaimed. "Since never, Mia. Tyrese *fucking* Black. Why can't you follow what I'm saying?"

I smiled. "Thank you, Glory. I don't know what you do in your office, but here I actually have work to do."

"Is this the way you repay me for what I did for you back in college?"

For some reason, Glory always felt the need to bring up what happened back at NYU, as if she wanted to remind me that I owed a debt to her. It aggravated me but in an attempt to avoid discussing the matter any further, I always let it slide.

"I never asked for your help, Glory," I forced a smile. "Please remember that. It's because of you I know what the inside of a psych hospital looks like and why I had to start seeing a therapist in the first place." Why did I even have to remind myself of that horrific time?

"Oh, get over it, already! First of all, stop placing blame on others by discounting your role in events. Secondly, you might as well not be seeing your therapist since you don't even take what she has to say seriously."

"It's a little more complicated than that," I said, hoping she'd back down and not continue any talk of my therapy sessions.

"It always is," Glory responded. "I hope it's complicated because you're over everything that caused your little college episode and not because it still lingers…"

Because she was blunt and sarcastic about everything she encountered, I always hesitated to talk to her about my depression, the reason why I suffered a dark moment in college that led to years of therapy. She didn't know the full extent of what I experienced as a result of it and I preferred it to stay that way.

"Please," I said, laughing it away. "It's so over that no one needs to even know that it ever happened."

"Not even Derek?" she challenged.

"Nope!" I said without hesitation. "And, once again, no one needs to know."

She eyed me curiously. "Interesting," she said, playfully. Standing abruptly, Glory retrieved her belongings from the other armchair, placed her jacket on her arm and secured her purse on her shoulder.

"Here's his business card," she said, throwing the card on my desk. "Listen to my message when you get a moment. Think: Tyrese *fucking* Black. He'll be in your next issue, guaranteed." She walked towards the door. "By the way, your man gets better looking every time I see him. Delicious. You better watch out before I take him away from you."

"When did you see him?" I asked.

"Saturday," she smiled. "I had a lunch meeting with him to talk about a personal development book by one of my authors. Didn't he tell you?"

I assumed a defensive position in response to the unexpected pang of jealousy that I suddenly experienced. "Believe it or not, Glory, we don't share every little thing that goes on in our professional lives."

"Well, I did ask him to say hello for me. I think it's kinda strange he didn't mention it." She opened the door to leave. "Anyway, tell him I said that next time, we'll try the new restaurant at Union Square. I heard good things about it. See ya!"

I didn't know when it happened, but I had just become a messenger.

Glory was a noteworthy character. She was the last out of eleven children. As the last child, Glory didn't experience an emotional relationship with her parents. Her older siblings practically raised her, and they had done so with contempt. She joked about not having a real relationship with her parents, but I believed it was that kind of attention she craved when she started having sex at the age of eleven with much older boys. For as long as I had known her, Glory never had a steady boyfriend but was never without a man.

That was why there was no doubt in my mind that she must have already slept with Tyrese *fucking* Black. It made sense. She could not have possibly come all the way to my office to talk up a painter when she wasn't at all a fan of the visual arts.

I decided to do what Glory suggested. I called in to listen to my voice messages. Hers was indeed the first one.

"Hey, girl, it's me. Just calling to tell you about this fine-ass man I met through the author Patrick Jerome. Mia, this man is so fucking fine. His name's Tyrese Black, and he's actually a pretty great painter. I was just wondering if you wanted to help a brother out and visit his gallery and possibly do a little story on him. His number is 212-555-0100, or you can just call me at work. I fucking told him about you, so you better have the damn decency to drop him a line. I'll call you some other time, okay? Bye, girl. Give my love to that beautiful man of yours. Oh, and don't be such a stranger. I might surprise you one day."

I chuckled. Had she not been so interested in Tyrese Black, she would have never asked me to do a story on him, no matter how great his work was.

Our October issue did need a feature story, and the fact that this Tyrese Black was not yet a mainstream discovery would be in our favor. I looked at the business card Glory threw on my desk and found his website address. The Powers Gallery. I checked it out.

What appeared on the screen was a fascinating combination of bright colors and powerful-looking African Americans in realistic-looking fantasy images: athletic women rescuing men from demons; men caring for their beauties, and children happily interacting with dangerous animals. There was also an entire section dedicated to black women in what seemed to be a collection of paintings following a specific theme. These were the works belonging to Mr. Tyrese Black. A picture of his chiseled face appeared on the lower right side of the screen. His skin was light brown, and his hair was cut low, close to his scalp. He was as good-looking as Glory boasted. I clicked on his picture and I was brought to a screen with a brief biography.

He started painting at the age of fifteen, and sold his first major piece for two thousand dollars at the age of twenty-three. His personal situation was typical for a young artist. He was a single, twenty-nine-year-old painter living in a brownstone in Williamsburg, Brooklyn. What was not so typical was the fact that he owned his own gallery in the heart of Chelsea. His biography explained that he worked at the gallery as the manager for eight years until the owner, who was very fond of him and the work he produced, died only one year before and left the gallery to him in his will.

I saw it already: *Brooklynite painter's rise from obscurity with the aid of his late mentor.* According to his biography, Tyrese took advantage of his ownership of the gallery to feature his own work. He quickly received a favorable response from the people who had been his customers when he used to sell his work from an apartment in Brooklyn. Through his shows at the gallery, Tyrese not only won new customers but gained many admirers as well. What kept the gallery open was not only his work but the works of the other local artists he exhibited.

I decided to give him a call and perhaps plan a visit to his gallery. When his machine picked up, I left him a message introducing myself and asked him to call me back at his earliest convenience.

Chapter 3

Thursday Evening, August 1, 2002

I stepped into the luncheonette on the corner of Third Avenue and East 73rd Street in Manhattan. On days that I didn't feel like cooking for myself, I'd pick up my usual grilled salmon avocado quinoa salad in the 50s-style diner. I liked it because the servers there were extremely friendly, and the food was amazing. But the most important feature of all was its convenience, located just a few feet away from my apartment building on East 73rd Street. The apartment had been my home since my boss at the magazine, Morgan Riley, hired me as an Editorial Assistant six years before when I was twenty-two. After Derek and I celebrated our second anniversary, he thought that it made sense for him to move in with me. However, I resisted, coming up with several different excuses why I was not yet ready to take our relationship further. *I'm too selfish*, I'd tell him. *Our relationship works because we give each other space. Statistics show that moving in together before getting married contributes to divorce.* The last one I wasn't sure about but he didn't fight me on it. He chose his battles.

Derek wanted us to get married and he used to mention it quite often. He never formally proposed but would often verbally insert me into his future plans for a large house and at least two kids. I assured Derek that my hesitation to marry him had nothing to do with him but with personal issues I could not discuss. The truth is that it was both. I just could not see myself being with him forever and the possibility of projecting my own past trauma onto my children terrified me. My disappointment in not yet being ready for marriage surprised me, knowing that opportunity was not the reason.

My therapist, Dr. Flare, agreed that there were too many emotional issues to resolve before I even thought about spending the rest of my life with someone. I never told Derek about my depression, the unfortunate incident in my dorm room, my brief stay at a psychiatric hospital where I was diagnosed with clinical depression or about the therapist I had been assigned to. How could I? Even Glory didn't take any of it seriously, chalking it up as an impulsive decision based on what one person did to me. If she never understood the depth of my despair, I didn't expect anyone else to, least of all Derek. As a result, I questioned my relationship with him. I never quite understood my need to hold onto him.

Feeling emotionally disconnected from Derek, I broke up with him three years into our relationship. I was comfortable with the decision until I started to feel desperately lonely and deeply depressed a few weeks later. He called one day to see how I was doing, and I simply broke down. I took him back into my life. My emotional dependence annoyed me; I didn't want to be that woman who clung to her man in order to feel whole. But that's exactly what I felt with him at the time. Whole.

What surprised me about Derek was his willingness to accept my terms for the relationship. He never asked me to move in again; nor did he ever mention getting married again. It confused me into thinking he was indeed the man for me. I felt like he understood the kind of relationship I needed.

I stepped into my one-bedroom apartment on the second floor of an old walk-up and set my things on the small end table by the couch. Taking my shoes off, I walked barefoot on the cold wooden floor before allowing my body to fall down onto the couch. My apartment was tiny, but I loved the comfort that the small space gave me. The entrance door opened into the minuscule living room area and to its left was an even smaller open kitchen, which I rarely used. Further beyond the living room to the right was my bedroom with an adjacent bathroom.

I picked myself up from the couch and, in the kitchen, poured my salad from the luncheonette into a bowl and fixed myself a glass of white wine. It was the brand my mother loved and I grew to love it too. I took a sip as I walked back to the living room, with the bowl of salad in one hand and my glass of wine in the other, and sat back down on the couch by the armrest. After placing the glass on the coffee table, I proceeded to sit back and exhale. It felt so good to relax and just do nothing. I took a few large bites of my salad, not realizing how hungry I actually was.

I stared at a framed painting that was leaning against the wall directly opposite me, sitting on the floor next to my large screen TV. The painting was of an African American woman, desperately grabbing her head as if the source of her pain lived there. She was crouched on the floor, with her legs held close to her body in a fetal position. That was how I often felt, like a helpless baby despite my need to feel in control of my life and feelings. The woman in the painting looked tormented. She lived in her own little box. Just like me.

My mother had gifted that painting to me only one month before she passed away. I didn't quite understand her gesture at the time, dismissing it as a quiet rebuke of how I had alienated myself from the family, especially from her. I accepted it, yes, but I never quite found it within myself to hang it on the wall—a sign, perhaps, of a resentment I had carefully nurtured over the last few years.

Setting my salad bowl aside, I walked to the coat closet by the front door and reached inside to retrieve a rather large cardboard box. Back on the couch, I opened the box. In it, there was a bright, yellow notebook with a cartoon image of a smiling black woman proudly displaying a large afro on it. My father had given it to me when I was in college because the smiling woman had reminded him of me. Though I was not yet wearing my natural, kinky curls at the time and I hardly ever smiled, he assured me that it was the notebook and pen she held in her hands that reminded him of my love for writing. I probably only used about four sheets of it.

Taking the notebook and putting it aside, I began to sift through the award-winning stories, poems and novellas that I had written when I was in college—stories of identity and self-acceptance; of race relations in our communities; and of the importance of a strong family unit—work that had been suppressed due to my mother's twisted guidance. My very first story that ever won an award highlighted a fictional account of how two young girls' complaints about a disrespectful generation of adolescent black Americans were justified through the actions of a young man under the influence of alcohol. I was proud of the work I had created, and all of my writing professors supported my work and tried to encourage me to pursue a career in literature. My entries in college writing contests and even state-wide literary contests always came in either first or second place. My work consistently appeared in the school's literary magazines as well as small anthologies and amateur literary magazines across the states. Writing was my life. I envisioned a life of fame with bestselling books that would be made into films. I would be a peer of other literary stars and win prominent book awards. Of course, my dreams may have been childish, but success begins with one small dream, a dream my mother didn't believe in.

I still remember my last interaction with her regarding my work. She was in her office one evening working on one of her cases involving reproductive rights for women. I had told her that I finally declared Creative Writing and Literature as my major. She carefully put her pen down, turned away from her computer screen and looked into my eyes, telling me that she would not pay my college tuition if that was the route I decided to take. It felt like a blow to my heart.

"Mom, I have a chance to impact the world through my writing," I responded, trying to plead my case.

"Writing stories does not impact the world, Mia. They are just stories. Why don't you use your writing talent as a political journalist, a school curriculum developer, a grant writer for nonprofit or advocacy groups? I don't know! Think bigger! You have a talent that can be very effective in helping disadvantaged people improve their situations. Why don't you do that?"

"Because that's not where my interest is." I was exasperated. "And you're wrong. Stories have the potential to impact people's imaginations and emotions and inspire them towards making decisions that empower themselves as well as the people that surround them. Stories have existed just as long as language has because it impacts the world. And even if it didn't, why can't you just support what I love to do?"

"You're asking me to do something that goes against everything I believe in. I'm sorry, Mia. Do what you will, but I can't support you." She said it with such a coldness in her tone that I couldn't understand where her contempt for me was coming from.

"What about Nancy?" I challenged.

"Your sister is still trying to find her way in the world. And once she does, I'll guide her, too."

I scoffed. "This is what you call guidance?"

"I'm done discussing this, Mia. I won't turn this into an argument."

That was her calm and quiet dominance over me and my aspirations. The way she spoke to me enraged me, yet I felt I had no voice because hers was so definitive, so authoritative, and so final.

Alas, I gave up on my dreams in order to win my mother's approval, the very thing I craved from her as a child. I failed to realize at that time how toxic her judgment was, like weeds threatening the life of a thriving flower by attempting to stifle its growth. I would have done anything to make her happy, but all I did was never enough. I decided instead to apply for the publishing program at NYU. My mother approved that decision but still harbored an insistence on maintaining her contempt for me. As desperate as I was for my mother's approval, which I wrongly confused with her love for me, I felt that I was meeting her halfway while still being true to myself.

I looked again at the painting my mother had given me. Yes, it was my resentment of her that prevented me from hanging it on the wall. Somehow, hanging it up meant that I had forgiven her of all the pain she caused me when she was alive. But leaving it there on the floor against the wall somehow brought me comfort. After all, my mother gave it to me. That was enough for me to keep it where I could look at it and contemplate it whenever I wanted.

Carefully standing to my feet, I placed my glass of wine down and walked over to the painting. I picked it up and studied the brush strokes. It was an original. At the bottom right were the initials TB. The dark blue background, the woman in agony, her pained expression—it drew me in and I felt comforted. It was no longer because it was a seemingly sentimental gesture from my mom—a woman whose many characteristics never included sentimentality. It was because I finally felt like someone understood my pain. I felt like the artist, this TB, reached into my heart, into my soul and found the thing I had been suffering with all of my adult life. It was almost as if I no longer needed to suffer alone.

I held the painting against my chest and almost immediately felt the need to exhale as I did so, releasing a sadness that had made its home in the pit of my stomach. I looked at the painting again and made the decision to finally hang it up. On the wall above my television screen, there was a smaller painting of a dirt path surrounded by trees and leading to a vast body of blue water and a fading sunset. That was going to have to come down. I dragged a chair from around the living room table and pushed it directly in front of my TV. Picking up my mother's painting, I turned it over to see where the hook was for me to mount it on the wall. And then I saw it. Tucked away inside the bottom left part of the frame was a piece of paper folded into a small square. I had never seen it before. I dislodged the paper, carefully placed the framed painting on the floor and unfolded the paper to find my mother's handwritten words: *"Someday, I hope to tell you the whole truth. Maybe you will forgive me for suppressing your dreams. And if I don't get the chance, I need you to know the truth. Look for it in my small wooden box."*

My chest tightened, and the pounding and racing of my heart filled me with a slight panic. I stared at the words, reading them over and over again as if they would produce an explanation for them, a reason why my mother would have written them to me. It took me a few seconds to realize that I was struggling to catch my breath. Suppressing my dreams? Forgive her? The words repeated in my mind as I tried to make sense of them. Did my mother secretly acknowledge that she had been wrong about my writing? What did this mean?

A flash of heat invaded my body. My breath became short and I struggled for air. A lump developed in my throat and with that lump came tears. I suddenly craved my mother's contempt, for that would mean she was still present in this world. This discovery was significant. My mother had tried to reach out to me. I closed my eyes and clenched my teeth in seething anger for having possibly missed an opportunity to connect with my mother before she died.

Unlike all the other times I suffered migraines, there was now no warning of the agony that would soon engulf me. A fierce, throbbing pain suddenly crashed into the left side of my head. It was torture. I scrambled up from the floor and ran into the bathroom. The last thing I wanted was to experience another migraine; it terrified me. I desperately searched through my medicine cabinet, looking for my prescribed migraine medication. There was only an empty bottle. Again, I panicked. I was supposed to refill my medication when I used the last pill almost three weeks before. Why couldn't I remember something so crucial? I breathed heavily, trying to calm myself but the severe pounding against my temples made it almost impossible. Sweat dampened my clothes despite the chill that had suddenly taken over my body. I found my backup: Motrin. I took double the recommended dosage in hopes of swiftly alleviating the throbbing in my head. The pain, however, was too sharp: a drumbeat; no, more like a hammer slamming into the left side of my head without mercy. I placed my hand on my temple, as if the touch alone would help soften the sharpness of the pounding.

I spent a good part of the next hour on the floor in the bathroom by the toilet bowl, regurgitating the grilled salmon salad I had consumed earlier. My throat burned. I rinsed my mouth out with water but was careful not to swallow any of it; the soreness in my throat prevented me from doing so. After a long, unbearable hour, the Motrin finally took effect, somewhat relieving my symptoms.

Ironically the very thing that had ignited my migraine was the same thing that gave me solace for the rest of the night. I read my mother's note over and over again with the increasing desire to find the wooden box my mother referred to. It was my chance to finally understand my mother and in turn, understand myself.

Chapter 4

Friday, August 2, 2002

The many plaques, awards, and certificates on the office walls with Dr. Flare's name on them impressed me. She also displayed pictures of herself shaking hands with prominent people. The accolades were probably meant to help the therapy patient feel secure with the fact that they were to entrust their mental health to a woman who knew nothing about them except the information they provided her. Sometimes I wondered if she were even qualified to advise me about my personal decisions just because she had so many credentials. As a white woman, she could never fully understand the challenges faced by black women.

Dr. Rose Flare sat in her chair and looked at me with eyes as warm as her level of compassion. Her tight, muscular facial features were hard to look at and seemed to contradict her empathetic personality. Long, brown hair fell over her shoulders, slightly softening her look. I was indifferent at first with having a white woman as my therapist. With time, I started to wonder whether an African American woman would be better suited to help me navigate my professional and personal experiences. I wasn't sure how much Dr. Flare factored my experience as an African American woman into her advice and counsel. I just always felt that she helped me see things clearly and in a different perspective. The part of me that did not wish to do any deep exploration within my psyche welcomed this woman as my therapist, afraid of finding a black therapist who would know just how to dive into the parts of myself I wished to keep hidden.

It was a possibility that Dr. Flare had always known that I kept some of my true feelings and thoughts to myself in an effort to prevent her from truly getting to know me and the way my mind worked. A part of me was always afraid to get to the core of what caused my own inner conflict. Yet, she had the incredible ability to understand me and somehow make me feel better when the situation called for it. Although she remained firm with me throughout our sessions, her firmness was always coupled with a warmth that would become a source of comfort for me. In many ways, she was the exact opposite of my mother. That brought me comfort at first as well. But I had to remind myself that she was getting paid to hear about my problems.

"Do you believe in coincidences," I asked Dr. Flare.

"I believe in making connections between certain situations that are meaningful to us."

A yes or no response was perhaps just too simple for her.

"*I* do," I said. "Yesterday was the anniversary of my mother's burial. I guess that's why I decided to finally hang up the painting she gave me just before she died."

"The painting of the woman in a fetal position?" She had a powerful memory, always using her ability for instant recall of the smallest details. Upon further thought, maybe this particular detail wasn't exactly small. Shortly after my mother's death, Dr. Flare seemed to only want me to talk about the painting and the significance of what it meant that my mother gifted it to me. I had brushed it off as an empty gesture, but I always knew and felt that it wasn't empty at all.

"Yes, that one," I responded.

"What made you decide to finally hang it up?"

I sighed. "I don't know. I was sitting on my couch looking at it and I guess I felt it was finally time."

I reached into my purse and took out the folded piece of paper that I had found tucked away behind the frame. "When I was looking for the hook to hang it up, I found this note." I read the note to Dr. Flare and she extended her hand to take a look at it herself. She read it silently.

"So your mother *was* trying to communicate with you," she said, the tone of her voice suggesting the importance of the revelation.

"But what am I supposed to do with this?" I answered. "I've always felt unsupported; I knew what to do with that lack of support. But what am I supposed to do with this note? With the knowledge that my mother was trying to make amends before she died and I never knew it?" The lump was there in my throat and the tears wanted to escape from my eyes, but I gently shut my eyes and prevented their release.

"But this is good news." Dr. Flare stated. "Your mother must have been deeply proud of you, Mia. It's a natural instinct when a woman becomes a mother- almost out of her control. Just like the instinct to love her child and protect her child. It's what nature does to keep the species alive."

"Yes, but, she never showed any of it. Maybe because I was the older sibling, my mother always gave me a hard time. Like she somehow resented me. She hated the fact that I took up writing in college, hoping I'd use my talent in a way that really matters—her words. And you should see the way Nancy is. She used to be so sweet, always wanting to help people when they felt sad. Now? She's always angry for no reason at all. Hanging out with the wrong people. She even dropped out of school in the middle of her freshman year in college. Got herself a job at some chain restaurant, I think. My mother didn't say anything to her about that. And who got the slack for studying writing and being focused? She resented me, Dr. Flare. And I will never understand why."

Dr. Flare sighed. "It's obvious that it was very difficult for her to express her feelings to you."

"But why was it so difficult for her? Why couldn't she share her feelings?"

"Her note is a way for you to begin to understand her. She was trying to give you the answers. Read the note again aloud."

"I know what it says," I said, stubbornly, refusing to follow Dr. Flare's instructions. "The note says *'Look for it in my small wooden box.'*"

"Mia, I really think this should be discussed with your father. Maybe he knows about this wooden box. Maybe he knows why your mother was the way she was toward you. Don't you think this is an ideal opportunity to finally reconnect with your Dad? Before it's too late?"

"I don't even know how to talk to him anymore," I said, softly.

My father had always been my biggest supporter until I was in college. It was my actions that rendered him emotionally paralyzed, distant from me, as if he no longer knew how to relate or connect to me. It all happened during that fateful year at NYU when I made the stupid decision to harm myself after something one guy did that almost got me expelled. No, that wasn't true and I had to keep reminding myself of that. It was that guy's that catapulted an idea that had been brewing in my mind as a result of years of untreated emotional pain.

Of course, the school had to notify my parents and that was what terrified me. Thankfully, my mother had been busy working an important case and did not pick up her phone when they tried to reach her. My father, however, was available. He had come to the school right away to make sure I was okay. I remember crying when he arrived, his hefty figure framing the doorway to the campus medical office. In that small room, his dark skin emanated a unique luminescence that had always brought me peace. Instead of fearing his reaction to my attempt, I found relief in the comfort of his unwavering support. I felt safe enough in his presence to release my pain in the form of tears that had long ago yearned to be shed.

"Please don't tell Mom," I had asked him quietly, fearing that my mother's disappointment would leave me forever disgraced. My father hesitated, understanding my need to keep the secret from her but also probably feeling that my mother had a right to know. He hugged me as he did whenever I scraped a knee as a child, and in his strong arms, I felt a sense of safety and a reassurance that I would be fine.

I had always loved the way his large, round eyes looked at me as if I was his world. But on that day, his eyes exhibited a quiet sadness that I knew was there because of my actions. "Mia, I don't think your mother will understand what happened here today." His already deep voice contained a lower baritone that I did not recognize. "So, I won't tell her as long as you promise me to take this treatment at the hospital seriously, okay? Their help is only as good as you allow it to be for you."

I apprehensively accepted his terms and appreciated his compliance to conceal my shame from my mother. Ever since that day, I had always been so cognizant of the fact that my father and I shared something that no one else in the family would ever know. I knew it bound us in a way that should have been special. However, it left me feeling uncomfortable and distant. I imagined my dad felt the same way. Every time I saw my father after that during my infrequent visits, he'd ask me if I was taking care of myself. We both knew what he meant by that question—indirectly asking me if I was getting the help that I needed to prevent another incident. I always assured him I was, carefully avoiding any possibility of discussion about what had transpired that day and why.

"So, you start off telling him that you don't really know how to talk to him anymore." Dr. Flare suggested, bringing me back to the present moment.

I exhaled. "You know, he used to be my biggest supporter. He used to defend me whenever my mother was on my case about something I'd done." I paused. "And that's when the thing happened in college…" I allowed my voice to disappear into the air.

Dr. Flare waited for probably ten seconds but it seemed more like ten minutes before saying, "Yes. I recall you telling me that that's when the two of you became withdrawn."

I nodded. "He calls me every once in a while, just to say hi and to make sure I'm—" I raised my arms, and with my fingers, made the familiar gesture for air quotes— "taking care of myself. I know he cares but he's also a little reserved. I don't think he knows how to really talk to me."

"How's your relationship been with him since the passing of your mother? Or maybe even in the last few months?"

"Nothing's changed much. We're still very distant. I just don't feel close to him like I did when I was a kid. It's like I never knew him at all."

"Have you tried talking to him?"

"Honestly, I can't bring myself to do it," I sighed. "He has tried to reach out, he really has. But at the same time, he works hard at keeping information from me." I looked at my mother's note once again. "But I will talk to him," I said, looking at Dr. Flare. "I need to find out about this."

Dr. Flare gave me her smile of approval. "Good. Now tell me how it's going with you and Derek."

I put my hand to my head in mild frustration. I didn't know if I wanted to get into my confused thoughts about Derek. But we still had some time and I had might as well make good use of it.

"I met Derek for lunch yesterday to break up with him." I was straightforward.

"You broke up with Derek?" she asked, surprised. "Why?"

"No, I almost broke up with him. But I got weak. Honestly, Dr. Flare, do you really think he's the one for me?"

"I think he genuinely cares about you. Tell me what happened."

I sighed. I told her the whole story of how I met up with him for lunch, sure that I wanted to break up with him. But the more I stayed talking to him, the more I felt like I was making a mistake.

She pensively stared at me before speaking. "So why do you feel that you and Derek are no good together?"

My eyes searched the room, trying to find the precise words. "I feel like I have no idea what I'm doing with him. I don't always feel that he is with me because he loves me. I think that we're together because we've gotten so used to each other. Yesterday, I was so confident that nothing he could say or do would make me change my mind about breaking up with him. Then, all he did was touch my arm and give me this look and I agreed that I wasn't going to break up with him."

"What are you so afraid of if you stay with him?"

"It's not about being afraid to stay with him. I think I'm just staying with him because I'm afraid of what's out there."

"Well, do you know what's out there?"

"Yes, as a matter of fact, I do! People like my first ever boyfriend David who manipulated me into staying with him by toying with my insecurities before he plagiarized my work in school, resulting in me having to take that journalism class a second time." My heart jumped with anger as I thought about him. "At least I can trust that Derek would never do something like that to me."

"Yes, I recall David the plagiarist, the reason why you attempted—"

"No! You and Glory keep thinking the same thing." I raised my voice slightly in an effort to make my point. "He's *not* the reason why I tried ending everything. It was what he *did* that brought me to the edge. I was already having an emotionally tough year and what he did and everything that transpired after that because of it just made me...just brought me to a really low place. It felt easier than to just deal with the pain."

"I understand that," Dr. Flare said. "But the point is, your hesitation to break up with Derek needs to be explored. There's a reason besides the look he gave you and that past relationship that made you decide to stay. Explore *that* reason."

"Well, that's easy," I said quickly. "The fear of being alone. The breathtaking, mind-numbing fear that I will not have a man to call my own. And that realization terrifies me because all I want to be is independent. Why am I so afraid of being alone?"

"Do you think your feelings have anything to do with your parents' relationship?"

"In what way?"

"Think about it. They stayed in a relationship you felt they should have left. Maybe subconsciously, you feel the fear they probably felt in their own relationship with each other."

"Oh." I was impressed. "I never thought about that."

"The fact that you are unsure of your decision either way means that you need more exploration. I want you to do something for me, Mia. Make a list of all the reasons why you should be with Derek and then a list of all the reasons why you should not be with him and think about it all. Really consider everything. And come back and talk to me. Okay?"

I went home that day with a little more hope than when I'd gone to her office. I was inspired to do two crucial things. I decided that I would visit my childhood home for the first time in a year to talk to my Dad. And the second thing I was going to do was give Derek another chance, truly exploring all the reasons why staying with him was a good thing for me. At the time, I had no idea how talking to my father would change my whole outlook on how I view myself in the world, and how I should have just trusted my initial instinct to end things with Derek once and for all.

Chapter 5.

Friday Evening, August 2, 2002

The house in which I grew up in Queens had gotten old and weather-beaten. It was situated on a long and windy road directly off of Hillside Avenue in Jamaica Estates, away from the noise and traffic of that very busy area. It was only a few minutes' walk from the train station and a collection of convenience stores on Hillside Avenue. Memories of happier times with my sister Nancy came rushing into my mind. We liked riding our bikes in the neighborhood because the winding roads filled us with excitement, not knowing when a car would turn onto a street and force us to the side of the road. It was also a treat to take the walk to Hillside Avenue, where it bustled with people scurrying off the buses and squeezing their way through others to run down the steps into the subway before they could miss their trains. To the right of the local bank, one of the small convenient stores, among the strip of many, aptly called *Convenience* was our favorite because it carried the gooey-filled Twizzlers that none of the other stores did. Our walks home were usually quiet as we savored the sweetness of the candies, which temporarily made us the happiest people alive.

Presently, I stood gazing at the large brick house that I once called home. My mother had always been proud of the fact that we never covered up the dark red brick with the aluminum siding that so many of our neighbors chose to use. My mother's love for the stone inspired my own appreciation of it. The uneven texture of the brick used to feel like hardened sand underneath my fingers. To me, it formed the sturdy foundation of our house, exuding a strength and character that always reminded me of my mom's own strength and spirit.

Now, the house simply looked beaten, no longer a structure of strength but one of debility. The front gate, which had been carelessly left open, was already overtaken by rust. The walkway leading from the gate to the broken front steps was overtaken by weeds, reaching out from the cracks of the fractured pavement. The house looked spotted; the white paint that had once shone so brightly on the side panels had already started to chip away. Only the brick layering in front that I once admired remained intact, although not for long, as the grout was starting to come loose. After so many years without giving us any problems, some of the shingles on the roof finally gave up and started falling off. There were two windows on either side of the double front doors that bore at least a year's worth of dirt and grime. On the porch, the wooden bench my father loved to sit on reading his newspapers during lazy summer days for so many years was now rotting away. A small rock path that led from the side of the porch to the entrance of the back yard could hardly be seen due to the wild overgrowth that extended from the front lawn. It was so sad for me to see that the house, although still inhabited, had long been abandoned. My mother most likely stopped overseeing its maintenance long before she passed away. In a way, the house's decay mirrored my mother's declining health. What stood before me now was the result of a slow death that further helped to deteriorate it and its surviving residents.

It had only been a year since I was last there but the degradation of the place indicated that it had been deteriorating for several years. It was actually still astounding how just a couple of years of not maintaining the house because of my mother's sickness and eventual death could make it look so terrible. What was once so meticulously maintained now looked abandoned. I knew that my mother had long ago found a landscaping company she was extremely pleased with to handle the lawn and another company to deal with the maintenance of the house. Perhaps my father didn't have the heart to keep up what he probably felt was her thing. It was difficult to believe that that was the same house my mother had once been so pleased to call hers. It looked out of place in the middle of a neighborhood where fine houses drew awe and admiration from passersby. I stood by the sidewalk where the cab had left me, taking a moment to absorb every detail of the house's exterior before moving.

Using the key that I never gave up after moving out, I stepped into the bleak house for the first time since my mother's funeral. The memory of that day was etched in my mind. It should have been a time for the family to finally come together by putting aside our petty differences, using my mother's death as an opportunity for reconciliation. Instead, Nancy and I got into a fight about what she perceived as my feelings of superiority and entitlement.

I still remembered it clearly in my mind's eye. Nancy's assumption that I didn't care about my mother's suffering had rendered me unable to properly defend myself. My relief was that she didn't blurt out her accusations in the presence of other mourners who came to the house for my mother's repast. Instead, she unleashed her rancor as we unwrapped the bereavement food in the kitchen.

"After all that Mom did for you all these years, you couldn't so much as come visit her once in a while to check in on her." She had taken a tray of lasagna and placed it in the heated oven. "You think being at her funeral today and being here right now make up for the fact that you left and never even bothered to come back? Must be nice being you. At least you won't have nightmares about the way she looked during her last few weeks." She shoved past me and continued to keep busy as she arranged bite-size sandwiches on a platter.

She was right. I had no excuse. My mother was dead and all I could think about in that kitchen with Nancy was how much anger I still held against the woman. How could I have gone to visit her with so much anger still in my heart?

"It was hard for me to—"

"No!" Nancy barked. "You don't get to say what's hard because you don't know what that is. Hard is coming home every day, watching your mother who was once so strong waste away to nothing but bones. Hard is watching the mother who you desperately wished you could finally have a conversation with slowly lose the strength to even whisper to you. That's what was hard. What you did was easy." She turned her back to me and rested her arms against the kitchen sink, breathing heavily.

Of course she was going to defend our mother. Nancy had clearly been her favorite. But I needed her to understand that my staying away was an act of self-preservation and there was nothing easy about that.

"Nancy, you can't understand why I had to stay away because you're not in the right frame of mind to hear me."

"Nope," she said, turning around to face me. "You are not gonna try your amateur psychological bullshit on me. The only thing I know is that you always thought you were too good to ever come visit. You thought you were better than us. It's because of Mom you got to where you are and you don't even have the decency to acknowledge that."

Because of that last encounter, I avoided coming to the house at all. Just thinking about visiting had always brought up terrible memories of the way we grew up, and the things my mother told me. And although I did not see her during her short battle with cancer, the house remained a representation of her sickness and eventual death.

My mother had died of ovarian cancer only a year before. My father and Nancy were right there with her during her last months. Her friends, neighbors and colleagues who paid their respects at the funeral and repast shared what they knew about her last days. They told me that my father never left her side on the days before her death. That surprised me a little—knowing that they never really showed any affection for one another. But learning that kind of gave me the sense that there was something that drove them apart. It was something that grew over the years until it took all they had ever shared and made them treat each other as strangers. It was a secret my younger sister Nancy and I never knew. We never dared ask; we simply accepted what we saw.

The house was dark; perhaps my father had stepped out for some fresh air. And either Nancy was out gallivanting with her friends or closed herself off from the rest of the world in her room upstairs. I made my way to my mother's home office: the room in which she had spent most of her time when she was still alive. I walked down the dark and dreary hallway, past the bathroom, all the way to the end of the hall. It was the last room on the left. I entered quietly as if I were afraid someone would hear me.

Despite the knowledge that she did not have much time left, I never came to visit her when she was sick. In fact, my last memory of her in her office was when she was still well. It was the semester before I graduated from high school and that night, in her office working on a legal brief, she had made it painfully clear to me that she would not support my decision to pursue a career in writing.

"Mia," she had said to me without looking up from her work. Her coarse hair was neatly pulled into a ponytail, creating a small, but seamlessly round afro puff at the end of it. Her small eyes didn't quite seem to match the high cheekbones that were so prominent on her diminutive face. She exhibited a rare beauty that was as hardened as her temperament. "You are so much more talented than you give yourself credit for. So, if you decide to use that talent to create literary fantasies which will only serve people by helping them to escape their current realities instead of helping to lift themselves higher than where they are already, I will not support you in any way, shape, or form. And please don't ever ask me to."

That was the night it hit me: I decided that I needed to stop living for her approval and start living for my own. The damage had already been done, though. I was never again to write for pleasure. Instead, her disapproval of my love for writing informed my decision to major in magazine publishing. That way, I could still be surrounded by literature while attempting to help people the way my mother wanted me to.

I stepped into my mother's office and turned on a rather dim lamp on the desk. With my back towards the start of my mother's library to the left of the room's entrance, I carefully inspected the large space. The room was just as it always was. Her law books were never out of place in the wooden bookcases that lined the opposite wall across the length of the room. Her desk was directly to the right, against the wall closest to me. And directly in front of her desk was a couch that seated three people comfortably. The room looked more dismal than I had ever remembered. The walls were of a deep burgundy color that I had always liked. Now it seemed to add to the joyless atmosphere of the room, especially with the greyish-brown couch, a dark wooden chair in the corner and the heavy beige window curtains that remained closed, protecting the room from seeing any sunshine at all. I turned my focus once again to my mother's desk. Shrouded with a thin layer of dust, the desk was neat, the way my mother had always kept it, and it still held her faithful *Dictionary of Modern Legal Usage,* which was the largest item on her desk.

My mother's note had instructed me to find her wooden box. A quick review of the things on her desk proved that her wooden box did not live there. Did I actually think it would be that easy? I put my purse down on the floor and proceeded to open up all three drawers of her desk. Nothing but office supplies like staplers, paperclips, notepads, a stress ball, tape, scissors and flash drives resided in the two smaller drawers on the left. The larger drawer on the right held legal books and dictionaries as well as a catalog to an art gallery located somewhere in Manhattan. But no wooden box.

"Mia."

I jumped, quickly turning around to find my twenty-six-year-old sister Nancy sitting cross-legged on the upholstered chair that was placed in the darkened corner of the room. I hadn't noticed her sitting there when I walked in. She looked at me with cold eyes, her anger penetrating the silence of the room. For the first time in my life, I saw my mother's face in Nancy's. It was my mother's small eyes that stared back at me with the same impatience. Though Nancy's skin was darker than my mother's, she still inherited the same high cheekbones and a mouth that was now ready to challenge me with whatever I dared to say to her.

"What were you doing here in the dark?" I asked her.

"Why are you even here?" She asked with a calmness that I didn't expect.

"I have as much right to be here as you do," I answered.

"We haven't even seen or heard from you in months!" she shot back, this time with a raised tone.

"What does that have to do with anything?"

"You never even cared about her."

"Oh, my goodness! Again, with this, Nancy? Stop it!!"

"I want the both of you out of this room now." The stern voice belonged to my father. He stood tall in the darkened hallway in his uniform, a pair of navy blue slacks, and a white button down shirt with a prominent badge on the short sleeve that identified his role within the corrections department of the city of New York.

As Nancy stood up, I quickly took notice of the fact that she had gained weight since the last time I saw her. It wasn't out of control, but Nancy was always the skinnier one, with large breasts that she was known to hide. Her breasts were definitely bigger, but it didn't look as though she accommodated them with a new bra that would completely support them. I could see now how her stomach slightly protruded from the small t-shirt she had on, and perhaps it was the shorts she was wearing, but her thighs did look especially large.

She headed towards the doorway, but I stayed, picking up my bag and producing my mother's note that I had found behind the painting my mother had given me.

"That means you too," my father said to me, pointing down the hall.

My father was a large, burly man with a deep voice to match. It seemed as though his eyes had grown smaller through the years but his nose remained large, as did his mouth. His dark skin seemed to have dulled—as if to reflect what he was probably feeling on the inside. It was clear to me that he was suffering from some type of depression. The darkness throughout the house wasn't the only physical indication of that.

"Hi, Dad," I said quickly. "I need to ask you something." I gave him the paper. He took it from my hand and quickly glanced at it.

"What is this?" he said as he handed it back to me.

"It's Mom's handwriting, isn't it?" I said, refusing to take it from him. Nancy quietly stood watching in the doorway.

"Where did you get it?" he asked, his arm still extended.

"I found it with a gift she gave me before she died," I said. "You didn't even read it."

"Get out of this room," he calmly repeated.

"I have a right to know. What truth was Mom talking about?"

My father gave me a cold stare. "Trust me. I don't know anything about this. Your mother had her own secrets."

I grew desperate. "Are you hiding something from me?"

"I can't do this, Mia. Not while the pain is still so strong."

"Pain?" I said with growing impatience. "The two of you were always so cold to each other."

"And you think that meant we didn't love each other?"

"What else would it mean, Dad?"

He sighed. "You should know better, Mia."

"Not if it's never been discussed." I found myself almost hysterical and had to take in a few deep breaths to calm myself down.

Seeming agitated, he groaned and read the note quietly. Did I detect a look of familiarity in his eyes? "This is your mother's private business," he finally said, neatly folding the note and handing it back to me.

"This is important to me," I replied, hoping he'd understand through the magic of those few words. But of course, he didn't understand. It only made sense in my mind. "If there is something I need to know about Mom's actions toward me, then I have a right to know. You can't keep it away from me."

He gave me a perplexed look and sighed. "It's always about you, isn't it?"

I had to admit that those words hurt. But I'd be damned if I let him see that, especially with Nancy still watching. I walked out of my mother's office with my father close behind me. Nancy joined us in the living room. My father took a seat on the sofa and stared at us, his large frame suddenly seeming to shrink right before my eyes.

My father was changing. I wasn't used to him this way. He had always been the type of man to intimidate everyone with his stern expressions and the deep bass of his voice. His firm disposition had always demanded a mixture of fear and respect from everyone he encountered. Those aspects of his demeanor served him well as a corrections officer for over 25 years at Rikers Island Correctional Facility. But ever since my mother became sick and especially after she died, my father transformed himself into a lost and withdrawn man whose quiet grief seemed to haunt the life out of him. His threatening words were no longer threatening but filled with pain.

He kept his eyes to the floor as he asked me, "Are you taking care of yourself, Mia?"

I knew what that question meant. It was our secret code. He always worded the question that way, given the fact that I had asked him to keep my secret between us. It brought me back to that time in college when I promised my father I'd cooperate with the doctors while I stayed at the hospital for a week shortly after the attempt, what I always referred to as the unfortunate incident. In exchange, he would help me conceal my true whereabouts to my mother and sister. According to them, I would rather stay in my dorm room than ever visit home.

"Yes, I am, Dad." My response let him know that I was still seeing my therapist. He slightly nodded his head, with his eyes still to the floor.

"Still getting your migraines?" my sister smiled childishly at me.

I sighed impatiently, turning to her to say, "Yea, actually I am, Nancy. Thanks for asking. I had to renew my migraine medication just this morning because I ran out. It would've been great to have it yesterday when I had my last attack but, oh well, at least I survived it! It's so nice of you to ask me about my health, though."

She turned up the corner of her lip in disgust and annoyance.

"What does your doctor say about your migraines?" my father softly asked.

"He's not so useful," I said. "I have to try not to stress out."

My father ran his fingers across a framed 8x10 photo in his hands. Confused, I looked at the framed portrait as if it suddenly appeared in his hands because that's what it seemed like; I didn't even notice when he could have had the opportunity to grab it as he had entered the living room and sat down. Upon closer scrutiny, I recognized the image in the frame as the very last family picture we took only five years earlier at my mother's strange insistence. Nancy and I had not understood our mother's need to capture the four of us in a false display of family unity. Yet we obliged and my mother encased the result in wood and made its home above the mantelpiece across from where we sat. Instinct made me check the mantelpiece upon recognition of the photo in my father's hands even though I knew it would not be there.

"What were you two doing in your mother's office?" my father asked, as he delicately clutched the framed image.

"I go there to feel closer to Mom," Nancy said. "And you can't stop me, Dad."

He shot her a quick look.

"I wanted to find the wooden box that Mom referred to in that note." I turned to Nancy. "Nancy, please. Do you know anything about a wooden box Mom left behind?"

"Nope," Nancy said, pursing her lips together and rolling her eyes as if we were back in the fifth grade.

My father looked up at me. "I called you today at work, but they said you were at lunch."

I sighed, feeling defeated and knowing when to cut my losses. "And my assistant didn't give me my message," I said as I sat next to him, placing my bag on the floor. "Next time just ask her to transfer you to my voicemail. Or..." I reached into my bag and pulled out my business card and a pen. "Just call me on my cell phone. I just got the phone last month." I wrote down my cell phone number on the back of my card and handed it to him.

My father took it and remained silent as he read the number. Then, not knowing where to place the card, he inserted it into the corner of the photo frame and shot me a look of embittered disappointment.

"What?" I asked him.

He looked at me with confusion and anger on his face. "Don't you even want to know why I called?"

I sighed. He was feeling emotional, and I hadn't taken heed. I wasn't yet used to his new emotional cues. He was hurting. I looked away from him, realizing I messed up.

"What has happened to you, Mia?" he asked.

I sighed. "I think you know, Dad. I didn't become like this overnight. You saw the change happening in me." He needed to understand that the way my mother treated me contributed to the change in my personality. "And what about Nancy, Dad?"

"Leave me out of this," Nancy said, angrily.

"She changed too," I said, ignoring my sister. "But, you and mom never even wanted to deal with the reason why she changed. Did you ever ask her the same question?"

"Stop talking about me as if I'm not here!"

"Your mother... did the best she could..." my father softly said as he touched her face on the family picture.

In an attempt to appeal to his softer side, I took the hand that was not holding the photo and squeezed it. "I miss her too," I said.

"Yeah, right!" Nancy retorted. "You miss Mom? Yeah. So much that you went back to work the day after she died and the day after her funeral. You have the nerve coming here talking about you miss her? Just leave, Mia. We don't want you here."

What she didn't know—what I could not tell either one of them—was that I didn't go to work on either of those days. Instead, I stayed home and contemplated ideas, things I could do to myself to follow my mother into the grave.

Nancy wanted a rise out of me, but I wasn't going to give it to her. "Everyone copes differently, Nancy," I said, calmly. "You let your anger handle your emotions and I turn to my work to help me deal. At least my way is productive."

"Screw you, Mia." Her words were bitter.

"See?" I said, allowing her to realize that her reaction confirmed my observation.

"Don't be turning this around on me. You're the one who never came back."

"Some people have their own way of grieving, alright?" I shot back. "Just let it go."

"Whatever," she responded with an eye roll.

"Yeah, that's cause you got nothing left to say," I said.

At that statement, Nancy didn't hesitate to charge toward me. My heart leaped in my chest as I stood up and quickly backed away from her. My father instantly rose to his feet and stepped between us, his enormity causing Nancy to retreat.

"Did you two girls ever grow up?" my father said with disgust. "Mia, I don't expect you to fight with your sister like this anymore. You've got two years on her but you're acting like you're the younger one. And Nancy, what you need to do is calm down. Now let me talk to your sister alone."

"Fine," she said as she walked out of the room. "Just as long as she's not here when I come back. I still don't know what Derek wants with your sorry ass anyway."

"Well, that's my own damn business, Nancy, so don't worry about it," I said.

"Fine! I won't!" Nancy said as she walked out.

I shook my head at her in disgust. I turned to discover my father picking up the framed family portrait, whose glass was now cracked on the floor.

"You two have never stopped," he sighed, carefully placing the broken glass fragments onto the coffee table.

"Well, if she wants to keep acting like a child, I'm not gonna stop her."

"Listen to me, Mia. I know you have your own way of coping, but Nancy often takes your actions the wrong way. Believe it or not, she's trying to do better with herself. I think she's finally talking to someone who could help her sort out her anger issues. But you...we've only seen you once in the last few months. And it'll be a miracle if you pick up the phone to call us."

"What do you want me to say, Dad? I've been busy."

"Is that all it is or is there something more? God, Mia. Look at you. You look like you haven't had a decent night's rest in days, and you've lost so much weight since the last time I saw you. Are you sure you're taking care of yourself?"

"Yes, Dad. I promise."

"Talk to me, Mia. Is there something on your mind?"

"There is," I answered. "But you already shut me up back in Mom's office. So I'm sorry, but I'm fresh out of things to discuss with you."

He sighed, cautiously removing the large pieces of broken glass from the frame but keeping the picture there. "Your mother had her demons," my father admitted. "But she loved you girls more than she could ever show. And honestly, Mia, I don't know anything about a wooden box."

I sighed too. For some reason, that was enough for me. I grabbed my bag to go. Even though she was supposed to be in the other room, I felt Nancy's angry eyes penetrate my back and turned to find my suspicion confirmed. She was hate personified when it came to me. She was so different from the caring, intuitive girl who always picked up on the quiet suffering of others and would offer kind words of comfort that magically assuaged their distress.

"I'm exhausted," I said. "I'm going home now." I awkwardly placed my hand on my dad's shoulder. "Dad, do you want me to call someone to fix the way the house looks outside? They can fix the lawn, the bench, and everything. It could look just as pretty as it used to."

"Sometimes when things change," he said, his eyes glued to the glassless family portrait, "there's no use in even fixing them. Your mother took care of this place. She's the only one who should."

His pain was palpable. What was ironic was that my mother never physically took care of the house. She hired people to do it for her. But it was *her* thing, and it was obvious my father didn't want to take it away from her, even if she was no longer with us.

It was too depressing to stay in that place for another minute. As I walked out of the house, I heard Nancy say, "Just get your black ass outta here."

I ignored her comment. As I stepped out into the night, I thought about coming back in the middle of the day when I knew they would both be out. I had to search for my mother's wooden box while the house was unoccupied by those two individuals who were now strangers to me.

Chapter 6.

Saturday, August 3, 2002

I decided to sleep in on a rainy Saturday afternoon. I was feeling so dejected that I had no desire to get out of bed and do anything. It was just one of those days where staying in all day and not answering phone calls would be so enjoyable. The apartment was dark and somehow that, and the rain tapping against the window gave me permission to do absolutely nothing. Taking a light blanket from my closet, I decided to simply spend my afternoon on the couch all day watching one movie after another on my DVD player. And that's what I did. With a large bag of chips and some water, I wrapped the blanket so snugly around me and used the soft cushions to rest my head. I was immediately drawn into the romantic comedies and dramedies I chose to watch, imagining what I would do in the same positions as the lead characters. This was escapism in its truest form. I welcomed the absence of responsibility and acted as if the thoughts that had troubled me in the last few days did not exist. Everything was right with the world and for a moment, I actually believed that nothing could take me away from the feelings of blissful distraction from the recent issues that have plagued my life.

I was wrong. Seemingly out of nowhere, my father's words echoed in my mind.

"Your mother had her demons," he had said the night before. Instantly, my mind recalled a memory. It was the summer before starting my freshman year at NYU. I had just gotten back from work; that summer, I worked at the central library on Merrick Boulevard shelving books. I was heading to my room when I heard my parents arguing in hushed tones behind their bedroom door.

"Nancy needs you, Dolores," my father had exclaimed. "I've taken her to work with me at Rikers to show her the path she's on, but—."

"Oh, for heaven's sake, Myles! Nancy is not a criminal! She just needs guidance."

"And that's what I'm trying to give her! But there's only so much that I can do as her father. You've got to step up and talk to her too."

"Don't you think I know that?" my mother had shot back. Her voice was deep, betraying what seemed to be an insecurity about the way she parented Nancy. "I want to help Nancy with everything that I have inside of me but I just don't know how. I don't think I can."

"Why, Dolores?" My father's voice had seemed calmer then, softer. "Talk to me. What is it? What's happening with you?"

If my mother responded, it was too low for me to hear her. I risked a creak in the floorboard if I stepped closer to their door to listen to a conversation that I shouldn't have been privy to. So, I slowly tiptoed away and stepped into my bedroom.

My current movie marathon finally ceased to amuse me. I came across a film that portrayed a young woman who learned of her recently deceased mother's secret life when a long-lost daughter—her own sister whom she didn't know anything about—showed up at her doorstep. The premise contributed to the thoughts of my mother's note invading my mind, forcing me to confront something that I realized I didn't want to face. I felt it in the pit of my stomach: the dread of confronting my father again. The thought single-handedly obliterated all the feelings of relaxation my marathon had given me, coercing me to think about my own dead mother's secrets. *What did she mean when she wrote that she had to tell me the truth?* My father had insisted that he didn't know anything about what she wrote in the note, but Nancy stood there, unusually quiet. Did she receive a painting and a note just like I did? She had responded negatively and rolled her eyes at me when I asked about the box. The fact that she wasn't curious about my inquiry struck me as peculiar. Maybe she knew something but decided to say nothing.

I took my phone and dialed her phone number. She had installed her own landline in her room a few years before my mother was even diagnosed with cancer. She had insisted that no one was giving her the privacy she deserved. Of course she never shared the number with me; I had to ask my father for it.

"What do you want, Mia?" she answered.

"Hello to you too," I said.

"What do you want?"

I sighed. "I want to talk about the note."

There was a pause. "What note?"

She was playing games now. "The note I asked Dad about last night."

"I have no idea what you're talking about. I'm busy."

She hung up on me! That brat hung up on me! I shouldn't have been surprised, but I was. She was keeping something from me. I dialed her number again.

"Bitch, what do you want?" she asked angrily.

"Did Mom give you a note too? Did she give you a painting before she died as a token of apology, maybe?"

"No, fool. I don't know what you're talking about. She didn't give me anything before she died, okay? Now leave me alone." She hung up again.

Why was she so angry? She didn't even ask me what the note said. Wasn't she the least bit curious? Maybe if I read the note to her...

I dialed her number for the third time, not surprised when the answering machine picked up.

"Okay, Nancy. Please do not delete this message," I said, "I want to read you Mom's note. She wrote, 'Someday, I hope to tell you the whole truth. Maybe you will forgive me for suppressing your dreams. And if I don't get the chance, I need you to know the truth. Look for it in my small wooden box.' Nancy, please let me know if you received a note like that. Mom had given me a painting before she died and that note was in there except I only found it the other day. Just please let me know." I hung up.

I needed a distraction and decided to check my e-mail messages from work. In a quiet corner of my bedroom, I made myself comfortable in front of my computer. I sank myself into the soft cushion of my chair as I pressed the button to turn on the computer. I clicked on my America Online internet icon. My instant message window came on, indicating on my *buddy list* all of my contacts who were currently logged onto AOL. Derek was on-line; his screen name was JonesPress. There was a pounding in my chest. Was he going to write to me? I wanted him to write but was also afraid of what would happen if he did. Perhaps that moment would define where our relationship would go.

I heard the sound of a door creak open and checked my buddy list. GloryB2God had just signed on. Glory chose the perfect screen name; she did think she was God's gift to men. I didn't want to deal with her and hoped she wouldn't involve me in a chat.

I went onto the website where I retrieved my work email. But I couldn't concentrate, not while JonesPress was still online. I quickly scrolled my unopened email messages to see whether any pressing issues had to be immediately addressed. Nothing. I rechecked my buddy list; Derek was still there. Suddenly, my laptop sang, telling me I had received an instant message. My heart leaped.

GloryB2God: what r u doing 2nite?

At first, I completely dismissed Glory's screen name and thought Derek was sending me the instant message. My excitement, of course, quickly disappeared once I saw who it was.

MiaHill: Nothing. Actually, I needed you to help me with something.

I wanted to ask her to help me find my mother's wooden box. I waited for her to respond but she didn't, which I found a little odd. But it was Derek who still remained on my mind. Perhaps he was going to ignore the fact that I was online. I wanted him to write me, and I didn't. Although my mind was already made up, I still questioned myself. I was still bouncing back and forth about whether I made the right decision to give our relationship a chance. I had a gnawing feeling inside of me that my life would fall apart without him. If he decided to write, then we'd probably end up making plans to meet up to continue the discussion that started during lunch at the Dominican restaurant. After my session with Dr. Flare, I felt that I would not be opposed to it.

I stared at my buddy list, wondering if Derek would send me an instant message. Then, without so much as a goodbye, Glory signed off. Shortly after, Derek signed off as well.

Just as I released a sigh of relief, my phone rang. I looked at the number; it was Derek. My heart leaped again.

"Hi," I said. "How are you?" My mouth was dry.

"I'm good. You?"

"Tired. But other than that, I've been all right."

"Mia," he said softly into the phone. The tone of his voice made my heart stop. "Can I—can I take you to dinner tonight?"

I exhaled. Why was I so nervous? Anxiety rendered me speechless.

"Hello?" he asked.

"Thanks. But actually, I'm not really feeling well today." I honestly did not know why I said that. It was almost instinctual.

"Are you okay? What's wrong?" His concern seemed genuine and it warmed my heart.

"It's just been a long week. I'm fine," I answered.

Silence. I didn't know what else to say, but I wanted him to stay on the phone. Chatting with him made me realize that I had desperately missed him. The seconds seemed like minutes, but I welcomed them. I didn't want him to go.

"I don't want to lose you," he finally said.

My heart pounded; my mouth became dry. "Me too."

He saw an opportunity and took it. "So, what about tomorrow, then?"

Knowing full well that I was not too exhausted to go to dinner with him, I said, "I want to see you tonight, too. Is that okay? I should be feeling better by then. Do you still want to have dinner with me tonight?"

"Yes!" he said without a second's hesitation.

As soon as he stepped through the door of my apartment later that evening, we hugged each other with a passion, a fear of what we had almost lost. I couldn't tell him how much I had missed him. I could only show him through my embrace.

"Thank you for agreeing to see me tonight," he said.

Derek had made dinner reservations at an Italian restaurant on West 44th Street. He knew that I simply loved their Chicken Francese. After dinner, he informed me that we were going to my favorite dessert spot, replicating one of our first dates. He planned a superb evening for us, reminding me of the Derek I had met so long ago. It wasn't that he was so different, but his spontaneous surprises had diminished the longer we stayed together.

I didn't want it to but during dinner, the excitement of the evening was dying and I was once again reminded of our recent troubles. We ate in silence for quite some time. When we did speak, we exchanged polite formalities. Although I felt it would be difficult to say what was on my mind, I knew it had to be done. Finally, I spoke up.

"I wanted to talk about the reason why I felt the need the other day to break up with you."

"Okay," Derek said, as he placed a piece of steak in his mouth and chewed.

"It's hard for me to say." I placed my utensils on the table and gave him my full attention. He did the same. "A part of me wondered why we were together for so long if we're not making any plans to move forward."

"That's been *your* choice," Derek said quickly, like a child blaming me for making a mess of something and never going back to clean it up. "I simply wanted to be patient. You know, give you some space."

"Please, let me finish." My hands perspired, and my mouth was dry. "It's hard for me to share with you the reason why I am the way that I am. There are things you don't know and I'm sorry, but I'm not sure when I'll be ready to let you in. And I somehow feel that if I can't share certain things with you, then that means we're not meant for each other."

He looked deep into my eyes. "Nobody's perfect, Mia. We all have our issues. But just because there are certain things you can't share doesn't mean we're wrong for each other. It just means that you'll open up when you feel ready to."

"Yea, but it's been five years, Derek. When am I going to feel ready?"

"You seem to place a lot of emphasis on the amount of years we've been together. I just think of it as time that we're still learning about each other. There's no formula—not that I know of, anyway—for how a relationship should develop. There may be books on the subject or magazine articles but the fact that many of them do exist tells us that there is no one set formula. Be who you are, Mia. I've never asked for anything else."

"You don't find it troubling that I can't be a hundred percent honest with you about the way that I am?"

"No. To try to change that would be to try to change *you*. I'm not about that. I've understood a long time ago that you need your space to thrive. In the meantime, we continue to be supportive of one another and I'll be there for you once you decide to share. I'm here, Mia. I'm not going anywhere."

The flood of emotions was inexplicable. I felt the lump in my throat and the tears in my eyes. Where else would I be able to find that level of understanding from someone? I was moved by his words and felt that he didn't need to understand me fully to love me. All he needed to do was be there for me. And I wanted so much to be there for him. Yes, he'd won me over. I felt loved. And I also felt an incredible amount of love and appreciation for him.

"Thank you, Derek," I said through trembling lips. I held his hand across the table. "You have no idea how much that means to me."

His smile was one of pride. He kissed my hand before picking up his fork and knife to continue eating.

Taking a sip of wine, I thought about the events of my day and what led us to having dinner together. Then Glory's online chat made an unexpected appearance in my memory.

"Hey. I wanted to ask you," I said to Derek. "Did you chat with Glory online at all today?"

"No. Was she on?"

"Well, all three of us were online together—just before you called me to ask me to dinner. She asked me about my plans for tonight and after I responded, she just signed off without saying goodbye."

"Well, she probably got kicked off," he said, never lifting his head from his plate.

"I guess. I just thought she might have told you something like she had something to rush off for."

He sighed, finally raising his eyes from his dinner. "Let's not talk about Glory, okay?"

So, we dropped her.

That night, after dinner, we went back to my apartment and had sex. Derek liked to call what we did making love. One would think that any kind of make-up sex is better than regular sex. However, sex for us was the same as always, our usual routine. What was once so phenomenal was now commonplace. Sex with Derek had waned with each passing year. It was nothing like that first year we discovered each other. We were now so accustomed to each other's bodies that there was hardly any exploration anymore. It was as if we now had sex out of obligation to one another. Nevertheless, I enjoyed it enough that I never complained; I just took it for what it was: sex with Derek.

Although what we did that night was no different than any other time, there was something different about the way I felt afterward. We lay in bed naked, holding onto one another until the morning came. And with the morning, there arrived an unmistakable feeling of doubt and fear. I doubted whether staying with Derek was a good idea and at the same time, I feared losing him.

Chapter 7.

Sunday Morning, August 4, 2002

Derek squeezed me in his arms as he woke up. "Good morning," he said. "Hi," I answered. "How did you sleep?"

"Better than I had in a long time. I've been so stressed about work."

I had a feeling about what was troubling Derek. There was another company that wanted to merge with Jones Press. Words-in-Rhythm, Inc. was a successful black publishing and distribution company with which he was in constant collaboration. He met the president and CEO of the company in Chicago during the same conference where I had first met Derek and heard him speak. Apparently, the president/CEO was very impressed with Derek's small publishing house and wanted to know if Derek wanted to join forces with his conglomerate. That meant Derek would have to uproot what he had already established here in New York, and continue his work in Chicago. Derek had expressed his hesitance about moving to another state and deferred making a definite decision.

"Derek?"

"Yeah?"

"That publisher from Chicago—from Words-in-Rhythm —is he still proposing that the two of you merge? I know you mentioned it recently. You haven't confirmed anything with him, have you?"

He placed his arm across my stomach. "I've been stalling. They want to buy my company, not merge. I'd still be publisher of Jones Press but all the major financial decisions would effectively be out of my control. They've given me time to think about it but it's been a couple of months now. I don't know how much longer the offer will stand. I mean, if it weren't for them, I wouldn't be able to afford the book release party we're having for Patrick Jerome later this month."

Jones Press's most prominent author, Patrick Jerome, was known for his morbid, realistic writing and made Derek one of the leading black publishers in the industry. Having the release party for him almost guaranteed that his latest book would shoot to the top of many of the bestseller lists, possibly even the highly coveted New York Times bestseller list.

Derek sighed. "I just don't know yet."

"Well, what's keeping you from knowing?"

He was silent.

"What's keeping you from knowing, Derek?"

He didn't answer me; instead he carefully lifted himself off the bed and put on his pants.

Was I being selfish in thinking about how his decision for his own company would affect me and my career? As I contemplated the future, I wondered what turn our relationship was going to take. I pondered whether he would expect me to move with him if he did accept the offer. He was probably thinking the same thing; something in my gut told me that was the reason why he had not given them a response yet. The questions gnawed at me and I feared learning the answers.

"I have a lunch meeting with a potential author today," he said.

"But today's Sunday."

"I couldn't get her during the week, so I had to settle for today when we were both free. I'll just grab my things and head on out."

"You can take a shower here if you want."

He did not expect my kindness, and frankly, neither did I. With a stunned expression, he said, "Well, I have to change my suit anyway, so I might as well shower at home. But thanks for the offer."

I didn't ask myself at what point things between us had become so awkward. I knew exactly when it happened. Rather, I knew when it was happening. All Derek knew was the strong, independent woman who commanded respect from everyone around her. I liked that he saw me as a strong individual. I didn't want him to see me in any other light. That was clearly a result of my inability to be completely open with him. Therefore, my inauthenticity created our strained relationship. The question I needed to ask, however, was why he wanted to stay with me. At dinner the night before, he admitted his patience with me with finally opening up when I was ready. Why wait?

He went into the bathroom and closed the door. My heart raced. *What was happening to me?* Was it love I was feeling for him? Why did I feel so awkward in expressing that love? Why was it so difficult for me to become comfortable with the way I felt for him? Yes, I was feeling some affection for him, but I was suddenly afraid that in a few days this new feeling would vanish, and once again I would ask him to let me be.

Derek opened the bathroom door and stepped out fully dressed. He had washed his face, and I could smell mouthwash on his breath. I lifted myself up from the bed and retrieved a t-shirt from my dresser. He stopped short and smiled at me as I put it on.

"What are your plans for today?" he asked me.

"I'll probably be heading to my dad's house later. I have something I need to do." I wasn't ready to tell him yet about the note I found behind the painting my mother had given me and the box she instructed me to find.

"I'll call you later." Derek said.

"Okay." I smiled.

He reached for my hand and kissed it. "Things will get better, Mia. We'll work hard together." He hesitated to continue, looking at me as if he were a nervous boy speaking with a girl for the very first time. His expression threw me off guard. I was not accustomed to seeing him that way; he was always so confident about everything in his life. "I was thinking maybe we should go away somewhere on vacation. Just the two of us, disconnected from the world. I feel like that may be our only chance."

It was sweet. However, I didn't have the heart to tell him how stressed a vacation would make me- missing days of work meant coming back to a collection of unanswered emails and a slew of voicemail messages. I had a dependable assistant but there were things I would rather handle myself. For that, a vacation didn't quite interest me. I politely smiled. "Thanks, Derek. That means a lot."

He searched my eyes as if he were not fully convinced that I meant what I had said. Alas, he would find nothing there because I knew that my eyes offered no promise. As much as I wanted to assure him, something was blocking me from doing so.

Disappointed, and maybe even a little desperate, he softly said, "I don't—I don't know what else to do, Mia. Tell me what to do."

It was the first time I had seen him look so defeated, and it was because of me. I wanted to reach out to him but was too afraid to get hurt. I felt like keeping him at a distance was what was protecting me from being taken advantage of. True, Derek never showed me any reason to doubt his love for me. He wasn't like the boys I dated in my adolescence. No, he was a man who loved me the way he thought I needed to be loved: from a distance. He was not overbearing and never pressured me because I think he feared that he would drive me away. And now he didn't know what else to do, for I was slipping away anyway, despite our renewed courtship. I was being difficult and I didn't understand why. I couldn't even find it within me to tell him about my depression and that one night in my dorm room when Glory saved my life.

The expression on his face told me he was desperate. The night before, he was confident in his assurance that he would wait until I was ready to open up. Now, he seemed distraught. I wanted to hold him in my arms, cradle his head against my chest and tell him that I loved him. But the mere thought of that action suddenly made me feel so uneasy. It was so unlike me to do that with him—so out of my character. But I wanted to console him and there was no way of doing that without stepping outside of my comfort zone. I felt like there was nothing else I could do for him other than finally telling him my story.

"Mia, look. I want to share my life with you." He took both of my hands in his and we stood looking at one another. "And I don't want to rush you either. But we have to start opening up to each other. You have to let me in. And know that I will always be here for you. No matter what."

My heart pounded, and I thought I could hear his heart pound as well. I couldn't tell him what he wanted to hear. But a part of me felt like I needed to. Was this it? Was I finally going to tell him about the night I've tried to avoid thinking about as much as I could?

"Are you in an absolute rush?" I asked, resolving to finally tell him.

In response, he sat down on the end of the bed and watched me as I sat down beside him. I finally felt ready to tell him about that night, about what transpired when I was at NYU. I could no longer keep him in the dark.

"When I was in college," I said, carefully. "Glory saved my life."

Derek stared at me for a minute, not quite understanding how to respond to my statement. "Okay...how?"

"For as long as I can remember, I've always been depressed. I was sad, I hated myself, and I had anger issues; all the things. I didn't quite understand what it was I was feeling or even how to express myself; I was just a kid. So I kept those feelings to myself. I didn't know at the time that what I had was clinical depression; I had never heard of it before. I couldn't talk to my mother because she never seemed to have any time for me. My dad was sweet and always told me to keep smiling, but I could tell my moods made him feel uncomfortable. And I never told my sister because I was the older one. I didn't want her to think I was weak."

Derek leaned in, fully engaged in my story. "I know you get into your moods sometimes but I never thought...Well, what do you think caused your depression?"

"Oh! It was totally my parents. More specifically my mom. But that's not the point of the story," I responded.

"Okay," Derek said, cautiously.

"So, when I got into the publishing program at NYU, I was finally writing what I wanted to write, my professors believed in my talent, and I met other student writers who made me feel like I belonged. I was finally happy. I was away from my mom and I could do whatever I wanted. And that's when I met David."

"I've never heard you mention him before."

"That's cause he's not worth even my thoughts. It sickens me now that I'm even talking about him because I don't want to give him that energy." I took in a deep breath and exhaled. "Anyway, David was in the same publishing program so he was in a lot of my classes. He was the first guy who ever showed me any kind of interest. I was so naive. We started dating and then, in our junior year, we did research together on a major project for our journalism class. He told me that he was having a hard time beginning his paper, so I made the mistake of giving him my draft copy just as an example." I shook my head. "Instead of using it to create his own paper like I thought he would, he just changed the name on the cover page from mine to his. My professor and the dean of students confronted us and David claimed that I was the one who stole the assignment from him. But because he submitted his work an entire day before I did, the professor believed him. I was so mad."

I paused. Derek took the opportunity to speak. "But wait. What about your draft copy? Didn't you save it? Couldn't you have shown your professor what you worked on?"

"My saved notes and documents on my computer were apparently not enough to prove that it was in fact my work that he plagiarized. I don't think it helped me that the dean of students was a man. Ugh!!!" My voice trembled with repressed fury. "Till this day it still makes me so angry!"

I could feel my nose flare up and I looked away from Derek.

"What happened next?" he coaxed.

My heart pounded against my ribcage as if demanding release from the rage that threatened to overpower me. "I didn't get kicked out of the program because my dad pulled some strings. Instead, I got put on probation, failed the class and had to re-register for it the next semester. My writing friends didn't even want to have anything to do with me. Everyone believed *him*. I hated him so much. I didn't understand how he could have done that to me. And I didn't know why everyone was so quick to believe his story."

As I recounted the story, my hands clenched into fists, my knuckles turning pale under the pressure. A fire ignited in my chest, each word fueling the flames of my anger. I had to close my eyes and take in a deep breath before I continued.

"I was heartbroken because I was so in love with him. I felt betrayed, taken advantage of. I felt so stupid for falling for him, thinking that he only dated me for my work. At least, that's what I started to believe. I stopped going to my classes, I stayed in bed all day, Glory tried to get me to hang out with her. I just wasn't interested in doing anything anymore. I was *done*. I just wanted to end it all; be done with it all. With *life*. So, one day, I took a bottle of pills—I don't even remember if they were over the counter or medication—whatever they were, I drank it down with alcohol. I was trying to end it all, Derek. Glory found me passed out in our dorm room."

"Oh my god," Derek said.

"She's the one who called 911. She thought I did it because of David but I tried to tell her it wasn't just him. It was because of everything that I had been going through with myself, my family, my life, my depression. She still jokes about it till this day. Whatever. They made me stay in a psychiatric hospital for a few weeks—well, it could've been days. I'm not even sure anymore. I met with therapists and doctors. I answered questions for them both verbally and on surveys while they figured out how severe my situation was. I just don't remember everything that happened because honestly, I have tried with everything inside of me to forget that dark time in my life. My mother never knew about it but my dad did. He was the parent they could get a hold of. And he kept my secret."

I looked at Derek for the first time since I began telling him my story and his eyes were glassy, his lips pressed together as if he were keeping himself from speaking. He pulled me toward him so that my head was now leaning on his shoulder.

"Why didn't you ever tell me?" he asked.

I shrugged my shoulders. "I just don't like thinking about that time in my life."

"Well, thank you for telling me," he whispered. "I'm so sorry you had to go through that."

I took a sharp breath in and then I exhaled, suddenly feeling so much closer to him. It baffled me why I had let fear prevent me from telling him my secret. Though I couldn't bring myself to disclose my current therapy sessions, there was still a peace inside of me because I told him so much. The burden that had weighed my heart down was suddenly lifted and I felt like I could fly. Derek did that for me with his patience and his understanding. I gave him a chance and he gave me hope.

Chapter 8.

Sunday Afternoon, August 4, 2002

"Hello?" I shouted as I walked into my father's house. "Is anyone home?"

If I knew my father, he was probably working at Rikers until later in the evening. Working on Sundays was always a source of contention between my parents. My mother believed in Sunday as a day of rest but my father believed in his work as a corrections officer. He always argued that maintaining law and order was what they both did as their professions, but his duty to the system couldn't always allow for specific days off.

I had no idea where my sister was, but I felt like I had little time to care about that. I needed to quickly find my mother's wooden box and then leave. I swiftly walked down the dark hallway and into my mother's office. I glanced at her desk and it was the same as I had seen it on Friday evening. I quickly searched the bookshelf but how would a wooden box be hidden behind or among the books? I didn't even know what kind of box I was looking for. A small, dark wood box? Light wood? How big was this thing? I rummaged through the desk drawers again. As I knelt on the floor, I searched underneath the couch. Nothing. While I was on my knees, I took the opportunity to look under my mother's desk, and also the chair I had found Nancy sitting on the other night. Nothing.

With not even a thought of visiting my old room, I ran back down the hall, up the stairs and into the first bedroom on the right: Nancy's room. Clothes were thrown all over the floor and on her bed. Sheets of paper were everywhere. On the desk, next to her computer, was a dirty plate with the remains of what looked like the previous night's dinner. Next to that was a glass of water, half empty. But I couldn't stop to judge Nancy's lack of domestic hygiene. Time was not on my side.

I promptly searched her closet. Going back to her desk, I rifled through her papers and books. Sifting through her unpaid credit card bills told me she was in financial trouble. Moving those aside, my eyes fell upon something that was completely unexpected. There were two books about the psychological effects of parental neglect on children, left open presumably to save her place in the books. Questions of whether Nancy picked these books up herself or if they were recommended to her formed in my mind. Perhaps they belonged to my mother, and Nancy found them in her office. But the fact that she was reading them shined a different light on Nancy. Maybe she was trying to understand herself to make important changes in her life. My focus had shifted, and I had to consciously bring myself back.

I saw Nancy's answering machine by the books. There was no blinking light indicating any new messages. I pressed play. "No new messages," the automated voice said, proving that she did indeed listen to the message I left her yesterday about the painting and my mother's note.

I surveyed the room. There was a large, thin cardboard box leaning against the wall. There were some novels and other books on the floor but there was no wooden box. I knelt down and quickly scanned underneath her bed. It was surprisingly clear—given the condition of the rest of her room. But there was literally nothing under there. I lifted myself up and looked around me. It could very well be somewhere in there, but her room was too disordered. I couldn't, in a timely fashion, effectively look through it without her finding out that I had been there. I needed help. I had to recruit Glory.

I looked again at the thin cardboard box leaning against the wall. It looked big and wide enough to fit a painting the size that my mother had given me. Could it be? What if my mother had given Nancy a painting as well? I quickly moved toward the box to investigate.

Suddenly, the front door slammed shut downstairs. My heart jumped into my throat. Nancy. Taking calculated breaths, I slowly tiptoed my way out of the room. As I stepped, the floorboard creaked under me.

"Dad?" Nancy asked from downstairs. She jogged up the stairs as I quickly positioned myself away from her bedroom door to the entrance of my old room past the bathroom only a few feet away. As she reached the landing, she stayed quiet, and suspiciously eyed me.

The beating of my heart had now calmed itself. That's when I noticed the logo on the canvas bag she was carrying. "Nancy!" I exclaimed. "Are- are you taking classes at Queens Community College?" That had to be the reason why I saw those psychology books on her desk.

Nancy was in no mood to be cordial with me. She turned the bag around to hide its logo and said, "It may not be a fancy school like NYU but at least I'm going. Why are you here, Mia?"

"That's so great, Nancy! It doesn't matter where you go. You're right. At least you're going. I'm happy for you."

She would not be swayed. "You're never here, Mia," she said impatiently. "Why now?"

I got the picture: no small talk. "You know why I'm here," I said, slowly walking towards her. "I'm looking for Mom's wooden box. I know you listened to the message I left you yesterday. Nancy, did Mom give you a painting too?"

Her steps toward me were slow and deliberate. She raised her index finger to my face and said, "If I find out you've been in my room looking for that box..."

My breath quickened, but I remained calm. I said, "Get your finger out of my face."

She slowly backed away, still staring at me with angry eyes, turned the doorknob and walked into her room. I sighed with relief. She was a bit scary.

There was no way I was letting this go. My thoughts were fixated on that big cardboard box in her room. In my heart, I felt it. I think my mother gifted my sister a painting as well. I decided to continue my investigation at a time when I could bring reinforcement.

Part 2

A Slut, a Liar, and a Cheater

Chapter 9

Monday Morning, August 5, 2002

I stepped into the conference room Monday morning. The staff had already gathered for an editorial meeting to which I arrived late. The room, surrounded by glass paneled walls, was quite large, enabling it to fit a sizeable table that seated about thirty people. There were always a few people who remained standing during those meetings; this time, I was one of those people. After a quick scan of the room, I noticed Morgan Riley, the publisher of *Fresh Voices*, and the man who happened to be very crucial to my role in the company, positioned at the front of the room. His newest golden boy, Bill Anderson was standing right beside him.

I politely nodded to the art director, a rather good-looking young man of mixed heritage who helped me once with a project I worked on that garnered much recognition. From across the room, I spotted my assistant, Sophia, seated at the table, and looking paler than usual due to the tanned publicity assistant sitting next to her. I squeezed through the small spaces between chairs and people and found a spot right next to Morgan Riley. I purposely stood between him and Bill Anderson in an effort to stand as close as possible to Morgan.

Morgan Riley, a large, homely dark-skinned man in his fifties, shot me a reprimanding look as I took my place in front of the room right next to him. It was his way of reminding me that my career was still in his hands. He had agreed to discuss the position of Editor in Chief with me if he were pleased with my next project. He admitted that my current position as Executive Director was not challenging enough for me and agreed that I would no doubt successfully take on the challenges of editor in chief. But I had to first prove to him that I still had it in me to turn in excellent work.

"So, we have most of the articles we're using for our October issue," Morgan said, addressing the room. "Is that correct?"

"That will be correct by the end of this week, Morgan," an editorial assistant answered. He was a tall and skinny light skinned man whose good looks made him a star among the younger women working at the magazine. "I'm fact-checking just two articles, and then we'll be set."

"What about the Patrick Jerome piece?"

"Won't be ready until deadlines for the November issue." Mandy, the book editor, was a short and wide middle-aged woman, whose complexion reminded me of milk chocolate. She rocked back and forth in her chair, her custom when she was nervous.

"But his book is coming out at the end of next month. Come on, folks. We need to stay on top of these things."

I saw the opportunity and seized it. "I happen to know Patrick Jerome's publisher," I interjected, "and because of that, I know that on the tenth of this month, there will be a party held in honor of Mr. Jerome's latest book, *Moment of Truth,* and he'll be signing copies. We mentioned this in last month's issue, but in retrospect, we should have done more. Let me talk with his publicist to perhaps arrange an on-site interview for the November issue. Also, Mr. Jerome has another book that will be in stores in May of next year. All we have to do is have a feature article on him in November's issue, highlighting *Moment of Truth* and his forthcoming book. We could have a photo of the author on the cover, and because he's so photogenic, that issue, guaranteed, will be flying off the shelves."

I purposely said all of that as I stared at Mandy, who should have been on top of Patrick Jerome for an article. She continued her rocking motion as she avoided my eyes by fixing her gaze on Morgan.

I continued, "I'll be glad to secure the interview with Mr. Jerome. I can also talk to Mr. Jerome's publicist about arranging a signing for us in February, during our Fourth Annual Fresh Voices Talent Conference. A large number of our female readership will no doubt attend solely because of him. November's issue will be fabulous."

The room was silent. I noticed many, including Mandy, looking at me with cold, spiteful eyes. Others awkwardly avoided eye contact with Mandy. The goal was to be quick in landing a situation one desired. If the book editor could not handle an author as popular as Patrick Jerome, then someone else had to step up to the task. It was the only solution. I was planning for big changes within the company that would propel me to the top.

I felt Mandy's eyes burning through my back, so I turned to smile at her. She rolled her eyes at me and then turned to look at Morgan, who began to speak again.

"So, it's settled," he said. "You take care of the Patrick Jerome piece for November's issue. I do expect you to turn in high quality work."

"Don't I always?" I said with a confident smile.

"So, we still need a feature story for October," Morgan resumed.

I quickly stepped in again. "Actually, I do have a proposal for a feature story."

I heard some sucking of teeth and some groans, but I only paid attention to what Morgan said: "Well, let's hear it."

I handed to him the information I had collected from the Internet on Glory's painter. "His name is Tyrese Black," I said. "He's twenty-nine years old and is quite a talented, fairly unknown painter in the mainstream world but has a small and loyal local following. He happens to own his own gallery in Manhattan, which is doing quite well. Fans of Patrick Jerome's books will recognize that Tyrese Black is the artist for all of the covers. We only need to expose him to the mainstream consumer."

"Have you spoken with him yet?"

"I've made an appointment to meet with him this afternoon." In my mind, I felt it wasn't a lie because my intention was to procure that appointment.

Morgan perused the packet I had handed him as soft murmurs filled the room. His face remained fixed in a pensive expression of concentration. "Hmm. I like this. It certainly catches the eye." He looked around the room. "Has anyone here ever heard of him?"

There were no nods, and no one raised a hand.

"See?" I said quickly. "We are a cultural magazine, and we don't even make it our business to know about young and promising local artists. A feature story on his work will finally give him the recognition he deserves. And we'll be highlighted as the publication that gave him that exposure."

"Well, it *is* worth looking into," Morgan told me. "We may even make him and his work the subject of our feature article. I assume that you will be taking care of this project."

"Of course," I responded. "As I said, I will be interviewing him today."

"Okay then. Just remember you only have until Monday to get everything in so that Camilla could start reviewing the pages. That also includes photos to go with your article, Mia. And if you can't handle it, let me know now because we haven't got much time."

"I can handle it," I assured him.

There were a few more logistical matters attended to before Morgan ended the meeting. As everyone gathered their things and left the room, I stayed behind to speak with Morgan.

"Mia, this Tyrese Black looks as if he has excellent work. If you can write up a great article within the space of a week, I will surely consider you for the position of Editor in Chief."

Consider me? I always thought I was the sole and obvious candidate. My heart began to pound. Okay, it was finally time to use the negotiation skills that Derek and I practiced so many times together. I inhaled deeply and exhaled all of the nervous anxiety that suddenly made its appearance upon understanding that I had to stand up for what I felt I deserved. "I don't mean to sound forward," I said hesitantly, "but I didn't think there was any consideration involved when it came to my filling the position of Editor in Chief."

"Bill Anderson has also expressed interest in the position, Mia. You are not the only candidate."

"Bill Anderson?" Was he serious? That raised the stakes for me. My apprehension to be aggressive politely gave way to a Mia Hill that surprised me. "Think about what it would look like if you hired a white man as the editor in chief of a prolific magazine that is consumed by mostly African American women. What message are you sending to our readers and supporters?"

"The message is that we do not discriminate. We hire those we know are fit for the job—no matter their race or background. And besides, he has a lot of connections and can help make our audience wider and bigger than it already is. Think of your work in the magazine reaching the mainstream audience, which means more recognition for *you*."

Anger boiled inside of me. "Our focus should cater to our current readership."

"Mia, if you're not willing to help this magazine grow…" He didn't need to finish his statement because his point was clearly made. I had to try a different angle. How would Derek direct me in this situation? Okay, it wasn't about Bill Anderson. It was about me and what I could do for the company. "Morgan, who else do you know that can turn in a feature article within one week's time while performing the many other duties I've taken over since becoming the Executive Director? What has Bill Anderson done recently for *Fresh Voices*? I need to know that I will definitely get the position."

He seemed dumbfounded. "Are you *demanding* the position?"

I couldn't back down now. I had to remain stalwart; this was too important to me. "I know I do brilliant work. Bill is just a newbie. He doesn't have the experience I have and you know it. If I don't get the position, Morgan, I will just have to bow out as Executive Director and take a higher position elsewhere. We both know that no one here—not even Bill—can take over my duties, which means you'll have to hire outside the company. Hiring outside the company will not only cost you the money it takes to advertise, but also the time to interview and train, and we all know that time is money. And who's to say the new person—even if it's Bill—will be as successful in this position as I am? I need to know that if I turn in good product, which I never fail to do, I will get this position with a $30,000 increase in my salary. Anything less and I walk out of the building today without looking back." The words escaped my mouth faster than I had time to think about them and their repercussions. I wasn't sure whether that was a bluff or if I was really serious.

Morgan seemed to be thinking the same thing. "Thirty thousand dollars? Are you serious?"

I smiled. The smile was of pride in myself for remaining so steadfast. I didn't know where this bravery came from but I liked it. It gave me the motivation to continue and I allowed it to control my thoughts and my words. "I know for a fact that it is equivalent to how much Daniel was making before he made his exit as the editor in chief last month. The fact that you haven't yet hired anyone to replace him proves you haven't yet found a qualified candidate. I'm the one, Morgan. And I'm worth that much. Everyone here knows it." The more I spoke, the more inspired I felt.

He sighed and lifted his head as if to assert his authority.

"Morgan," I said, in an effort to reassure him of my skills. "Who was the one who suggested that we include the LGBTQ art section in our magazine? Sales shot up sixty percent that month, and we have been doing well since then. Whose idea was it to create and then organize the *Annual Fresh Voices Talent Conference,* which for the past three years has brought many people in the publishing and music industries together? The conference has been such a huge success that with each passing year we've gained major promoters and dozens of sponsors."

Morgan cut me off. "I'm well aware of the results of your successes within the company, Mia. No need to go through all of them."

"Then you know how good I am for this company, Morgan, and I know I can do better in a higher position." I thought about Derek suddenly and how proud he would be that I used his tactics.

Morgan sighed. "Yes, I know you're good for the magazine. I saw how you used your knowledge of Patrick Jerome's future projects to take that assignment out of Sandy's hands."

"Sandy?"

He looked at me strangely. "The book editor."

"Oh! All this time I thought her name was Mandy."

He shook his head and smiled. "Okay, Mia. Provided your article is flawless and we do get a great response, the position is yours."

"With a $30,000 increase?"

"We'll still need to negotiate that."

"Very well," I said, now with a natural confidence that seemed to be born from my sudden boldness. "I'm assuming the position and the salary are already mine, then." And to close out the negotiation, I ended with the question Derek had me memorize: "Should I expect a written statement based on this conversation by the end of the day?"

He looked at me again as if I threatened his authority in some way. I guessed that he didn't like my being so forward, as if I had somehow tricked him into giving me the promotion. I had always had the feeling that he didn't like me very much. Maybe it was because each time we exchanged words, I was requesting overtime pay or demanding more resources for specific projects. I think my requisitions have always rubbed him the wrong way. However, he knew that his personal feelings against me were no basis on which to make business decisions. He also knew he could not afford to lose me.

"You'll get your written statement," Morgan responded. "And for God's sake, Mia, at least try to remember the names of *some* of the people you work with. As Editor in Chief, the creative, managing and executive directors have to report directly to *you*. I expect you to know who they are."

"Kate and Eileen are the creative and managing editors respectively," I quickly responded. "And I haven't yet had the pleasure of meeting my replacement as the Executive Director."

Morgan nodded as he walked out of the conference room and headed to his office.

As soon as he left, I had to hold myself up on the conference table as I laughed to myself. *I just did that!* I thought. I didn't quite understand where the arrogance came from but I liked it. It showed up for me like a reliable advocate whose only job is to attend to my personal—and in this case—professional welfare.

Feeling encouraged, I went back into my office and retrieved Tyrese Black's business card from my desk. I dialed the number and waited.

"Tyrese Black," he answered.

"Good afternoon, Mr. Black. My name is Mia Hill. I left you a message not too long ago. I'm calling from *Fresh Voices: The African American Magazine for the Arts*."

"Oh, yeah. Didn't you get a call from Michael, the gallery director? He told me he left you a message."

I wasn't prepared for what I heard on the other end. His voice, low and deep, was intoxicating, sexy and seductive. It made me smile in a way only teenage girls would when a boy expressed attraction to them.

"Oh. Well, I actually didn't get a chance to check my messages today," I stammered. "I understand you must be a very busy person, so I won't take much of your time. Glory Williams is a friend of mine, and she suggested I give you a call. I was just wondering if I could come by your gallery soon and interview you for our October feature article. Your work is perfect for our magazine."

"Hey!" he laughed. He did it again. He melted me with the simple sound of his voice. "Here I thought it'd be just another interview but an actual feature article? And for *Fresh Voices* no less! That sounds good to me. Would you like to come by the gallery sometime this week?"

"Actually," I stuttered, "I was hoping to come by today if that's not too soon for you."

"Today?" he chuckled. "You got deadlines, huh?"

My heart leaped. "Excuse me?" I asked in a tone of disbelief.

"I've never made an interview appointment with someone on the same day they want to see me. I'm just wondering if *Fresh Voices* is a bit desperate right now."

I couldn't believe he had the audacity to joke with me; it was disturbingly unprofessional. "Mr. Black, I really do find your work fascinating and think that exposure in our magazine would be great publicity for you."

"And I completely agree with you. Nothing wrong with a little humor, I think. I'm sorry if I offended. Let me check my appointment schedule with Michael."

The man had the nerve to transfer me to his director! After a short exchange with the director Michael Knowles, I arranged a meeting with Tyrese Black for five o'clock that evening.

I needed to gather more information about him but I still had other phone calls to make regarding the other articles I was working on. I picked up the phone and dialed my assistant's extension.

"Good morning, Mia."

"Good morning." I wanted to say Cynthia but doubted myself. "Can you please come into my office for a minute?"

"Of course," she said.

I quickly scribbled Tyrese Black's name on a sheet of paper, followed by the words *gallery*, *Patrick Jerome*, *NY artist*, and *painting*.

My assistant walked in and approached my desk. She was tall and slender with small breasts and no hips. Her milky white skin, which could possibly bruise at the touch of a finger, screamed for at least one whole week at the beach. If it weren't for the fact that she looked rather dowdy, I would have believed she was supermodel material.

"I've made an appointment to interview Tyrese Black this afternoon." I handed her the sheet of paper. "Please find out everything you can about him by doing a quick search using these tags. Can I have your results by one o'clock?"

"No problem," she said as she scanned the paper. "Anything else?"

"No, that's it. Thanks."

Cynthia, or Sophia, always pulled through for me. Her commitment to her position and to what I needed was never something I had to question. I had wanted to hire an African American assistant when I first took my current position, but Morgan assigned her to me and would not budge to change his mind. She did come highly recommended and I always felt she did great work. I wasn't quite sure what the psychology behind my not remembering her name was. I trusted her with everything that needed to be done in the office yet it wasn't enough to remember whether her name was Cynthia or Sophia. Maybe because I wasn't the one who hired her. There was no time to consider that now. I depended on Cynthia-Sophia to be effective, as her efficiency would help me achieve success at my own job.

It was no surprise, then, that she found everything I needed in order to prepare for the interview. Cynthia-Sophia did not disappoint. At one o'clock, she handed me printed information, pictures, short articles and anything else that was relevant to Tyrese Black. From her gathered research, I created my interview questions and was ready for my meeting with Tyrese Black. I didn't know at the time that meeting Tyrese was going to change my life.

Chapter 10.

Monday Afternoon, August 5, 2002

An hour before the scheduled meeting, I left work, grabbed a cab, and despite the unbearable traffic, arrived in Chelsea fifteen minutes before my scheduled appointment with the artist. As usual, 23rd Street was lively with a mixture of bohemian type people in their 20s, students from the nearby schools as well as people in business attire, which made it a welcoming environment where everyone seemed to both stand out in their own style and blend into the rich diversity of the neighborhood. The shops and boutiques seemed larger than life, beckoning some to support their love of extravagance, while others were content to indulge in window shopping. The street vendors fared well themselves, for they carried unique pieces of jewelry and other accessories anyone would be happy to add to their growing collections.

I walked half a block before I spotted the address of the unassuming gallery, housed in a large, white-columned building, whose architectural structure seemed so classic that it could have been on display as its own art show. Inside the main lobby, the marble floors shined and the large, open space left room for people to sit and chat while enjoying their lunches or simply make time as they perhaps waited for potential clients or business associates. The security guard was having a conversation with the desk clerk when I stepped up and asked for The Powers Gallery. After presenting my ID, I was instructed to take the elevator to the third floor, make a right out of the elevator and then go straight down the hall to the last room on the left.

It wasn't what I envisioned but then again, this was Chelsea, an area where many galleries were known to exist; they had to be kept somewhere. I followed the desk clerk's directions and found the gallery at the end of a long and narrow hallway on the third floor. The glass door was modest with the words *The Powers Gallery* written in a plain font. However, there was nothing plain about what I was about to experience through that door.

As soon as I walked into the gallery, I was greeted by the powerfully rich and vibrant colors of the paintings that graced the walls. A security guard stood erect to my right by a table with pamphlets and flyers carefully and creatively arranged. Looking around the room, I acknowledged that the gallery wasn't just a room; it was actually quite larger than one would have guessed judging by the hallway alone. During my quick scan of the gallery, I noticed three other connected rooms holding specific collections. I took a quick tour around the gallery by myself and was engulfed by the peaceful and relaxing energy the room gave off. I felt it all over my body: a feeling of serenity. It was unnerving.

There was another African American woman in the space with me, scrutinizing one of the paintings so deeply and intently that I moved ever so softly so as not to disturb her concentration. She was a tall, thin woman with dark skin and a completely shaved head. She was regal.

The gallery's director, a short, pale-skinned man, introduced himself as Michael Knowles before leaving to alert Tyrese Black of my arrival.

"I'm sorry," the regal woman said. "Did he just say you're Mia Hill?" She said it as if that were not the first time she had heard my name. Resembling a fashion model, her make-up looked like it was the result of a professional's creativity.

"I am," I said, looking at her inquisitively.

She stuck out a hand with exquisitely manicured nails for me to shake. Her handshake was firm and powerful.

"My name is Tiana Brown. I'm a follower of your work at *Fresh Voices Magazine*. I've attended all of the talent conferences your magazine hosts and I have to say that I love what you're doing for the community."

I was quite literally speechless. I had never met anyone who knew me without first mentioning the magazine.

She smiled and then took out a small case from her bag and produced a business card and handed it to me. "I just started my own magazine although I know better than to compete with *Fresh Voices*!" She laughed a laugh that exuded with confidence.

I took the card and read her name. Below it were the words *Black Prose Literary, Founder.*

She continued. "Your magazine actually inspired me to start my own. It's strictly literary so it doesn't go into the different art forms like yours does. And my focus is on Black women and our stories. If it's possible, I would love to keep in touch with you. Maybe pick your brain every once in while if that's all right with you."

While I was trying to move up at *Fresh Voices*, this woman did something so bold as to start her own magazine. I didn't feel like I could ever make a move as brazen as that. I was impressed with her. In fact, I felt that I should probably be asking her for advice rather than the other way around.

I finally found my voice. "That- that would be great. Yes. I would love to connect with you. And congratulations on this endeavor. It's not easy taking such big risks."

She sighed as she nodded her head in agreement. "Well, you know. When you get the calling, you have to answer or else the inspiration leaves a hole in your soul."

She excused herself after telling me that it was great to meet me and walked out of the gallery. I pondered her statement for a moment and thought about the hole—perhaps holes—in my own soul.

I took a deep breath and briefly glanced at the paintings. Each wall was dedicated to a certain theme. There were a few paintings I recognized from the website. I studied a painting that would have been depressing had it not been for the gorgeous bright colors. A woman dressed in black extended her arms up to a brilliant sky. What was seen behind her could be determined as a blue-green sea meeting a winter green land of trees or shrubbery. Her face was distorted, revealing an unmistakable expression of pain. Its radiant green and blue did not take away from the strength of the piece at all. It was called *Comfort in Pain*. It was a thought-provoking concept, and I questioned its contradicting possibility. How can one ever find comfort in a feeling and emotion we all try to avoid at any cost?

As I stood by the entrance examining the painting, I heard footsteps approaching. I turned to find a striking man walking toward me, and I literally lost my breath. He greeted me with a smile that told me he knew who I was. Mesmerized, I took in a deep breath, trying to calm my heart rate. The man who approached me was a gorgeous specimen, not too pretty but beautifully crafted. Looking much better in person than in his online photo, he was, simply put, a vision of rugged perfection.

I remembered that his biography said he was twenty-nine years old. The brawny man approaching me certainly looked his age and looked amazing.

His roughly chiseled face had the shadow of a beard. He walked towards me with a confident swagger as his small, light brown eyes fixated on me. His most remarkable feature, however, was his dreadlocks—a complementary mixture of black and brown, neither too thin nor too thick, descending just below his shoulder blades. He was magnificent. He had on a fitted, black short sleeve shirt that revealed a muscular physique and I quickly lowered my head as if his chest was a secret not meant for me to see. But in doing so, I noticed his finely molded hands and found myself staring at the veins that popped out around his wrists. And as I surveyed his arms, I discovered a tattoo peeking out from under the short shirtsleeve of his left arm. I could not make out what the image was, but I definitely saw a pair of feet. I looked at the man standing before me. He had to be almost six feet tall and was extremely well defined. He was—in a word—beautiful.

"You must be Mia Hill," he smiled as he extended his hand for me to shake. I firmly took it in my own. His grasp was strong. Was there anything about him that wasn't sexy?

"I am," I said, trying to sound professional. "Tyrese Black?"

"The one and only." Even his smile had a beauty all its own. Tyrese *fucking* Black. Glory was so not kidding.

"It's good to meet you," I said. "I have to admit, the photo on your website is a little deceiving."

"I know; a lot of people say that. I took that picture just before I started growing my hair and I never had the web designer change it for me."

I wanted to tell him just how much his website photo did not do him justice. But I had to maintain my professional composure.

"Well, Tyrese, I want to thank you for giving me this opportunity."

"Of course," he said, eyeing me up and down. "I believe in supporting our own. Especially when I find out that our own looks as good as you." His eyes regarded my hair in appraisal. "I'm loving your natural fro. It's bold."

"Thanks." I felt myself blushing. He was as smooth as he looked. His flirtatious words surprisingly put me at ease.

"Well, welcome to The Powers Gallery. Do you want to take a look through before we start the interview?"

"That would be great. Thank you."

We walked through the halls as he briefly explained the inspiration for some of his pieces. His artwork was awe-inspiring, and I thought it was a shame that not many people were familiar with his work. Perhaps my feature story on him would positively change that.

"I have a question about the title of this painting," I said, pointing to *Comfort in Pain*.

"Many people do," he answered with a delightful smile.

"I'm not too sure people can actually find comfort in their pain. I know I certainly don't. What do you mean by it?"

He continued to smile. "Of course, you can find comfort in your pain. Some people would rather live their lives in emotional pain than try to find the reason behind that pain for fear of releasing demons they thought long dead. Containing demons can inspire comfort."

I stared at him, his wry smile testing me. "Do all of your paintings have such grim interpretations?"

"Actually," he laughed, "someone I recently met described the painting in that way. It wasn't my intention, but it makes sense if you think about it. I did this during a time in my life when I was in a lot of emotional pain, and I just wanted it to go away. I started to think: why do we experience such pain at all? There has to be a reason. Then I thought of it this way: When someone experiences pain, physical or emotional, that pain is a sign that life still exists within that person. When I studied martial arts years ago, my instructor taught us to welcome the physical pain we endured during our intense training and testing. That was how we knew we were still alive. And the fact that we were still alive meant that we still had a chance to give it our all. The same goes for emotional pain. Emotional pain is simply an indication that one is not cold and dead inside. And if something should pain you emotionally, take comfort in the fact that you still have feelings to spare. The woman in this painting is rejoicing because she knows she is emotionally alive. It's a beautiful thing. I don't envy people who are emotionally dead."

I felt exposed. It was as if he could see right through me.

"I-I've never thought about it that way," I stammered. "It's actually brilliant." He spoke about it with such passion that I had to ask: "Is it a favorite of yours?"

"As a matter of fact, it's not," he answered. "Let me show you which is. I only have a reproduction of it, but I love it."

We walked to the end of the hallway, and there it was, looking absolutely breathtaking. My heart jumped as my eyes traced the familiar lines and images that had already been branded in my mind. My breath was shallow. The print reproduction I looked at was a frontal view of a brown woman in the nude curled up in a fetal position, her hands desperately clamped against her temples. Her face was clearly that of a woman in agonizing pain. The background was midnight blue, and if one looked carefully, as I did for the first time that day, vague, faint facial images of people looking at the brown woman could be seen. Some of these faces extended their arms out to her, all of them behind her. Seeing those vague images for the first time gave me an odd feeling of comfort. I was completely absorbed in the image. It was called *The Box*. I knew because it was the same painting that was hanging in my living room, only I had not known that Tyrese Black was the artist.

I felt a sudden wave of a hot flash overtake my entire body for half a second before it went away. I had to compose myself. "Wh-why is it your favorite?" I managed to ask.

He stared at the reproduction, utterly enchanted by his own work. "She's so deeply depressed. Her vulnerability shows in the fact that she's nude and in a fetal position. You see the tears? She's in a lot of pain, and her pain adds to that vulnerability. She's at her darkest hour but doesn't realize that if she just turns around and opens her eyes, there would be hope for her because people care about her and want to help her. They're trying to reach out to her, but she won't let them in. She has her back turned to them. The fetal position is a sign that she really doesn't want anyone inside her world. I think it's kind of sad."

I swallowed the lump that had found its way into my throat. The man described not only his painting with eloquence but also aspects my own life. I stared at him in amazement as he continued to study the piece. He was truly gifted and, given how he described the painting, that hit was evident that he believed in his own artistry.

"*The Box*," I whispered in some sort of trance. "Perfectly titled."

He stepped back a bit, and eyed me expectantly. "Really?" he said. "How so?"

I should have known he would want me to explain. Inside, I felt oppressed by an intense heat that the sun's rays alone could never produce but perhaps could only be achieved with the aid of a magnifying glass. Clearing my throat, I said, "Well, clearly there's no box in this image. They say that some people build walls around themselves so that others can't touch them emotionally." I exhaled as I continued speaking, trying to disguise my trembling voice. "If you think about it, anyone can climb over a wall and get to the other side, thus actually reaching someone emotionally. But this woman has built herself a box, making sure no one ever gets in. Those people reaching out to her are close to her but still can't physically connect with her. So, she's trapped in her own sorrow forever."

He stepped away and looked at me with an expression that told me he was deeply impressed. His lips curled into a sly smile as if he didn't quite know what to make of me.

"Are you familiar with this painting?" he asked.

"I own it, actually," I said. "It's hanging on my living room wall."

He laughed a hearty laugh filled with pride. "But you-you're not the one who bought it. I specifically remembered an older woman purchased it."

My mother. It suddenly clicked. The initials on the bottom right were TB. Tyrese Black. I couldn't believe that this was really happening.

An abrupt sensation overcame me. Although I was taking in deep breaths, it felt like something was inside my throat, blocking the air from getting through.

"Restroom," I somehow managed to say.

"Down the hall to the right," Tyrese Black quickly stammered as he pointed me in the right direction.

As I rushed down the hall, I had to admit that I was a bit horrified about what I must have looked like to the beautiful painter. As soon as I entered the restroom, I took in a long and deep breath and slowly closed my eyes, counting backward from ten. It was a technique Dr. Flare had taught me and it worked for me each time I suffered a panic attack. I stared at myself in the mirror. The man knew my mother, or at least he had met her. This was my chance. I had to ask him about his encounter with her. But how would I do that and remain focused on the whole reason why I was there in the first place?

A knock on the door pulled me out of my thoughts. I inhaled one last time, released the air and then opened the door to find a concerned Mr. Black standing before me.

"Are you okay?" he asked.

"I am," I said quickly, trying to make the whole incident just go away. "I think I just need some water."

"I thought you might!" he said, producing a bottle of cold water and handing it to me.

I smiled my thank you and drank the entire bottle down as if I were afraid another panic attack would come over me if I didn't drink it all up. He watched in astonishment.

"Are you sure you're okay?" he asked again.

I nodded.

"I'm sorry, but can I ask you something? You said you had my painting...um...was it a gift from the woman who bought it?" He looked at me expectantly.

"Can we just continue with the tour, please? I said.

He smiled uncomfortably, then cleared his throat. He walked me back to the main room where the print of *The Box* was on exhibit. Making his way over to a display table by the entrance, he picked up a catalog. "*The Box* is actually part of a set or a pair," he said as he opened the catalog. He flipped to a double-page spread. *The Box*, along with its details underneath the image was on the left page and on the right page was an equally captivating image of what seemed like the same poor woman once again in a position that reflected her pain and torment. This time, she was crouched down vertically in what seemed like the corner of a room. Her painful expression was haunting; her face was partially hidden from the shadows that gave the painting a gloomy mood. Her hands gripped the sides of her head as her fingers disappeared into her hair. He used the same color of midnight blue as in *The Box*. I looked away from the painting as I wiped away the sweat that had formed on the back of my neck. This woman's pain reminded me too much of my own. The details beneath the picture informed me that the title of the piece was *Solitary Agony*. In an effort to curb my uneasiness, I quickly lifted my head and looked around the room.

"Why *Solitary Agony*?" I asked, avoiding any more attention to the image.

"She's in a prison of her own agony," Tyrese said softly.

I could not respond. There was something inside of me preventing me from doing so. I had no desire to think about my own small agonies. His paintings stirred up so much emotion within me.

Tyrese took his cue from my silence. "Maybe we should start with the interview," he said.

I watched him as he marched ahead of me. He walked as if he owned the world. And while I admired his walk, all I could think about was how to broach the topic of my mother to him and still get my interview recorded. I had to make a quick decision: focus on this interview and then ask him about my mother directly after.

He led me into his office—a smaller room within one of the exhibition rooms—and invited me to sit down on the chair that faced his desk. He walked over to a small refrigerator and took out two bottles of water and placed one on the desk directly in front of me.

"Thank you." I took my small digital voice recorder from my purse and asked him, "Do you mind if I record this interview?"

"Not at all," he said. My eyes followed him as he sat down. I noticed another painting on the wall directly behind him. The piece showed a nude brown man and a somewhat paler woman in an embrace with their bodies wrapped around each other. The background was a deep and radiant yellow. It didn't look like the others. The colors were a bit off, and the technique seemed amateurish.

I hit the record button on my digital recorder. "The one behind you there is romantic," I said. "Is it yours too?"

"*Intertwined*," he said. "My very first non-fantasy piece. It was experimental."

I reviewed the painting for a few more seconds. The figures were disproportioned yet fit into each other perfectly. "Soul mates," I said. "Nobody's perfect, but we each have someone with whom we were meant to be, someone who fits us."

He smiled. "You're beginning to scare me. You're the first person to ever say what I was thinking when I painted it. A lot of people tell me sex or just two people enjoying each other, passion, lust, that kind of stuff."

I quickly scrawled the title in my notebook. I wanted to feature that painting in the article as well as *The Box, Solitary Agony* and *Comfort in Pain*.

"Do you study the art of painting?" he asked me, with a curious smile.

"Not formally," I answered. "But I do admire any art form from sculpture and painting to animation and writing. I find it all quite fascinating."

"I like the way you analyze the work."

"Thank you," I said, surprised at how difficult his presence made it for me to maintain my professionalism. I proceeded to ask him questions about the types of paints he used in order to create his works, about his background and training in the art as well as his creative influences.

I continued with the interview, touching on how he got his start selling his paintings, his inspiration for his new collection, and his mentor Simon Powers—a prominent African American artist in his own right and Tyrese's late employer who left him the gallery.

About his current works Tyrese said, "Among the countless letters and emails I receive, a lot of them came from women who needed closure with their daughters and from daughters talking about difficult relationships with their mothers. People see themselves in my work, you know. So I figured I'd just create a collection where I could address those issues."

I asked him where his studio was located and he responded: "In Williamsburg, Brooklyn, one room in a two-bedroom brownstone." And then he added with a sly smile, "You should come by one day."

He flirted and I loved every second of it. His suggestion was tempting. I wondered how he decorated his apartment and whether it matched his personality. I found myself quietly intrigued by him. But I cleared my head of lustful thoughts and continued with the interview. Focusing on my questions and his responses prevented me from my attention to two distinct thoughts: his encounter with my mother and the things I wanted to do with him...

I cleared my throat and asked him if he worked on commission. He handed me a small portfolio album that displayed his work. "I was recently commissioned to do something for a benefit against domestic violence and child abuse. I was really proud of that. You might have also seen my work on the covers of the books written by Patrick Jerome, an African American novelist."

"Yes. I am familiar with his work. I know his publisher very well," I said as I flipped through his portfolio, which included works for AIDS research, domestic violence, and breast cancer. I was particularly interested in the work he did for depression awareness. The image was of a woman sitting on the floor, resting her arms on her raised knees, her face disappearing into the safety of her arms. The color blue seemed appropriate once again to depict someone in emotional agony. The woman could have easily been me.

I looked at him. "Do these charities carry any special significance for you?"

"The one for depression does," he responded but offered nothing else. Perhaps it was too personal for him to share with me.

I continued flipping through prints commissioned for low-budget movies, personal galleries, and book covers for authors other than Patrick Jerome.

"Let me ask you," I addressed him. "Would you consider yourself successful?"

He smiled in an almost humble way. "I've been blessed with a talent I chose to develop. I've been blessed with people who have helped me succeed. Success is only a result of my being blessed."

"That's a good quote."

"My mother's phrase."

"I noticed the same theme running through many of your paintings: women in pain. Is your mother your inspiration for that?"

"She was my inspiration, yes," he said, though he seemed a bit hesitant.

"She *was* your inspiration?" I asked.

Looking away from my eyes, Tyrese said, "She passed away. Suicide. Ten years ago."

My heart pounded, and I didn't exactly know why. "Oh my God," I said. "I'm so sorry to hear." I took the bottle of water he had given me and put it to my mouth, not removing it until I finished the entire bottle.

Tyrese smiled at me. "You okay?"

"Yes. Of course. Why did—why did your mother kill herself?"

He sighed. "I don't know the answer to that question. I can only guess that she was in pain. What caused her pain? I will never know."

"Did she even say goodbye? What about a note? Was there a history of depression?" I suddenly caught myself asking personal questions that had nothing to do with his interview. "I'm sorry. I'm prying."

"Actually, I don't mind talking about it. But the interview's about me, not my mother."

"Well, okay, if you don't mind, I'd like to ask you one more question about that. How has your mother's death affected your work?"

He sighed again. "I chose to develop my talent just after she died. It was my way of grieving, I guess."

"Is there a message you're trying to share through your paintings?"

"Yeah, actually, there is. People don't have to suffer alone. People should not have to ever be alone. Just one person by your side is enough. Whether they are the aliens and monsters from my earlier stuff, or individuals expressing a specific emotion, all of my paintings refer to one basic theme: relationships. God created Eve to be with Adam, side by side, companions. Why should anyone ever be alone? We were made to accompany each other through life, to help those in need and laugh with those who are happy. Why are there so many people in pain, people who feel as if they can't turn to anyone else for help, you know? My mother had me, her parents, her sister and countless other people who cared. But, she still felt too lost to ask any of us for help. Why? What my paintings portray—despite the despair and pain we experience so often in our lives—is connection, communication, companionship and love."

A slight chill ran throughout my entire body.

"Do you feel your message has come across to people?"

"Yup. I receive a lot of mail from people all over the country telling me how much my work has helped them cope with relationships in their lives. Some of them have bought paintings; some just see the prints from the Internet. Others write about the peace and feelings of warmth my prints give them. And then there are those who keep the truth to themselves." He smiled, almost as if he did not really want to say what he was about to. "I met a woman just today who was like that. She told me that she had one of my paintings, but she refused to share her feelings about it when I asked her."

A sudden annoyance rose up from deep within me. The arrogance of this man! "But it's not always about you, Mr. Black," I said, knowing full well that I was the woman he referred to. I wanted to know why he felt it was so necessary to mention it during the interview. "Maybe she didn't want to get into something personal."

"Fair enough." He stared intently into my eyes as he spoke.

That wasn't enough for me. "Not everyone has to share what they're going through just because they have one of your paintings, Mr. Black."

"See, Ms. Hill, I've always had a natural talent for painting, but I never used it to connect to people until after my mother passed. I was given this gift not to become successful but to reach people. But I never knew that until *after* my mother was gone. It makes me feel good when someone benefits from my work, and I'd like to know about it to help others. By refusing to talk about what bothers you, you're not being true to yourself."

I grew defensive. "So, one person didn't share her feelings. Why would that affect you, knowing that you already have a loyal following?"

"It's not about the following. It's about who I've touched and how through my work. We were all put in this world to touch somebody, but most of us don't realize that until after a tragedy happens. And the unlucky ones, the ones not paying attention, never achieve the full potential of their talents, thus never realizing that they could have made a profound difference in at least one person's life. We were given our talents to help each other, not to profit from them."

Again, I felt exposed, as if he knew about the box of writings I had hidden in my apartment. I felt a shiver throughout my body and saw the goose pimples on my arms appear. I knew in some way his words were meant for me only. God! Everything about what this man was saying was profoundly affecting me in a way I had never imagined I could feel! I redirected my focus.

"'Not to profit from them'? But you profit from your own work, Mr. Black. How do you explain that?"

"I profit to eat, pay my rent and to keep paint on my paintbrush to continue to inspire. My gallery is flourishing, yes. But, there are months that treat me very well and then there are months that don't. My success has nothing to do with the amount of money I'm pulling in."

"Okay, so what would you say to the people who have not yet discovered their talents?"

"I would say that life is too short to *not* be doing something that makes you happy. Plain and simple. You are the first person you need to please before you can please anyone else. We are all creative beings. You need to find that specific talent— because we all have many talents—but find that *one* that makes you happy before you use it to make others happy. And if you are using your talent to create, then share it with others. The sheer satisfaction of touching just one person is enough to make you burst with pride."

I was moved. The man was my age, yet I looked at him as if he were an elder who inspired respect for the wisdom he had acquired during his many years. Glory didn't tell me he was so profound. Admittedly, he wasn't really saying anything new; many artists shared his beliefs and I had the privilege of meeting many of them through my work at the magazine. But what he said—or maybe *how* he said it—resonated with me. And the more he spoke, the more I looked at him as a genius. I remembered the way I first fell for Derek when he talked about his desire to give young people a chance to realize their own dreams. There was one difference: I felt more intensely for the painter than I did when I first met Derek.

I was in complete awe of Tyrese Black, an intriguing man who knew exactly what he wanted out of life. Knowing he was perfect for the readers of the magazine, I felt I had to give him the cover page. He sold me. His whole attitude about life was reflected in his paintings. His philosophy about why people embraced their creative abilities—for the connection rather than the profit—captivated me. For the first time, although I'd been exposed to different forms of art throughout my career, I truly started to understand the idea that artists create out of their love and desire to communicate. In college, I recalled loving to write because it was something that came naturally to me but I also remembered my aspirations to share them with others as well. And when I didn't do that, yes, my depression worsened. But I had a desire to share and that sharing wasn't about connecting with anyone else. It was solely about my pride in something I thought was beautiful. Yes, I had always recognized the need an artist has in sharing her work. But genuinely connecting with others through art was something I had forgotten as a result of my years in the business.

After the interview, I firmly shook the artist's hand and informed him that a camera crew would accompany my assistant and me to his gallery the following day.

"I'll be looking forward to seeing you, then," he said, showing off dimples that made me weak.

I flashed him a polite smile and turned around to walk away. *Courage.* I didn't think it would take courage to ask the man a simple question about my mother. Perhaps it was because I felt deeply attracted to the man. I couldn't nurse my feelings for him because I needed to remain strictly professional. There was no chance of anything ever happening between us. I would not allow myself to start something I couldn't finish. Besides, he was probably already involved with a very lucky woman. Tiana Brown, the woman I met just moments before he made his entrance introducing himself to me, was probably that lucky woman.

I needed to ask him about my mother's purchase, but I didn't quite understand why I was struggling with it. *Just ask him. This is your chance. You won't regret it.*

He opened the door to his office in order to lead me out.

I didn't know where the courage came from, but I was glad for its appearance. Avoiding his eyes, I said "That older woman who bought your painting was my mother."

"Oh," he said, sounding surprised, slowly removing his hand from the doorknob.

"And," I continued. "I wanted to ask you some questions about her."

There was a dryness in my mouth that forced me to attempt swallowing, but even that proved to be difficult. So I took a few steps away from him, as if the distance between us could help me focus long enough to ask him my questions.

"I know it was over a year ago when my mother bought the painting from you," I said as soon as I felt comfortable enough to speak. "But do you remember anything about your encounter with her?"

Tyrese sighed and looked up, as if he were trying to find the answer to my question on the ceiling. "She was very serious," he finally said. "I don't remember her smiling or anything. She came into the gallery already knowing what she wanted. She asked for the paintings by name—I don't remember if she told me where she had seen them or how she knew about me."

My heart leaped. "Paintings?" I repeated. "You mean she bought more than one?"

"Yes..." Tyrese stammered. "*The Box* and *Solitary Agony*. She purchased both of them on the spot. Cash."

Both paintings? I knew it! She must have given the other one to Nancy! That must have been the large box I saw in Nancy's room.

Tyrese expectantly gaped at me and I felt I owed him an explanation.

"My mother and I had a very strained relationship. She gave me *The Box* just before she passed away last year."

"Oh, man. I'm sorry."

"Irony has an interesting way of making itself known. It took the anniversary of her death for me to hang it up this past Friday, just before meeting you today. While I was putting it up, I noticed for the first time that tucked away behind the frame was a note she wrote to me telling me that..." I let my words trail off. I didn't want to share the details of the note with him. "Now," I continued, "it seems like my mother may have given my sister a painting too. Suddenly, I want to know everything I can about her, but my father and sister don't seem to want to talk about it."

That old familiar lump in my throat emerged and I fought to keep it at bay. I refused to shed tears in the presence of this beautiful man I hardly knew.

"That's—that's heavy," Tyrese said. "I'm sorry I couldn't tell you anything else about that day. I never had any more contact with her."

I smiled. "No, Tyrese. You helped plenty. Thank you."

I couldn't keep my eyes away from him. In the few minutes after the interview, I told him more about my recent revelation than I even thought to share with Derek. I was grateful for his presence and glad that I asked him about my mother. I now knew what direction I needed to take in my investigation of the wooden box my mother had instructed me to find.

Chapter 11

Tuesday, August 6, 2002

Instead of accompanying Cynthia-Sophia and our publicity guy to the photo shoot with Tyrese Black, I worked on the article in my office the entire morning the following day. I was more than halfway done with it, finding myself experiencing a bit of writer's block. Maybe it was only because I kept thinking about the fact that my mother had met Tyrese Black. My mother. He had met my mother. Her inner turmoil undoubtedly pushed her to buy those paintings. I wanted to understand why she couldn't she tell me in person what she felt I needed to learn from her box. The whereabouts of this mysterious box and its contents remained heavily on my mind. I closed my eyes. *Focus.*

I turned my attention to my computer screen once again, reading the words that I had already written down. Tyrese Black. His words of inspiration jumped off the screen and landed in the part of my mind that gave me hope. During the interview, he somehow personalized his message in a way that made me believe in my power as a positive being. I couldn't remember the last time I thought of myself in a positive light. In fact, the last time I experienced such inspiration was a distant memory involving Derek when I first met him.

Derek accepted me the way I was and no longer challenged me to become a better person. I once felt that it was important that Derek accept me for the person I was without trying to change me. I seemed to have forgotten, however, that Derek was indeed an inspiring force behind my rise to my current position at the magazine. But as soon as I achieved my current status, his encouragement practically disappeared. I knew it wasn't his responsibility to help inspire me, but it had been quite a while since I'd felt any kind of support or push from him when it came to my career. I didn't suspect a loss of interest in me; he and I were simply drifting apart. But in one afternoon, an artist, a stranger, had me believing in my creativity again and in my life. I thought about the stories and poems I created during my college years—work that I had long since abandoned due to a lack of support from the one person whom I had idolized.

I played my interview with Tyrese on my digital voice recorder as I stared at the unfinished article on my computer screen. It was important for me to capture Tyrese's passion for using his talent to reach out to people. I pressed play on my mini-cassette recorder and listened to Tyrese's voice: "We were all put in this world to touch somebody, but most of us don't realize that until after a tragedy has occurred. And the unlucky ones, the ones not paying attention, never achieve the full potential of their talents, thus never realizing that they could have made a profound difference in at least one person's life. We were given our talents to—"

I heard a knock on the door, and I quickly pressed the stop button on the digital recorder. I looked up to find Mr. Tyrese Black standing in my office doorway with his locks pulled back in a ponytail, a shirt that defined his muscular physique and slacks that welcomed me in. My heart jumped. *Why was he here?* He was breathtaking. I quickly collapsed all the windows on my computer screen in order to subtly check my reflection and ensure my hair wasn't flat.

"I thought I'd drop in to see if you'd had lunch yet."

My heart pounded. The dimples in his cheeks softened his rather chiseled features.

"How did you get past my assistant?" I asked.

I knew he saw it in my face how I wanted him, but I couldn't allow my voice to betray me.

"I told her you were expecting me."

"It was that easy?" I asked, not necessarily to him but he answered anyway: "I think she likes me."

I couldn't act like I didn't want him there because I thoroughly enjoyed seeing him again. There was an excitement building inside me with the knowledge that he came to see me and spend time with me. I was at a loss for words and I could tell he sensed that.

"Is it okay if I sit?" he asked as he placed himself in the chair in front of my desk without waiting for my response. A sudden image of the both of us on my desk naked and wrapped around each other like the painting in his office came to my mind before I shook it out. I had to maintain my composure.

He smiled at me and I felt my body relax—almost against my will. I still had no words to speak, finding myself completely awestruck and trying to pull myself out of it.

He smiled again. "Hey, I'm sorry for coming in here like this," he said. "But ever since you left the other day, I couldn't wait to see you again. And I was so disappointed when you didn't show up this morning with Cynthia and the camera crew."

I finally snapped out of it. The photo shoot! "Oh right!" I said. "You had the photo shoot this morning. How did it go?"

"It was good," he smiled. "Cynthia told me that you guys would choose the pictures later today and send me the mock-up of the cover later this week."

I found myself lost in his eyes. "Who's Cynthia?" I asked, in a pleasant daze.

He looked confused. "Cynthia, your assistant. At least that's who she told me she was. I don't—"

"Oh, right! Of course. Cynthia." My attempt to retain her name by remembering that it rhymed with mine apparently did not work. "I keep thinking her name's Sophia."

"Oh," he said. "Did you just hire her?"

"No." I offered nothing else.

I was in a euphoric trance. It was exciting to know that he had actually looked forward to seeing me again. Maybe he liked me as much as I liked him. Wait—was I back in high school? My heart pounded as I repeatedly and desperately tried to think of my boyfriend, *Derek*. It didn't work; there was no way I could expect to concentrate on anything else when this beautiful man was in the room. I was actually acting like a teenager in love! I shook my head, tensing my body and throwing myself back into reality.

"The editor agreed with me," I said. "She thinks you should take the cover page. Of course, the decision will go to the production department, but I'm curious: which painting would you like to see on the cover of the magazine?"

Without hesitation, he said, "*The Box*."

"Why that one?" I asked.

"If it spoke to you, no telling who else it might speak to."

"Does that painting have any special significance to you?"

He slouched a little in his seat. "My mother was the reason why I painted it. Too many people hide their depression through false smiles like my mother did. You're the only one I've met, though, who doesn't try to hide her dissatisfaction with life."

My heart jumped. "Excuse me?" I said with an assertiveness I hoped would intimidate him.

He seemed reluctant to continue. "There was a whole lot more I wanted to say to you yesterday about the painting, but I felt it was inappropriate."

"Oh really?" He was beautiful. But I had to remain focused. "Like what?"

"I mean no disrespect to you, please understand that, but I read up on you too. I found your story "Respect" in a literary magazine from when you were in college. I loved the social message about how our young people are keeping negative racial stereotypes alive. You went through your college years studying creative writing and journalism, and you're a reporter for a great magazine—"

"Excuse me. I'm not a reporter. I am the Executive Director, soon to be Editor in Chief. I do interviews because, along with the many other responsibilities that are associated with my position, I happen to enjoy them."

He laughed in spite of himself. "Correction noted, Ms. Hill. But what I wanted to say is that you've never published your work outside of *Fresh Voices*. I think you have a story to tell to inspire the world. But maybe the time hasn't come to tell it yet. It will. And you will be known as the woman who brought that story to our attention. But right now, something is keeping you from your destiny. And until you recognize what that something is, you'll never write to inspire. You'll just write to work."

A shallow breath, a pounding heart, and a quick hot flash all at once were a result of my absolute disbelief in the fact that he had the nerve to tell me what he thought about me without my provocation. I was furious! Who did he think he was to analyze me in such a manner?

"Don't pat yourself on the back because you've assumed that I have personal issues to resolve."

His smile was one of embarrassment. "No, no. I wasn't trying to assume. We all have our own issues, don't we? But with you, it's just a vibe I picked up on when I met you. And, well, knowing about your educational and professional background, I just felt like I knew enough to say what I said."

Enraged, I said, "Just because I understand one of your pieces, you think you've got me all figured out? Well, you don't know a thing about me, Mr. Black. Stop pretending to know me."

He had the nerve to laugh! "My apologies, Ms. Hill. I'm being sincere. Really. How can I make it up to you?" His smile infuriated me even more.

"You can start by keeping your thoughts to yourself."

"How about I take you to lunch, Mia, or am I gonna have to beg you?"

My heart pounded, and a hot flash shimmered through my entire body. I found myself wanting him despite his presumptions. It was strange how the more he angered me, the more I wanted him. "I don't appreciate that comment about me."

"I don't know why I just said that and I apologize. I didn't mean it." His laugh was one of embarrassment. "All I seem to do is offend you. I'm sorry for what I said about your dissatisfaction with life."

I felt my body loosen up. "You don't need to be sorry about anything," I sighed, looking away. "We both know you only spoke the truth."

His eyes lit up with opportunity. "Am I gonna have to sit here all day or can I take you to lunch?"

"I won't allow you to sit here all day, Mr. Black. As you can see by the papers on my desk, I do have a lot of work to do."

"Enough said," he chuckled. "I can take a hint."

Lifting myself from my chair, I walked to the door and held it open for him.

He slowly and carefully inched himself towards me, standing so close that I could feel his hot breath against my face. His breath smelled sweet, a mixture of sandalwood and Egyptian musk oil. Was that his breath or the scent coming from his hair or clothing or his rock-hard body? My mouth went dry, my nipples hardened, and I felt moist down below. I enjoyed every second of it.

"I really do hope I see you again," he whispered before slightly rubbing his cheek with mine. "Sincerely." He looked into my eyes, and for the first time, I noticed how stunning his were. He had the kind of eyes that boasted promises of passionate affairs full of noncommittal lust and eventual heartbreak and agony—a promise some women would love to gamble with given the slightest chance. He smiled as if he knew that I couldn't help but fall prey to the promise in his eyes. And then he walked away, taking with him all the passion I had forgotten existed within me.

I shut the door and leaned against it, closing my eyes. Not since the first time I met Derek had another man made me feel so hot, so desired, so listened to. It was exciting. His persistence and confidence were so sexy, not to mention the fact that he was just so magnificent. I wanted to see him again, yet I prayed that I wouldn't. I was afraid that he would become a new reason why I should not stay with Derek.

Chapter 12.

Tuesday Evening, August 6, 2002

"**I** got another email from a college student who graduated from the school where I gave the commencement speech in June," Derek said.

Derek and I had dinner together that evening in his Madison Avenue apartment. He cooked his favorite dish, seared salmon and roasted asparagus, to culinary perfection. The soft music coming from his sound system in the living room was just loud enough to drown out the clinking noise of the forks and knives hitting his ceramic plates as we ate.

"My speech was on fire that day," Derek continued. "It was one of the best ones I wrote. Anyway, this college student who emailed me wanted to know if he could intern with me. That makes the third kid who wants to work with me because of my speech and a few others sent me their works in progress. I want to give more speeches. There's something powerful about commanding an entire room. Like when I spoke at the conference where we met. Remember that, Mia?"

While he spoke, I thought about what transpired after my interview with Tyrese. I couldn't believe that my mother had purchased *two* paintings. The night I went to my father's house, I questioned my father about the note but not Nancy. I only asked her if she knew about the wooden box. And she had avoided answering my question about the painting when she caught me at the house on Sunday. I needed to talk to Nancy. Perhaps another visit to the house was in order; I wanted to see what was inside that thin cardboard box in her room. I resolved to call her after dinner.

"Hello?" Derek said. "You okay?"

"What?" I asked.

He chuckled. "Where are you? I mean, you're here but you're not."

"I'm sorry, Derek. I just got a lot on my mind."

"Anything I can help with?"

I didn't know why. I didn't understand why I felt like I couldn't talk to him about the paintings and the note and my dad and Nancy. There was something keeping me from telling him.

"Is it about your mom?" Derek asked quietly. "The anniversary of her death and funeral?"

I raised my head and my eyes met his. I decided to tell him. "I just found out that my mom left me a note in the frame of the painting she gave me. But my dad and Nancy claim they know nothing about it."

He wiped his mouth with his napkin. "What did the note say?"

"She wants me to find some type of box that will help explain why she treated me the way she did."

"Wow," Derek said. "That's huge. That's great, Mia. I noticed that when I was there the other night the painting was finally up on the wall. Is that when you found the note?"

I responded in the affirmative.

After a few moments of silence, Derek asked, "Can I do anything to help?"

"I don't think there's anything you can really do. I mean, I'm just gonna have to do my own investigation in the house when they're not there."

Derek once again offered to help me if I needed it, and I politely thanked him. We fell silent again, long enough for me to realize that my fear or reluctance to talk to Derek had been unfounded. It wasn't as hard as I thought it would be.

"How's work going?" Derek asked, breaking the silence. "Anything new from Morgan? By the way, I'm still so proud of you for using my negotiation tactics."

I was glad for the change in subject. "No, nothing from Morgan yet. I figured I'd at least wait until the end of the week."

"Yeah, I think that's enough time."

"Oh! And you know the painting I finally hung up on the wall?"

Derek nodded in acknowledgement.

"Can you believe I'm actually working on a story on the artist who painted it?"

Derek's eyes and mouth opened wide in surprise. "Really?" he stammered.

"In fact, you should know him," I said. "Tyrese Black."

His face suddenly morphed into a strange expression that resembled something between anger and guilt. "Why would I know him?" he asked.

Was he serious? "Umm...because he does the artwork for all the covers for *your author,* Patrick Jerome. Aren't you involved in the choice of cover design for the books you publish? Especially for your biggest author?"

"My concern is with my authors, Mia," he said with an air of self-importance. "Not cover designers or the artists they hire. Yea, I approve all the covers but you should know that I deal with so many different people in different areas of publishing on a daily basis. I can't keep track of them all."

"No need for the attitude," I said, rolling my eyes. "I just assumed you would have known him or at least know more about him. That's all."

"Yea, w-well," he stammered, avoiding my eyes. He was acting peculiar, and I didn't understand why. "I've never met him; I just know his work because of Patrick Jerome's books. And now, of course, the painting your mom gave you."

"See? I didn't even realize that painting was his until I saw a print of it in his gallery yesterday when I went to interview him. What an interesting interview."

"Oh," Derek said, putting his knife and fork down and looking at me. "You met him? You interviewed him?"

"Yea. For the magazine. He's actually really interesting. He has this great theory about why artists turn to their creative side. It makes a lot of sense. I mean, the idea that we were given our talents to help people and profit from them only to be able to continue using our talents to help others is something that I never really thought about. Not from that perspective, anyway. I thought it was profound. I think he's such an interesting person. Quite talented."

"Yes, Mia, it's called the creative mind," he said in a way that seemed to mock me. "Half of my writers feel the same way and the other half feels that the world should bow down to their genius *because* they are giving so much of themselves. It's nothing more than what any creative person would think." Then he looked at me and smiled. "You know what? It sounds like you've got yourself a little crush."

"What?" Maybe I was laying it on a bit too thick. I tried to put it another way: "All I'm saying is that I find his way of thinking very intriguing."

"Nothing more?" he smiled.

"Of course not, Derek. I'm a professional."

He chuckled. "You used the word *interesting* three times within the space of two minutes to describe this guy. Just calling it like I see it."

"Well, you're seeing wrong." I rolled my eyes. "And I'm sorry if I don't have access to vocabulary like you do. That's just the word that I thought most suited Tyrese Black."

He leaned back in his chair. "I think I'm starting to feel a bit jealous," he said, playfully.

"Don't be ridiculous, Derek. You have nothing to be jealous about." A feeling of invigoration swept over me. I had to admit that his jealousy and my adolescent feelings towards Tyrese were both so intoxicating. I had absolutely no intention to act on my feelings for Tyrese, but it certainly made things between Derek and me much more exciting.

"The last time I saw you this excited about meeting someone was when you first met me years ago. I forgot what it was like to see you so captivated by a man." He glared at me as if he had just caught me doing something illicit.

"I have absolutely nothing to say in response to your statement." I was not going to let him take the conversation further.

He looked at me through squinted eyes. "Just making an observation."

He mumbled something about laying down as he stood up, leaving his unfinished plate of food, and walking into his bedroom. Standing up, I gathered both of our plates before throwing the rejected food in the garbage and carefully placed the plates in the dishwasher. I collected dirty spoons and bowls from the sink, finished loading the dishwasher, placed the detergent pod in its compartment and started the machine.

"I'll be right in!" I raised my voice loud enough for Derek to clearly hear me. I searched my bag for my cell phone and quickly dialed my sister's number when I retrieved it. Answering machine. "Nancy. I'm calling again because I need to know if Mom gave you a painting before she died. Or at least left you a note. Please, Nancy. Call me whenever. Thanks."

In my gut, I knew she wouldn't call me back but it was the best I could do at the moment. Maybe she knew where the box was, or maybe we could both look for it together. That would mean we would have to stop bickering long enough to work in solidarity with each other. I was willing to do it. Truth be told, I missed my sister.

I walked into Derek's bedroom and found him sitting on his bed, his back leaning against the headboard.

"Everything okay?" he asked me.

"Yeah. I just had to ask Nancy something. I left her a message."

He reached for me to sit beside him. I sat down next to him as he placed his arm around me. "I still feel like I'm losing you, Mia."

"I'm not going anywhere," I whispered. "I need you in my life."

"Good," he answered. "That's what I need to hear."

He turned the music off with his remote, and we held each other until we fell asleep. This time, the morning had not brought with it a feeling of peace as it had only a few days before, and I was surprisingly okay with that. The absence of peace, however, did not mean I felt any form of agitation or distress. What I did feel, instead, was a certain safety. Derek's arm remained around my shoulder all night into the morning, protecting me from the potential heartbreak that only someone like Tyrese could bring.

Chapter 13.

Wednesday Evening, August 7, 2002

I worked late the following night, finishing up work for deadlines I had ignored the previous two weeks in preparation for the October issue. The first draft of my article on Tyrese Black was already finished and on Morgan's desk awaiting his comments and edits.

I was so engrossed in my work that when I happened to glance up, I was startled to find Bill Anderson, Morgan's favorite flavor of the month, standing in my office. I didn't even think there was anyone left working on the floor.

"Hi," I said, hesitantly. There was a soft pounding in my chest.

"Hey, Mia. Sorry to bother you."

"What can I do for you, Bill?" I had absolutely no patience for the man. There was no reason for him to be in my office, and I needed him to say his peace and let me be.

He showed me a document in his hand. "Yea. Morgan had asked me to take a look at your article on Tyrese Black."

The soft pounding in my chest quickly became quite violent, forcing me to speak before I was ready to. "Excuse me? Why are you editing my article?" I was now breathing hard and loudly.

"Uh..." he spoke with caution. I could tell he did not expect my reaction to be so strong. "Morgan just thought it would be a good idea to take a look at—"

I stood up. "You already said that, Bill. Why? Why does Morgan want you to take a look at *my* work?" I spoke firmly, making him understand where I stood regarding Morgan's insulting request.

His voice trembled. "He thought it would be good to collaborate on this with you."

"Collaborate? Are you serious?" I stepped away from my desk and walked towards the pale man. "After I did all the work, Morgan suddenly wants us to work together?" I snatched the pages from his hand and threw them on my desk. "I have no intention of collaborating with you, Bill. Please leave my office."

Suddenly, the hesitant newbie who stood before me magically transformed into a confident and cocky man, with a wry smile clearly displayed across his face.

"You need to watch your attitude, Mia. Don't think that just because you've been here longer than I have you automatically get the position you want. I'm the one who makes more sense for this position if you expect the magazine to go mainstream."

"And by mainstream, you mean, when people who look like you start buying the magazine? I like the readership we already have." Moisture began to form in the pits of my arms.

"Then you're not progressive enough to help the magazine thrive. It's plain and simple."

"Just get out of my office, Bill." I said it with a calm forcefulness that was quite contrary to the fury I felt inside.

He held his hands up in surrender as he backed out of the office, saying, "Hey. I don't make the rules."

I leaned over the desk as I caught my breath. The coward waited until everyone had gone home for the day to bully me. After I had calmed down, I stood up straight, took the pages from my desk, and skimmed through them. It looked like Morgan was the only one who actually did make some edits on the article. I couldn't believe Bill had the gall to confront me the way he did. I was not going to let Bill or Morgan break me. I was going to fight for this position.

· · · ·

AS I LEFT MY OFFICE late that night, I found Mr. Tyrese Black waiting for me just outside my work building. It seemed that he had been waiting for me as he flipped through the pages of a magazine. Flattery and surprise were the least of the feelings I had when I saw his hard body shine in the soft moonlight and bright night, illuminated by street lamps and storefronts that remained open long into the night. His locks were pulled back into a ponytail. Naughty thoughts of the two of us forced their way into my mind as I watched him. My body against his lean and toned body, our lips seductively teasing each other, his arms around my waist. I could only imagine what he looked like with no clothes on. My heart jumped with excitement as I saw him look my way. He quickly straightened up and smiled at me, showing off that set of darling dimples. He was something like an angel to show up at a time when he did, helping to melt away the experience of that horrible encounter I had just had with Bill Anderson.

"I figured since I couldn't take you to lunch, I'd take you to dinner—if that's all right with you, of course," he said as I approached him.

I felt astoundingly happy and thrilled and excited and amazed, and I didn't care if my smile gave it all away. I couldn't remember the last time I felt deserving of such a sweet and unexpected surprise. For a second, I forgot about the paintings and my mother and lost opportunities I even forgot about Morgan and Bill Anderson. I concentrated only on the innocent excitement Tyrese inspired within me, the same euphoria that schoolgirls experience with that first awareness that a cute boy has a crush on them.

"How long have you been waiting out here?" I asked.

"Only about twenty minutes. But don't worry," he said, showing me the cover to his magazine. "I had last month's issue of *Fresh Voices* to read through."

Yes, I did find that amusing. I smiled at him, then I caught myself. Trying to avoid his eyes, I said, "I'm not that hungry but why don't we go for a few drinks?"

"Sounds like a plan to me," he said as he extended an arm to the street to flag down an available cab.

Surprisingly, we didn't have to wait long before a cab driver pulled over to let us in. We slipped into the back seat as the rhythmic beating of my heart escalated in such a fury that I was forced to take deep breaths to calm it. A fear—or was it an excitement? —of what might transpire in that small intimate space swept over me. I kept my eyes on my hands, which rested on my lap, for the entire time I was with him in the car. I felt reduced to a child, afraid to speak to the person sitting next to me because he was a boy—a boy I liked. I could tell that he sensed my uneasiness.

"You okay?" he asked me.

I smiled and nodded before diverting my attention to the moving city outside the car window.

We arrived at a casual lounge just blocks away from my office building. We were led to a remote corner where we sat at a booth with a small round table directly in front of us. The flame from the small candle provided a wonderful and romantic glow in the darkened bar. I swear he was trying to make me crazy by taking his hair out of the ponytail, releasing his finely twisted locks to fall over his perfectly molded shoulders and revealing the beauty they suddenly gave to his face.

"What were you thinking when you saw me standing outside your office tonight?" Tyrese asked me after we ordered our drinks.

"I liked the way you looked," I said, trying desperately hard not to flirt with him. "And I was flattered, I have to admit. What about you? What were you thinking?"

"That you were gonna turn me away," he laughed.

"Am I that bad?"

"Yeah, Ms. Hill. I'm afraid you are. But you knew that already, didn't you?"

"Yes, I guess so," I said.

"I'm just gonna put it out there," he said with a sweet smile. "I can't stop thinking about you."

Whoa. His blunt confession took me by surprise.

"And I have to be honest with you," he continued. "Your interpretation of the title of my painting impressed the hell out of me. Every thought I've had since then has been of you. I mean, I don't mean to make you uncomfortable by saying that. You just fucking blew me away, and I wanted you to know that."

I couldn't believe how taken I was by those words. I was suddenly living a scene out of a romantic movie.

"I just made you uncomfortable, didn't I?" he asked.

"You didn't," I carefully said. "It's just that—you think about me all the time? We just met, Tyrese."

"Well, do you think it's so impossible to have feelings for someone you just met?"

I knew it wasn't because I had already developed feelings for him as well. Hot flashes invaded my body. I wanted him to kiss me, but it didn't happen, which was perhaps for the best. The waitress suddenly appeared and placed our drinks on our small table, a Jim Beam bourbon whiskey for him and an apple martini for me.

I gulped my apple martini in one shot, and my glass was empty.

"Wow," Tyrese smiled.

"I so desperately needed that." I signaled to the waitress to get me another apple martini.

"Be careful with those," Tyrese said. "I wouldn't want anyone getting the wrong idea about us."

What was I doing?

"I have a boyfriend, Tyrese," I finally said. "I've been with him for five years."

His smiled looked to me to be one of disappointment. "Of course you do."

"I'm not here to lead you on."

The waitress placed another apple martini on the table. This time I took only a sip.

"I don't think you're leading me on. I just wanted to take you out for lunch, that's all. And when that didn't happen, I figured dinner would be better. But now that I'm having drinks with you, I wouldn't have it any other way." He raised his glass, so I did as well. "I want to make a toast to the unbreakably cold, straightforward, no shit-taking, no smile-having, no-nonsense Mia Hill."

I laughed as we touched glasses. I was tickled. The man's cleverness captivated me and there was nothing I could do about it.

"Wow," he said softly. "I think the world would like to see you smiling more often."

Yes, I blushed. He was saying all the right things and I was taking it all in. Everything about him was wonderful, from the way he held his drink, to the way he smiled, to the way he sat on the lounge chair—as if he were completely aware of his perfection, and no one could tell him differently.

I thought about the beautiful woman I had seen at his gallery the other day. "Do you have a girlfriend, Tyrese?"

"No," he answered, eying me carefully.

But I still wanted to know who that woman was to him. "I met a woman the other day before my interview with you. Tiana Brown? Who's she?" I watched carefully for any facial expression that would tell me anything that would contradict his response to me.

"Oh, Tiana was there? She didn't even tell me. She stops by every once in a while to check out the work. She's my cousin. From my mom's side."

I had to admit that I quite liked that answer. I didn't want him to be taken; I wanted him all to myself.

"So why don't you have a girlfriend?"

"It just hasn't happened yet," he smiled. "I mean, don't get me wrong. I've been in a few relationships, but for one reason or another, things just never worked out."

"I see." I took another sip of my drink. "Did anyone ever break your heart?"

"Hell yeah!" He laughed. "Hasn't it happened to everyone at one time or another?"

"I guess so. I'm not exempt."

"Oh yeah?" he smiled. "Tell me about it."

"Not tonight, my friend." My story was too depressing.

He didn't respond to that. Instead, we stared at each other for what seemed like minutes. He finally broke the silence: "Anyway, other than being really busy? I guess I haven't been looking for that special someone. The truth is I haven't found anyone who challenges me like you do."

My heart skipped. "But how have I challenged you?"

"Well, I never know what you're thinking. I find myself wanting to get you to open up. Thus, the challenge. And you make me think about my concepts and ideas again and the reasons why I paint." He took a sip of his drink and looked back into my eyes. "You're a hard person to figure out."

"Stop trying to figure me out."

"Already stopped."

I felt myself falling into a state of vulnerability as I thought about how much I wanted him for myself. I had worked so hard to make sure that no man ever took advantage of me again like David the plagiarist did that I forgot completely what it was like to give in to a moment. In that second, I concluded that I didn't want to be that tough, impenetrable woman I'd spent years constructing. I just wanted to have fun, let my guard down, and just fully experience my time with him. During my interview with Tyrese, I had felt vulnerable as he spoke about creating art but now, I craved full exposure. Yet, the part of me that spent years cultivating a cautious personality understood it could not happen in one night simply because I willed it so.

Tyrese Black. I wanted him as my little secret and wished that Glory had never brought him to my attention. I wished I had met him on my own. I resented the fact that Glory was the one to open my eyes to this fantastic man. Without warning, Glory's exaltation of this man created feelings of envy and jealousy within me as I thought about the way she must have thrown herself onto him when she met him. Based on the little I knew about Tyrese, I guessed that she was not his type. But men are men and some of them are weaker than others.

"Let me ask you something," I said. "What do you think of my friend Glory Williams?"

"Glory!" he said while he laughed. "She's—I think she's a unique individual,"

I looked at him curiously. "What's so funny?"

"Nothing." He covered his mouth with his hand.

"Did you two happen to hit it off?"

"I guess you can say I had the chance."

"What do you mean?" I challenged. "Come on. If I know Glory, then I know you two have already—"

He didn't let me finish. "And if you knew me, *which you don't*, you'd know that I would never mess with a girl like that."

"A girl like what?" I suddenly felt like I had to defend her honor.

He put his hands up in the air as if to surrender. "Look. I know she's your friend and everything, so I don't want to offend you, but I get turned off by aggressive women like her."

"Oh, come on!"

"No, really! Glory didn't do anything for me intellectually. You spent five minutes looking at my paintings and analyzed them with such precise skill. Glory only acknowledged my work as art after she saw what I looked like.

Don't get me wrong, I don't want it to be all about me, but you gotta let me know that you got more going on in your head than just money and sex."

"Glory is a very intelligent woman."

"I don't doubt that. But she was a little too forward, especially in a professional setting. It was nonstop, and that was a huge turn-off for me. Guys like to sleep with girls like her but that's about it."

I was annoyed with what he was saying about Glory, although I agreed with it all. But then again, I *did* ask him. And I received my answer—he was not the least bit attracted to her. She was no longer my competition.

"Well, that's Glory," I said in an attempt to finish our conversation about her. I didn't want to ruin the friendly exchange we had going. "You gotta love her for that."

He shook his head. "If you say so."

I put my martini glass to my mouth and took another sip as I felt him carefully watching me.

"Can I ask you a personal question?" he asked.

"Uh oh," I responded.

"I hope you don't mind my saying but I get this feeling of deep sadness from you and I'm wondering why. I mean, you got a man who I'm guessing loves you and a job you seem to enjoy. It seems as though you got a real good life. But you seem so unhappy. Can I ask why?"

"First of all," I said, taking another sip of my martini, I dramatically stalled. "Someone can have all the things in life they've ever wanted yet still be unhappy. It's something I can't really explain. It just is. And secondly, just because it looks like I have a man who loves me and a job I enjoy does not mean I have it all together. It doesn't mean I don't ever have the right to be sad."

He hesitated. "You—you had such a strong reaction over my painting. Can I ask what happened?"

I chuckled more to myself, and stared at the contents of my glass. "I've wanted to stay angry at my mother for how she treated me when she was still alive. Never supporting my writing career. Pretty much never supporting anything I did. But with that one note, she expressed, I guess, a kind of apology. An olive branch. And the coincidence of meeting you just days after I discovered the note was a bit bewildering."

A soft lump grew in my throat before I realized I was getting emotional. A wave of sadness engulfed me. "Why am I even telling you all this?" I asked him. Tears started to push their way through my tear ducts. I had never spoken about my feelings to anyone outside of my therapy sessions. But there I was, so quick to share them with Tyrese. I quickly wiped the tears from my eyes, and Tyrese politely looked away, pretending he did not see, as if he knew that was what I needed.

He cleared his throat and took a large gulp of his drink.

I decided to change the subject. "Did you know your mother, Tyrese? I mean, really know her?"

"No. Actually, I didn't. I got to know her through my aunt, which was her sister, and my cousin. She spent a lot of time with them too before she—" he hesitated "—you know, ended things."

"It must have been so hard for you."

"Yeah. You start telling yourself shit like, 'If only I told her I loved her every day.' A major regret is that I didn't get to know her while she was still alive. I was nineteen years old, into meeting girls and hanging with the guys and just having fun. I took advantage of always having her around. Her death changed my life." He kept his eyes on his hands, which were wrapped around his glass.

"How so?" I asked, finding myself wanting to hear more, feeling the desire to be enveloped in his own story of tragedy.

"There are always sacrifices to be made in life. I guess I have a good life now because my mother took hers then."

"What do you mean by that?"

"Well, I chose to develop my talent because of her death. Circumstances and events would not have been what they were if she didn't do what she did."

I sighed. He spoke of her suicide not with anger or pain but as something he had long ago come to terms with and accepted.

"What about your dad?" I asked, cautiously. He was revealing so much; I wasn't sure just how much more he was willing to divulge.

"Never knew him. My mom raised me alone. She told me all about him, though. Left out the part that he abandoned her only a few weeks after I was born." He smiled and said, "I was proud of my mom. Still am."

He was quiet for a moment. I felt the martini now in my head, affecting my thinking and perception.

"My mom died of cancer about a year ago," I said, "and despite all the pain she went through during her final months, I still can't find it in me to forgive her for every wrong I felt she ever did me. I want to forgive her, to just let it go. But there's this resentment inside of me that just insists on holding on to that anger. It's a constant battle and it's exhausting."

After a moment's thought, Tyrese said, "That's deep."

The silence between us stretched. I sighed. "I have so many regrets about her and my relationship with her."

"Like what?"

"I'm sorry that we didn't get along, for one thing. See, I wasn't her favorite, but *God,* I loved her. I loved her so much that I used to hate myself for loving her. Twisted, I know. But I looked up to her because I thought she was brilliant. And you were right, Tyrese, about what you told me at the end of the interview. She has always been that thing that has kept me from my destiny, as you had called it. She dissuaded my interest in writing and told me I'd never get anywhere with it. You have to understand something about my mother. She studied journalism and political science and then went to Harvard to study law and I guess she expected me to follow in her footsteps."

A memory of the time I told my mother about my first-place win in a state short story contest entered my mind. "I once let her read a short story I wrote that I thought was profound about a young man whose poverty forced him into a life of violence. It was one among thousands of submissions from other writers throughout the state and I won first place. So, you can imagine how excited I was to let my mother read it. I remember waiting anxiously on her couch in her home office as she read the story. I remember everything about her from that day. Her hair was in a short ponytail and her makeup wasn't on yet and I thought the expression on her face as she read my story was one of pride. Maybe it was. After she finished reading it, she flipped through the pages as she said to me, 'Wow. I can see why it won. This is really good, Mia.' Oh, my goodness. To hear my mother say that was like the best dream come true. I remember tears in my eyes, and I tried to wipe them away so that she wouldn't see them. Then, just like that, she burst my bubble. She said, 'You have an incredible talent here. You're able to make the reader feel everything the character is feeling in a way that catches the reader off guard. But wouldn't that talent be better served in a way that can help other people? Think about what I do as a lawyer to help others. As good as it is, Mia, how can this story help anyone with their problems in life? You're better than just a story. Use your talent in a way that really matters.'"

Both Tyrese and I were silent as I thought about the words that had been ingrained in my memory for so many years. I felt the tears forming in my eyes once again, but this time, I wasn't going to allow them to be set free. It was not the time to feel sorry for myself. I didn't share the story to upset myself or receive any sympathy from the resplendent man sitting across from me. Still, I couldn't help feeling exposed, as if a shroud of protection had been pulled away to reveal all of my truths and vulnerabilities. Something inside of me, which had long been waiting to unburden itself from those vulnerabilities, however, kept going; it finally had someone who was willing to listen.

"I thought she was a genius," I continued. "She could have owned that law firm she worked for, that's how great I thought she was. That's why when she said my fiction didn't matter, I believed her. It hurt, and I was angry, but I still believed her. The woman was my idol, Tyrese. I mean, my pride doesn't come from the person I once was. It comes from my mother, the person who has molded me into the woman I now am. And I don't even like myself! I'm proud of the way she helped me to become a strong person, yet I hate myself the way I am. If that's not twisted, then I don't know what is! She was so cold to me, and I couldn't help feeling both love *and* hate for her. She treated me so differently than my sister, Tyrese, and I *saw* it and I *knew* and *felt* it but I *still* thought she was so remarkable. She spoiled my sister and let her do whatever the hell she wanted, but she was always so firm with me. I vied for my mother's affections and did whatever I could just to feel some appreciation from her. And it never happened."

It wasn't until after I finished my monologue that I realized I was slowly growing angry. But the alcohol in my system overpowered that anger, which was the reason why I rambled on, telling Tyrese more about my feelings for my mother than he needed to know. The weight I had been carrying had finally been lifted and I somehow felt free of it. It felt different from talking about it with Dr. Flarc. I closed my eyes and permitted myself to indulge in the lightness of my head.

"You're drunk, aren't you?" Tyrese asked me.

"Just a little tipsy," I answered, putting my index finger and thumb close together. "I'm sorry, Tyrese. It's just that my mother raised me in a state of negativity; it defines who I am. I guess I'm proud of the no-nonsense Mia but hate the socially inept Mia as well."

"She fucked you up, that's what she did," he bluntly said.

"Tell me about it," I agreed.

"But why do you hate yourself so much?"

"Because." I chuckled. "I'm not always that nice, and sometimes I really don't understand why. It's like my mother's coldness rubbed off onto me. And I live in this perpetual anger and resentment of everyone around me." I sighed. "I can't seem to change no matter what I do."

He pursed his lips together in a polite smile. "Maybe you don't want to change."

"Why would anyone want to be so bitter? I'll end up just as unhappy as my mother was."

He took a sip of his drink and then looked at me with a seriousness that seemed to counter his disposition. "You didn't tell me what was in the note that your mother wrote you with the gift of the painting. You said it was her olive branch. Maybe it was her way of asking for your forgiveness."

Almost instantly and without any warning, a flood of tears escaped me in a raw demonstration of the feelings I harbored in the past few days since I had discovered my mother's note. I realized at that moment that I had not been able to really talk about the discovery or the content of my mother's note to anyone but Dr. Flare though it was something constantly on my mind. Keeping the palms of my hands over my eyes, I released the emotions I had kept hidden from everyone who had come into contact with me—everyone including me. I didn't know what Tyrese was doing at that moment or how uncomfortable he might have felt. All I knew was that I finally allowed myself to really feel the guilt, the shame, the relief, the hope of changing the story of my mother's behavior towards me when she was still alive. Meeting Tyrese almost immediately after I discovered her note felt like a serendipitous sign that things were going to get better. Maybe Tyrese was supposed to help me figure things out. I needed to believe in the idea of the universe aligning itself in such a way just for my benefit.

Removing my hands from my eyes, I found that Tyrese was patiently waiting for my breakdown to end so that he could provide me with tissue that he managed to get from somewhere. I graciously took it and dabbed my eyes.

"I am so sorry about that," I said, chuckling to let him know my moment was over.

"No need," he responded.

I took another sip of my martini, and we sat in silence.

"Were your parents divorced?" Tyrese asked after a few minutes.

"No. Why do you ask?"

"The way you talk about your mother and never mention your father puts them at different levels. It almost sounds to me like you never lived with your father."

"Well, I never really got to know him," I answered. "I remember when he used to read to me in our living room. And before he went to work on some days, he'd let us stand on his feet as he walked around the kitchen, holding onto us so that we couldn't fall." I smiled at the memory. "My happiest memories of him are when we were kids. He was always there for us. We kind of grew distant in my college years, though. But no, my parents never divorced. They should have. Instead, they stayed together in a marriage that had no love or affection. My biggest fear is ending up like them."

"Won't happen." He said it so quickly.

"What makes you so sure?"

"Because it's your biggest fear. You'll make sure it doesn't happen."

I nodded. "Good point. But it can go either way, can't it? Some people follow the same emotional patterns their parents had. And look at how I turned out. I grew up with such a twisted model of relationships, and it shows through in the fucked-up relationships I've been in."

"Really?" he said curiously, as if yearning to learn more about my failed relationships.

"I'm sorry," I said. "I'm rambling again. Must be the martini."

He smiled. "Would you like some more?"

"You trying to get me drunk?" I flirted.

"No, ma'am. Just trying to make sure you're satisfied."

I chuckled. "*You* don't have to worry about that."

"I'm sure your man's got that all covered, huh?"

"He sure as hell does. What about you, Tyrese? I know you don't have a special lady, but is there anyone available to satisfy *you*?"

He leaned back in his chair and smiled. "You applying for the position?" he asked.

"Calm down," I said. "I'm just asking a question."

"I have friends."

"Good for you! People should always have friends they can call when they have needs that need to be met. These friends of yours—girls, I hope."

"No doubt," he smiled, moving closer to me.

"I want to ask you something that has been on my mind since I first met you." I said.

"Go right ahead."

"I want to see your tattoo."

"Well," he said as he pulled the sleeve up from his left arm. "Even though it's not a question but a statement, I'll let you see it anyway." There it was, the image of a smiling angel looking up towards the sky. Her arms were crossed over her chest with the palm of her right hand touching her left shoulder and the palm of her left hand touching her right shoulder. Her wings were so large that they wrapped themselves around her body, just below the elbows of her arms. The intricate details of the wings and her smile were extraordinary. The tattoo was so beautiful that I wondered whether it was his design.

"Your guardian angel?" I asked.

"Not mine, my mother's." He pulled a silver chain from underneath his shirt and revealed a pendant with the same design on his arm. "My mother was given this pendant as a child. It belonged to her grandmother, my great grandmother. She was told it would always protect her, so she kept it on a chain close to her heart. That's where I keep it now. And if someday I should lose it, knock on wood, I'll still have it on my arm."

I stared at him. There was something so genuine about him.

"Do *you* have a guardian angel?" he asked me.

"No," I responded. "I don't believe there's something like an angel watching out for me and 'guarding' me. If that were the case, I don't think I would have experienced so many terrible things in my life."

"But everyone goes through bad times, Mia. No one is exempt."

"Well, there you go. That proves my point."

"Fair enough."

Changing the subject, I said, "Can I ask you something personal?"

"Go ahead."

"Why did your mother kill herself? Wasn't she happy?"

"You asked me this question already at my interview."

"Yeah. I know, but at the time you didn't know me, and it was during a professional interview. Your answer may not have been complete. You said she may have been in pain, emotionally. Was there anything you learned about her after her death?"

He sighed. "All I know is that she never gave any signs that she was sad. We got along so great, and she seemed like she was always such a happy person. She never complained about having to raise me on her own, especially after my father left her when I was born. I would have never known that my mother was depressed; she hid it so well behind smiles that made her shine like heaven. No one knew what she was going through inside, not even my aunt. And they were so close. I don't know what the cause or the root of my mother's pain was. Maybe it was my father leaving her. Maybe I was the reason for her pain. I just don't know."

"Couldn't have been you. You said that the two of you got along great. She must have been proud of you."

"But I'll never know what caused her pain. It used to eat me up inside, but I've learned to accept the fact that I'll never know."

"Isn't it amazing, though, how your feelings can be so deep within you that the only way to alleviate them—the only way to *kill* them—is to kill yourself? I don't care what anybody says. That's got to take courage."

"But doesn't it also take a greater amount of courage to live through that pain and not take your own life? Taking your life is giving up, and I commend anyone who doesn't give up because *that* takes more strength than the guts needed to just end it all. A cop-out."

He didn't look at me. He simply took another sip of his drink.

"Are you angry with her for what she did?" I asked, thinking of my own attempt back in college.

"No, I'm not angry." He said, his voice low. "Not anymore. I'm just sad every now and then. My mom was so cool. I miss her. I miss the talks we had, the arguments, just my time with her. She was the best person in my life."

I stared at him, realizing that I would never say those words, or anything like them, to anyone—least of all to myself—about my own mother. He was quiet, so I remained silent as well. In one gulp, I finished my martini. "You're a fortunate man, Tyrese, to have known the true love of your mother."

"I guess I am. But she's still gone."

I looked into his eyes and said, "So is mine."

We stared at each other for several seconds before we both burst into laughter. I was so light-headed and tipsy, and it made me feel like such a different person. I loved the person I became when I had alcohol in my system, and I had to laugh to express that feeling. I was happy to be with him, and I didn't want my time with him to end.

"Your man's a lucky man," Tyrese said after catching his breath.

"Why do you say that?" I asked, wiping the tears of laughter from the corners of my eyes.

"He gets to call you his girlfriend." Tyrese stopped laughing, but the beautiful smile stayed.

I stared into his brown eyes, feeling myself falling for him in a way that was more than just an innocent crush.

"My boyfriend," I said, "doesn't always make me feel lucky to be with him."

Upon moving closer to me where I could feel his breath on my face, Tyrese said, "If you were my girlfriend, you'd never doubt how lucky we both are to be together. Sincerely."

His words. They captivated me as we held each other's gaze. The longing grew from the pit of my stomach where the alcohol currently made its home. It was the alcohol that gave me clarity. That night was all about me and Tyrese. I made the decision right there that Tyrese would come home with me.

• • • •

THE MARTINIS MADE ME do it. Alcohol loosens me up and helps the daring and pleasant Mia make an appearance. No wonder I told Tyrese all that I did. But there was also something about him that made me open up to him so easily. What was it? I loved the time I spent with him that night at the lounge bar; I hadn't had that much fun in years. He made me laugh, and I loved myself when I was laughing. I longed to forever be in Tyrese's presence, just because he made me laugh. I was deeply attracted to him; I felt a powerful connection to him, and I was comfortable with him. It was as though he brought out the best in me, and I liked that.

The thoughts I had of him lingered not on our conversation at the bar but on what he said as he stood outside my apartment door. He had wanted to make sure I got home okay, and I was more than willing to accept his kindness. As I stumbled out of the cab, he quickly got out and ran to my side to keep me from falling to the ground. I was only a bit tipsy, so I knew I wouldn't fall, but I loved having him there to give me that kind of attention. He took the stairs with me and walked me to my door, all the while keeping his arm around my waist to keep me steady. And just after I opened the door with my key, I turned and said to him, "I had a good time tonight, Tyrese. Thank you for the drinks."

"Always," he answered. That was it. He didn't say, *You're welcome*, or *Anytime*, or *No problem*. Instead, he said, "Always." And he said it with a conviction that meant everything he did not say in response to my thank you. I knew then that my physical attraction to him and his to me had reached a new level.

He smiled and stared deeply into my eyes as if he were not afraid of what he might find there. I couldn't resist him any longer. I reached over, placing my hand behind his neck and pulling his body closer to mine. I kissed him with urgency, recalling the day I first met him and how much I had wanted him then. He returned my kiss with a fierceness, moving his hands down to the small of my back and then lower still. Our bodies were pressed up against each other with an uninhibited passion. I felt him grow hard against me and I loved the feeling. My heart pounded as his mouth moved down to my neck.

Derek.

I quickly pushed Tyrese away from me and, breathlessly, I said, "I really do have a boyfriend."

In between breaths, Tyrese answered, "I believed you then, and I believe you now."

And then we ravished each other. It was such an unbelievably glorious moment that I didn't care about anything else but fucking him. And I did. I would have loved to recount the raw details of my sexual encounter with Tyrese. As it was, I had not actually had dinner when Tyrese asked me earlier that night, but I lied in order to prevent the awkward situation a dinner can so often create. I was very aware of everything I did that night while I was doing it. However, without any food in my stomach, the three martinis that I consumed traveled easily through my system, altering my perception, making me feel bold while triggering a slight impairment of my memory.

I could not recall all of the details the next morning, but I did remember what was important. The act itself was fuzzy to me, but I know that I enjoyed him immensely. There was no bed involved; the carpeted living room floor served us well. I recalled being on top of him, looking down at his beautiful face as his hands caressed my lower back. At some point, he was behind me, placing his hands on my back. His hands were soft against my skin and made me feel delicate, as a woman should feel. I remembered him gently cupping my breasts as he rocked me. I had never before felt so aroused by that alone. My breasts missed the soft touch of a man who was unfamiliar with them. Tyrese explored my body as he enjoyed me, something Derek had not done in quite some time. We laughed together, especially when a leg cramp threatened my performance. But Tyrese didn't let my cramp stop him from enjoying our moment. He gently massaged my leg as he kept his rhythm.

I had fun with Tyrese that night and realized how important that was for me. Sex with Derek had become mundane, a duty. I had forgotten how remarkable sex could be. Tyrese awakened the sexual person that I long thought was dead, and in doing so, triggered such an intense sensation that mere words could not describe the explosion I felt within my body, forcing me to scream out his name louder than I'd ever imagined.

The knowledge that Derek had a key to my apartment and could walk in on us at any moment heightened my excitement. It was absolutely, deliciously perverse. And I'll say it again, the martinis made me do it.

Chapter 14

Early Thursday Morning, August 8, 2002

My eyes beheld the painting that now hung proudly on my living room wall. I marveled at the idea that my act of finally placing it on the wall possibly manifested its creator into my life. With a bit of irony, I appreciated the surreal nature of its new home as Tyrese and I lay in each other's arms. We were on the floor in front of the couch in my living room, his body so close against mine. He moved his body closer still from behind and wrapped his arms around me, resting his hands on my naked stomach. We both sighed. I relished the thought of what had happened between us and how absolutely amazing it was. I knew exactly what I was doing the night before—the martinis simply gave me the courage to go through with what I had wanted since the moment we met. Giving into my weakness like that was something I would normally never do, knowing that I was completely wrong for doing so. But with it came such a feeling of empowerment and freedom.

With the alcohol no longer in my system, the sense of tranquility I felt jolted me into reality. *What was I doing?* I had to get dressed. I sat up and searched for my thong.

"What's wrong?" Tyrese asked.

"Nothing. I need to find my underwear. I suggest you find your clothes, too." Suddenly, a feeling of trepidation overcame me. "My boyfriend has a key to this apartment. You have to go."

He was silent as I found my underwear and put them on. I walked into the bathroom and put on my bathrobe, and secured it with a knot in the front.

Tyrese lifted himself up and stood before me in his naked glory. I had never seen a man who looked so sexy naked. He started to dress, and I watched. There was something sensual about the way he put on his pants, not zipping them up until after he buttoned his shirt, even though he didn't tuck his shirt into his pants. As he finished dressing, he motioned to his painting, *The Box,* which was hanging on my wall.

"I just realized something," he said.

"What?" I asked, also looking at the painting.

Never taking his eyes away from it, he said, "The woman in my painting is you."

Chapter 15.

Thursday Afternoon, August 8, 2002

"I felt highly insulted yesterday when Bill had the audacity to walk into my office and hand me the pages that were meant only for you, Morgan." I glared at him, for effect. He sat at his desk in his large corner office and smiled smugly at me, as if he were enjoying a show I was putting on for him.

"Mia, I'm not to blame for how you feel when all someone does is deliver marked pages to you from me."

"He wasn't just delivering them, Morgan, and you know it. He was trying to intimidate me, to make me feel like he had the upper hand. You need to keep your boy in check."

He leaned back in his chair. "I'll talk to him about taking the pages from my office, but if you want to be the editor in chief, you'll have to check your emotions at the door. I can't have you bursting into my office each time someone here upsets you."

I saw red. He was trivializing my complaint and turning it into a matter of me being too emotional for a position that I knew I was more than capable of handling.

"Keep your boy in check," I repeated. I stormed out of his office and walked right back into mine.

I sat at my desk, closed my eyes and took a deep breath in. I was not going to allow those two men to affect my work. I began to question whether I still wanted to work there. The obvious display of male ego was disgusting and I had to wonder whether that would be something that I would have to consistently deal with moving forward.

I took another deep breath and exhaled. Taking the pages in my hand, I read the edits Morgan had made on my article on Tyrese Black. Morgan seemed to like it and had made few changes. I was surprised he didn't find more things wrong with it. I pulled the article up on my computer screen and started to revise. I was grateful for the distraction that kept me from thinking about my office drama. Working on a piece about Tyrese of course made me think about him and our incredible time together. I still couldn't believe it happened. I didn't think I could ever be unfaithful to Derek.

I didn't feel guilty about cheating on Derek and that unnerved me. Derek had always been so good to me. He would never cheat on me. I knew what I did was wrong, but I wasn't sorry for it. I suppose that if my tryst with Tyrese had been one of disappointment, I would have felt guilty for risking my relationship with Derek for a dissatisfying night. Either that or I would have been too disappointed to feel guilty. But the fact that I felt no guilt at all was strangely disconcerting. Maybe it was because I knew that the truth was safeguarded somewhere deep inside my heart. I felt that I was meant to be with Tyrese and not Derek.

"Mia?" That was the voice belonging to one Mr. Tyrese Black. He poked his head through the doorway of my office before stepping in. My goodness, how can a man wearing a simple t-shirt and a pair of jeans look so good? But as happy as I was to see him, I was still a little annoyed with the way he popped in without calling me first. It seemed like all the men that surrounded me suddenly acted as if they were entitled.

"Hi," he said, standing in my office as if he had been invited. "Am I disturbing you?"

I leaned back in my chair. Still annoyed about my encounter with Morgan and his apathetic attitude to my concern, I had to let Tyrese know that his visit was not okay.

"Don't you have a gallery to run?" I asked.

"I do, but I also take lunches. I assumed you did the same. Besides, Michael is my right and left-hand man."

"Your gallery's in Chelsea. You came all the way uptown just to have lunch?"

"It's really no big deal, Mia. A few minutes out of my way."

"I'm sorry, Tyrese," I said, looking at the work on my desk. "I do have deadlines to meet."

"Oh. So, I guess now's not a good time."

I smiled politely. "It isn't."

"All right, then. I'll give you a call later." Confidently, he turned to walk out of my office.

"Tyrese," I called to him.

He turned to look at me.

"It was just sex. Please don't mistake that for anything else."

He stared at me for a few seconds in disbelief. "Wow," he said with a slight smile before walking out. "At least you're sincere."

My intention was to make sure I didn't become attached. Becoming attached would only make me vulnerable. Yes, I felt that he and I were better together than Derek and I were but I could also be telling myself that because Tyrese was still so new to me. As much as I liked Tyrese, I could not allow myself to nurse any feelings for him because I was very much in love with Derek. Well, at least, that's what I tried to convince myself.

Chapter 16

Thursday Evening, August 8, 2002

Derek cooked me dinner that night in his apartment—oven baked chicken breast with steamed vegetables and scalloped potatoes. He was quiet as he cooked, and during dinner, he seemed preoccupied. I could sense that something was wrong. My only guess was that Jones Press weighed heavily on his mind.

I had to keep reminding myself that Derek was going through his own dilemmas. Though the press was doing well, there were still some financial setbacks that prevented him from truly enjoying his success. He had been collaborating with the CEO of Words-in-Rhythm, Inc., which was a distribution company based in Chicago. For some time now, he had been stalling his decision on whether he would enter into a joint venture with the distribution company. I assumed Derek, not unlike myself, sometimes found it difficult to make important decisions.

"You haven't said a word all night," I said.

He sighed. "I guess I've got a lot on my mind."

"Do you want to share?"

He looked at me, and I suddenly remembered my night with Tyrese. I felt like he had somehow learned about my infidelity. But that was close to impossible. I hadn't shared that information with anyone.

"Words-in-Rhythm offered me more money to buy out Jones Press."

I sighed. "What did you tell them?"

"I told them I needed some more time."

I looked away.

"Why don't we just get married, Mia? Look at us, playing around for so long."

I didn't know where it came from, but I snapped. "What, Derek? Marry you and then what? Have Words-in-Rhythm buy out Jones Press; we move to Chicago and then what happens with my career at *Fresh Voices*, Derek? I'm not giving up a job I spent so many years nurturing."

"Okay, so we get married; I tell Words-in-Rhythm I'm out; I take out a loan to help me out with Jones Press, and you stay at *Fresh Voices*, working your way up to becoming publisher. How does that sound?"

"Why do we have to think about this now, Derek? Why can't we just let things fall into place?"

"Because that's not me. I have to look ahead to the future."

"Well, then, *marriage* is simply not me. How many times are we going to discuss this?"

"Marriage is simply not you?" He repeated. "Or is it that marriage with *me* is not for you?"

He threw his napkin onto his plate, lifted himself up from his seat and walked over to the couch in his living room. I could tell he was under a lot of stress, and our fighting about our relationship was only adding fuel to his fire. He needed to relax. I needed to show him that this was not something we had to discuss at the moment. I didn't want there to always be tension between us when we were together. Following him into the living room, I knelt down in between his legs, unbuttoned his shirt and took it off. I slowly sucked on his neck and worked my way down his chest, lightly biting his nipples. He liked it when I did that.

"Mia," he whispered as he closed his eyes and exhaled. I unzipped his pants, reached inside, and started gently caressing him. I lowered my head but he stopped me.

"Sex doesn't fix everything, Mia."

I exhaled. "Apparently not," I answered, relaxing into my kneeling position before transitioning to sitting on the floor, still directly in front of him. He zipped his pants and leaned back, his head resting on the back of the couch. He sighed as he stared at the ceiling.

"When did things between us become so strained?" Derek asked. But he didn't wait for a response from me. "We don't even go out anymore."

"Don't be so dramatic, Derek," I quickly responded. "Don't we have plans for Saturday night? That counts as going out, doesn't it?"

"I'm sure if it weren't a book party for Patrick Jerome, you would have already conveniently made other plans to avoid being sociable for one night."

"What the hell is that supposed to mean?"

"I'm referring to your antisocial nature, Mia."

I looked at him as if he were crazy. "My antisocial nature? Are you kidding me? I have always supported you in everything that had to do with Jones Press."

"Yes! With Jones Press. You feel you have a duty to be at this party Saturday night because I'm Patrick's publisher and you have to show face. If it were any other circumstance, I'm sure I would be going solo."

"It's incredible how little you think of me," I said. "I've never given you any reason to feel that I don't like going out with you. We both lead very busy lives; maybe *that's* what's getting in the way of our social life together."

He said nothing.

And then, out of sudden curiosity, I asked him, "Why do you even want to get married, Derek?"

He sat up and looked at me with an intensity that I did not understand and said, "When I look at you, I see the perfect representation of a strong black woman who follows her passion and doesn't let anything get in the way of that. And I would be honored to have that admirable trait passed on to my children."

I didn't know what to say to that admission. I turned my head and looked away from him as guilt and shame coursed through my body. A part of me loved hearing him acknowledge my strength as a black woman and hearing him speak of his future children softened me in a way I had not expected. But, I couldn't possibly live up to his idea of perfection when I was so far from what he perceived me to be. I couldn't share with him his need or his want to get married. I didn't want it. It suddenly struck me that I couldn't understand why I was trying so hard to hold onto a man I didn't want to marry.

I decided to take another angle. "Look at the sad, bitter, depressed person that I am, Derek. How can I ever bring children into this world and raise them to become decent human beings? Look at the person that I am." It pained me to think of my parents and how their own bitterness and coldness contributed to the unbalanced person that I was. The thought of a life like that for Derek, or for our potential children, saddened me.

"I'm looking. And I see a woman who's working through her grief to come back stronger than ever before."

I shook my head as I looked down to the floor to avoid eye contact with him. "I'm not strong, Derek. I still haven't gotten over any of my issues even though I've been in therapy for years. My fears dictate all of my actions. And slowly, I feel myself unraveling again. What you see is not a strong woman. It's a representation of who I wish I was because it's all been an act. At home, at work and with you."

He lifted my chin with his finger. "You're still here, Mia. That means you are stronger than you think you are. Resilient. Valiant. That's what I see. That's what I know about you. You haven't been beat down. And that's the strength that matters. That's the strength I want our kids to have."

As beautiful as his sentiment was, what stayed in my mind was the fact that he never said he wanted to marry me because he loved me.

Chapter 17.

Friday Afternoon, August 9, 2002

"I went to visit my fucking parents the other day," Glory said as we had lunch outside of a Thai restaurant at Union Square. The outdoor markets were open for business and masses of people traveled there to shop the great deals they found on the vegetable stands. Cyclists rode through the crowded streets, in the midst of yellow cabs, elongated buses, cars and pedestrians, all trying to get to their destinations. The honking and the general noise of the area were a welcomed distraction to my day. Among all of the restaurants with outdoor seating at Union Square, we were very lucky to be seated almost immediately.

Glory explained her latest attempt to reconnect with parents who showed so little interest in her and her life. As the last child out of eleven siblings, Glory never quite reconciled with the fact that her parents never showed her much attention, or love for that matter. They welcomed her with excitement for the way she could financially support their many vices but they didn't seem to care about how she had made a successful career for herself. Because her older siblings had been burdened with the responsibility of being her caretakers, they had treated her with derision and no longer kept in touch with her. Therefore, Glory explained, she had no family.

"Anyway," Glory said in an effort to wave the discussion away. "Whatever. That's the last time I waste my time going to see them."

"You have to try to talk to them, Glory. If only to relieve yourself of feeling so badly about the whole thing."

"I don't see you taking your own fucking advice." Glory said this without even looking at me.

"You don't want to end up like me, Glory. Every day I beat myself up for never making up with my mother before she died."

Our waiter came and placed our meals before us: a Caesar salad with grilled chicken sprinkled with parmesan cheese on top for me and for Glory, a rice pilaf dish. We both thanked the waiter as he walked away.

"I keep telling you," Glory said, holding a forkful of her meal in her hand. "You did the best you could. Your mom was mean to you and she stifled you. You did what you needed to do to survive under her oppression."

Her words were comforting but they also brought me pain because of my recent knowledge that my mother was indeed trying to reach out to me for forgiveness before she died, yet I never took heed.

I suddenly lost my appetite and didn't even want my food. "Glory, I think I might have done something terrible."

Glory stopped eating and focused her attention onto me. "What?"

I took in a deep breath and then I spoke. "Remember the painting my mother gave me before she died?'

"Yeah."

"She had left a note behind it asking for forgiveness but I never knew until a few days ago because I finally decided to hang it up. I'm so stupid. I should have known that she wasn't just giving me a painting."

"I understand why that's so upsetting," Glory said. "But calling yourself stupid isn't going to change what happened. Stop beating yourself up over it. It's not doing you any good. Why don't you honor her memory maybe through an article in your magazine or visiting her grave or something?"

I closed my eyes to let the tears fall and then exhaled, feeling grateful for Glory's words, her advice and her friendship. "Thank you," I said softly with a broken voice.

"I know it hurts," she whispered, reaching for my hand. "I'm hurting too and I just wish it didn't have to fucking hurt so much."

I wiped my tears away, and with a stronger voice said, "You're hurting because you care."

"Yeah, no shit. I always have these stupid fantasies that the next time I see my parents, they'll be genuinely happy to see me. But dreams are only fucking dreams. Whatever." She slumped her back. "Can we not talk about this anymore?"

"Forgotten," I quickly said.

It suddenly dawned on me how little I thought about Glory and her familial relationships. My problems with my family were something I discussed and shared with Glory often, yet perhaps I was always too inconsiderate to remember that she was suffering too. The difference between Glory and me was that she was selfless enough to consistently put her problems aside to tend to mine. I felt terrible.

"You okay?" I asked.

"Yeah, I'll be fine."

I finally took a bite of my salad and quite enjoyed the flavor. My appetite had been awakened.

"Hey, Glory. There's something I've been meaning to ask you. Last Saturday we were both online and you sent me an instant message asking me what my plans were for the evening, and when I responded you signed off without even saying goodbye. What was up with that?"

"Oh. I got kicked offline." She said it without looking up from her food.

"Got kicked off?"

"Yeah. Look, I was checking my email, and all of a sudden, I was kicked off. It happens sometimes, doesn't it? What the fuck is this third degree about? Damn. Hasn't it ever happened to you?"

I was stunned into silence. I didn't expect her to react so defensively. "No. I mean I didn't mean to offend you," I said. "It's just a question."

Annoyed, Glory said, "Whatever. So, what's going on with you and Derek?"

I hesitated. "You okay?"

She smiled and looked at me. "Yeah. Just ignore me. I'll be fine. So what's up with Derek?"

I told her that Derek and I had been expressing our differences a lot lately and that I didn't want to think about it right now, which she respected. We continued eating our meals. In our silence, the bustle of the street and restaurants and people simply enjoying the square on such a beautiful day drowned out my thoughts. I was not yet ready to tell Glory about my time with Tyrese; I wanted to keep him as my little secret for just a little bit longer. Besides, knowing how much she was attracted to him, I wasn't sure if she'd react with jealousy or congratulations. I didn't really know if I wanted to find out, so I said nothing about it.

Instead, I decided to ask Glory for her help. "So remember the note I said my mother left me? Well, in it, she said that I would find the answers to all my questions in a wooden box. I have no idea where this box is in the house. Both my father and my sister claim they know nothing about it.

Nancy refuses to return my calls. But I really need to find this box. I really feel like it'll help me push aside the angry and upsetting feelings I have about my mother. Will you help me?"

With a mischievous smile, Glory leaned into me and said, "Done!"

• • • •

BACK IN MY OFFICE, I checked my email in anticipation of an announcement from Morgan about my promotion. There was nothing from him. He never even sent me the written agreement he had promised me. What was taking him so long? I rolled my eyes in annoyance at the memory of Bill Anderson coming into my office the other night.

My phone rang.

"Mia speaking."

"Mia, it's Cynthia. Tyrese Black is on line one."

"Thank you, Cynthia,"

I didn't know what he wanted to say to me but the last time I spoke to Tyrese, I was rather cold. I had to take in a deep breath before I picked up line one. "Mia Hill."

"I figured I'd give you some time to cool off after you shot my ego down so quick yesterday. Is it a good time for you to talk?"

"It is," I said, becoming aware of a thrill inside of me. Yes, it certainly was exciting to hear from him again.

"I just wanted you to know that saying that whole shit about it just being sex was really not cool. I hope you didn't think I wanted you to be my girl. I thought we could be friends."

"Was what I said to you that much of a shock?" I challenged.

"No. I guess it wasn't. I just had such a great time with you the other night that I wanted to tell you how I felt. That was it. I'm being sincere. I didn't expect anything else 'cause I know you got a man. Best to leave what happened the other night alone. I just wanted to be straight up with you. The other night was something else. I mean no disrespect, but I really like you."

I could tell he was smiling on the other end but I didn't say anything. I secretly commended him, actually, for not making a scene in my office but giving me some space before approaching me again. He had my full attention. But I had to make myself clear about Derek.

"I have a boyfriend, Tyrese."

"I already know this."

"Then what do you want from me?"

"A friend, maybe—like I said before. Someone to talk to. Nothing else."

I believed him. I needed to push past my fears, my hesitations and the present was as good a time to start.

"Have dinner with me tonight, Tyrese. We can sit down and talk." I was surprised by my words.

"Why do you want to talk to me?" he asked.

"I got scared. Is that what you want to hear?"

"I just want the truth."

"You've got it. I got scared," I said softly into the phone. "I have a boyfriend, and I'm hanging out with you and fucking you as if I don't. I love him, but then I don't know what I'm feeling for you. Is it lust, infatuation, admiration, what? I don't know what it means, and it terrifies. Okay? Everyone I've ever felt anything for has hurt me. I don't want to risk that again, especially with someone who isn't my man."

He was silent for a long time. I figured I earned some points with him by confessing how I felt. Now I was truly vulnerable, and he knew it. He knew exactly what I was afraid of, and that was the last thing that I wanted.

"I won't ever hurt you," he finally said. "And I would be honored to have dinner with you tonight."

Chapter 18

Friday Evening, August 9, 2002

Tyrese and I planned to have dinner at a local restaurant that was supposed to be the hot spot in his neighborhood. He knew I was taking a cab, so he asked me to stop by at his brownstone in Brooklyn before walking to the restaurant together. The excitement I felt was palpable. I sat at the edge of the seat in the cab, looking anxiously around the neighborhoods that were as diverse and fascinating as some of the neighborhoods I knew in Manhattan. The beautifully lined brownstones upon approaching Tyrese's looked as picturesque as if they were on a movie screen. The schoolgirl in me was so impressed with the fact that Tyrese lived in Williamsburg. In only a few more minutes, Tyrese and I were going to be walking through streets that I had never explored, getting to know more of each other on a deeper level.

My heart raced as the cab approached Tyrese's home, slowing to a full stop. *Derek.* My heart leaped. The thought of Derek initiated the immediate sensation of what could transform into a serious headache. I fumbled through my bag until I came across my medication. I quickly swallowed a pill, paid the cab driver, and slowly walked up the stairs and rang the front doorbell.

I waited a few minutes before Tyrese opened the door, wearing a white t-shirt and a pair of light blue jeans, both soiled with paint. His locks were pulled back into a ponytail, forcing me to notice some dried blue paint smeared on his forehead and the lovely smile splashed across his face.

"What kind of restaurant were you planning on taking me to?" I asked.

He placed his paint-stained hand on his forehead. "Oh, shit! You're gonna hate me, Mia. I got caught up painting and lost track of time. Would you mind if we saved dinner for another time?"

I sighed. What was happening to me? If Derek had pulled something like this, I'd turn right back around, flag the cab down and head home with no plans of accepting any of Derek's calls or apologies for at least the next few days. But here Tyrese was, cancelling our date and all I wanted to do was invite myself in. "Well," I said, "I'd like to at least see where you create your work, if you don't mind."

"It would be my pleasure," he smiled.

His apartment was up a flight of creaky stairs. He opened the door for me, and I stepped inside. I was immediately greeted by paint fumes but dismissed the uncomfortable odor as I marveled at the space. It was huge. Directly to my left, near the door, stood a small, upholstered bench. The firm grey padded cushion stood atop four legs that were carved from dark wood. Straight across from me was the bathroom; the door was slightly ajar, and I saw a beige bathtub peeking through. I walked down the hall to find a small, rather charming kitchen on the right. When I walked further, I found myself in a spacious dining room connected to the living room. An old-fashioned television set (with an actual knob to turn the channel), art books in a small wooden bookcase, a black stereo, a large grey couch and a small black rocking chair made the place look comforting and homey. Abstract paintings and line drawings graced the walls of his home.

"Welcome to my humble abode," he said.

"Wow," I said. "There's something wonderful about this place that just draws you in. It's comfortable and almost familiar."

"Thank you. I'll show you the room that I turned into my studio," he said as I followed him into one of the two rooms. "The other room is where my bed is. I don't think I should show you that one yet. You might take advantage of me."

I laughed at his joke. I was excited to be with him in his apartment, realizing that simply being in his presence made me happy.

We stepped into his studio, an inspiration in itself. Blotches of multi-colored paints decorated the floor, and on the walls hung future masterpieces that I had not seen on his website or in his gallery. The vibrant colors alone took my breath away. Each piece, bearing Tyrese's trademark theme of some crucial moment of life, had its own individuality. The way he used a paintbrush to invoke an emotion through his characters was nothing short of brilliant. His works told stories of pain and happiness, of suffering and comfort, mixing the negative with the positive to portray what life is really all about. Through his paintings, I gathered that true contentment could never exist without the experience of despair. He was an extraordinary man with exceptional talent.

"These are amazing, Tyrese."

"I'm glad you think so. The paintings on the walls are my latest works. I still haven't decided what I'm gonna do with them. They don't fit in with my next theme, but I like them a lot."

"I do too," I said. Then I turned to him. "I say you should definitely exhibit these."

He stared into my eyes. "Well, if Mia says I should, then I will."

In the corner of the room, close to the walls, I located a canvas that had nothing on it but a side profile view of a child with closed eyes and a big round cheek formed from a sweet smile. "So, what were you working on?" I said, pointing to it.

"Mother and child—that's the theme for my next show. I don't know what this particular one will be like, though. Maybe I'll have her mom hugging her or something. I think that's what I'll do."

"Is that how you paint? You create as you go along?"

"Not all the time. It just happened to be that way this time. I usually know exactly what I want to portray in my paintings. But this one—I don't know. Would you believe me if I told you I was thinking of you when I started?"

I smiled. "In case you haven't noticed, Tyrese, I'm hardly a little girl."

"On the contrary, I see a little girl wishing she was loved by her mother. Maybe that's where I was going with this."

"That's sweet," I said.

I stared at him. His eyes were bright, once again promising me moments of lustful pleasure coupled with personal agony—the kind of pleasure one would want to indulge in only because of the promise of such an adventure. Though I wanted no part of that anguish, I still wanted him badly.

He pointed to a lone brown futon in the corner, the only real piece of furniture in the small room. "Please make yourself comfortable. It's been a while since someone has watched me as I work. I'd like it very much if you would."

He said it so seductively, with a huskiness to his voice, that I wanted nothing more than to comply with his wishes; I was in a trance. I put my purse down and sat on the futon.

"Can I get you something to drink?" he asked me.

"No, thank you. I'm fine."

"I got an idea. You want to order pizza?"

I smiled. "I'm not hungry just yet. Don't worry about me. Do what you gotta do."

He grabbed a small stool and placed it directly in front of his canvas. He sat down to continue painting and looked at me. "Why do you look so tired?"

"Thanks for pointing it out. I didn't think it showed."

"Well," he whispered, "I think you're beautiful when you look tired. And that's being sincere."

I smiled. He turned to his canvas and began to study his work. He took his paintbrush and with a few strokes, miraculously created a body that would represent the mother figure. With a few more strokes, he shaped the face of the mother, and painted an arm that gently caressed the child's cheek. The mother's eyes were closed and a warm smile of maternal love was displayed on her face.

"I want to ask you something personal," he said as he studied his painting again. "Why are you still with your man?"

The question caught me off guard; I was curious about why he thought of that while he was painting a child and her mother. "Why do you ask?"

He looked at me. "Earlier today, you said that you love him. But the other day, you said that he doesn't even make you feel lucky to be with him. This may not be my business, but it's something I was thinking about, and I thought I'd ask you. Now, I don't know the guy, but I'm guessing there was something great about him that attracted you to him in the first place and kept you with him. And I guess I just wanted to know why you're still with him. If that thing that first attracted you to him still exists."

That was a loaded question. "Yeah, it still exists," I said. "He's the same career-driven, intelligent, handsome man I first fell in love with. I guess I'm the one who changed. He loves me and wants to take care of me, but I keep him at a distance...Maybe that's why I don't feel lucky to be with him.

Sometimes I get the feeling that he's with me because of what I represent as a strong, successful black woman."

"Why are *you* with him?"

I sighed. "I know where you're going with this. I've been with him for five long years. It's just that, well, now he's become sort of like my comfort blanket. Ours is not a perfect relationship, but the truth is, Tyrese, I've been in dysfunctional relationships all my life; this is nothing new. In fact, my very first dysfunctional relationship was with my parents."

"How was it dysfunctional?"

It had to have been the paint fumes that made me open up to him without any hesitation. Or maybe it was because, despite what I said about Derek, Tyrese was the one I would rather be with.

"Ugh! Where do I begin?" I said. "I don't ever remember my parents telling me they loved me. They never showed me any type of affection. Well, at least when I grew older. As a kid, I don't remember my father saying it a lot, but he showed me he cared. He'd read books to me and he'd hug me when I was sad about something." I paused in my memory. "It was weird, but it was also our normal. I knew they loved me; it was just never spoken. My mom was very detached from me and my sister—I don't know what happened there. She was just never a loving mother. She did what she needed to keep us safe and taken care of, but there was never any affection from her. The older we got, the more..." I tried to find the right word. "...aloof she became. And my dad got quiet and distant when I..." I allowed my words to hang there, not wanting to tell him about the attempt when I was in college. "Let's just say that as a teenager and even as an adult, I just didn't feel any feelings of warmth from them. And it affected me much more than I thought it would. And then I had a really bad relationship in college that we don't need to talk about. Let's just say that for a very long time, Derek's been the best person in my life."

"Derek?" He suddenly stopped painting. He removed his paintbrush from the canvas after fixing the mother's long, braided hair and looked at me. "Wait a minute," he laughed. He put his paintbrush down and looked at me. "Your boyfriend's name is Derek?"

"Yeah. You knew that."

"No! I didn't." His disposition suddenly changed. "Let me get this straight. You said you knew Patrick Jerome's publisher. Do *not* tell me your boyfriend is Derek, as in Derek Jones, as in Jones Press, as in the publishing house that publishes Patrick Jerome's books. Derek Jones. He's your man?"

"Yes! What's the big deal?"

He rubbed his hand behind his neck. "No, it's just that I never put two and two together. That's all. I've heard of him; I even met him a few times. I just never made the connection."

"You've met Derek?" Tyrese must have been mistaken. Derek had told me he didn't recall ever meeting Tyrese, and Derek had no reason to lie about that.

"Well, yeah. I've seen him once or twice at Jones Press. And I've seen him...around."

He couldn't be right. Why would Derek lie to me about that? I didn't understand.

"Are- are you sure?" I stammered. "He told me he'd never met you."

"Well, we were never officially introduced. But you know what? That doesn't matter. He probably meets so many people that it's hard for him to keep track." He picked his paintbrush back up to continue painting.

"Yeah. That must be it," I said, deciding to put the mystery away to think about later. I made a mental note to ask Derek about that. In the meantime, I wanted to stay present, in the moment.

Tyrese was quiet as he kept his eyes on his work. The mother's face and hair complete, he was now working on the little girl's face, caressed by the mother's soft and gentle touch. Both of their eyes were closed as they held their sweet embrace. The way Tyrese used the paintbrush to create strokes on the canvas turned me on, though I didn't really know why. I watched him as if he were my prey. His brush flattened as it touched the surface of the canvas and he slowly moved away to inspect what he had created. I took it upon myself to regard his demeanor. The veins that popped from his soiled arms, the fitted paint-riddled t-shirt and the loose and baggy jeans that promised to plunge down to his ankles with a slight, but sudden movement all seemed to intoxicate me. No—perhaps I was getting that titillation confused with the paint fumes. I continued my focus on him. The colors from his paintbrush moved across the canvas with a salacious fluidity, magically creating an image out of nothing. I observed the concentration Tyrese's face exhibited as the brush made soft sounds with every move of his hand. His hair, pulled back into a ponytail save for two locked strands, completed a picture of masculine energy. Yes, I was enjoying myself. An almost animalistic urge came over me and I knew I wouldn't be satisfied until he was in my clutches.

I took such great delight in talking with him. He asked me questions that made me think about the type of person I was and how that affected my decisions. Not even Dr. Flare did that for me. Or perhaps I refused to let her in, just as I refused to let Derek in. With Tyrese, I didn't mind telling him how I felt. I didn't mind opening up to him. I *wanted* him to get to know me. It felt good; it felt natural.

"He wants to get married, doesn't he?" Tyrese asked me.

I sighed and nodded my head, choosing not to respond with a verbal affirmative.

"And you don't want that?"

"It'll never work," I answered. "Relationships are doomed once they're sealed with the sacred vows of marriage."

"Woa!" he exclaimed. "That's dark!"

"It's realistic. One can say that the institution of marriage isn't what it used to be. But that's not necessarily true. It's always been the same. The only difference is that up until a few decades ago, divorce wasn't as accepted by society as it now is. It's all around us. I don't want to go through that kind of pain."

"But you won't."

The certainty in his voice was both thrilling and annoying. "I remember you saying that before. What makes you so sure about that?"

"Because it's what you don't want. However, if you believe that your marriage will fail, then everything you do and say will lead to that inevitable result because you believe in it so much."

"That makes sense, I guess."

"You're honest with yourself on some levels," Tyrese said. "But most of the time, I think you're just trying to protect yourself from getting hurt."

"It's not a revelation, Tyrese. I just now admitted that with my own mouth."

"So he wants you to marry him but you said no," he said, disregarding my response. "But he stayed with you anyway. That's interesting. Well, I'm sure he'd never purposely do anything to mess up the relationship. You may be a tad bit difficult to handle, but I think you're worth it. Any man can see that. You do have your moments."

I smiled in spite of myself. "You flatter me, Tyrese."

"I only speak what I believe to be truth."

"Do you analyze everyone who comes into your life?"

"Only the people who hold my interest. Not many people do."

I had to admit it was intoxicating receiving so much attention from him. It had been a long time since I heard anyone say such good things about me. "I suppose I should feel flattered once again."

He smiled at me. "You are an enigma, Mia."

Ooh...I liked that. "I only present myself to be the enigma you say I am," I replied. "In a few short months, you'll see that I'm just as ordinary as everyone else. It's only a front."

"Why do I doubt that?" he smiled.

"Believe what you will, Tyrese. I've been analyzed enough for one day."

"Ah, you see that, little one?" he said to the little girl in his painting. "Mia doesn't like to hear people tell truths about her."

It could have possibly been that my body was hungry for the feelings he had ignited in me that first night I slept with him. Or perhaps it was all that talk about Derek, and the naughty girl inside of me wanting to do something that I knew I could get away with. Maybe the paint fumes had started to alter my behavior—they had already affected my thoughts and words. Or quite possibly, it was simply his beautiful self, sitting on that stool, doing what he loved to do, what he was meant to do. Whatever the reason, I found myself slowly approaching him. He was already transfixed by his work, for his face bore an expression of sweet surprise to find me so close to him. I took the paintbrush from his hand. He slowly stood up and I placed the paintbrush on his stool, careful not to get any paint on my clothing. Releasing the rubber band that had held his dreadlocks away from his face, I ran my fingers through his thick, locked hair and studied the beauty I saw before me.

"And I thought keeping you away from my bedroom would keep me safe," he whispered.

He kissed me, not with the passion he had once before, but with a sensuous softness he must have known I had long craved. And then he undressed me as carefully as I had placed his paintbrush down moments before. He unstrapped my bra as we stared into each other's eyes. I took the bra off, letting it fall onto the floor, no longer caring about the specks of paint there. There was an area in the corner of the room that was almost paint-free, and he slowly led me there as we kissed. We both knelt down, still staring at each other. I lifted his t-shirt as he raised his arms to help me undress him. His chest was hard, muscular, and beautiful. I pulled down his pants and underwear and he maneuvered himself to finish the job. As he did so, I took my own pants and underwear off. My heart pounded, for I was feeling strangely nervous and excited about what was happening. Again, we stared at each other, making use of no words, for discourse was not necessary at that moment. He came closer to me, both of us still kneeling. I used my hands to explore his body, and my eyes to guide the way. His eyes moved from my stomach, lingered a moment at my breasts, and then focused on my neck, which he lightly rubbed. He softly kissed my neck as he caressed my shoulders. Gently kissing him on the neck underneath his chin and down his chest, I bit his nipples lightly and slowly licked my way down to his stomach. He kissed me on my shoulders and up my neck, placing his hands on my collarbone and moving them down my arms. From my arms, he continued down to my stomach, softly rubbing it, putting his mouth to my belly button and tenderly kissing the area. We positioned ourselves down on to the floor. He kissed my neck as his fingers moved down my stomach, softly feeling what I had to offer him down below before entering me.

There we were: two souls brought together because of the beauty that one created. He couldn't promise to keep paint away from my skin, nor did I expect him to. Speckles of paint that were not yet dry on the floor spotted parts of our bodies. We were soon entangled in each other's embrace, and it brought to my mind his first piece, *Intertwined*. My own words rang in my head from that day in his office. *Nobody's perfect,* I had said of the painting, *but we each have someone with whom we were meant to be, someone we fit with.* We had become the intertwined couple in his painting. I wasn't sure if that night we fucked, had sex, or made love. Whatever we did, it was more tenderness than I could handle. Fear entered my heart and made itself a home.

"That was nice," I whispered after our tender moment had passed. We were both lying on our left sides on the floor, our arms covered with paint particles. He curved his body behind me, molding himself to the shape of my body, and placed his right hand across my stomach.

"I thought it was just sex with you," he whispered back.

"It is," I said. "That's why we have to stop."

"Why?"

I wanted to say that it was because I was starting to fall in love with him. I wanted to say that his affection was the kind that would force me into a state of madness if I were to ever let it possess my soul. But that confession would give Tyrese permission to break my heart, so I opted to give him the simplest response.

"Because I'm with Derek and that's not going to change."

He didn't say anything, and I didn't know him well enough to even guess what he was thinking. He was behind me, so I could not see the expression on his face. But I kept my word. I didn't change my mind. Derek was the one I chose to stay with.

Chapter 19

Saturday Evening, August 10, 2002

Derek and I attended a catered book release party Saturday evening in Manhattan for Jones Press's most prominent author, Patrick Jerome. His much-anticipated book, *Moment of Truth*, had been recently published and was the recipient of several book awards in the black literary community. There were a few of Derek's first-time authors at the event, wide-eyed and excited to be present among photographers, novelists, other publishers, and journalists alike. The whole affair was put together nicely, and Derek had his assistant Gerry Baker to thank for the well-organized event. Along the perimeter of the room, there were stations of hot food that boasted an impressive menu of a variety of dishes including vegetarian options. The raw and grilled vegetables and sliced fruits were tastefully displayed on a large table in the center of the banquet room. Servers passed out hors d'oeuvres and hostesses served drinks.

A large poster board in the lobby displayed the cover of *Moment of Truth*. The cover art was created by the one and only Tyrese Black. It portrayed a young, unhappy mother sitting on an old, worn couch cuddling her three young, unhappy children. A man in the background had a sinister expression. Although I didn't know the book's content, given what Patrick Jerome's was known for writing, I assumed it addressed domestic violence.

As the publisher's long-time girlfriend, I knew I had to look flawless. I wore a long, slim-fitting navy-blue strapless dress that tastefully exposed my cleavage. Subtle blue beads delicately sewn onto my dress reflected the light softly. I managed to find navy blue open-toe heels that completed the dress, and, of course, I carried a matching purse. I had to admit that I looked absolutely stunning. Derek loved the way I looked, calling me "a vision" when he came to pick me up earlier that evening. At the reception, he proudly introduced me as the soon-to-be editor in chief of *Fresh Voices* magazine to everyone I had not already met. This included the very dignified Patrick Jerome, the author whose book we were celebrating.

"It's a pleasure to finally meet you, Patrick," I said as I shook his hand.

"The pleasure's all mine, Mia. I've heard so many great things about you."

I looked at Derek and said, "I can't imagine what great things Derek must have told you about me, but it's good to know I'm talked about. Congratulations on yet another successful publication."

"Thank you, but I want you to know that I couldn't do it without this man right here." Patrick hit Derek on the shoulder, and they both laughed.

"Plan nothing for the first weekend of February 2003," I told Patrick.

"Why? What happens the first weekend in February?"

"I already spoke to your publicist this evening about you doing a book signing at The Fourth Annual Fresh Voices Talent Conference."

"Well, okay. That sounds great!"

"You can get all of the details about it from your publicist. Oh. And don't forget. The book editor at my magazine was supposed to have arranged something for you tonight."

"Yes, right," Patrick said. "A brief interview for the magazine."

"Yes, I hope that's not too much trouble."

"Not at all. I'm always happy to talk about my work."

"That's Mia for you," Derek said. "Never putting her work aside." I assumed Derek said that because he felt left out of the conversation.

From across the room, I noticed a beautiful, statuesque woman with dark skin. I recognized her as Tiana Brown, Tyrese's cousin, who I had met at the gallery the day I interviewed him. She wore a stunning black strapless gown with a side slit that teased viewers with a peek at her right leg. I knew that many people in the industry were invited to the event, but I was particularly curious about her connection to Derek, if there even was one. *"When you get the calling, you have to answer or else the inspiration leaves a hole in your soul."* Her statement still made me think about my lost inspiration.

"I hear good things are happening with your magazine," Patrick said, pulling me away from a deep contemplation I had not even realized I was in.

"Oh, *Fresh Voices* is not mine. *Yet*," I answered. "But, I promise you one day it will be. It's doing quite well, thank you."

"She's got her mother to thank for that," Derek chimed in, like an outcast who needed to find a way into the popular group at school. "Mia's goals have always been to be a published fiction writer until her mother helped her understand how she could put her talent to better use."

Confusion and horror set in as I contemplated Derek's insensitive comment about things I had told him in confidence. Not only was it inappropriate for him to say that, but I hadn't realized that Derek held the same perspective about my work as my mother. Both rendered me speechless.

"Hold on now," Patrick chuckled. "Are you saying that authors who write fiction could be doing something better with their talents? I mean, where would that leave you as our publisher?"

"W-Well," Derek stammered, struggling to find words to defend what he had said.

No longer speechless, I continued my conversation with Patrick as if Derek had never said a thing. "I actually interviewed a colleague of yours only recently. Tyrese Black."

Patrick's face lit up. "Really? That's great!"

"He's a wonderful artist and quite the philosopher."

Patrick laughed. "That's Tyrese, all right." He glanced around the room. "I thought he'd be here by now."

A sudden hot flash invaded my body as my heart leaped into my throat. I should have known Tyrese would be expected at the party! Of course! It made sense. After all, it was Tyrese's own artwork reproduced on the poster board, showing off the cover of Patrick's book. I was panic-stricken as I tried to deliberate what I would do if Tyrese did wind up at the event.

"I see Tyrese now," Derek said, looking over my shoulder.

I stared at Derek, once again horrified. How did he recognize Tyrese if they'd never met? I quickly recalled Tyrese telling me in his studio the previous day that he had met Derek before. But Derek had acted as if he'd never met Tyrese. And there Derek was, referring to Tyrese by his first name. The name rolled from his tongue with such familiar ease as if they were old friends. Instead of focusing on how I would react in the presence of my man once I was standing face to face with Tyrese, I decided to question Derek.

"You told me you didn't know Tyrese," I challenged him.

"I don't," he answered. "I met him once. That doesn't constitute knowing him."

I couldn't believe it. First of all, Derek had blatantly lied to me about ever meeting Tyrese, and I wondered why. Secondly, the thought of Tyrese and Derek at the same function terrified me. I was caught in the middle. What if I revealed my infidelity with the expression on my face or the guilt in my voice?

"Looks like he got himself a good-looking date, too," Patrick said.

Tyrese was dating someone. The surprises that evening were never-ending. I quickly turned to see who Tyrese was with, half expecting it be his boldly beautiful cousin Tiana Brown but instead found that it was my very own little minx, Glory Williams. I felt jealousy overcome me. Tyrese had come with Glory. Tyrese with Glory. But my jealousy quickly dissipated as the man before me willed it away with his beauty. I was enthralled.

Tyrese was radiant. His long locks appeared wavy and freshly twisted. They appeared crisp and shone as if they had their own spotlight. His black suit made him look absolutely ravishing. It seemed impossible for a man to look as spellbinding as he did. His rough, rugged style and high-quality formal wear came together in such a splendid marriage of extremes. It must have been my imagination because I could actually hear music playing just for him as he made his way through the crowd. So caught up in the image of Tyrese in a suit that I almost forgot where I was and who I was with. I snapped out of my daze, realizing only a few seconds had passed.

Glory saw us looking and waved. She gently tugged at Tyrese's hand, and they walked towards us. She was sexy in her short and sheer black dress, but I was elegant in my blue gown. No competition there.

"My favorite people in the publishing industry!" Glory said as she hugged Derek and me. She turned to Patrick to shake his hand. "Nice to see you again."

"Same here," Patrick replied. "You look wonderful tonight."

"As always," she smiled.

I thought I saw her winking at Derek, but I couldn't be sure.

I cleared my throat and shook Tyrese's hand. "It's good to see you again, Tyrese. Your work on the cover of the book looks magnificent."

He took my hand and discreetly massaged it inside his own. "Thank you," he smiled. My heart leaped; I felt like Derek might have been watching it all as if it were happening in extra-slow motion.

"Tyrese," Patrick said, "Mia was just telling me that she interviewed you not long ago for her magazine."

"Best interview I've ever had," Tyrese said, smiling. I couldn't believe it. He was flirting with me through Patrick with Derek standing right next to me!

"Well, it was quite informative," I said. "Tyrese, this is my boyfriend, Derek. I've heard you two have already met."

He extended his hand to Derek. "Good to see you again, Derek," Tyrese said.

"Likewise," Derek answered with a cold smile. "We're all looking forward to your next show."

"Thanks, man," Tyrese said, answering the smile with a smirk. "It's good to know where my support is coming from."

Tyrese then gave me a knowing glance and a smile that told me we had found ourselves in an awkward situation.

I grabbed Glory's arm. "Will you excuse us for one minute, please?" I led Glory to the buffet table. "What are you doing here with him?" I asked as soon as we were a safe distance from the men.

"Are we jealous?" Glory playfully asked.

"Don't be ridiculous," I said, rolling my eyes.

"Well, then, I suggest you erase that look of excitement from your face before facing your man. I didn't come with Tyrese, if you must know. I'm still trying to fuck him since you didn't attack what I threw at you."

I still hadn't told her of my recent trysts with Tyrese, although I had planned to. Now was not the time to do so.

"Tyrese *fucking* Black. It should be a crime for a man to look that good," Glory said, salaciously staring at him. "Tonight just might be my lucky night with him."

"Patrick looks good too," I said, trying to dissuade her thoughts about Tyrese. *He was mine.*

"Yeah, well, he's got a wife and a newborn kid. The man ain't going nowhere but home tonight. As for me, I need a little action, and I might get it with Tyrese." She shamelessly squeezed her breasts together. "Who can resist these?"

I wanted her focus to remain far away from Tyrese. "You know," I said, "Tyrese just might end up being a prude."

Glory slowly turned her eyes to me. "You fucking slut!"

I was sure I had given myself away—that she had figured out my secret.

"'Patrick looks good too'? Hmmm. There's a reason why you're trying to distract my attention. You want Tyrese for yourself, don't you?" She curled her lips into a smile that taunted me.

I sighed in relief. "I never said that."

"You don't have to. It's written all over your goddamn face! As if you don't already have enough with your man." Then, with a seductive smile, she said, "If you don't want Derek, *I'll* take him."

"Ladies!" Derek said, coming from behind us. "May I interject?"

Now where was Tyrese? I looked over Derek's shoulder and saw that Tyrese and Patrick Jerome were deep in conversation.

"Derek!" Glory laughed loudly. "I was just telling Mia how great you look tonight. She better watch out before I steal you away from her."

Derek smiled as he looked away and said, "Mia would never have to worry about that with you."

"Very nice comeback," Glory said seductively. "But I'll have you know that I can be very persuasive."

I couldn't believe it. She was actually trying to seduce Derek.

"So I've heard," Derek said, oddly avoiding eye contact with her.

His dismissive attitude, I had to admit, made me feel better about her brazen advances. I knew how flirtatious Glory could be, but she had never before so blatantly flirted with Derek in my presence. I suddenly felt threatened. She had an incredible power over men. Up until that night, I had never felt intimidated by her ways when it came to Derek, not even when we had both met him at the publisher's conference in Chicago five years ago. I placed my arm inside of Derek's, claiming him as my own, and Glory shot me a curious look.

"I can tell when I'm not wanted," she said, still eyeing me curiously. "I'm gonna find Tyrese. Derek, it was good to see you again."

Derek nodded as she walked away.

I took a deep breath. "She was flirting with you."

"She was being *Glory*," he answered.

I looked over at her as she approached Tyrese and Patrick. Tyrese looked at me, smiled, and raised his glass. He was having way too much fun. I quickly turned my head; luckily, Derek did not see that.

"You know," I challenged him, "when I asked you about Tyrese Black, when Glory first mentioned him to me last week, you came off as if you'd never even heard of him."

He stared at me as if I had just said something wrong. "Mia, is there a reason why you're bringing this up? It's no big deal."

"If it's no big deal, then why did you lie to me?"

"I never lied to you."

"You withheld information that led to a certain conclusion that you wanted me to have. That's the same thing as lying. And during my interview with Tyrese, he seemed shocked to find out that you were my boyfriend. Why was he shocked, Derek?"

"I really don't know, Mia," he said, challenging me with his eyes.

"And what the hell was that comment you said about my mom?" I needed to understand why he felt it was necessary to say something so personal about my relationship with my mother to a virtual stranger.

"I'm sorry about that. It just slipped out."

That apology seemed so artificial and insincere and it fed my anger. "You're sorry?" I said. "That was way out of line, Derek."

"I'm not doing this right now. Okay, Mia? I won't feed this need you have to ruin a perfectly good evening by being the disputatious person that you are."

He walked away from me, heading towards Glory, Tyrese and Patrick, but stopping a passing server carrying a tray of hors d'oeuvres before joining them.

I took in a deep breath to calm my pounding heart.

"Hello, Mia."

I turned and found Tiana Brown standing there, smiling at me.

"Hi, Tiana. It's so good to see you again." As I stuck out my hand for a handshake, Tiana extended her arms for a hug and what resulted was an extremely awkward handshake-hug that left us both laughing uneasily.

"I didn't expect to see you here," I said, after our uneasy laughter turned into uneasy silence. "You look great!"

"Well, thanks. I'm unofficially my cousin's plus one. He told me about it and I thought it would be a great opportunity to rub elbows with people who could help me with my magazine *Black Prose Literary*." She shrugged. "Call me an opportunist."

I smiled. "We are all opportunists in some way, aren't we? We know how to play the game."

"I couldn't agree with you more." She raised her hand to someone in the distance. "I'll catch up with you later. Enjoy the event." She glamorously walked away, toward the person she had waved to.

I looked around the room. Glory and Patrick were deep in conversation while Tyrese and Derek attentively listened. I stood alone for a short while before I decided to join and complete the unlikely group that consisted of a slut, a liar, two cheaters and the author who could write about it all.

Part 3: The Opened Box

Chapter 20.

Monday, August 12, 2002

"At our last session, you showed me the note your mother had left you with the painting she gave you. Has anything transpired from that?" Dr. Flare plunged directly into our session that Monday morning.

I admitted to her that I was a bit disappointed in myself for not further pursuing my mother's wooden box. I told her that I went back to the house looking for the box in my mom's old office and then in my sister's room. When I didn't find anything, I thought of maybe bringing Glory with me next time to help me look. She seemed a bit curious about my wanting Glory with me but didn't press it any further.

To my surprise, the news of my meeting Tyrese and sleeping with him didn't seem to faze her at all. When she told me that it seemed like Tyrese was a better suitor (her word, not mine) for me and suggested I "explore" a relationship with him, I became impatient.

"There's nothing to explore, Dr. Flare. Can we please change the subject?"

She sighed, and I glanced at my watch. I had twenty more minutes. These sessions were so emotionally exhausting. Having to always analyze my actions and thoughts and words week after week was sometimes just too much for me. Every week, I fantasized about just running out of the room, telling Dr. Flare that harping on all my experiences and thoughts and feelings was doing me no good. Yet, I knew in some small way they were. So I stayed. I always stayed.

"How are you feeling, Mia?"

I looked up to the ceiling, feeling a bit exasperated, not wanting to delve into a description I would rather avoid. "This thing that I feel. This cloud...hanging over me. It never goes away," I droned.

"Tell me more about that."

I shifted in the chair. "There are times when I feel so incredibly lonely and desperately alone. Like I'm somewhere dark and far away where no one will ever reach me. It doesn't matter where I am or who I'm with. It doesn't matter if I'm talking to someone or even having an intimate moment with Derek. It's just there...like always in the background. My own hell, my very own hell. And I've been feeling it more in the last few days. Quietly waiting to bury me the second something goes wrong. It scares me."

I heard the sound of my own voice drifting away until only its memory remained in the air. I cleared my throat. "I know if I keep myself focused on my job, I'll be okay."

Dr. Flare looked confused. "What does your job have to do with you feeling better inside?"

"For one, it's a welcome distraction," I said. "And once I have everything I want in terms of my career, I'll feel more secure and my life will be better."

"I know you don't believe that."

"I can beat this depression as long as I keep coming to therapy," I said, trying to convince myself. "I'll eventually get over it."

"You can't just get over it, Mia. It doesn't just go away. We've gone over this already. It's a mental disorder, a chemical imbalance in the brain that needs to be treated. Yes, you come to therapy but you also have to put in the work. While I respect your reluctance to take medication, I do highly recommend it. Mia, it can be very effective and doesn't have to be forever. Medication can help with the imbalance while you work through the depression. This is not just a phase for you, Mia. It's a mental disorder. And very likely a disorder your mother may have suffered with also."

"My mother?" I scoffed. "What are you talking about? I never even saw her cry or anything."

"Some people don't necessarily need to cry as a result of their depression. They may become overwhelmed at times, but they are not always likely to cry..." and then she emphasized the words "in someone's presence."

Confused, I asked, "So what are you saying?"

"Just because you never saw your mother cry doesn't mean she didn't express her depression in other ways."

She said it again. Depression? My mother? I never told Dr. Flare such a thing. It never even crossed my mind. "Why do you think she was depressed?"

"Mia. The very fact alone that your mother was unable to show her own children affection tells a great deal about her emotional stability. It's a mother's natural instinct to want to show her children love and comfort. You yourself admitted how shocked you were as a child when you realized that her behavior was not normal. There was something there, hindering her from loving you and your sister as a mother should."

"So, I'm confused. Can you please tell me what causes depression in the first place?" I said.

"We've gone over all this before, Mia."

"I know but—" I hesitated before admitting it. "I wasn't always ready to accept the truth."

Dr. Flare crossed one leg over the other. "There is no one thing that causes depression. A number of things can trigger it. The loss of a loved one, perhaps abuse or trauma, whether it be mental, physical, emotional, or psychological."

"But my mother was so strong, so sure of herself."

"Yes, on the outside, Mia. But that doesn't mean she wasn't hurting inside. Something might have happened in her life to cause her depression. That's one possibility. And then there are people who are genetically predisposed to suffer from depression. Depression can run in the family, as, I believe, in your case."

"Excuse me?" I interjected.

"Yes, Mia. Just listen. Some people suffer from depression all of their lives without anything triggering it. They remain in constant despair. They may have everything they had ever wanted in life: a fabulous and admirable career and job, a supportive family, a roof over their head, food on the table and a spouse who loves them very much. Yet they suffer. And it's not to say they're not grateful for all their blessings; they just can't help that feeling of utter hopelessness. There is always something bothering them, making them miserably sad. Maybe there's something in their life that hasn't yet been fulfilled. Maybe there's not. But whatever is bothering them is heightened ten times over due to their depression. I've seen a lot of people come and go, Mia. I've seen what it's done to them. I've seen some people treat it and go on to live full lives. But the fact remains that there are not enough people who seek professional help. There are those who are ashamed to admit that they have a mental condition because of the stigma that has always been associated with it. Others think depression's just something else they need to get over or that it will pass when they achieve some goal. It's not that simple."

She dramatically paused before continuing. "In your case, Mia, based on what I've learned about you, your depression is a result of your family history."

"Can't it just be a chemical imbalance in my brain?"

"It can be, yes, but I see other forces at work here. You were emotionally neglected as a child, your parents never supported your creative endeavors, and you never got along with your sister. You feel as if you don't belong, as if you were cast out of your own family. Not only did someone steal your work at school but you were the one who was blamed for plagiarizing and that too was traumatic. It is my professional belief that your mother suffered from depression, Mia. And it is theorized that depression can be passed on from one generation to another."

"Then in your professional opinion, what do you think caused my mother's supposed depression?"

"The same thing that prevented her from showing you and your sister the love you two deserved as children. That's what your mother wants to reveal to you when you find the wooden box. I'm sure of it."

"And what about my sister? Why doesn't she suffer from depression like I do?"

Dr. Flare didn't miss a beat. "Don't be too sure about that. The way she is always angry with you is a sure indication that there's something deeper there that no one is talking about. Suicide, crying and restlessness are not the only signs of depression."

My mind quickly wandered to the two books about the psychological effects of parental neglect on children that I had found in Nancy's bedroom that Sunday I decided to go snooping around for any clue about my mother's wooden box.

"Okay, I know you said that I can't just get over it. But what can I do to move on with my life? I feel stuck. "

"You have to do the work, Mia. Assess the things in your life that cause you grief, for starters. You have to talk about them, understand what lessons you've learned."

I thought about the things that could have possibly caused my mother grief. Perhaps it was Nancy and me. My mother was never emotional with us, maybe because our very presence caused her grief. *Why?*

"I remember once, my mom had just come home from work and she went straight into her office. I was in high school at the time and I had been waiting for her to come home so that she could read an essay I wrote for—I think it was my history class. I remember walking into her office and asking her to look at the paper. She said, 'Mia, what did I tell you about bothering me when I come home from work?' I felt so bad, like I really did something wrong. So, I told her I was sorry and asked her if she could look at it later. And she didn't even look at me. She just said, 'I don't have time for this today, Mia.' And she asked me to shut the door on my way out. I just wanted to cry. I walked out of there so fast. I thought that she was angry at me. But I'm starting to understand that her job was stressful, and she didn't separate that stress from her home life that well. In fact, I don't ever remember a time when she wasn't stressed."

"Mia, I think it's time for you to have a talk with your father about your mother and what caused her to behave the way she did towards you and your sister."

"Why? What do you mean?" I said.

"I mean that you need to speak with your father again about the whereabouts of this wooden box. Ask him for help. You don't know what can come of it. But don't involve Glory. This is a family issue that needs to be resolved. You need to talk to your family."

Chapter 21.

Tuesday Afternoon, August 13, 2002

"Derek and I aren't talking."

"So, what else is fucking new?" Glory asked.

Glory and I met each other downtown for lunch in a rather small Mexican restaurant. With multicolored sombreros of varying sizes lining the walls, and portraits and images of Mexican figures and food, the atmosphere of the restaurant pulled us into its authenticity. As most eateries in the area, the crowded restaurant left little room for complete privacy, as the voices from most of its diners blended together into a noisy racket. It was an early weekday afternoon, and at Glory's impulsive suggestion, I took a long lunch with her at La Contenta, her favorite Mexican restaurant. I really had no business going for a long lunch as there were so many emails and phone messages I knew I had to respond to back at the office. However, I really felt like I desperately needed some *best-friend time*.

"So, why is he angry with you?" Glory asked.

"It was actually about Saturday night."

"The party?" Glory seemed a bit surprised. "Why? What happened?"

"Well, listen to this. When I first told him last week that I was writing an article on Tyrese Black, he acted like he had never met him. But Saturday night, he made it fully clear that he did know him."

"That's weird. Why do you think he lied?"

"My guess is as good as yours. And get this: when Tyrese found out that Derek Jones of Jones Press was actually my boyfriend, he was speechless. Like he knew something he didn't want to tell me. I didn't press him on the issue, but something tells me I should have."

"What could Tyrese possibly know about your man that you don't already know?"

"Beats the hell out of me. But when I talked to Derek about it at the party, he got all defensive and didn't want to talk about it. We haven't spoken since then."

"Damn. It's always something with you two."

Our waiter, a tall man of Latino descent dressed in a typical Mexican entertainer's outfit appeared with our meals.

"One Cecina a la Mexicana," he said as he placed the plate of beef and vegetables on the table in front of Glory.

"And for you, miss, pollo enchilada." He placed my plate on the table as Glory and I thanked him.

We started our meals, with Glory moaning with each bite that she put into her mouth. I, however, kept thinking about Derek. Unable to concentrate on my food, I decided to tell Glory about Derek's recent request.

"He brought it up again the other night," I offered. "It's been a while, but he finally mentioned wanting to marry me again. I guess he thinks I'll eventually come to realize that I need to marry him."

"Seriously, Mia," Glory said after she swallowed. "What's the problem? Why don't you even consider marrying him? I mean, you've been with him for five fucking years."

"A fact I'm well aware of, thank you."

"So, what are you waiting for? Either you marry him or leave him. What's the damn problem?" She took a sip of water.

I hesitated before answering. "I guess I'm afraid to be alone. Okay? And Derek has already proven he'll never leave. But at the same time, I feel he's not meant for me. And if he's not meant for me, then why marry him? But until something else comes up, I'll stay with him so that I won't be lonely."

"That's twisted and fucked up. You're using him."

"Trust me, I've thought about that too."

"So, why do you think that Derek's not the one for you?"

"I don't know. Deep down, I just don't feel right about being with him for the rest of my life."

"So why don't you just fucking dump him, Mia? You know that's not fair to him."

"I told you already. I can't be alone right now, and he treats me so well. He really does."

"Yea. So well that he's not even talking to you right now."

I said nothing.

Glory sighed. "Do you really, honestly think you'll find *the* one?"

"Maybe."

Glory looked at me curiously.

"Someone else has got me seriously second-guessing my relationship with Derek."

"Ooh! A mystery man?" Glory's voice elevated with interest. "*Now*, we're talking! Who is it?"

I sighed. "Tyrese Black."

Glory's eyes immediately popped wide open. I could tell she wanted to scream but the waiter inconveniently prevented her from doing so by stepping in between us to fill up our water glasses.

"What about him?!" Glory excitedly screeched as he walked away.

"Ssh!!" I motioned to the elderly couple sitting next to us. I smiled as I shook my head in disbelief. "You told me he looked good, but *damn*."

"Tyrese *fucking* Black!" she exclaimed as if she could no longer hold it in. "Why did you not believe me when I told you? Everything about the man screams sex!"

"Yes!" I exclaimed, matching Glory's excitement. The elderly couple beside us looked at us uncomfortably. I placed my finger on my lips as a way to tell Glory to lower her voice.

"So," Glory said in a loud whisper. "Tell me! What happened?"

I sat in silence and looked at Glory, smiling, waiting for her to identify my silence as a confession of my infidelity.

She finally opened her mouth and pointed her finger at me as a child would. "Do not tell me you fucked him! You fucked Tyrese! Girl, when did this shit happen? Not Saturday night?"

"Oh no," I sighed. "It happened last week." Something told me not to tell her about Friday night as well. "That's why I was acting so strangely at the party the other night."

Glory playfully hit me on my shoulder and screeched, "And you didn't even fucking tell me, you stank ho! I always knew you were a slut!"

"Trust me: I wanted to tell you at the party, but it was too risky. And honestly, I didn't know if you'd be angry with me for sleeping with someone I knew you were into."

"Oh girl, please! I practically gift-wrapped him for you! If I couldn't have him, I would've definitely wanted you to have him. And I must say I have gained a deep respect for you, girl. Oh! But wait a *goddamn* minute!" she teased. "What about Derek?"

I looked away. "It's not something I'm especially proud of, but at the same time, I don't feel terribly guilty about it. And I sort of feel guilty for not feeling guilty. Does that make any sense?"

"You *are* feeling guilty about it," Glory said, matter-of-factly. "Feeling guilty about *not* feeling guilty about the very thing you *should* be feeling guilty about only shows that you are *actually* feeling guilty about the very thing you *thought* you weren't feeling guilty about. Now. How did it happen?"

I sighed. "I don't know. He kept asking me out to dinner after the interview last Monday and the man is just so fine. Everything about him—"

"You don't have to fucking tell me! I already know!" Glory giggled mischievously. "Go on."

"The more he came by my office, the more I couldn't resist. And while Derek keeps pressuring me to marry him, all this guy wanted was to eat some food."

"Yeah, from the secret fucking garden," Glory laughed.

I had to admit that Glory's joke had me laughing too. When I caught my breath, I said, "It was more than just sex, though. We clicked. I had a chance to really speak with him. He told me things about myself that I tried to hide. Things like why I'm so unhappy. He helped me open up to myself, and he is so deep that I began to seriously doubt my relationship with Derek."

"But you've always doubted your relationship with Derek. That's nothing new."

"Yeah, but now it's different. I'm looking at it now with the possibility of being with Tyrese instead of Derek. This is a very big deal for me. We talk. Derek and I don't do that."

"That's because you never allowed it."

I sighed. She was absolutely right. "You know how when someone mispronounces your name and you never correct them and so they keep mispronouncing your name every time you see them? And then it's weeks or maybe months later and now it's awkward to say, 'Oh by the way, my name is pronounced *mee-ya* and not *my-a?*"

"Oh, yeah. There are still people at my job who call me Gloria. Ugh. I've grown to hate that name."

"Yes! It's like that. After a certain amount of time with Derek, it was just easier not telling him about my depression or my therapist. It was only a few days ago that I finally told him about what happened in our dorm room."

Glory was surprised. "Really? That's huge, Mia. What did he say?"

"Nothing really. He just thanked me for trusting him enough to tell him."

Glory turned her nose up in disgust. "Ugh! Men are so limited when it comes to the exposure of feelings and emotions."

"And I still haven't told him about my regular sessions with Dr. Flare. If I tell him now, it'll change everything between us, the way he sees me and the way he treats me. It's too much."

"So, you're saving yourself from an awkward situation?"

"It's not like that. At first, I didn't tell Derek because he was so perfect, and I didn't want him to see my major flaws. So, I kept it all hidden to the point where it's actually become easier for me to continue acting like I'm okay now. It's just easier."

Glory said nothing.

"I don't even know the reasons why I'm with Derek anymore," I said, finally. "I do love him. But now I'm starting to think a real connection was never really there."

"Hmm," Glory said, staring me up and down. "Sex with Tyrese was that good, huh? I fucking knew it. Come on, now. You got to give me the details."

"It doesn't have anything to do with the sex. We actually connect."

"Good sex can make anybody talk like that. Was he big? He's huge, right?"

I smiled. "He wasn't that big, I have to admit that. But he was sure as hell not small either! He was the perfect size. And oh my goodness did he knew what to do with it! And he was kind of rough, you know? We were almost like animals—like we both wanted it so bad and we finally got to the point where we couldn't take it anymore and we just had to do it. And we sure as hell did it! We did it again and again and—"

"Oh shit, girl!"

"Need I go on?"

"I think I just came!" We both burst into crazed laughter.

The elderly couple looked at us again, this time making it clear that they did not appreciate our conversation.

"Don't act like you never talked like this when you were our age!" Glory said to them. I felt a heat wave through my body. I couldn't even lift my head to apologize to the couple. The old man raised his hand to the waiter and said, "Check, please!"

Glory turned back to me and acted as though nothing had happened. "So, make up your mind girl. It's obvious to me who you should be with."

"Well, I do like the idea of being with Tyrese more than the idea of being with Derek. Oh my goodness! I'm such a terrible person!" I held my head in my hand, with my elbow on the table.

Glory sighed. "Can you see your life with Derek? Be honest with yourself."

"Yes, I can. Derek would provide for me and take care of me. But, I still feel deep down he's not meant for me. I don't think I enjoy my time with him anymore. Sometimes he seems so full of himself."

"So, then it's settled. Why are we even having this conversation? It's obvious you found the person to help you not feel lonely when you break up with Derek. Can you see your life with Tyrese?"

I nodded. "I do and I don't. I want to be with him, but it may be for all the wrong reasons. Yeah, the sex was great, but we just met. And now I feel like we're friends more than anything else. We're—we're more like colleagues in the office space of life."

"I can't believe you just said that."

"What if he ends up breaking my heart? I don't think I could handle that type of rejection."

"What?" Glory gave me a look like I was a stupid, confused fool. "Why do you even think about that? Just go with the flow, girl. Enjoy your present moments with him instead of being afraid of what *might* happen with someone who's not even your man. It seems to me like you trying to give yourself reasons *not* to be with Tyrese just as you always give yourself reasons why you *should* stay with Derek."

"Maybe I am," I agreed. "I went to Tyrese's studio the other day and talked to him as he painted. We talked, Glory. The kind of connection I have with Tyrese is the kind of connection I should have with Derek. Do you see what I'm saying? I'm not emotionally available to Derek like that."

"Then there's no question about it! The answer's staring you in the face!"

"No, I feel like I have to first discontinue my friendship with Tyrese and then maybe break my relationship with Derek."

"Why let go of something that's going so great?" Glory asked. "I think you should dump Derek and go with Tyrese."

The elderly couple stood up to leave and being in such close proximity, it forced me and Glory to shove our chairs over in order for them to make their way out. The old lady turned to look at us shamefully as they walked away.

"Have a lovely day!" Glory called out to them, laughing.

"But Derek is such a good person," I said, motioning for her attention again.

"What does your therapist say?"

"She thinks I should give it a shot with Tyrese."

"There you go! And you yourself said that you connect more with Tyrese than you do with Derek on an emotional level. Okay, maybe you don't allow it with Derek but look at the bigger picture here. The fact that you allowed it with Tyrese is a very big deal. You never open up to *any*one anymore. It doesn't matter how long you've known Tyrese. The fact is you have something deep and emotional going on with this guy that I don't think you should dismiss so easily. I mean I like Derek and all cause he's a fine brother, but I'm looking out for your best interest here."

I didn't expect such advice from Glory. I did, however, continue thinking about my main reason for staying with Derek.

"But I've invested too many years into this relationship to just let it go."

"And some couples get divorced after twenty or forty fucking years of marriage," Glory countered. "Get over it."

"But is that what I really want to do?" I asked. "Let go of Derek? He's been there for me through so much."

"I understand what you're saying, Mia, I do. But honestly, like you said before, I just don't know if Derek is the one for you. He doesn't even know you've been seeing a therapist since you've been in college. You've been with him for five years, and he doesn't know *that*? You have to ask yourself why and then start exploring all your options."

Glory certainly gave me something to think about. She really pushed the idea of letting Derek go, never even exploring the reasons why I should stay with him. Perhaps what I really needed to do was break *both* relationships to be by myself for a while. The decision seemed like an easy one to make, but I found it to be such a challenge. I couldn't bear the thought of letting Derek go. I honestly didn't understand the omnipotent hold Derek had over me. And it scared me like nothing I had ever known.

Chapter 22.

Wednesday Evening, August 14, 2002

I let myself into my father's house with the key I had kept when I moved out. The darkness welcomed me in. A soft light coming from the living room guided my feet towards it. I found my father sitting on the couch, reading the day's paper under a dim lamp light that contrasted the light that used to shine within him. My father was once a vibrant soul whose very presence exuded an infectious enthusiasm with which he embraced life. Now sitting there, he seemed wasted away to a ghost of himself. His vitality was gone, along with the light that once drew so many people into his world.

On the coffee table was the 8x10 wood framed family portrait that he had been looking at the first time I came to talk to him about my mother's note. The glassless frame was positioned directly in front of him, as if he had deliberately placed it there for some type of comfort or consolation. The image in the frame had become something real my father could hold onto after the collapse of our family, which proved to be as fragile as the glass that had once protected it.

My memory recalled a time when I must have been about six years old and Nancy was four. My father was sitting right at the same spot on the couch, reading our favorite story book, *The Giving Tree* to me. I was sitting right beside him and Nancy sat to my left, my legs dangling against the couch, my feet unable to reach the floor and Nancy's legs not even long enough to dangle yet. I remembered how thrilled we were that he was reading it to us at that moment, although it certainly wasn't the first time. We watched with delight as our father read the words we knew so well. And, as always, after he was done, he tickled our stomachs saying, "Who's always gonna give you everything you need?" Giggling with excitement, we always responded with a loud and enthusiastic "Daddy!"

Now I watched the man who seemed to have nothing left to give. I was determined to go through with my plan. My mouth was dry. *I can do this,* I thought, already terrified of what might transpire during my unexpected visit.

I remained standing in the entrance of the living room, studying the man who no longer seemed familiar to me. He looked as if he had lost weight, and though he was reading the paper, he looked very sad. There he was: a lonely old man who had nothing better to do with his life than to read about the troubles that other people were suffering. Perhaps reading about others' woes helped him overcome the grief in his own life.

I was suddenly aware of my beating heart as a flash of heat quickly took over my body. During my last session with the therapist, she had advised me to speak with my father about what could have possibly contributed to my mother's supposed depression.

I took in a deep breath, waiting for him to look up at me, which he did almost the second after I willed it.

"Hi," I barely said above a whisper.

"Mia," he said, putting the paper down. "How are you?"

"A little tired," I said as I entered the living room. I sat next to him.

"Are you—are you taking care of yourself?"

I smiled. "I never stopped, Dad. How about you?"

I worried about whether or not it was a good idea to start asking him questions about Mom. Would it open his wound and hurt him even more? I couldn't remember the last time I worried about my father's feelings. That was good, right? It made me feel a little lost—like I had somehow stumbled into an unfamiliar room in the house.

"I'm doing all right," my father answered. "Just fine."

I took his hands inside my own. "Dad, please let me call someone about the house. We could start small. We can get the lawn done and then move on from there. What do you say?" I was stalling, not wishing to follow through with the reason I was there.

He sighed and gently nodded his head.

"Or if you want," I said, trying to choose my words carefully. "I can get somebody in here to clean up. Make this place something you'd want to come home to. I feel like it's too depressing in here and that's not good for you or Nancy."

In a soft voice and with eyes fixed on the framed photo on the coffee table, my father replied in the affirmative. "We can start with outside."

I smiled, kissed his cheek and squeezed his hand tighter. We stayed in silence for a while before he spoke again.

"But that's not why you came here tonight, is it?" he asked, now with the look of concern displayed clearly on his face. "What is it?"

"I do have something important I wanted to discuss with you. It's about Mom."

He groaned, removing his hands from my grasp. "What about your mother?"

"Well, you know how I've been taking care of myself for the past few years now... by seeing a therapist? Dr. Flare."

"Yes. You feel it's helping you?"

"I do," I responded. "In fact, the last time I was at Dr. Flare's office, she mentioned something about finally talking to you about Mom's behavior towards me and Nancy." I gently placed my hand on his knee. "Dad, I'm sorry but I need to know. Why did Mom resent me so much? And please don't tell me I'm just imagining it. There was something there. Something happened that made her resent me and be so cold to me."

He looked away. The once burly man seemed so frail, unable to withstand any more of life's hurdles. "The truth is not worth the pain it will cause you," he whispered.

"Dad just think about it. You yourself told me once that it's not good keeping feelings locked inside; they need to be shared. You have remained silent for so many years. And what good has come out of it? Nothing. Just a rebellious daughter who no longer has respect for herself or her life and another daughter who has become so mean-spirited that you can't even stand to be around her anymore. And look at yourself, Dad. You are not the man who raised us. I think these secrets are slowly killing you from the inside. The truth will be worth the pain because it is the truth, Dad. *You* need to release that pain from inside of you and I *need* to know." I was suddenly aware of how much I wanted to know, almost to the point of desperation. And seeing the pained look on my father's face made me emotional. I could feel the goose pimples rise on my arms and legs. Swallowing in an attempt to push down the lump that found its way in my throat was futile, for my throat was far too dry to finish the process.

"Just leave things the way they are, Mia. Why go and deliberately cause yourself pain?"

"*Cause* myself pain? Dad, I've been living *in* pain practically all my life. You got a glimpse of it back when I was at NYU." How could he not know? How did he not realize that the bitter person I became was a result of the pain that I'd been living with for so many years? Pain that was caused by a parent who could not love her children and another parent who turned his back on the neglect that existed in the family? I didn't want to say it but the questions in my mind brought me to a feeling of annoyance. He was doing the same thing he'd done all our lives—trying to deny what was happening.

"Dad," I finally said, "Now it's time I find out why. Why was Mom the way she was toward us, especially me? What happened?"

His eyes became like glass as he turned away from me.

"Mia," he said, as if telling me to just let it go.

"Dad," I responded, gently but firmly.

"All right," he sighed. He stood up, gingerly moved the family portrait aside and sat on the coffee table directly in front of me, so as to look at me straight in my eyes. Having him so close quite startled me. I wasn't prepared to fully see how much he had deteriorated. The sagging of his eyes, the paleness of his skin, the wrinkles that didn't seem to be there moments before were all so apparent to me now. He no longer resembled the father I once knew. It was all quite an aching shock to me.

He hesitated before he started. "You know that your mother's career was the most important thing to her."

"She worked so hard, I know. She was working at making partner, wasn't she? But she never made it."

My father nodded. "She was going to be made partner at her law firm. And that's when she got pregnant with you." He said it softly, possibly knowing what effect the truth would have on me.

I held my breath. Of course. It made sense. I stood in the way of her career, so she did the same to me. The lump in my throat grew bigger and I was unable to make it disappear. The tears burned my eyes. I finally understood; I couldn't even blame her. How would I feel if something stood in the way of my career at *Fresh Voices*? I tried to see myself in her situation—belly swelling, something growing inside of me, threatening the career I carefully molded for myself. I tried, but I couldn't even imagine it. Was that how she felt? Was that enough of a reason to resent her child throughout the child's life?

"So, what? Did she have to take leave? How did her pregnancy keep her from becoming a partner?"

"Remember that this was in the seventies. The laws regarding pregnant working women were not as developed as they are now. She was promised her position as long as she was physically capable of working. It wasn't against the law to deny her the partnership because of her pregnancy."

The truth, no matter how much you wanted it, no matter how minor it seemed, and no matter how much you prepared yourself for it, was always hard to accept.

"I wasn't wanted," I whispered.

"Yes, you *were* wanted but—"

"Not at the right time," I tried to finish my father's sentence the way I could make sense of what he was telling me. I attempted to swallow but my mouth was too dry. "Then why did you guys keep me?" I continued. "She could have had an abortion. It would have been better to be happy without a child than miserable with."

"She wasn't miserable with you, Mia. And besides, it wasn't that easy. Your mother and I were married for five years and could not get pregnant. We tried everything the doctors recommended. Fertility tests, diet change, health diaries, and so many other things but still nothing. Artificial insemination and IVF treatments were not even available to us at the time. That's when, your mother was told that she had a chance to be a partner at her firm. We discussed it and decided we would stop trying to conceive so that she could pursue her career. We even talked about adopting after she made partner. It was actually a few months after we stopped trying that you were conceived. The doctor said it was because we both were no longer stressed about it. But she was physically incapable of working because it was a very delicate pregnancy. The doctors were afraid that she wouldn't carry you to term. Chances were if she had a miscarriage with you, she would never be able to conceive again. Since she couldn't work, she never got the partnership. But Mia, you have to know that an abortion never crossed our minds."

"The thing is," my father continued, "as devastated as she was to know that she could not have children, I think she got used to the idea that she could continue with her career. It excited her. A black woman becoming partner—that was a real accomplishment thirty years ago. Still is, but—you know your mom. She was fiercely proud. She knew her own mother and grandmother never had such an opportunity. She didn't expect anything to come in between her and that, not even me. I'm sorry, Mia. I never wanted you to know because–"

"Because I was a mistake."

"You were a *miracle*," he said, emphasizing the word. "You were what we wanted, a blessing."

"How can a blessing drive two people away and throw one of them into a deep depression that probably caused the illness that eventually killed her?"

"You think your birth drove your mother and me apart and developed her cancer?"

"Well, what else am I supposed to think, Dad? We've never talked about these things. I have to reason them out myself. I can appreciate and understand all you're telling me. But you know the facts just as I do. Mom did treat me differently, like I needed to repay her for something I didn't know I owed. I always felt like that. So maybe I was paying for her not making partner or even the failure of your marriage. I don't know."

"Let me explain something, Mia. The failure of my marriage to your mother was due to things that are completely unrelated to you. The truth is that I fell out of love with your mother long before you were conceived, and she knew it. I still loved her, but I was no longer *in* love with her."

"But *why*? What happened to change your feelings?"

"It's so complicated." He sighed as if he did not want to continue with the conversation. "I'll understand if you lose respect for me because of what I'm about to say."

"Just say it."

He sighed again. "Your mother was a very difficult person to get along with. At first, she blamed me for the problems we had conceiving, before we found out that it had something to do with her ovaries. The whole experience of trying to get pregnant was just so—so stressful. We were constantly fighting. She was always angry. We grew distant. I secretly resented her for making it so hard on the both of us. I had to admit that it turned me off."

Wow. Trying to conceive a child through the bond and love of marriage became so tedious that it led to resentment. I felt sad for him and at the same time, disgusted.

"Her body wasn't cooperating," I finally said. "It wasn't her fault. But you placed the blame on her anyway."

"I didn't place the blame on her. She was difficult to deal with, under so much pressure to conceive. She didn't seem quite like herself, yet I pursued, despite my growing resentment. *That*, I should not have done. I realized it then but who can really make sense out of the irrational? I just want you to know that I understand my mistake."

"What mistake, Dad? It was how you *felt*. Your feelings can't be a mistake. What *was* a mistake was staying in a marriage with a woman you were no longer in love with."

"We were distant, yes. But I tried the best I could to love your mother. What turned me off wasn't us trying to conceive, please understand that. It was her negative attitude about it and what felt like a resistance against me. *She* turned away from *me*." With a far off look in his eyes, my father spoke as if he were understanding something about my mother for the very first time. "And with you girls, I can't explain it. It was like she wasn't comfortable with you and Nancy. Not that she didn't know how to physically take care of you. But she cared for you girls as if you weren't her children. She was reprimanding to you but never nurturing. She was easy on Nancy but never supportive. It was almost as if she didn't know *how* to love you. She did what she was supposed to do as a mother but the love and nurturing and compassion were never there. There was never any warmth towards you girls and that was always strange to me. It worried me, especially since she refused to talk about it with me. I knew I had to be the one to show you girls love, so I did what I felt was natural to me. I read to you girls, I played games with you, I watched movies with you. I made sure I was always there for you. At least until you girls were in high school."

"You never told us you loved us," I said.

He had a look of confusion on his face as he shook his head. "And I don't even know why. I don't even know what happened after that. Why we grew so apart."

"I know why," I responded. "You got the promotion at work and started working more hours. That's when Mom took over with her oppressive ways."

"Your mother wasn't always like that. It's as if she became joyless and bitter after you and Nancy were born. She was battling personal demons and she refused my help. I couldn't leave you girls with the woman your mother had become. I stayed with her for you and Nancy."

I was quiet, trying to process my feelings as best I could. I was hurt and confused and angry and relieved to know everything, all at the same time.

My father continued. "We all make mistakes and sometimes not only we suffer for the mistakes, but our children suffer as well. Look at your sister. Your mother turned Nancy into a spoiled brat because of her guilt for treating you the way she did. Now Nancy is suffering because of it, you know. Being out there in the real world is teaching her a hard lesson that the world will not stop everything to cater to Nancy Hill. She's taking classes right now at Queens Community College and she's having a hard time not only with her professors but with the students in her classes that she's paired with to do group work. And she's been looking for office work going on a year now. She's trying to fix her attitude and get used to hearing the word *no*. But the damage has already been done. She's angry with you, Mia, because she envies you and the way you were brought up. I used to hear her argue with your mother. She had no control over her life, and she knew it. She's trying, but she's still got a long way to go. But you, you're fierce, and you project yourself well. I think we all envy that about you. As far as I'm concerned, I cherish the fact that I was able to love such a strong person as you."

"Strong?!" I hollered. "Dad, do you want to know how weak I really am?"

"What happened at NYU was so long ago and you were under a lot of pressure."

"No, Dad. The way I carry on pretending nothing ever pains me is a sign of weakness, not strength. And slowly, I'm making an enemy of you. Just look at how Mom's treatment of me has ruined my emotional life. I won't even marry a good man like Derek! Dad, do you want to know why I tried to end everything?"

"You were stressed out at school. I understand that."

"No, Dad," I pleaded. "I was always able to handle school and good grades. I tried to kill myself because I felt beaten down. The stress of dealing with what David had done to me when he plagiarized my work and everything that happened after that because of it just ripped me up inside. And on top of that, I didn't understand why Mom was so against everything about me when all I tried to do was please her. It got to the point where I didn't know what else to do but to end the pattern that brought me pain. At the time, I thought ending it all was my best solution. Strong people do not go around trying to end their lives because other people hurt their feelings." The verbal admission unburdened me; the unspoken reality had quietly weighed me down for so many years and I hadn't even realized it.

My father's eyes became glassy again and he wore a pained expression on his face. He put his hand on his chest in an expression of sad surprise. I saw so much love in his eyes as he softly tried to understand my misery. "Mia," he said softly. "I didn't know."

"I've never been able to handle my emotions or anything that was remotely hurtful to me. I couldn't talk to you because you were never around. Couldn't talk to Mom because she was emotionally unavailable. Nancy doesn't give a shit about me. Who was I supposed to turn to? I was alone in the world, Dad. I should have developed a thick skin, but instead I tried to take the easy way out."

"Mia honey, I'm so sorry. I never knew you were going through so much pain."

"Well, you were just as afraid as I was to talk about it. I understand. It wasn't easy to talk about."

He sighed, "I don't know what to say, Mia. I wish we had been there for you. I wish you had talked to us."

"Yeah. Me too. But the fact remains that I didn't. Now look at me. I hate the way I turned out. I really do. I struggle every day with my personality, and I don't know how to change it."

He looked at me as if he realized something. "But this is the person you were meant to be. If you want to change, make sure you retain the essence of what makes you Mia Hill— your strength, your power, your confidence. Why can't you retain those excellent qualities while working hard to be a pleasant person, absorbing the positive in all situations and not the negative?"

"I don't know how."

"I'll help you!" he said. "We can try together. I love you, Mia. Don't ever forget that. The thoughts of the past can't affect the way I feel for you now. Don't be angry with your mother. It takes two to screw things up the way your mother and I did. Your mother has paid her dues. Be angry with me if you need to direct your pain onto someone."

I was inundated with a flood of emotions. I had spoken such harsh words to my father but now realized that those words came from a pained place deep inside of me and not from an actual anger towards him. I couldn't be angry with him when I was just as flawed as he was. We both handled our pain terribly.

I found myself crying as a result of his words, and it shocked me. He believed in me. I wanted to be the pleasant person he desired me to be; and for the first time, I felt hope that I actually could be. I had a vision of myself as someone who had finally learned to use the painful memories of her past to transform herself into someone that she could always be proud of. Maybe knowing what my mother went through could finally help me push past all the wrong that I felt she had committed against me.

"I don't even know what to think about all of this," I sobbed.

He put his arm around me. "I don't know what to say, Mia, except that I'm sorry."

"Did Mom blame me for how her life turned out?"

"She blamed the circumstances, not you. Please trust me on that."

"Then why did she treat me the way she did?"

"She was angry with the situation. She probably blamed herself, on some level, and took it out on you."

"*I* know. She wanted me to follow in her footsteps. That's why she discouraged my writing. She wanted me to become the lawyer that she wasn't. I took that away from her and so I owed it to her."

"Maybe." My father sighed. "I'm sorry, Mia. I tried to protect you from that truth."

"I didn't need your protection, Dad. Don't you understand? I deserved the complete truth."

"I see that now. God, Mia. If I could turn back the hands of time with the knowledge I've gained as a weapon, believe me when I tell you I would."

"I was the right thing at the wrong time."

"Now you listen to me." He sought my eyes and held them within his gaze. "You were the right thing at the right time. Your mother and I both knew it. You were meant to be and God, Mia, for what it's worth, I am so proud to be your father right now."

He hugged me for the first time in years and cried. The strength in his arms reminded me of how he'd hug me when I was a child. He had always made me feel safe and that was exactly what I was feeling at the moment. I felt safe from the world, safe from myself, safe from the secret that had been kept hidden for over twenty years.

"I'm so sorry for the way things turned out," he said.

I accepted his hug, rubbing his back as he released what looked to me like years of personal pain. It was a side of my father I never knew; I didn't feel comfortable with him in such a vulnerable state. I wanted to gently suppress his tears, but I knew that I shouldn't. He needed the emotional liberation. It was real. It made me remember when I was a little girl, waiting for him to come home from work. I didn't know how old I was exactly—just the fragment of memory: excitement. *Daddy's coming!* Just knowing that he was home made the world right for me. It felt so special. Somehow, I was starting to feel at home again. In his arms, I knew that everything was eventually going to be all right with us.

But there was something that was still bothering me. Maybe my father was still keeping something from me. Or, there might have been things about my mother that my father perhaps didn't know. The way he described their marriage—and what I knew of it—of course she had secrets. If he had known everything in her heart, there wouldn't have been so much tension in our home.

"Dad?"

My father looked at me, and quickly wiped his eyes with his forearm.

"There has to be more to mom's story than what you just told me. It just doesn't add up."

"What do you mean?" my father asked. "What doesn't add up?"

"Well, why did she let a partnership come in between her and the family she so desperately wanted? I mean, mom was brilliant; she could have easily started her own firm. And why couldn't she show her affection to me and Nancy—the children that she wanted so badly? Why was she so cold to us?"

My father met with me with a blank stare, looking like he wanted to answer my questions but did not know how. "Mia, I really wish I knew. Your mother...her state of mind...her actions...were all a mystery to me. Like I said before, it was like she was uncomfortable with you and Nancy. She cared for you girls as if you weren't her children. I can't explain it because she never confided in me. But maybe that's the same reason why she never tried for a partnership again. Mia, I wish I had the answers."

I was sure, suddenly, that those answers could be found in the wooden box mentioned in my mother's note.

I retrieved the note from my bag.

"Dad. Do you remember me asking you about this?"

He took the note from my hand. "Yeah. A couple of weeks ago."

"What you just told me tonight—do you think it's the truth Mom was referring to in this note?"

"I—" my father hesitated. "I honestly don't know, Mia."

"I don't think so. There's more going on here and it has to do with the reason why she was never loving to me and Nancy. If that was the truth she was referring to, she would have simply told me to talk to you about it. So there must be something in that wooden box that even you didn't know about."

My father suddenly perked up with the enthusiasm of a small boy ready for an adventure. "Do you want me to help you find the box tonight? We could look in her office. Maybe she hid it in our bedroom."

The thought of spending more energy into this mystery seemed more than I could bear. It had been exhausting enough dealing with emotions and a truth I thought I was ready to handle. I desperately wanted to take my father up on his offer. In fact, I was quite pleased to have his support in the endeavor. But no, it all felt too confounding, like a cloud growing into an overpowering storm. The memory of those days before my suicide attempt in college rose up—how battered I felt, my inner voices insisting that life was just too hard, that I was unworthy—yes, extreme feelings of despondency crept in.

"You know what?" I finally said, smiling. "Maybe another time. Maybe the weekend?"

"Fine," my father said, returning my smile. He slowly kissed me on my forehead. "You'll let me know when you're ready. In the meantime, I'll search through her things in our bedroom."

I was relieved that my father was willing to share the burden of searching for that box. As much as I longed to know what my mother's secrets were, I found myself too afraid of the truth to continue the investigation on my own. So, I put my curiosity aside. What my father told me was more than enough for the time being. I couldn't handle any more news. The fact that I was a mistake was already too much.

Chapter 23

Thursday Afternoon, August 15, 2002

Although I was busy at the office working on the final layout of the issue in which Tyrese was to be featured, I found it difficult to concentrate. The events between my parents weighed heavily in my thoughts. I couldn't imagine dealing with a situation like that. There was only one time in my life that I thought I might be pregnant, and it was a scary time for me, thinking about what my options were and imagining each option's consequence. But to finally get pregnant after one's conscious decision to not have a family must have come with its own traumas. It was hard for me to know for sure what I was actually feeling, armed with the information my father had shared with me. One part of me felt special—as if I had come into existence on my own, even when odds seemed against me. Another part of me still viewed my existence as a mistake. But thinking of myself as a mistake was too painful to bear.

I needed to talk about what I had recently learned about my mother. Tyrese had already made it so easy for me to talk to him, so I invited him to lunch.

We met up at a small bistro on the corner of Thompson and Spring streets. From where we sat outside the bistro, we could see boys playing basketball at the park across the street. The air was warm, but the breeze was cool, making it a perfect day to enjoy what nature had given us.

"I was a mistake," I told Tyrese. He took a bite out of his hamburger while I absentmindedly mixed the raspberry vinaigrette dressing into my garden salad. "My parents had given up trying to have a baby and then, surprise! I came along. My mother finally had the baby she desperately wanted, but I came at an unbelievably high price."

"I don't believe in mistakes," he said in between bites. "What's meant to be will be and always is. You were like a miracle baby."

"It kept me up all last night, though. I kept thinking that my parents really didn't want me. I was an inconvenience to my mother's career. And I feel like there's more to the story that my father doesn't know."

"What about your sister? *She* may know something."

I shook my head in disagreement. "The thought of learning another secret is too much right now."

"So, you'd rather be kept in the dark than learn the truth about something that's been bugging you for years?"

I grew defensive. "I know it's not something you would do, Tyrese, but I'm not like you."

Tyrese sighed. "Well, in that case, why focus on a past you didn't even know about until yesterday? What matters is now. Okay, so you were an unexpected surprise. Turn that around and make that something people will celebrate for years to come. You were put in this world to do something wonderful, Mia. Stop thinking the negative and finally do what you were meant to do."

I swallowed my food and stared at him, the fork in my hand midway between my mouth and my plate of food. Those words were the words I needed to hear, the reason why I told him about my father's confession and not Glory or Derek. I somehow innately knew that he would be the one that could tell me what I needed to hear to help me through the pain of learning the truth.

"Thank you, Tyrese," I said. "I truly look forward to the day when I could be as positive as you because right now, I can't do that no matter how hard I try."

"Well, you have to really want to be positive."

"Easier said than done," I said in response.

His smile disappeared, and he suddenly bore a serious expression. "Mia. When my mother . . . did what she did, it was the darkest, most painful moment of my life. I cursed God, my mother, myself. I didn't see the good in life or what it had to offer. My faith in people and in life just started to wane until it completely—it no longer existed."

"So how did you get your faith back?"

"The miracle came in the form of letters from people telling me how my paintings touched them. I don't know. I guess that did it for me, restored my faith."

So that was it. I recalled that during the interview, he had mentioned how important it was for him to know what people thought of his paintings.

And now he described it as a miracle. He was sort of a miracle himself. My feelings for him had extended from mere physical attraction to so much more in such a short amount of time. I knew I had already fallen in love with him. Was it love or lust? Whatever it was, it scared me.

"So, yeah," he said. "It *is* easier said than done, but it's not impossible, Mia. Remaining optimistic during the day-to-day pressures of life is a challenge, but a challenge worth taking."

I sighed. Tyrese was such a wonderful influence on me. He exuded positive energy and a strength that told me outside forces could not break him down. Derek, on the other hand, never had me look at life quite the way Tyrese did. Derek had a way of just being; he wasn't a negative person, for he would not have achieved the things he had in his life if he were. But there was something inspiring about Tyrese that I didn't find in Derek—at least not anymore. Perhaps it wasn't fair of me to expect Derek to be the optimistic person who could influence my life. I had to share that burden as well. And I couldn't help but wonder if my pessimistic nature ever stifled Derek's own potential. Who knows if he could've achieved more without me?

The waitress came out to our table and poured us some more water. "Are you two okay over here or can I get you anything else?" she asked.

"We're fine," Tyrese answered.

"Thank you," I added as she walked back into the bistro.

Tyrese and I remained silent as we continued our lunch. I didn't know why but I suddenly thought about his painting, the one that was hanging on my living room wall.

Taking a sip of water, I said, "When I first saw your painting after my mother had given it to me, it didn't mean anything to me. I mean, I saw the colors, the composition, and realized it was a good painting. And during the reading of my mother's will, I guess I was disappointed my mother hadn't left me something that could help me understand her. Her favorite books, maybe, or something that was precious to her when she was my age. Anything. And I kept questioning why she would give me that painting. It was only a few months ago that I began thinking about the title's message. I finally understood the significance of the painting in my life and in my mother's. I understood the significance of my mother gifting it to me. And then I knew she did leave me something by which I could understand her.

I didn't need anything special from her will." I paused. "It speaks to me, I guess."

"What does it say?"

"She was trying to give me a message, I think. That people are trying to help me and that I shouldn't turn my back on them. That I should be careful not to close myself off in a box like she did. To open my box...let people in."

"Do you think maybe she thought you felt all alone?"

I suddenly felt exposed, wishing I could hide under my very own shroud of seclusion. I'd always presented myself as a strong individual who had control over her life and over the people she allowed into her world. It was important for me to hide the fact that I indeed felt alone in a world that crawled with dishonest people who had selfish agendas. I knew he knew the answer, but I just didn't feel like sharing all of that with him. I wanted to shut down; I didn't want to discuss it.

"You know what?" I finally said. "Let's just forget it."

"Why won't you let me in, Mia?"

"Are you serious? I have let you in, Tyrese. More than I ever thought I would. Just leave it at that!"

He responded in a reassuring tone. "I just want to get to know you, Mia."

"Don't bother, Tyrese. It's not like we have a relationship to pursue here." I fought it; I didn't know why but I did.

He sat up in his chair, then. "Mia, what are the chances of me coming into your life this way and you having my painting hanging on your living room wall? You think it was an accident we met? We were meant to meet by a force greater and more powerful than us. My guardian angel is hooking me up and I think yours is looking out for you too." I smiled before he continued. "All I ask is to be your friend. I didn't know how much I needed that until I met you. This is the most interaction I've had in months with anyone else. I'm always working! If I'm not at the gallery, I'm in the studio painting. I don't hang out. I don't socialize."

I suddenly saw him in a different light. "Do you ever feel lonely, Tyrese?"

"Hell, yeah," he responded. "I'm an artist. I think it's in the job description."

I chuckled at his joke and he did too. I softened.

"I feel lonely too," I said. "I always feel lonely. Sometimes I think that I don't have an outlet for the way I feel because my writing was taken away from me. I don't even feel compelled to write about my feelings anymore. That's one of the reasons why I'm still seeing a therapist."

"You're seeing a therapist?"

I shut my eyes; I couldn't believe I let it slip. "Damn. Pretend you didn't hear that."

"No. But wait. Why are you seeing a therapist?"

I sighed. "I'm depressed, Tyrese. I don't want to get into it."

He didn't need to know about the unfortunate incident in dorm room. But he wasn't letting me off the hook just yet.

"There's no judgement here," he said, softly. "Talk to me."

I looked away, angry with him for not letting it go but at the same time, grateful for his concern.

"I don't think my mom is the only reason why I stopped writing."

"What do you mean?" he asked, putting his fork down and focusing his attention on me.

"David," I said. "He plagiarized my work in college and no one believed me. I have the magazine to back me up now but what if it happens again with my own work? It will break me." I felt the tears in my eyes and I did nothing to stop them from falling.

"Why will it break you?" Tyrese asked, seeming completely absorbed in my declaration.

"He's the reason why," I hesitated to continue. I still didn't want to tell him about the incident in my dorm room. "I broke down after it happened. No one but my dad and Glory believed me. My professor, the administration, and my writing group all believed that I was the one who plagiarized. My reputation as a writer was ruined and I wanted...I wanted to end it all." One version of the truth was better than nothing. "It was the school that connected me to my therapist. And I've been seeing her since then."

Tyrese sighed, then leaned forward in his chair, wiped a tear that had fallen and said, "See? I knew you had a story to tell."

I smiled. I felt the goosebumps rise on my arms and my legs. I took a deep breath in and exhaled. Yes, my story was a powerful one. Perhaps I was meant to write it; but it wasn't finished yet.

I looked at Tyrese, who now continued enjoying his meal.

"What about you, Mr. Black?" I said. "What's *your* story?"

"If you read the next issue of *Fresh Voices* magazine you'll find out," he laughed. "I got the cover page."

I smiled. "I never told Derek about my love for writing fiction and poetry," I said, softly. "He knows I used to write, but he doesn't know how important it is to me." I finished the last of my salad and took a sip of water. "It's one of many things I've never told Derek. He doesn't ask me much about myself. Or what takes up most of my time for that matter. He just accepts me the way I am."

"Isn't that what we all want, though? Someone to love us just the way we are?"

"We also want someone to be interested in everything about us, right? Our thoughts, our loves, our passions. How can Derek love me so much yet never ask me why I am the way I am? He's never asked me why I love working at the magazine. Or what I dreamed of becoming as a young girl."

"Well, why not just tell him instead of waiting for him to ask you?"

"Because I've never been that person to volunteer information about myself unless it's asked of me. I'm not going to just start talking about myself, not knowing if the person listening to me is actually interested. It can be rude and awkward."

"But he's your man. He'll be interested in anything you have to say about yourself."

"I know people who just go on and on about things in their lives that no one cares about, and they keep making fools of themselves because everyone is too polite to tell them that they just don't care. I don't want to be one of those people. Whether Derek's my man or not, it would be nice to know that he was interested in something about me."

"Maybe he's afraid of unlocking the mystery that is Mia Hill," Tyrese smiled. "Or maybe he acts the way he does with you because he thinks that's how you want him to act."

I took in a deep breath and exhaled. I shifted my weight on my seat. Yes, that was how I had always felt. Derek followed my cues. During the beginning of our relationship, he was much more open and yes, he did ask me questions about myself—safe, superficial questions. He never delved into anything too deep like why my relationship with my parents was so strained. Once I started to shut down with Derek, he sensed it and shut down as well. It was hard to admit that.

"I think you're right," I said softly.

We remained silent for minutes as I finished my water. He placed his elbow on the table and rested his head on his fist and stared at me, smiling slightly.

"What?" I asked.

"You don't have a box around you anymore," he answered.

"Really?" I said, smiling. I didn't know how else to respond to that.

"Yeah," he said, mostly to himself, then he continued to address me. "No. Now, you just have really tall walls. But I can see the walls slowly chipping away. And I'll be there when they're finally down and gone for good."

I exhaled and looked down at the table. His words were so powerful. I could feel them penetrate. I was letting my guard down. He saw my vulnerability, and that no longer scared me.

"So. Therapy, huh?" Tyrese said. I'm sure he picked up on my slight discomfort in the moment. "What happens in therapy?"

I sighed, not wanting to share that part of my life with him but also drawn to do so. "I do a lot of talking, mostly about how I feel about myself right now. And she talks to me about how I need to be a more active participant in my therapy, blah blah blah. But most of all, we just talk about what's caused me pain in the past."

"Well, why do you talk about that?"

"According to my therapist, I need to first understand what has caused my depression before I can move on."

"It doesn't make any sense. Isn't therapy supposed to concentrate on finding solutions to your current problems and focusing on a positive future? If you keep talking about past hurts, you'll get even more depressed and never get any better. Kind of defeats the purpose of therapy, don't you think?"

I looked at him. He was acting as if he were in a position to actually judge the situation and it frankly annoyed me. "So, you're an expert at talk therapy now?" I said, sarcastically. "Why are you being so judgmental?"

"I'm sorry. I just—" he hesitated, looking very foolish, perhaps embarrassed. "It just seems like her style of therapy is counterproductive to what you need."

"But how would you know this?" I asked, annoyed.

The waitress came, placed the bill on the table directly in front of Tyrese and took our plates away.

"I've been seeing her for a while now. I'm actually starting to feel better now than I did when I first started," I said, defensively.

"Okay. I'm just an outsider here looking in and my knowledge of depression and therapy are very basic, but could it be possible that because she's focusing on past hurts, she's been talking you into a deeper depression?"

I sighed, releasing my annoyance because I appreciated that it was a valid question. "But she's not talking me into a deeper depression." I searched my thoughts. "I used to go just to have someone to be angry with. I don't know why. Sometimes I don't want anyone to know how I truly feel on the inside, but I need to let it out. I feel like I've become more receptive to how she's trying to help me. She wasn't really able to help me before because I wasn't willing to be helped. Now, I want to start getting better. Ever since I found my mother's note, it—it changed the way I'm responding to therapy. Yeah, my therapist talks about my past a lot and there are still certain things about my past that I don't want to talk about; I just make sure they're not brought up." I paused. "I guess it's all right that we discuss my parents. She's the one who insisted I talk to my dad about my mom. If she didn't suggest it, I wouldn't have found out the story of them having me." I paused again. "I believe in talk therapy. I think it's important for people to release the demons they have hidden inside of them."

"Fair enough," Tyrese said.

I watched the boys in the park across the street play ball. One boy had left the game in order to flirt with a girl who was apparently reciprocating his feelings. They won't last, I thought. Teenage love rarely lasts, and adult romance is usually too complicated to not struggle through, no matter what the outcome.

"I don't think Derek and I will make it," I finally said.

"Why do you say that?"

"Because," I answered, "he and I have never talked like this."

Chapter 24

Thursday Evening, August 15, 2002

Luck was on my side earlier in the afternoon when I called Dr. Flare right after my lunch with Tyrese. I had asked for an emergency meeting to discuss the family details my father told me the day before. She told me another patient had just called to cancel and that she could fit me in at six o'clock. I quickly agreed. Although Tyrese helped me to think of myself as not a mistake but as a miracle, the news was still quite difficult for me to process. It consumed me, so I felt like I needed her perspective. As I sat in Dr. Flare's office sharing with her, I found myself becoming emotional about it all over again. She listened carefully as I spoke, jotting notes onto her notepad every so often. When I finished, she took in a deep breath and exhaled.

"That's quite a story, Mia. How did it make you feel when he told you this?"

"Hurt," I said without hesitation. "I had a right to know about my mother. I think it was wrong of him to keep that information to himself for all of these years."

"I completely agree." She looked at me with soft, understanding eyes. "But remember that your mother never shared this information with you either. Aren't you just as upset with her?"

She made an excellent point. "With my mother, I guess I would have expected her to keep something like that from me. But my father and I were once close so I guess that's why I'm more upset with him than I am with her."

"Given the state of your relationship with your father the past few years, do you think it would have been easy for him to simply share those details with you? Especially while your mother was still alive? It was the responsibility of the two of them to share that story with you and your sister *together*. It is not your father's fault more than your mother's."

"It's more than just blame, Dr. Flare. I feel..." I hesitated.

"Go on," she coaxed me, "What else do you feel?"

"I feel like I'm a mistake. I feel hurt, upset, sad, lost."

"Did you tell your father how you felt?"

"Not really. He knows I was upset, but I've been trying to process these feelings as best as I could since I left the house. It feels weird and strange. Tyrese told me that I should celebrate the fact that I'm here, that there's a reason why I'm here. But I almost feel like I wasn't meant to be here. What if I wasn't meant to be alive? What if that's the reason why I've always been depressed? Somehow my soul or my spirit knows it doesn't belong here?"

"Let's back track a little." Dr. Flare put up her right palm to tell me to stop. "You talked to Tyrese and not to Derek. Why?"

"I feel more comfortable talking to Tyrese."

"Why?" Her facial expression was one of confusion.

"I just do." She was beginning to aggravate me.

"I'm not taking that for an answer. This is your opportunity to really look inside of yourself and analyze your actions. Your father just gave you some unsettling news and instead of confiding in your boyfriend, whom you say you love, you tell Tyrese, whom you've just met. Why do you feel more comfortable talking to Tyrese?"

I could feel my head growing hot with frustration. "I came here to talk about what my father told me, not why I spoke with Tyrese first."

"Okay," she said, giving in. "You feel that perhaps the reason why you suffer from depression is because you were not meant to exist."

I exhaled, releasing the growing frustration I felt towards the doctor. "Is that a possibility?"

"I wouldn't discount it but then again, I don't know enough about existentialism or philosophy to answer that question."

"I just don't know what to do with all of these feelings, Dr. Flare."

"Try to think about it this way, if you can. Your parents put a wish out into the world and for a long time their wish did not come true. When it finally did, they understood its importance. They understood that their wish was fulfilled but they were confused too, because they didn't understand why their fulfilled wish did not come when they first asked for it. In an effort to love and to protect their wish, they made a series of mistakes that resulted in pain for them and for you. Yes, it is painful. But did they get the wish they had asked for?"

"Yes."

"Then you were meant to be here. Plain and simple. I think it's healthy to feel lost and angry and unhinged, Mia. It can be very disconcerting and confusing to learn such a secret that affects the way you think about yourself and others."

"Exactly," I responded, grateful that she understood my perspective. However, in a much unexpected turn, she threw it right back at me.

"Now, I want you to listen to me very carefully, and consider what I'm saying here."

"Okay." She had my attention.

"Do you realize that you are doing the same thing to Derek?"

My heart jumped into my throat. I thought she was on my side; that she truly understood me and I could trust her to help me.

"What do you mean?" I asked her, my heart pounding.

"You wanted your father to be honest with you, but you've never been completely honest with Derek and the reason why you're with him, which is also the reason why you can't seem to break away from him."

I felt a rush of heat travel throughout my body. I could feel myself becoming enraged. "You know nothing about me except what I've told you."

She sighed. "I look at you, Mia, and I see someone who wants and needs to be in complete control of her life."

"I *am* in control."

"No. You're not," she said sympathetically. "And I'll tell you why. Your thoughts get in your way. Thinking so much about your life with Derek and why you're hurting just confuses you and makes you lose focus. It's all caused you to lose control of your life and of what you actually want. You know what you want but then you don't know. Do you see what I'm saying?"

"I'm afraid I don't," I said crossing my arms, preparing to resist anything she had to say.

"Take your life right now, for instance. You love Derek, yes, but the main reason why you're still with him is because you're afraid of getting hurt again. You claim it's because you can't see your life without him, and you feel you need him. But it's actually because you know he is safe. Derek has already proven that he will always be there for you and never hurt you. But you can't fully focus on your present life with Derek, or with Tyrese for that matter, because of the pain you've endured in past romantic and familial relationships. As soon as you experience any type of happiness in a relationship, you want out because you are afraid emotional pain will follow. Am I right? It takes you right back to the plagiarist, that first romantic association where you were taken advantage of. You come across as if you've moved past the pain of that early relationship but in actuality, that is what continues to drive your life with Derek and now, how you are handling things with Tyrese. I don't think you realize that if you don't address this fear you have, you will continue the same pattern with Tyrese if he's the one you choose to be with."

My heart pounded. My breath became heavier. My mouth lost all of its moisture. I felt the dampness build on the surface of my skin. I didn't understand how she knew all of that. I tried to hide it even from myself. The relationship that broke me before I met Derek still haunted me and did indeed inform the way I behaved with Derek and now Tyrese. I never told her those things, though. Or did I? I thought I made it a point never to discuss them with Dr. Flare because I didn't want to admit it to myself. It was possible I might had indeed discussed them with her during one of my many sessions with her and I forgot. No, I could not have possibly forgotten something like that. I needed to feel in control of my therapy with Dr. Flare. That was why I never harped on the plagiarist—I never wanted to actually believe that that insignificant boy whose inconsiderate use of me and my work was actually an important part of my development. I wanted to believe that Derek was indeed safe but that my feelings of safety stemmed only from my desire for a reliable man in my life. She wasn't supposed to know how I truly felt and because she did, it changed everything. In that moment, I decided that I would never visit her office again. But in my need to feel that I was still one step ahead of her, I stayed, allowing her to continue her ramblings, all the while having her believe that her words were finally getting through to me.

"Now you're probably wondering how I know all of this about you. It's my job as your therapist to read between the lines and your actions."

I said nothing.

"What you can't seem to grasp is that unless you change all your current thoughts and fears, you won't be able to move forward, and you won't ever get out of this depression."

I sat in silence, already resigning myself to the idea that she was no longer my therapist and reveling in the fact that she was not yet aware of it.

She continued. "Depression is a complex illness, Mia, with many contributing factors. If it's left untreated for too long, it can get worse, causing untold suffering that could end in suicide. I don't want that happening to you."

I sighed, already annoyed with her but staying and listening, allowing it to feed my growing anger with her. It would be easier to leave her if I began to hate her.

"I come, don't I?" I shot back. "What more do you want from me?"

Then she answered me in an irritatingly calm tone: "You have to be willing to really evaluate your thoughts and behaviors about life, Derek and your family because those are the issues that plague you the most. You need to learn to identify all the stresses that contribute to your depression and work to modify all of them. You need to work on that, Mia. I can help you; that's what I'm here for. But you have to be willing to do more than just talk about what's bothering you. Therapy is not a quick fix. It takes quite a bit of time to begin working, but its effects are extremely beneficial, more so than medicines and drug therapy alone. Trust me. You suffer from one of the mildest forms of depression. You should not have been in therapy this long if you were really serious about getting better. Do you wish to prolong your depression, Mia?"

"How dare you!" I snapped. "Why do you think that's what I'm trying to do?"

"To me it seems like you're trying to nurse your depression instead of getting rid of it. Do you think that's a possibility?"

"Unbelievable! I can't believe you're asking me these questions!"

"They're serious questions to consider." She spoke with more passion now as if she felt like she were losing me, and this was her last chance to convince me that I did need more help. "Do you even understand how therapy with me is designed to treat your depression? There's no reason for you to be here if you don't. Therapy is supposed to help prevent depression from coming back by correcting the beliefs, perceptions, and behaviors that contribute to your depression. Because it takes a great deal of effort, you have to be ready and more than willing to make that effort. But you're not trying to correct anything."

"Why are you saying these things to me? I've been listening to you for the past couple of weeks. I've done what you suggested. I talked to my father, I tried talking to my sister."

She shook her head. "Yes, you've made progress. I can grant you that. However, you haven't addressed the issue with Derek, and then you made things even more complicated by starting something with Tyrese that you don't plan on finishing."

"That's where I need your guidance!" I yelled it. I didn't mean for my voice to get so loud but there it was, still hanging in the air like a threatening cloud ready for a downpour. But there was no downpour, only a big realization: "I don't think this is good for me anymore."

"Mia!" She exclaimed in shock. "But you're doing so well! You talked to your father. You finally did what I have been suggesting you do for so long! You can't give this up now!"

"Talking to my father only caused me a different kind of pain, Dr. Flare. I can't keep going through this."

"This is what I suggest you do, Mia." She stood up and walked over to the empty seat beside me and sat down, holding onto my hand with urgency. "You need to take the time to take care of yourself and pamper yourself. Depressed, you are no good to anyone. You need to take the time to relax and just take inventory of how you treat yourself and your body. Have you ever considered massage therapy or acupuncture or maybe even yoga? They can all be very effective ways to reflect and ponder your situation and to handle them with a clear and open mind. And you don't have to stop there. There are many other alternatives that can help you relax, and I think that's what you need. Take that time for yourself, Mia."

"That's where your advice is useless," I told her. "I simply don't have that kind of time. And honestly, I don't have time for *this*. Thank you, Dr. Flare, but I have to get going now."

"Mia, you can't get better unless you help *yourself*," she pleaded.

"Why did I think you could help me all this time?" I asked as I made my way out of her office. "You don't know the first thing about the pressures of being a professional black woman and you can't understand our experience in the world. You just sat there for all of these years listening to—but not understanding—what I had to say, and then you formed your own damn conclusions about me and had the nerve to spit them back to me in the form of therapy. I'm done with this." In an effort to be dramatic, I purposely left her door open as I left.

Take care of myself? Did she not know the pressure of being the executive director of one of the leading black magazines in the country? Her suggestion was ludicrous!

That was, indeed, the last time I visited her office. She was getting too close and that terrified me. I couldn't let her into my world and my thoughts. And most importantly, I couldn't risk hearing any more in words what I already knew about myself. It was just too painful.

Chapter 25

Friday Afternoon, August 16, 2002

Tyrese and I met for lunch outside of a small restaurant at Union Square. I wanted to let him read the final draft of my article before the issue went to the printer. Though the chicken salad on the table in front of me was absolutely delicious, it was hard for me to enjoy it. I waited anxiously as Tyrese silently read the article. It was important to me that he approve it; I wanted him to feel that I had done justice to him, his work, and his beliefs. After he finished reading, he smiled, held the article in his hand, and read the last few words aloud, dramatizing each sentence as if he were presenting it to a room full of people.

"Among the many pieces of advice Black enjoys sharing, one of them reigns true above all the others. "You need to find that specific talent—because we all have many talents—but find that one that makes you happy before you use it to make others happy," Black counsels. "And if you are using your talent to create, then share it with others. The sheer satisfaction of touching one person alone is enough to make you burst with pride."

'Perhaps we can all gain something from the lessons Tyrese Black was forced to learn. He welcomed his natural God-given talents at his darkest hour and, in finding a way to grieve his loss, he found his way into the hearts and homes of hundreds of people all across the country.'"

Tyrese placed the stapled sheets of paper on the table and kept his eyes focused on it.

"Well, Ms. Hill," he said, taking a sip of water. "I would have never guessed this article came from you."

I chuckled. "I'll take that as a compliment."

"I didn't know that someone with such a negative outlook on life could write something so inspirational. And you do it well."

"Well, there is a reason why I get paid so much to do what I do. Some people may not like me or like working with me, but they can never say that I don't create and produce excellent work."

"I loved the article."

"I'm glad you did," I said. "You deserve the recognition I hope this article will bring. I think people need to hear what you have to say and see what you have to paint."

He nodded his head. "Thank you, Mia."

"No thanks needed."

"On the contrary, I think it's very much deserved. You know, I have a feeling that you're not as completely negative as you think. I was looking through some back issues of *Fresh Voices* and noticed that you write exceptionally powerful and inspirational pieces. It seems to me like you always reach deep down inside your heart to find something positive to say, and I think you should be commended for that."

I proudly smiled, quickly recalling what he had told me after I had interviewed him: that other than just writing articles for *Fresh Voices*, I needed to write something to inspire people. Reading the article about his own work seemed to have changed his opinion. Though I wrote for my job and not for myself, he recognized my talent and saw how I used it to try to touch other people's lives by promoting issues I believed in.

"As a matter of fact," he continued, smiling as if proud to have made some kind of discovery, "this may just be the story that you were meant to tell to inspire the world. I mean, not necessarily about me but about what you *wrote* about me. Maybe I was wrong. Maybe your *articles* and *not* your fiction were meant to inspire. You knew exactly what to pull from my interview to use in an article meant to introduce people to my work and simultaneously show them that they can do wonderful things too. That's your gift, Mia. Your talent is to inspire others through the articles you write about people who have already found their inspiration."

It wasn't until after he had finished talking that I realized I had not been breathing. It astounded me how he saw something in me that I myself had never taken the time to acknowledge. I slowly exhaled, concentrating on the air that was being released from my body and then stared at him in admiration. I actually felt a sensation of warmth on my face and neck. As soon as the sensation disappeared, I was very aware of the sweat that had suddenly built up in the pits of my arms.

"You really think so?" I asked, feeling strangely like the wide-eyed child I was when my father used to devotedly read the little stories that I had written for him.

"I sincerely do."

"Life is funny," I said. "My mother thought that I couldn't reach anyone with my writing and so discouraged me from pursuing a writing career. So instead of becoming the novelist I thought I'd be, I pursued a career in magazine publishing. I didn't know at the time how much I would love it. My first big break was when I wrote about a local music artist who wasn't well-known. But, so many subscribers wrote to *Fresh Voices* telling us how much they loved it and felt inspired. It made me so proud! And it was because of my article on the gay and lesbian community that so many people wrote me after they read it, saying how liberated they felt because they felt seen. That's when we incorporated the LGBTQ section of the magazine."

"And then there's the annual talent convention that you started."

"Yeah, the Annual Fresh Voices Talent Conference. Tyrese, if it weren't for my mother disapproving of what I wanted to do, I would never have ended up at *Fresh Voices*."

"So, you have your mother to thank."

"I guess..."

My thoughts drifted as I was suddenly overcome with emotion, recalling Derek's insensitive comment about my mother's rebuke of my writing talent. I hated the fact that both Derek and Tyrese saw it before I could acknowledge it for myself. Yes, my mother discouraged me in an effort to challenge me to do more than what I was already doing at the time. In the end, I did in fact use my writing to help uplift the community, just as she always advocated. The tears were there; I could feel them forming and I did not block them from falling down my cheek. There was no need to hide or deny them. For a moment, I thought of my mother differently. I think she might have been really looking out for me. I took a sip of water to soothe the sandpaper in my mouth.

"I think my mom saw the same thing in me that you do and that's what her discouragement was about." I said, trying to swallow away the notorious lump in my throat. Tyrese nodded in agreement.

"And if it weren't for you," I continued, "I would have never realized all this for myself."

"You would have eventually," Tyrese assured me.

It all became so clear to me. Everything I had ever done in my entire life was meant to happen the way it did. Befriending Glory in college, meeting Derek at the publishing conference, and working at *Fresh Voices* were all meant to happen to enrich my life. And I was meant to meet Tyrese so that love and inspiration could be breathed into me. But why had I come into Tyrese's life?

"Why do you think you met me?" I asked him. "I mean, what purpose do you think I serve in your life?"

He smiled as he looked down at the table. What was so strange about that reaction was that he suddenly appeared so shy. It didn't suit his personality at all. The color in his face completely changed from light brown to crimson. Right in front of my eyes, his demeanor changed to that of a shy teenage boy who didn't know how to talk to a more mature woman.

He avoided my eyes as he stared down at his plate. "If I told you why I think you're in my life, you'd probably never want to see me again."

I didn't expect that response. "What do you mean?"

He hesitated, as his eyes continued to survey the food on his plate. "Like you said once in my office . . ." And then his voice simply drifted as if he had forgotten he was in the middle of a thought. A shy smile came across his face and he tried to hide it by putting his head down.

"Tyrese?"

He looked at me and smiled. "Um, it's like you said once, each and every person has someone they were meant to be with, a soul mate. Now if I–" he stopped himself and laughed. But his expression quickly changed, and he became serious once again. Finally, he continued, slowly pronouncing each word as if to produce some kind of dramatic effect. "Mia, if I told you that I found in you the person I was born to be with, I'm scared you would find a way to prevent that from happening."

A sudden hot flash invaded my body. I felt it, too, like we were born to be with each other. Fear, however, overpowered me because I knew what that meant. We had both allowed ourselves to become vulnerable with each other.

I reached across the table and took his hand in my own. "We're together now, Tyrese. I mean, we're friends. Isn't that what you want?"

"It's not enough," he quickly responded, his voice suddenly becoming deeper. "Not anymore. I want us to be more than just friends."

In a panic, I released his hand and nearly spilled my glass of water. That was the first time he admitted he wanted more than just friendship with me. He wanted to be with me despite the knowledge of my depression and its effects on me. I suddenly resented him for complicating our current arrangement. He knew my reasons for staying with Derek. But he couldn't understand the fear in my heart that would never allow me to love him the way he deserved to be loved.

There were so many ideas, fears, and worries running around in my head. I was the one who invited this response from him by posing the question in the first place and now I resented him for putting me on the spot. My stomach ached from the pressure. Just as I had done with Derek, I allowed Tyrese to know only a part of me and the thought that he would learn about the really indecisive, confused, dissatisfied Mia if we were to enter a real relationship made my stomach knot up in dread and apprehension. If we entered a real relationship, the magic between us would disappear. I pictured us arguing and him feeling defeated, frustrated with my behavior. Derek was patient with me but I doubted that Tyrese would tolerate such conduct. I felt afraid that Tyrese would grow tired of me, yet I also felt he could be my biggest ally. Tyrese would never be able to understand that incommunicable fear I had because I myself was completely and utterly baffled by it.

I took my glass of water and gulped it down in one shot, hoping to drive away the uneasiness in my stomach. I then looked at him and found him staring at me with eyes that no longer boasted promises of lust and passion. His eyes now promised sincerity and kindness, friendship and compassion forever. His eyes promised understanding, togetherness, and love. I stared into his eyes, wanting and needing to give him what he wanted because it was what I wanted as well. But it would be too difficult for me. I didn't have the confidence in us that he seemed to have. Love would be the end of me; I knew that.

I could picture it. Scenes of a supposed future life together flashed before me. The euphoria felt as a result of my finally allowing Tyrese into my mind, my life, and my heart replaced with the anguish of infertility experienced as punishment for not having reconciled with my mother before she passed. The joy of finally feeling free to love with all of its uncertainties replaced with the madness associated with the loss of a love I thought was truly rare. Then, an awareness: anytime I envisioned a life with Tyrese, the thought of pain and heartache were also present. I didn't feel that with Derek. No, with Derek, I felt like I could have an untroubled future with someone who learned to keep his distance. There was comfort in that.

My stomach started to hurt again, this time with a mixture of emotions that included fear, anxiety, regret, and love. I desperately tried to ignore the pain as I took a deep breath in and then exhaled.

"Tyrese," I whispered. "I can't promise that we could ever be more than friends."

Growing very serious, he said, "So, how do you think this friendship will work? Us getting together every once in a while, to have pleasant lunches? Maybe fuck every now and then whenever the mood strikes us? And in between all of that, we have deep, meaningful conversations with each other because we can't seem to open up to our significant others? Well, that's not the kind of relationship I want, Mia."

I couldn't look into his eyes. He was right. Continuing a friendship like ours would not work. We'd be hurting ourselves more than anything. At some point, he would meet someone who would want to give him everything he wanted in a relationship. I'd be left alone, heartbroken and jealous, feeling cursed that I finally experienced the thing I tried to avoid all this time with Derek.

"Then," I said, unable to believe the words that I was about to say, "I guess we won't even be friends."

The expression on his face was blank; I couldn't read it. "I was afraid of that," he answered, taking a sip of his water. He didn't make a fuss. I somehow expected him to fight for me like Derek always did, but Tyrese simply accepted my choice. It confused me. I didn't know whether I wanted him to fight for me, or if I wanted him to make it easy for me and just let it go.

He looked at the article and said, "Damn, Mia. This issue will be great. You keep writing like this and people will want to know who you are. Can I keep this?"

I stared at him awhile and smiled awkwardly. "Uh, yes; of course. I brought that copy here just for you."

He flashed me a splendid smile and said, "Yup, this is great. Even *I'm* inspired by the way you wrote the article. You make me want to go home right now just to paint."

But he didn't. He stayed with me and finished eating his lunch, as I remained quiet. He was remarkable. Even after I could not tell him what he wanted to hear, he didn't fixate on it. Instead, he continued to talk about how powerful my article was. He wasn't petty. He wasn't selfish. No. Instead, he was cheerful. In fact, he believed I was his inspiration, never once realizing that I was the fortunate one to have him as my very own personal muse.

Chapter 26

Friday Evening, August 16, 2002

The clock on my office computer read 7:45 pm. Work once again managed to occupy my mind, allowing me to forget for a moment my afternoon lunch with Tyrese, my complicated feelings about Derek, my dysfunctional relationship with my sister and father, and the stress I suffered from learning the story behind my conception. I was busy working on the magazine's final layout in preparation for the production meeting in which the upcoming issue would be discussed. So engrossed was I in my work that it took me a few minutes to realize that someone had been knocking on my door.

"Come in," I answered.

My assistant walked in. With a pair of blue jeans, she wore a black V-neck sleeveless top, which made her look even paler than she already was. Sophia? Cynthia? I glanced at her email messages to me on my computer screen to confirm her name was Sophia. Nope. There had to be a reason why it was so difficult for me to remember her name.

"Hi, Cynthia. What can I do for you?"

"I just wanted you to know that I spoke with Patrick Jerome's publicist. Mr. Jerome is now officially booked for the *Fourth Annual Fresh Voices Talent Conference* in February. All arrangements have been made. In December, I'll place an order for 750 copies of the book to arrive at the center in time for the conference."

For the first time in a long time, I truly felt appreciative of all the hard work she actually did for me. She was a quiet but reliable assistant. "That's wonderful news, Cynthia."

"Was there anything else you needed me to do? I'm working on a few things now but if there is anything immediate—"

"No. That'll be all, Cynthia." I repeated her name, hoping that I could finally commit it to memory.

She turned to walk away, and I felt a strange urge to express my appreciation for a job well done.

"Thanks for booking Patrick Jerome for the conference, Cynthia. Thanks for your help with everything."

She turned around and looked at me, confused, as though I had just said something very wrong.

"Are you all right, Mia?"

"I'm fine," I quickly said, knowing that thanking her was out of the ordinary for me. "You know, there's really no need for you to stay so late in the office."

"I had some things to take care of."

My office phone rang, giving me an opportunity to escape the awkward moment.

"Okay then. See you Monday," I said, shooing her away. Still looking confused, she turned back around and walked out, closing the door behind her.

I picked up the receiver. "Mia speaking."

"Hi, Mia."

"Nancy?" I barely recognized the voice; it didn't carry the anger that I had grown accustomed to.

"Yeah."

Why was my sister calling me? My heart pounded. "What's wrong? Is Dad all right?"

"Yea, he's fine. Nothing's wrong."

"Oh." I exhaled, releasing my tense muscles as I leaned back on my chair. "So why are you calling?"

"Damn! I can't call you to say hello?"

"Of course, you can, Nancy. It's just that you've never done it before, so I didn't expect it."

She was silent for some time, which prompted me to say, "Hello?"

She cleared her throat. "I just wanted you to know that Mom did give me a painting, too," she said softly, and my heart dropped.

"She...she did?" I sat bolt upright, pressing the phone to my ear, as if that action alone would tell me more of what I wanted to hear.

"Yea." Nancy practically whispered the word, her tone betraying a sense of shame in having to admit it at all. She was finally opening up.

"Nancy. Remember the note I said that mom tucked away in my painting? I think I called you about it like two weeks ago."

"Yea," Nancy said. "I got the message." I heard a deep exhale and then she said, her voice broken, "I got a note from Mom too."

My heart leaped. "I'm coming over right now."

I quickly hung up the phone, called Cynthia into my office and told her that it was urgent that she get me the company car as soon as possible. In under an hour, I was at my father's house. Nancy invited me into her room, which was not in a state of disarray like it had been the last time I saw it. This time, it appeared as though she had quickly rearranged her mess—putting order to her chaos. Her desk still held books and papers but now they were in a slightly disorganized pile. There was nothing on her floor besides a pair of shoes and a pile of worn clothing in the corner. Her closet door was closed. But none of those things held my interest as much as the large, thin cardboard box that was prominently leaning against the wall. It was the same box I saw when I was sneaking around in her room. The box that I had suspected contained a painting from my mother to Nancy. My suspicion was now confirmed.

Nancy kept her eyes down, avoiding any visual contact with me. It was probably shame or embarrassment, but I couldn't tell. I never knew Nancy to be either ashamed about anything or ever embarrassed. So what was it?

"Nancy," I said, carefully allowing my voice to sound as supportive as I could. "Are you all right?"

She nodded.

It had been a long time since I had actually seen my sister as someone who was beautiful. She was always angry and the scowl that seemed to live on her face perhaps had erased any of the beauty one could find there. But now, the scowl had been lost to a child-like expression of pain. And what remained was the face of a woman whose beauty was desperate to make itself known. Surprisingly, she looked more like my mother than she had before. With the natural expression of anger now gone from her face, I saw more clearly than ever the resemblance to my mother's own small eyes and high cheekbones. Nancy finally looked at me.

"It's still in the box." Then, almost hesitantly, she added: "It was always too painful to look at."

The pounding in my chest was slight but still perceptible. I carefully watched my sister as she walked toward the thin, cardboard box. Carefully, she removed the painting and laid it flat on her bed.

There it was. The second painting that my mother had purchased from Tyrese Black, *Solitary Agony*. Being able to see the brushstrokes and the care to detail filled my body with an intense chill that, for some reason, I welcomed. Crouched down in the corner of a room, the distressed woman sat in a position that reflected her pain and torment. The misery she embodied was palpable; it reached out to me. I felt her pain—it was *my* pain. Her hands gripped the sides of her head, her fingers disappearing into her hair. Her face was partially hidden by her arms and her elbows were touching her knees, which disappeared into the shadow of the darkened room.

Nancy touched my shoulder; I turned to look at her and only then did I realize I was crying. My eyes weren't just filled with tears. I was crying full-on, as if the woman in the painting had transferred all of her pain to me. I cried as if the woman *was* me. And I was not the only one so emotionally moved in the quiet room. My sister removed her hand from my shoulder and moved her body closer to mine, embracing me. In my arms, Nancy allowed her pained emotion to escape her mouth as she wept aloud.

• • • •

HAD IT BEEN AN HOUR? Maybe two? I was sitting cross legged at the end of Nancy's bed while she was sitting against her pillows, hugging one knee to her chest as her other leg remained extended by the flattened painting.

"She gave me this painting like the month before she died. June of last year, I think. And when I first saw it, I felt it, Mia. Like the way you were crying when you just saw it was the same way I reacted. But I didn't know what the hell to do with those feelings. I didn't know what to say to Mom about it. I kept it in the box all this time. I never once looked at it again cause..." she paused. "I was so scared." She shook her head, seemingly disappointed in herself.

"Is that why you didn't admit to all of this when I first asked you?"

"Yup," she nodded. "I didn't know how to deal with all this shit, Mia. All my life, I was always so angry and I hated you because Mom cared more about you than she cared about me."

"Wait! " I said. "What? What are you talking about? That's what I thought about you!"

"Come on, Mia. She always talked about how you could do so much with your talent and she encouraged you to go beyond than just writing stories. She believed that you could actually do something great with your life. But me?" She scoffed. "She just let me do whatever I wanted. She didn't guide me in any direction. She never took interest in my future like she did for you."

"Perspective is such a funny thing," I said. Nancy looked up at me.

I shook my head. "I always felt like Mom favored you and that she treated me the way she did because I owed her something or because she was disappointed in me. To me, she wasn't encouraging. In fact, she *discouraged* what I actually wanted to do in my life. And she did it by making my dreams seem so juvenile or silly. But you- I always thought she was so easy on you and I resented you for that."

We stared at each other. We didn't need to exchange words because we both understood that whatever our mother was going through had unfortunately resulted in the different ways in which she chose to rear us. We sat in silence for quite some time, each of us ruminating on the confessions of hidden feelings that had kept us enemies for far too many years. In my heart, I was secretly ecstatic that Nancy and I were finally being civil to one another. We were finally behaving like sisters; I didn't want to ruin that by telling her I had been in her room looking for clues to our mother's wooden box. And I didn't want her to know how very happy I was to be sitting with her, finally confiding in each other. I simply didn't know her well enough anymore to know how she would take it.

Nancy reached toward her bedside table and retrieved a small piece of paper. She unfolded it and said, "This is the note Mom tucked inside my painting. '*Someday, I hope to tell you the whole truth. Maybe you will forgive me for not providing you with the guidance you needed in your life. And if I don't get the chance, I need you to know the truth. Look for it in my small wooden box.*'"

Almost the exact same note.

"Why did she assume that we'd automatically know where this wooden box would be?" I asked incredulously.

Though I meant it to be a rhetorical question, Nancy responded anyway. "I have no clue."

I looked at her and sighed. "You've had this for a year now, Nancy. So why tell me about this now?"

She sighed, looked up at me quickly and then shifted her eyes back down to the fabric on her bed.

"I heard you and Dad talking the last time you were here."

She had been eavesdropping. I didn't even know she had been home.

"You heard everything Dad said about them trying to get pregnant before she got pregnant with me?"

"Yup."

I sighed. "Well, now neither one of us is in the dark about that," I said.

"Yeah, I guess." She had the look of guilt in her eyes and I suddenly made the connection.

Feelings of nausea suddenly replaced the warm, happy feelings I had started to experience. A sudden panic arose from deep inside me, causing my stomach to churn.

"Wait. If you heard our conversation," I said, slowly, "then you know about what I tried to do in my dorm room."

She was silent for a moment—never once looking at me—before she quietly responded, "Yea."

I came to a harrowing realization. I stood up and turned my back to her, wrapping my arms around my stomach as if that was where my shame lived. My breath became shallow; I couldn't control it. Taking in a deep breath was such an unbelievable challenge. *She knows. She knows!* The secret I had kept hidden for so many years between me and my dad had at long last been revealed without my knowledge of it. Through her eavesdropping, Nancy had inadvertently learned that I had once tried to kill myself. *She knows my secret. She knows my secret. What must she think of me?* I felt like a loser. I felt vulnerable, as if Nancy now had access to a side of me that I had carefully kept buried in secrecy and shame. The tightness in my chest, the sweat that I felt all over my body, the continuance of my shallow breathing were all a result of my disgrace, my embarrassment, the disgust I didn't know I had for the darkest moment in my life.

"I'm sorry you went through that," she said softly. I closed my eyes and quietly sighed in relief, my back still turned toward her. Her words of commiseration were unexpected but also surprisingly reassuring. Slowly, I found the ability to take the deep breath that I needed to help calm me down.

I waited until my breath became regular. I turned to face her, my arms still wrapped around my stomach. "Thank you, Nancy." I had nothing else to say.

"You're welcome," she gently murmured. "The psychology classes at QCC are helping me to understand the psychological effects we both suffered because of the way Mom treated us."

"Wow," I said, feeling a growing pride in my heart for a sister I no longer knew. "That's- that's great."

She forced a smile and said, "I think I finally know what I want to do with my life. Thanks to Mom," she chuckled. "I want to become a child psychologist to help kids with traumatic childhoods. And it's helping me so much to deal with my own issues."

"That's amazing," I said, as I sat back down on the bed. "I'm so proud of you."

An awkward smile of what could have been pride came across her face. "Thanks," she said.

If that was finally our reconciliation, I was happy to accept it as such. I wanted to be trapped in this moment of mutual connection forever, finally feeling the sisterly bond I long thought was dead. Maybe Nancy was being nice to me only because she knew about the unfortunate incident in my dorm room. I didn't know what to think of it. We were actually finally talking. It felt at once strange and gratifying. For the first time in years, I actually felt something special with my sister. It brought me back to the days before she entered high school. The days when she'd take notes on what happened in other households and compared them with our home experiences. The days when we'd stroll around the neighborhood, lacking anything better to do, talking about the books we'd read. Nancy's interest always centered on the flawed characters in those stories and how she would have helped them if she were their friend.

The rift that separated us so many years ago was perhaps finally beginning to close and I liked to think it was because of Nancy's initial phone call to me earlier that evening. She actually cared enough about me to call and she cared enough about our mother to try to understand the woman who raised us amidst her own trauma and pain. Nancy had a compassionate side after all, with an unspoken love for her mother and her sister, a love that showed through her actions much too rarely. Thinking of Nancy as someone who could be caring and unselfish was foreign to me, but I welcomed it.

Yet, there had to be a time in her young life when she was always caring and selfless. For some reason, her coldness seemed to quickly define her. There wasn't even a smooth transition from her original mild-mannered nature to what I currently knew her as. In fact, the first time I had confronted Nancy about her growing hostility was the day I felt completely defeated by her. She was a freshman in high school, and I was a junior. I had asked her why she was starting to behave so badly and hanging out with the types of people she had once ignored. Her response had been so cold, so angry, and so full of a pain that I didn't yet understand. She told me that if Mom and Dad were going to treat her like she wasn't important, then she was going to act like it too.

I had tried a few times to reach out to Nancy, but admittedly, those times were not enough. I never quite understood the depth of her resentment. She had acted as if it were all somehow my fault and, as a result, I avoided speaking to her altogether.

I had long ago mourned the breakdown of my relationship with my sister, almost believing that we would never be able to rectify things between us. A part of me had already accepted the fact that we were no longer friends. Incredibly, I never even considered making amends with her. I simply accepted the person she had become. But sitting in her room with her helped me to think differently about that.

"Well," I said, slowly gathering my things. "It's getting late and I am emotionally drained. But we need to find this wooden box Mom left for us. Do you think it might be in Dad's room?"

"Trust me," Nancy said, "I already looked through that room more times than I could count. It ain't in there."

"Then it must be somewhere in Mom's office."

"Looked there too. But I guess I could look again."

"You don't think Dad found it and did something with it, do you?"

"Well, up until a couple weeks ago, there was a whole lot of shit he was keeping from us."

"Oh, but no," I said, recalling my last conversation with my father just before I left him that night. "When I asked him about it, he was willing to help me look for it. So he can't be keeping it a secret."

I was at a loss and I could see that Nancy sensed that from me because she added: "I'll keep looking—the basement, the attic, any extra cupboards or closets I missed."

"You shouldn't do this on your own," I offered. "She wanted both of us to find it. We should do this together."

Nancy shrugged. "Okay. In the meantime, I guess I'll have my own one-on-one with Dad and see what else I can find out. Maybe he'll look for the box too."

I stared at the painting on the bed and found myself unable to speak, unable to even move.

"I was thinking of hanging it here above my bed," Nancy said, pointing to the wall. "Is yours already hung up?"

"Yes," I answered. "I hung it up a couple of weeks ago. That's when I found the note."

Nancy nodded, tears forming in her eyes. "Maybe I could stop by and see it one day?" Her voice broke as she spoke.

"I can't think of anything I'd like more," I said.

She released a sigh of relief. We walked out of her room and downstairs toward the front door.

"Thank you for coming," Nancy said softly as she held the door open for me.

"Always," I smiled back. I stepped out of the large, dark house, called for a cab and waited in the cool night, feeling completely and utterly exhausted.

Chapter 27

Friday Night, August 16, 2002

Later that evening, I stepped into my apartment and found Derek sitting on my couch. We hadn't seen or spoken to each other since Patrick Jerome's book release party. It was amazing how time could heal so many wounds.

His tie was loosened around his neck, and his Oxford shirt had been pulled from inside his pants. His jacket was neatly placed on the armrest. He looked relaxed. There was something sexy about finding him in my apartment waiting for me despite the fact that he knew I would not approve. I welcomed his presence, not realizing how much I had missed him.

He had been following the news program when I walked in and so turned the TV off with the remote. His eyes were fiercely focused on me as I spoke not a word, placing my bag and jacket by his feet. He leaned back, his eyes playfully challenging me to come toward him. I deliberately positioned myself between his legs, kneeling directly in front of him. I removed his loosened tie and set it by his jacket.

"What's gotten into you?" he asked, his voice seductive.

I wanted to tell him. Rather, I wanted to talk about the breakthrough I had with my sister, but I didn't want to discuss it with him. It was suddenly clear to me that I wanted to share the confusion I felt, the relief I experienced, and the hope I had that I would find my mother's wooden box and finally learn what she could not tell me when she was alive. Yes, that was my current wish, my current need. However, the person I craved to share all of that with was Tyrese. And the guilt that resided in my stomach because of that fact forced me to accept Derek for the evening—for what he came to my apartment to do. I pushed my need aside to tend to the man I no longer wished to be with but, for some uncertain reason, could not let go of.

Needing to break away from the routine that had become our sex life together, I proceeded to unbutton his shirt and helped him out of it. I massaged his chest and his stomach, sensually feeling my way around his body, something I hadn't done in months. But for some reason, he could not break out of the routine we had grown so accustomed to. He picked me up and carried me to my bedroom where he politely undressed me before making love to me. There was passion there; I could feel by his rhythm that he had missed me and wanted to be with me. I wanted him as well but found myself becoming annoyed with his pattern. Even the way his strong left hand cupped my right breast as he rocked me didn't ignite the excitement and passion it had so many times before. The biting kisses on my neck that used to drive me wild now felt like a dog's unwanted slobbery tongue on my skin. In an attempt to try something new, I climbed on top of him, but he quickly pushed me back onto the bed, and we assumed the missionary position. Giving up, I went with it. I closed my eyes and thought of Tyrese. Tyrese's naked body was intertwined with mine. It was Tyrese's hand that fondled my breasts, Tyrese's mouth that bit my nipples, and Tyrese himself that I welcomed inside of me. Though I should have been ashamed of inviting someone else into the bedroom that night, I wasn't, because as a result of my wandering thoughts, I ended up enjoying Derek so much more than I ever had, even more than when we'd first met. And then we arrived together in a place where it no longer mattered how we got there, just that we were there together. He squeezed my body in his arms as he silently took in the pleasure of the moment. Feeling the pressure of his arms around my body, I exclaimed my praises to God, and then secretly to Tyrese. And we simply lay there, Derek on top of me, breathing heavily with his forehead leaning against the place where my neck met my shoulder.

We stayed in each other's arms, catching our breath for minutes. Silence thickened the air. I thought about Tyrese and about how much I wanted to be with him then. The shame I hadn't felt before slowly crept inside me, finding a place in my stomach where guilt had once resided. Yes, it was wrong of me to think of him during such an intimate moment with Derek. Although I felt deep within my heart that I still loved Derek, something inside me knew for certain that my many reasons for staying with him were starting to become weak. Yes, my heart knew that Tyrese and I were right for each other, but my mind couldn't allow myself to get mixed up in emotions that could potentially shatter my heart. Logic told me that it was fear that prevented me from truly accepting my connection to Tyrese, but still, I fought it. I'd kept my distance with Derek in order to counter any possibilities of heartbreak because I always knew he would be true. Now I was facing those same possibilities head-on by allowing Tyrese into my thoughts at the most inappropriate time. By doing so, I felt like I reached a point where the possibility of heartbreak was surely inevitable.

"How's the Tyrese Black article coming along?" Derek unexpectedly asked me as he rolled over onto his back.

His voice drifted, and I could sense a little sadness in it. He was keeping something from me; I had a feeling he suspected something was going on between me and Tyrese. Perhaps he sensed my wandering thoughts during our moment of intimacy. Why else would he mention the man he supposedly hated minutes after we had sex? I probably gave myself away; Derek was not a stupid man.

"Is everything all right, Derek?"

"Yeah. Everything's cool."

He squeezed me tightly in his arms. Suddenly everything that I had been going through with the magazine, my mom and my father and sister were no longer the main focus on my mind. I didn't care about anything else when I was with Derek. I only thought about being with Tyrese.

Chapter 28.

Saturday Morning, August 17, 2002

"Do you think we're soul mates? Like we were meant to be together forever?" Derek asked during breakfast the next morning. I fixed us a quick meal of scrambled eggs, with cheese thrown in for flavor and toast with whipped butter.

"I've known you long enough to know that you don't believe in that stuff," I said as I placed a glass of orange juice by his plate.

"Well, I'm trying to figure out why you don't want to marry me. Maybe you simply feel that you haven't met your soul mate yet."

I was not in the mood to discuss our relationship.

"Stop trying to analyze everything, Derek." I tried to keep the tone light.

"Well, you haven't disagreed with me."

The resulting outburst to his line of conversation surprised me: "Why?!" I said, slamming my hand down on the table. "Why must you always do this? You're deliberately picking a fight with me!"

"I'm not," he said, calmly. "I'm just trying to understand my possible future here."

"I don't want to listen to this." I massaged my now stinging hand as I looked down on my plate.

"You think I'm blind, Mia? You think I haven't noticed the change in your attitude the past few weeks? It started when you met Tyrese Black. All of a sudden, I see you less and less, and when I *do* see you, you always want to have sex. Your attitude is starting to change for the better, which is great. But we've been together for five years, Mia, and I have to work hard to do something as simple as put a smile on your face. This guy Tyrese does it with the snap of a finger. And what the hell was going on last night? You came home and fucked me in some kind of trance. Did you think I wouldn't notice? What were you thinking of, Mia? Were you thinking of *him* while we were making love? Am I supposed to sit back and think there's nothing wrong with that?"

"Think what you will, Derek. He's only a friend. Believe me."

"But am I right? Hasn't your attitude changed because of him?"

"If it has, I haven't noticed it."

"All lies," he said. "I won't be made a fool of."

"No one is making a fool of you, Derek."

"You just did by staring me in the face and telling me that!"

"Oh my God!" I exclaimed. "What the hell, Derek?"

"You slept with him, didn't you?"

"Well, since we're asking questions about the guy, why don't you tell me why you lied to me about knowing him?"

"The man acts like he knows everything and everything he says is a philosophy that the world needs to adopt in order to live fulfilling lives. He's a conman—a modern day swindler, and I knew the second you mentioned him that he'd gotten to you. And, yeah, I was thinking selfishly when I lied, I admit that. I wanted to know what you would say about him without the knowledge that I knew him."

"I don't buy that story."

"Hate to disappoint you, but it's the only story I got. What's your story? You slept with him yet?"

"I love you, Derek," I said, sidestepping the question. "That will never change."

"Well, then, maybe it should."

"Why are you always so dramatic?"

"Because I happen to care about this relationship."

"You care about our relationship?" I scoffed. "What about you and Glory?"

"What *about* me and Glory?"

"I've seen the way the two of you flirt. And you have lunches together without even including me or so much as telling me."

The shock in his eyes and clenched jaw revealed not only that I was correct but that he was prepared to defend himself against any types of accusation.

"Your boy-toy Tyrese Black told you that?" The expression on his face dissolved into one of disgust.

"Tyrese?" I said confused. "What does Tyrese have to do with this?"

The guilt on his face was apparent. "Okay," he said. "I've had lunch with her, yes. But it was always with her authors."

"Why didn't you just say that from the beginning?"

"I can't deal with your jealousy. I can't, Mia. You got a problem with Glory? You go and talk to her. She's *your* best friend."

"Jealousy?" Again, I was confused. "Since when have you known *me* to be jealous?"

He said nothing. He crossed his arms and looked the other way as an angry child who couldn't find the words to voice his frustrations would.

I sighed. "What are we doing, Derek?" I asked. "All we do is argue now. And it's clear that we don't trust each other. I don't even recognize us anymore."

"It's the people we love the most that end up breaking our hearts," he said softly, his eyes focused on the kitchen floor.

"What are you saying, Derek?" I said, placing myself in his line of vision so that his focus would be on me.

He looked into my eyes. "Nothing," he said. And then, to my surprise, he wrapped his arms around me and held me, kissing my forehead once. "Mia. Don't leave me. I don't know what I'd do if I lost you."

Those last words ended our discussion. I closed my eyes and inhaled as I took in his scent, recognizing the fragrance of his fading Armani cologne. Once again, I found myself unable to extricate myself from the grasp he had on me. The physical grasp was one from which I was able to easily remove myself; it was that unspoken hold that proved difficult to loosen.

Part 4

Secrets Uncovered

Chapter 29

Tuesday Evening, August 20, 2002

"Thank you for meeting with me like this, Tyrese. My message was vague, so I appreciate you coming at such short notice."

His hair was loose, hanging over his shoulders; he looked unbelievably beautiful on the one night I decided to end my relationship with him. Most of the people in the office had already gone home. My mind quickly raced with thoughts of one last fling with him.

"Not a problem," he said, placing his hands in his pockets. He didn't smile. He probably knew that what I had to tell him was not good.

I remained seated behind my desk in a feeble attempt to shield myself from the inevitability of experiencing any emotional distress.

"Do you mind sitting down?" I said motioning to the chair directly in front of my desk. My hands were shaking, as was my voice. In retrospect it seemed silly of me to think that it would be simple to break the news to him. I foolishly didn't expect that my feelings for him would get in the way. But they did. My palms were clammy, and I had to inhale a few times to calm the pace of my heart. I felt tears trying to push through, but I held them back. I wouldn't cry. Despite the gnawing feeling that my actions were probably wrong, I decided to go through with my plans.

Tyrese deliberately did not sit in the chair I motioned to. He took a seat, instead, by the corner of my office on the couch and slouched as he placed his right calf over his left knee.

"What's going on, Mia?" he asked.

I leaned back in my chair, taking both sides of my cardigan and wrapped them across my chest.

"Um," I started, clearing my throat. "You don't know how you have affected my life in such a short time. Meeting you when I did was probably the best thing that has ever happened to me." I stopped. Feeling the need to control the tremble in my voice, I inhaled deep within my diaphragm and then closed my eyes. My exhale was slow and measured. I continued. "But as much as I appreciate your friendship, Tyrese, I think it would be best if we, um, if we stopped seeing each other and contacting each other altogether."

"Why?" he said quickly, firmly.

I avoided his eyes. "Tyrese, I cheated on Derek with you on a physical and emotional level. I want things to work with Derek, and I can't have that if the guy I cheated with continues a friendship with me. It can't work." My voice continued to tremble, and I knew he heard it.

He put his right foot down and leaned forward with his elbows resting on his knees. "You yourself said that you and Derek wouldn't last because you two don't talk the way we do. Obviously, that's very important to you."

I reached for the bottle of water on my desk and in doing so, I knocked the *Fresh Voices* mug that contained all of my pens and pencils all over the desk. I immediately stood up, aware of the violent beating of my heart.

"I've made my decision, and you'll just have to respect that, alright?" I desperately worked to get all of the pencils and pens back into the mug.

"And what if I don't?"

I stopped what I was doing and stared at him in silence. My mind became preoccupied with the sudden sensation of heat that seemed to engulf my body. I didn't know how to feel about his boldness. And I certainly did not expect to feel as lost and confused as I did.

"I can tell that you're upset," he said, getting up and walking closer toward me. "What happened, Mia? Did he give you some type of ultimatum?" The concern in his eyes was more than I could bear.

I looked away. "I made this decision on my own, Tyrese. Please understand that I have to do this. We can't go on the way we had."

His face hardened. "I should have known that you'd drop me sooner or later," he said. "That's your thing, isn't it?"

"What's my thing?" I asked, the quiver in my voice an obvious indication of how upset I really was.

"You're at your happiest when you're miserable. That's why once you get close to someone, it scares you and so you back off."

"Tyrese, please don't do this. I already have a boyfriend." I took off my cardigan.

"Then why did you take the time to get to know me?" He leaned on my desk.

I wanted so desperately for the tears to fall, to stop pretending that what I was doing was not actually hurting me by breaking my relationship with the one person I actually wanted to be with. But I reasoned that a broken heart now was better than a broken heart down the line, which would, no doubt, be an even more painful ordeal. So, I swallowed the lump in my throat and spoke slowly to hide the tremor in my voice.

"You were a distraction," I whispered, as I sat back down. Again, my eyes avoided his, seemingly of their own accord.

He nodded his head and exhaled. "Of course I was. Why did I think differently?" He turned around and walked to the door. "The three of you are close, aren't you?"

I looked up at him. "The three of us, who?" Why didn't he just leave so that I could have the freedom to cry in peace?

"Your man, your girl and you. Or is it just Derek and Glory who are close. They leave you outside of their closed circle."

What was he talking about? "If you have something to say, Tyrese, just say it."

"Long before I met you, Mia, I always thought that Derek and Glory were an item. It's just something to think about."

My heart pounded against the inside wall of my chest. The heat I now felt was concentrated in my temples. He only said that to hurt me; that was simply his technique. I couldn't take what he said seriously. Derek was one of the good guys; he would never cheat on me. Tyrese was only trying to hurt me because I was hurting him.

"You know, Mia," Tyrese said, "All I asked of you was friendship. And I know I mentioned once that I wanted more. But fuck that. I consider you my friend, and I thought you considered me one too. Friends just don't go around throwing each other away like this. I think you know how sincere I was when I told you that I would be happy just being your friend. But I'll respect your wishes because that's what friends do. *That's* being sincere."

With that, he left my office and my life. I was unsure about the decision at first. My mind raced with the reality of what I had just done. I stood up and stepped in front of my desk, contemplating the details of what had just transpired. I wrapped my arms around my stomach because that was where I felt the sting. A mixture of nausea and butterflies came together to create the strange feeling that brought about the uncontrollable sobbing. I placed my hand on my mouth in an effort to silence the painful sounds coming from it. I didn't even try to suppress my tears because telling Tyrese I could no longer see him was like a malicious blow to the gut. The tears felt necessary to help me wrap my head around the whole situation.

I tried convincing myself that it was the right thing to do. I was trying to prepare myself for a life with Derek, so that I would one day soon be ready to commit myself to him in the sacrament of marriage. Derek had remained by my side for five years. He deserved a commitment from me. Once I made it, I'd feel better. I'd stop thinking so much; I'd be able to move forward. Right? I felt so lost, like that was the worst mistake I could have ever made.

Although I truly did value my friendship with Tyrese, the fact that I had actually slept with him would not allow me to continue the relationship while thinking about a possible marriage with Derek. That much I knew was wrong. The guilt I had previously denied feeling came crashing down on me with a vengeance. I could only have Tyrese if I gave up Derek, and I wasn't going to do that. I tried doing that before, and I went right back to him. I needed Derek. I owed it to him to stay, I owed it to myself. But above all else, I did love him, and he loved me. No matter how much I felt for Tyrese, the proof was always there. So, my decision was final. Sometimes important sacrifices must be made in life. It was just unfortunate that Tyrese had to be mine.

Chapter 30

Tuesday Night, August 20, 2002

As I approached the door to my apartment, I heard soft romantic music coming from inside. My heart pounded; my mouth was dry. Derek was waiting for me. Thoughts of our last impassioned interaction raced through my mind. I didn't know if I was going to confront the Derek who was still angry with me or the Derek who insisted we still belonged together. The music suggested it could be the latter. He was probably inside preparing to surprise me with an intimate dinner. Although my heart raced with gratitude, it was also full of dread.

I didn't want him anymore. There it was, the truth. Hearing the music inside made me realize that I didn't want *us* anymore. Maybe it was because I managed to do something as hard as letting Tyrese go that I gained the courage to finally break free from Derek. I didn't need him and everything inside of me told me that I never did. It was suddenly so very clear to me what I had to do. I wanted so much to tell him that I had finally chosen to marry him, but it was too late. Our relationship had to end. No matter what he would try to say or do, the truth was that we were simply incompatible. I finally admitted the truth to myself. I had been holding onto a fantasy, a fictional belief that I would somehow never get hurt if I always had him by my side. How could I have believed this monumental lie based on one failed relationship in college? I took in a deep breath and exhaled. No matter what romantic evening he had planned, I promised myself that I would be strong and not put it off any longer. I was finally going to give Derek valid reasons why I could not stay with him.

I opened the door. No, my eyes did not deceive me. But my mind did select the memories it would have me retain. I could now only remember what I witnessed at that moment through a series of quick flashes: Derek and Glory, his mouth on her neck, her shirt on the floor, his hand on her thigh, a bra strap down her shoulder, his other hand on the sofa's armrest, her eyes closed, her mouth open, her hands clawing his back. My heart sank so low that for about a half a minute, I literally could not breathe. Those were the longest thirty seconds of my life. I stared at them, frozen in utter shock, literally unable to speak. I found myself starting to take deep breaths to regulate my breathing pattern. There was no doubt in my mind that if I had not walked in when I did, my best friend and my boyfriend would start screwing on my living room sofa! And to make it worse, they were both uninvited guests in my apartment!

"Damn it!" Derek whispered aloud as he saw me. He quickly jumped off of Glory and ran to the stereo to turn the music off.

Glory sprang from the sofa and immediately put on her shirt. Both Glory and Derek remained silent. Nothing they could say or do would ever erase what I saw happening between them.

My heart pounded furiously, and I felt my fingernails digging deep into my palms before I realized I was actually making fists. I felt my temperature rise and my eyes burned, a precursor for the tears that wanted to flood through my tear ducts. My heart was crushed. I was desperately dejected, but I knew that my dejection had lost to the power of my anger when I became aware of how badly I bruised the palms of my hands.

"Should I leave you two alone and come back in the morning?" I said. It was only my sarcasm that kept me from crying.

Glory nervously began to collect her things. "I was just leaving."

"No, you weren't," I said quickly.

She looked at me, shocked at first, but then an expression that told me that she was impressed with the way I handled her replaced that shock. She didn't even apologize for what had just happened. She simply crossed her arms and looked at me as though she was ready for a challenge.

"Mia," Derek said, panicking. "I can explain!"

I didn't even look at him. Glory seemed to want a challenge, so I wanted to do just that. "Derek, can you leave us alone for a minute?"

"Mia, just listen to me—"

"God, Derek!" I snapped. "Please, can I talk to Glory for two minutes alone?"

He sighed, looked nervously at Glory, and then reluctantly walked into my bedroom and shut the door.

I turned to Glory and confessed, "You don't know how hurt and betrayed I feel right now."

"Well, I'm sorry you had to see that." She said it so coldly, as if she didn't even care about our friendship.

"Are you moving in on my man?"

"I don't think you appreciate how great Derek actually is." She answered me with such a fierce attitude, as if she was the only one in the room who had the right to be angry.

"So, you fucking him is supposed to make me realize how great my man really is?"

"I never fucked him, Mia."

"And why am I supposed to believe that? That's all you ever do with men!"

"You're my best friend, dammit."

"I walked in on you and Derek on my couch!" I shouted. "Is that what best friends do?"

"Well, if you fucking gave him what he *needed*, he wouldn't need to come to me to get the attention that I give him."

I slapped her face so hard that my hand instantly felt inflamed. Specks of blood from my bruised palm smeared onto her cheek. I felt tears in my eyes and as angry as I was, I did not want to get emotional. But sometimes one's feelings fail to cooperate.

"*That* was what he needed?" I said, my voice shaking. "I can't believe you would do this to me!"

"The man needs you, Mia!" she screamed. "But you're never there for him. Physically or emotionally. He loves you so much that it fucking pains even *me* to see him like this. I may not know much about being with a man in a fucking relationship, but I know that if I had somebody like Derek in my life, I'd do everything in my goddamn power to keep him. Your problem is you don't know what the fuck you got. Yeah, I've come across a lot of men and I fucked a whole lot of fucking losers, but Derek is the only man I've ever met that has some fucking dignity and class, and on top of that, he's a decent human being. I see the way he loves you, but you can't see it for yourself. And you're trying to throw it all away because you don't know what the fuck you want!"

"Do not even talk to me about knowing what I want. Look at you. You're twenty-eight years old and you don't even know what kind of man *you* want in your life, so you take a sample from every single man you meet. You can have any man you want, and you usually do. So why would you move in on Derek, who's not even your type?"

"After all these years, you still don't fucking get it. We're not that different, the two of us. We both try to find comfort in men for the love we wished we had at home as children. But the only difference is, you found yourself a good man and you can't even appreciate that because you're always fucking it up with him."

She was attacking me, but she couldn't appreciate the fact that it was my depression that made me behave the way I did. Why couldn't she understand that I had an illness that affected the way I handled my relationships? She had always been so dismissive of anything I ever told her about my depression.

"You don't understand what I've been through," I said, weakly pleading my case.

"Oh please! You can save the 'poor me' shit for your fucking shrink. I've got three words for you, Mia. Get over it! So, your mother treated you badly and you never felt loved. Get over it! I had an entire family who didn't care that I existed. Open your fucking eyes and finally recognize what you have in your life and what you have in a man like Derek! You've got the perfect job, a family that could be the perfect family if you gave them half a chance, and a great guy who actually loves you. What I wouldn't give to have all of that. You take it all for granted and act like it's not enough."

I stared at her in shock. She was so angry with me, and she sounded almost envious, taking all of my issues personally. For the first time, I figured out Glory's reasons for befriending me when we were in college.

"You're jealous, aren't you?" I said. I was now no longer crying. "You wish you had what I have and so tried to steal it away from me. That's why you were pushing me to let Derek go and be with Tyrese: because you wanted Derek for yourself. That's it, isn't it? After you got my boyfriend, what were you going to steal next? My job? My apartment? My fucking family?!"

"Now you're taking all of this shit out of proportion and dramatizing it the way you dramatize everything. All I did was flirt with your man. I never fucked him."

"You were on my couch messing around with him!" I screamed.

"You over there fucking Tyrese and you mad at *me* because I kissed your man?"

I quickly looked in the direction of my bedroom door. I could imagine Derek listening to the whole conversation with his ear pressed against it. I was suddenly terrified that he should find out about Tyrese. "You keep your voice down about that!"

"He's not stupid, Mia. You don't think he figured it out already?"

Anger boiled my blood. I continued in a loud whisper, still conscious of Derek's presence in the next room. "You *wanted* me to meet Tyrese. You used me as bait to reel him into your twisted little plan!"

"Get over yourself, Mia."

"You were probably trying to scheme something up ever since we both met Derek at that conference five years ago."

"How pathetic do you really think I am?"

"It all makes so much sense! It's killing you inside, isn't it? You couldn't believe that he chose me over you and so you started to think of a plan to get him all to yourself. What makes all this so sad is that it took you five years to get this far. Meeting Tyrese must have been a big deal for you. You knew I'd fall for him. Oh my God! Why didn't I see this coming?"

"You miserable, selfish little *bitch*. If you ask me, you wanted your relationship with Derek to end long before Tyrese came into your life. Tyrese was an excellent excuse for you to let things go with Derek, and now you're trying to blame that shit on *me*?"

"Keep your voice down about that!" I whispered aloud, once again looking in the direction of my bedroom. "It happened *once*," I lied.

"Once is enough, Mia. Cheating is fucking cheating, no matter how many times you done it. Do not fuck with me, okay? If you *ever* accuse me of sleeping with your man again, your secret will not only be shared with the one person you claim you love, but I will bring you down so low that your family will never want anything to do with you. You will lose your job and credibility so fast that you will have no *choice* but to finally fucking kill yourself. Now leave me the *fuck* alone and consider this friendship over."

What just happened?! She turned and walked out the door, leaving me confused as all hell. I had suspected Glory the previous weeks and was *completely* stunned to find her with Derek, but *none* of that prepared me for that confrontation. I was hurt that things turned out the way they did, but my anger superseded my hurt. I was not only angry with myself for not seeing what was happening between the two of them, but I was furious with her for pretending to be my friend since college. I was sure I was right about that: everything fit.

The Saturday afternoon when we were all online and she sent me a message asking what I was doing that night must have been meant for Derek, which is why she never responded but instead abruptly signed off. And when I had asked her about it—it didn't occur to me at the time—she had grown defensive so quickly about my line of simple questioning. I had wondered why she kept pushing for me to break things off with Derek and it suddenly made sense why. All their secret lunches together supposedly with clients now made sense to me. *Everything fit.*

I had to be careful. She was now an enemy who had a secret about me to hang over my head. Glory never made empty threats. I believed her promise of shame and humiliating exposure that would kill my career; *that* was not something I wanted to risk. However, she only had that leverage as long as I kept what happened between me and Tyrese a secret. I had to confront Derek.

The door to my bedroom opened and Derek slowly and cautiously walked out and entered the living room. He stood there looking at me, resembling a sorrowful child who knew he had done something wrong. I didn't even want to look at him.

Placing my arms across my chest, I spoke softly and calmly, keeping my eyes to the floor ahead of me. "You wanted to make me believe that I was going out of my mind when I questioned you about you and Glory."

"Mia," he pleaded. "Let me just tell you what happened here tonight."

"I saw what happened, Derek."

"I came here to see you because I wanted to surprise you with dinner."

"I don't see any dinner."

"I know. I got distracted. Glory came by looking for you. We got to talking, and like nothing out of the ordinary, she flirted innocently with me. It was innocent, Mia." He paused. "But I reciprocated. I swear nothing more would have happened; nothing more *has* ever happened. We never slept together. I wouldn't lie to you about that."

I sighed. I wanted to believe him, and I didn't want to be angry with him, but I couldn't help feeling betrayed not only by my boyfriend but by my best friend. Memories of Glory telling me how fine Derek was, of her flirting with Derek at the book party, of what Tyrese said about them seeming like a couple all came rushing back to me in a new light. It had been so obvious.

"The way you two flirted," I began, "always seemed a bit inappropriate to me, but what do I know? And the fact that my best friend and my boyfriend find each other remotely attractive and have the potential and opportunity to act on it is a clear indication that something is very wrong between us. There's always been something wrong, Derek. You were just too blind to see it, and I chose to ignore that."

"Mia, just listen to me."

"Do you know what I did for you earlier today? I told Tyrese that I didn't want to continue my friendship with him because I wanted to be with you."

"You didn't do that for me," he said softly but with a curtness in his voice. "You did that for yourself."

"Do you know what he said to me?"

"I don't really care what he said."

"He said that long before he met me, he thought you and Glory were a couple. Why would he think that, Derek?"

"Simple. The man is trying to mess with you. Didn't I tell you about what he does to manipulate people?"

"It's curious how he seems to have known you a lot longer than you say you knew him. Now I get it. Now I see why you distrust the man so much. He's a threat to you. I know why you got so angry when I mentioned him on Saturday. You were afraid that if I befriended this guy, he would eventually tell me your secret about this thing with you and Glory."

"What the hell are you talking about, Mia? There's never been a *thing*."

"It all makes perfect sense now. And Glory played you, too. She introduced me to Tyrese so that I could sleep with him and so Tyrese could tell me about you and Glory. Oh! It was foolproof! And then, being so upset that Tyrese told me, Glory expected me to go ahead and break up with you for the final time, leaving you available for her. Naturally you'd turn to her for comfort because she planned it that way. She's made sure to know everything about our relationship by befriending me for so many years. And what do girls talk about with their best friends? Their relationships." I sat down on the couch, placing my head in my hands as I leaned forward. "I can't believe I didn't see this happening."

"Mia! Do you have any idea how crazy all of that sounds? It's too good a plan for Glory to have come up with."

I looked up at him. "You obviously underestimate the power of an envious woman."

"This is just too much for me to take," he said, rubbing his hands over his hair.

"If you don't mind, Derek, I'd really like to be alone."

"Mia, please believe me when I say that I wouldn't want to do anything to jeopardize our relationship."

"And yet, you did." I stared at him with an anger that I hoped would make him feel guilty.

"Don't do that, Mia," he said, his expression filled with disgust. "I know about you and Tyrese Black."

"What?" I quickly said, standing up. My heart leaped. "Are you talking about what Glory was saying before?" I was thinking about fabricating a story to keep him from finding out the truth.

"Your walls are thin, Mia. Yes, I heard everything. But that was only confirmation for what I already figured out for myself. It was so damn obvious."

My eyes were now glued to his. A shame I had never known suddenly washed over me. I was uncertain how to escape the predicament in which I found myself. "How long have you known?" I said, looking away.

"I knew it the moment you fucked me as if I was someone else."

A wave of intense heat flooded my body. My eyes refused to meet his for fear that he would see the shame I harbored in them.

He continued. "I know we haven't been right for a long time, and things like this are bound to happen when relationships go wrong. But I swear to you: my feelings for you never went away. What you need to do, Mia, is think about who you're really angry with. Don't blame me for what you saw here tonight until you accept some of that blame."

I stared at him, enraged. I knew he was right, but the fact that he said those words to me with such power rendered me incapable of a response, so I simply said: "Get out of my apartment."

He sighed. "Mia, I think—"

"Just go," I snapped. "Please just leave me alone."

He stood there looking at me with pain in his eyes. He did not budge. I knew that he was hurting. A part of me felt that he deserved to suffer more. But the other part of me, the one that loved him deeply, wanted to embrace him and tell him that it would be all right and that I forgave him. However, the image of him and Glory together was still too raw. I felt like it was seared on my eyeballs. He inched toward me, and I backed away.

Sighing, Derek grabbed his jacket from the sofa and headed toward the front door. He paused as he opened the door and turned to look at me. I stared right back at him, waiting for him to leave. He turned back around and reluctantly left, softly closing the door behind him. I looked around the room as I hugged myself, images of what had transpired only moments before surging through my mind. Allowing a sigh to escape my mouth, I slowly sat on the couch. Almost involuntarily, I jumped up and stared at it. Ugh. It smelled like Glory. No, I had to move away from it. A moment, a flash of the two of them together on my couch, entered my mind. I imagined Derek seeing me entwined with another man—with Tyrese—and I was filled with so much shame.

Derek was right. Who was I to be upset with him? In my moment of anger, I had completely dismissed—until he mentioned it—the fact that I had carried on a relationship with Tyrese Black. The more I thought about it, the more I felt sick in the pit of my stomach. I had condemned Derek for something of which I myself was guilty. What was wrong with me?

Chapter 31

Wednesday Morning, August 21, 2002

I asked Derek to have lunch with me at Alimento. It was clear to the both of us what that meant. I was going to tell him what I felt just before I had opened the door to my apartment to find him with Glory the night before.

Waiting for Derek to arrive, I sat at the table feeling nauseous. The waiter had already filled my water glass three times. My nervous feelings grew much stronger as I saw him walking towards me. He had on a dark blue tailored suit that made him look so handsome. I couldn't believe what I was about to do.

"How you doing, Mia?" he said as he sat down. He looked different. He didn't seem as though he was ready to challenge me with reasons why we were so good together, but rather as if he had resigned himself to an inevitable fate.

"Drained," I answered. "You seem preoccupied, though. Can I ask you the same?" I spoke formally; it was my way of distancing myself from the situation.

He looked at me with cautious eyes and took a sip of his water.

"You invited me here to tell me something, Mia. Well, I have to say that I did a whole lot of thinking after I left your apartment last night. There are a few things I need to tell you myself."

His somber tone, his sexy, serious expression, and the confident look in his eyes piqued my interest.

"Why don't you go first then," I said.

He sighed as he took another sip of his water. "Nothing more ever happened between me and Glory than what you saw last night. Truthfully, I picked up on the signs a long time ago. I knew she was playing games to get me. The night you and I got back together earlier this month, she sent me an instant message on AIM asking me out to dinner."

Just as I had suspected. Glory must have written that message to Derek but accidentally sent the message to me. And when I responded, she probably panicked, sent the message to the correct recipient and signed off after he declined. I knew Glory well; I had just underestimated her all the years we were supposedly friends.

"So, you lied to me about that during our dinner that night," I said.

"I did. I didn't see the point in bringing it up then. I've always known that Glory was trying to win me over. I'm not proud of it, but I think I liked playing her games; they made me remember what it was like to feel wanted. Another thing: Glory and I did have a lot of lunches alone together upon her suggestion; no more lies about that. She'd tell me about her family and how much she was hurting and what they had put her through. She shared a lot with me. The woman was looking for sympathy. I stopped wondering a long time ago why she wanted that sympathy from me and not from you."

"So why didn't you ever stop it?"

"I liked the attention, Mia. Someone actually needed comfort from me again. And I guess, being a guy, I didn't care that it was coming from my girlfriend's best friend." He cleared his throat. "And about Tyrese: I lied about him too."

"So, you *have* known him for a while?"

"Yes. I met him almost two years ago. I was with Glory at the time and he simply assumed we were together. I never corrected him. I don't even know why. Each and every time I ran into the guy after that, I just happened to be with Glory. And when you first mentioned him, *my God*, I thought I was done for. I thought that he'd tell you about my meetings with Glory and then you'd want to leave me. So, I played it off as if I hated him so that you wouldn't believe him if he said anything about Glory and me. But you were so taken with him that I got jealous. I hated him because I think something inside me knew that you two were so compatible. I knew straight up that we were wrong for each other. But matters of the heart are rarely dealt with logic."

He kept quiet and I had absolutely nothing to say about his confession. I appreciated his honesty, but I had to remind myself that this honesty had only shown itself after I caught him with my best friend.

"Mia," he continued, "our problems go much deeper than Glory and Tyrese. I love you more than I think you care. I've loved you for five years despite the fact that I know you can never share your emotional feelings with me. Even after your mother's death, when our relationship got worse, I thought, 'she's just going through a rough time.' But Mia, I have loved you despite the wall you've created to keep me out of your life. All this time that I have loved you, I have, by the same token, been afraid of you."

"Afraid?" I asked. "Why would you be afraid of me?"

"Afraid that one day you'll finally tell me it's over and mean it. Afraid that you'll take advantage of my love for you in a way that's unforgivable. For once, Mia, I'm thinking of myself and my heart. For once, I'm actually willing to take this chance to free myself and not live in more fear of an uncertain future because you keep dancing with our relationship. My logic has finally won over my heart."

My heart pounded, and I had to take a breath before I passed out. I took a gulp of water from the full glass in front of me. He was breaking up with me. The entire time we were together, he never once tried to break up with me.

"What are you saying, Derek?"

"I know I told you that I'd always be by your side. I meant it, Mia. But I'm coming to the realization that you don't want me by your side, much less need me, especially now. I've thought a lot about this and decided to leave this relationship once and for all."

I stared at him for what seemed like hours. Was it really happening? Shock rendered me speechless. I suddenly felt like the unlovable little girl that yearned for her mother's affection. The man I loved was letting me go, and even though it was my intention to break up with him since the night before, I still felt wounded. A part of me wished that I was the one to speak first. My ego and my pride reminded me why I had invited him there. But all I could think about was the one truth that remained.

"I love you, Derek," I said, possibly for the last time.

"And I love you, but it's time I start protecting myself."

I couldn't stand hearing those words with the knowledge that he was leaving me. *I love you.* What did it mean after all? "See, I don't think you really do love me, Derek. You used to say that you'd try anything and would go so far as to spend time in therapy. Yet you never even asked me about what was important to me—my writing. You're a publisher but when I first told you about my writing and awards and all the accolades, do you realize you never once showed any interest in seeing any of that work? You never supported my passion for writing fiction and poetry. In fact, you had the same view my mother had. Having the nerve to be so insensitive as to mention it to Patrick Jerome at the book party." I shook my head in disgust. "And you told me once that you wanted to be that thing that made me happy. But how can you be that thing when you never even knew *how* to make me happy? You don't even know me, Derek, and sometimes I feel as if you don't even care to know me."

He lowered his head.

I continued. "I was a convenient girlfriend to a workaholic who could not or would not find the time in his schedule to get to know me."

He remained silent. The expression on his face was hard to read. He took a sip of his water and kept his eyes on the table. Did he feel guilty? Was I wrong in assuming he didn't care to know me?

He sighed. "You're right. I think I was afraid to find out how to make you happy."

I gave him a questioning look.

"What if I tried to find the thing that could make you happy and I still couldn't do it? What if I failed? What if I read your work and didn't like it? How would you feel about me then? My pride as a man, Mia..." He trailed off. "I don't know, Mia. With you, I always felt like I had to prove myself as a man."

I looked at him possibly for the first time in years at that moment. The man suffered from what I understood as narcissism. It was all about him.

"This relationship has put such a strain on me," he continued, "that Jones Press is actually suffering. I've put off making an important decision about Words-in-Rhythm just in case you would agree to marry me. Do I move out to Chicago or try to make Jones Press work by staying here with you? *My* business, Mia. My dream, my *life*. By no means am I blaming you. I'm blaming myself for letting it get this far."

I had to set him straight. "But see, Derek? Every time you mentioned marriage, it was never because you loved me. You always talked about my resilience and strength and how you want your children—not ours—to have the same traits. It was always about your offspring, never about your love for me. And even after I told you about what happened in my dorm room, you never brought it up again, as if you were afraid to mention it."

He looked at his hands on the table. "You're right. And I'm ashamed of myself for all of that. And truth be told, talk of depression and suicide makes me uncomfortable and I just didn't know how to talk to you about it. That and everything else between us got me thinking: what the hell have we been doing together for so long if we're not going to get married?"

It was torture. "Then just go, Derek. There's nothing more to be said."

"There is, Mia. Just one more thing," he said with concern. He turned his eyes from me to focus on his plate as he spoke. "I've made arrangements to move Jones Press to Chicago. I finally signed the papers. Jones Press will now be an imprint of Words-in-Rhythm, Inc. This is an excellent opportunity for me not only because Jones Press will no longer suffer financially, but also because the books we published together were bestsellers. And you know I've been toying with the possibility of them buying me out. I signed the papers yesterday."

It was a blow to my heart. I didn't know what to say or how to react. I invited him to lunch because I wanted to break up with him. Now that I knew his final decision, I was scared to envision a life without him. My stomach became queasy; I was nauseous. I put the full cup of water to my mouth and swallowed in one gulp. I didn't understand why I was feeling this way if a break-up was what I wanted as well. Maybe it was because the idea of breaking up with me was one thing but to move to another state expressed the finality of it all.

"I'm sorry, Mia. But I have to do what's best for me."

"What finally drove you to make this decision?" I asked softly.

"I came to the decision on Saturday after our argument. In fact, that was why I was at your apartment last night: to let you in on the news." He stopped. His face bore a genuine expression of concern.

"Mia," he whispered.

I looked into his eyes.

"Five long years, Mia, and we are at the same place we were three years ago. I can't live my life like this. As much as I care about you, I have to let us go."

"Well, you've—" I cleared my throat, "you've certainly thought a lot about this." I tried to hide the tremor in my voice. I wanted to cry so desperately, but I reserved my tears for the comfort of my own company.

"It wasn't an easy decision," Derek said. "How can it be when I'm about to lose everything that I based my life on for the past five years?"

"Okay. I get the picture, five years!" I said, raising my voice. A lump materialized in my throat, but I promised myself I would not give him the satisfaction of my tears. Was this foreign feeling a result of lost love? A part of me wanted to follow him to Chicago and another part of me knew that I *only* felt this way because he was the one breaking up with me, nothing more. I knew and understood that this was the best thing for the both of us. So why was I feeling so distraught?

He sat there in silence with a hopeless expression on his face. "I have to go," he finally said. "As soon as I'm settled in Chicago, I'll give you my contact information and I'd like you to call me whenever you need to talk. Anytime. I hope everything turns out all right for you. I do. I wish it didn't have to end this way, but I can't change that now."

"Just go, Derek. Stop stalling with your wonderfully rehearsed speeches." I leaned back in my chair and crossed my arms. I was hurt and being a bitch about it helped me deal with how much I felt like a child.

He sighed, as if he wanted to stay there for a few minutes longer.

"Well, you have to understand that this is hard for me too, Mia."

"Then why don't I make it easier for the both of us?" I stood up, grabbed my purse and sweater, and walked out. I fought back the tears, stifling all of my emotions.

Chapter 32

Wednesday Afternoon, August 21, 2002

The only way I could deal with this breakup was to immerse myself in work. As I walked the few blocks towards my office building, I found myself scowling and cursing at people as they bumped into me on the crowded sidewalks. I kept my head down and walked quickly, my head racing with the words that Derek and I had exchanged. I didn't want to think about what just happened. All I wanted to do was get back to work; that was the only thing that could help me survive the day. I simply wanted to get back to the place where I made an impact, the place where I was valued. It was my only remaining solace.

I stepped out of the elevator on the seventeenth floor and walked through the cubicles towards my office. I noticed something peculiar as I walked. A number of people surrounded Bill Anderson at his small cubicle. It looked as though they were congratulating him. My heart dropped. I moved swiftly through the office floor, past my assistant's desk and into my office, throwing my things onto the couch. I turned on my computer and waited impatiently for it to load up, my heart pounding through my chest.

"Please, please, please," I whispered before silently praying that I did indeed get the position, and that the crowd of people around Bill Anderson was there to console him.

And that's when I saw the email. Upon opening it, I learned that the email was sent to every member of the company, not announcing my well-deserved promotion, but Bill Anderson's.

Please join me in congratulating Bill Anderson in his promotion to Editor in Chief of Fresh Voices. *Bill came to us only two years ago as an Editor and has moved up the ladder and showed us the exemplary work he can do. I'm sure we can all agree that as Editor, Bill has helped turn out a great magazine month after month, putting* Fresh Voices *at the top of the list of the most popular African American magazine in the country. With his insightful articles, his propitious connections, and his knowledge of this competitive industry, Bill has attracted a strong intellectual and artistic readership, sponsorships and promoters...*

I couldn't even finish reading it. Rage. That was what I felt. Red. That was what I saw. Tears slid down my cheeks without permission. My jaw started to hurt before I realized how tightly I was gritting my teeth in seething anger. Morgan decided to go with the candidate that made our magazine seem more inclusive. Bill's resume was not half as impressive as mine yet there it was in black and white. Bill Anderson, a man who was by all accounts my subordinate now held a position higher than my own.

Incensed, I marched into Morgan's office, deliberately intruding on a meeting with one of the editors.

"How dare you!" I screamed, feeling a fire of rage burning within me.

The editor jumped and turned to me in utter astonishment. Morgan calmly lifted himself up from his chair and said, "Francine, please give us a moment."

As Francine rushed out of the office, I repeated myself. "How dare you promote this man who is not *nearly* as qualified for the position, as you know that I am?!"

"Mia," Morgan said, continuing to remain calm, "Think of your own history here, how you moved up so quickly from the position of Editorial Assistant. This company prides itself on giving well-deserved opportunities to people who prove that they are worthy through their efforts and dedication. Why not give Bill the same consideration that you have been given since your first year here?"

"No," I said firmly, "That's not what this is and you know it. It was just too much to ask you to disappoint the white man by giving a black woman the higher title. You disgust me. Look yourself in the mirror, Morgan, and remind yourself that you are a black man running a black company. Diversity is something white companies have to contend with. We need to hire our own people to represent the community we are serving. A wider audience should not be on your priority list. We need to do right by the audience we already have."

He ignored my comment. "Now, Mia, I know you said that if you did not get the position that you would resign. I'd like to tell you that we value your work here very much and we hope you will reconsider. Thank you for closing the door behind you."

The man turned his back to me as he made his way back to his chair. Just like that, I was dismissed. And his dismissal of me made me feel smaller than I had ever felt in my life.

Intentionally leaving his office door open, I exited, instructing Cynthia to get me the company car immediately. I gathered my purse and sweater, leaving the office in a new kind of shame as others stopped what they were doing to watch me leave. The company car was already waiting for me outside and I practically threw myself inside it. Home. No, I didn't want to go home. All that waited for me at home was a lonely space where Derek and Glory were together, the same place where all I could do was think about my break up with Derek and Tyrese and how Morgan snubbed me for a chance to shamelessly showcase how liberal *Fresh Voices* can be.

"Where to, Ms. Hill?" the driver asked me.

Instead of going home, I instructed him to take me to Queens—straight to my father's place. A number of thoughts ran through my head as I sat in the back seat gazing out the window. Bill Anderson. Had I been too confident in thinking that the man was not a threat? Did I somehow let my guard down? How could this have happened on the same day that I broke up with Derek?

I stepped out of the car in front of my father's house, and immediately took notice of how the front lawn had been neatly groomed, trimmed and beautified. There was no more overgrowth and the weeds had been pulled out. What remained was reminiscent of the work that my mother had overseen when she was alive and well. The grass was a bright green and welcomed me down the cleared walkway toward the house. There was still the matter of the broken steps but my father's rotting wooden bench had been completely removed. My hope was that it would be replaced with a new one. What surrounded me was the promise of what the house could look like again.

Memories of the night I first invited Derek to dinner with my parents flooded my mind. My mother had liked him, and I remembered being annoyed with the way she smiled and joked with him. She had never acted that way with me before. That night at the dinner table, I promised myself that I would never allow Derek to come in contact with my parents again. I didn't even know why I had invited him to meet them when I myself never made much effort to be in their presence. In the following months, my mother often asked about him, insisting that he was the best thing that ever happened to me. I remembered hating her for that comment and at the same time feeling relieved that she had accepted him and had given me her blessing. It seemed as though everything I did, and thought were always in conflict with each other. Now, I realized how ironic it was that my mother approved a relationship that, in the end, resembled her relationship with my father. It suddenly dawned on me that could have been one of the reasons why it was so hard for me to let Derek go all of these years.

I used my spare key to get into the house.

"Nancy?" I called out at the base of the staircase. I knew she wasn't home but I decided to call out anyway. After I heard nothing, I felt the urge to go to my father's bedroom in pursuit of the elusive wooden box my mother had mentioned in her note to me. Would my mother have hidden it in there? My father had offered to help me find it himself, which meant if it were indeed in his room, it wasn't there as a result of his actions. Then I remembered that Nancy had said she already searched his room and found nothing. What if she were lying? That was now irrelevant because something inside of me compelled me to head to my mother's office. It took only a few seconds to come up with a plan that included investigating the contents of my father's room if my mother's office proved fruitless once again.

I slowly walked into her office and carefully sat on her chair at her desk. I had never seen anyone but my mother sit on that seat and it almost felt wrong to do so. The burgundy walls surrounded me, making me feel both despondent and protected at the same time. As always, her copy of the *Dictionary of Modern Legal Usage* was on her desk. And then, for the very first time, I noticed a postcard leaning against some of the other books that were stacked on her desk. I picked it up to take a closer look at it. The postcard held the image of a woman dressed in black holding her arms in the air, her face bearing an expression filled with unbearable pain. I recognized that woman and suddenly understood the comfort she felt in her pain. While

I was the woman in *The Box*, and my sister was the woman in *Solitary Agony*, my mother was the woman who found comfort only through her pain. My mother was one of the thousands of women Tyrese Black painted for. Still seated, I leaned forward in the chair, wrapping my arms around my stomach as I rocked back and forth. I felt an incredible sense of support in that very chair and in that very moment. My mind was suddenly clear with an understanding of a pain that I had never been aware of before. It was the kind of pain that existed only to release me from the things I held on to that no longer served me.

"Derek left me, Mom," I whispered. "I know how much you liked him. And now he's gone. Just like you. And everything I've worked so hard for at the office was given to someone who can't even measure up to me." I sat for a very long time, just lost in my thoughts about everything that had transpired in the past few weeks.

Despite the fact that I had already looked through the drawers weeks ago when I was first there to look for my mother's wooden box, I looked through them again. There was some irrational hope that I might find what I was looking for in there this time. No wooden box. Just some notepads, a stapler, a box of staples and some paperclips among other things. I found a couple of flash drives and picked them up to read the labels, on the off chance that one of them might be labeled as *The Wooden Box*. Nope; it was a longshot. I opened the larger door on the right side of the desk to find a few legal books, dictionaries and a catalog to Tyrese's art gallery. I looked though the catalog with a heavy heart, thinking about how I had severed my ties to him. It was a mistake. I knew it was. Considering the potential outcomes of reaching out to him again, I wondered if it could lead to a conversation, forgiveness, and the chance for us to be together. I sighed as I placed the catalog back in the drawer. No wooden box.

Not knowing where else to look, I placed my hands directly underneath the desk and felt my way around. No hidden compartments. I looked around the room and my eyes landed on her bookshelf. Standing up, I slowly walked toward it and looked at all of the books that were neatly stored with the words on their spines facing toward the left. There were novels, personal development books, law books and others—all various sizes and widths.

But there was one that stuck out to me. It was larger than all of the other books on the shelf and did not have any words on the spine. I carefully removed it from the shelf and upon holding it in my hands, I learned that it was not a book at all. It was a wooden box whose spine was meant to look like an actual book. It was a wooden box! *The* wooden box! My heart skipped a beat and a strange warming sensation suddenly overtook my entire body. I looked at the box I held in my hands in a strange spell, unable to move, unable to do anything but stare at it. *Was it really happening?* Did I find the actual thing I had been thinking about since the day I was made aware of its existence? *Finally*! The box was slightly heavy, as if something was inside of it, perhaps a book.

The box opened like the front cover of any book. Inside of it was a journal notebook the size of a novel with pictures of flowers that adorned the entire cover. What made my heart pound was the fact that the flowers were pink petunias and yellow marigolds, the same exact flowers I was inspired to purchase for my mother at the beginning of the month when I went to visit her grave. I didn't quite understand the significance behind why I chose those specific flowers and what it all meant.

I suddenly felt afraid of the information I would find inside of the journal. I didn't know if I had the courage to read its contents- details my mother wanted me to know. The question of how this would alter my perceptions of her, my father, and Nancy gnawed at me. I questioned whether the words within would permanently reshape both my understanding of them, and perhaps more significantly, my own self-perception.

I took the box in my hand and found my way to the couch directly in front of my mother's desk. Carefully taking the journal out of the box, I hesitated to do anything else. Nancy. *Nancy and I should do this together*, I thought.

I took my cellular phone from my purse and turned it on before realizing that I had no other number to call Nancy. I didn't know if she had her own cellular phone, nor did I have a number for her at work. Just to make sure I covered all my bases, I ran throughout the house and checked each room for Nancy. I took the stairs two steps at a time and knocked on Nancy's door.

"Nancy?" I said. Nothing.

I slowly turned the knob and peeked inside. On the wall, just above her bed, hung the painting our mother had given Nancy. It was stunning. I stared at it for a beat before snapping out of my trance. I couldn't turn my eyes away from the portrait, even as I closed the door. Running back downstairs, I entered my mother's office, where her journal waited on the couch for me. I had to do it on my own. I sat down. Holding the book in my hand, I felt the significance of the moment.

After all of this time, I was surprised at how unprepared I felt about the moment for which I had been waiting so many weeks. I slowly opened the journal to a random page. I struggled to read the words; the fading ink and scribbled handwriting made it a challenge. But they were her words. I recognized the handwriting as my mother's. Perhaps I was wrong, but the handwriting suggested that she must have written the words in a state of intense emotion, maybe during a time when she was deeply upset. But I did my best and started to read:

He doesn't know how much it hurts. He doesn't know how painful it is to have borne children for whom I could never show any love.

Yes, this confirmed it. Nancy had been starved for affection just as I had been. It made sense. Even though my mother spoiled my sister, she never showed Nancy the kind of love that I myself craved. She only showered Nancy with privileges that Nancy later took for granted.

I turned to a few pages before that one and read a passage that almost stopped my heart, a confession:

It was cruel, and at the same time, was life's sweet revenge. It was ironic and almost poetic how I spent my college years aborting babies - mere fetuses - that I felt would keep me from the life I thought I was meant to live. And when I fiercely wished and prayed for a child of my own to love and to cherish, it was not given to me. It was only given to me after I had healed from the heart-breaking fact that I could never conceive another child, after I used that painful fact as a sign or a permission to live the life I thought I was meant to live. It was only until I was blessed with exactly what I had once wished for that I knew that the life I was supposed to live was a life as a caring mother, not as a valued partner in a prestigious law firm as I had once thought. Even though I finally learned what my fate was, I could not accept it. For that, I would be punished. My punishment was spending the rest of my life desperately loving a family for whom I was unable to show my love. Instead, I found myself nurturing the cries of the babies that never were and ignoring the cries of the daughters who were meant to be.

Secrets I was afraid to learn mocked me as I repeatedly read the passage. My mind raced with the knowledge that a part of me and Nancy had been aborted long before either of us was conceived. I wondered if my father knew of the abortions my mother had—not just one, but it seemed like several. I had a feeling he didn't. Her past haunted her, prevented her from living a peaceful existence with her family—the family she created perhaps to atone for the babies that never had the chance to taste how sweet life is. I couldn't stop there; I had to go on. It was as if I was trying to make myself crazy by reading a book that now existed solely to spill secrets that should have been taken to the grave with its author.

Every day I was haunted by thoughts of my forsaken babies. Each time I held my first-born in my arms, I could think of nothing else but the ones that were never meant to be. With my second living child, I desperately wished and prayed that I would be granted the gift to finally show my love to my offspring. I foolishly allowed little Nancy certain liberties that slowly began to unravel an unstable character; someone who, before long, I would no longer be able to recognize.

All day, every day, dreadful thoughts of the discarded babies in the form of recurring questions threaten my sanity. Did they think me a murderer? Had I been punished for revoking their lives before they had a chance to even take their first breath outside of the womb? Did they curse me with babies who refused the nourishment I desperately tried to give them from my breast? Was it they who placed the belief in my mind that I did not deserve my living children? Were my doomed babies responsible for destroying my ability to love Mia and Nancy the way a mother would naturally love her children? Or was it my guilt that evoked all of the anguish that I have suffered as a result of my actions so many years ago?

It wasn't until I stopped reading that I realized I had not been breathing. I released a breath from deep inside me and sunk lower into the couch as I read more. The pain she suffered seemed utterly unimaginable. I would never have wished it upon my greatest enemy, yet, my mother chose to suffer it alone. I flipped through the pages of the journal, reading passages about how she hated her life, how she loved her husband but could no longer touch him, how she had made all the wrong decisions.

How could I confide in my husband when he himself has never known about the abominable actions I took before he and I ever met? How could I tell the love of my life about my heinous past without risking the loss of his love and respect? I could never find the courage to tell him.

My eyes happened to fall upon an admission of how old the babies would have been: *Had I allowed them all to survive, these children would have been six and eight years older than Mia.*

My mother also wrote about how she welcomed her dreadful disease and looked forward to the day it would finally consume her body, giving her emotional pain the release she long desired.

The memories of having one too many procedures stayed with me always. I had carelessly abused my ability to conceive once by engaging in unprotected sex. Learning my lesson proved fruitless, for my second—and last pregnancy before Mia—would have given me twins. Yet the torment of feeling that the time was not right led me to another accursed decision that would continue to persecute me for the rest of my days. Yes, the sweet relief of disease—for it was a promise of deliverance—was a welcomed misfortune. And the irony of ovarian cancer did occur to me, confirming to me that it was my final punishment for the loss of life that had resulted from my negligence.

The words were powerfully overwhelming. My mother's emotional agony was deeper than I had thought. She was tortured, more so than I could ever imagine. Her journal carried emotions which I could not even comprehend. My mother was so miserable that she longed for death.

Another page revealed my mother's feelings about my choice of career, solidifying my profound guilt for never reaching out to her while she was still alive. *Is it my ego or shame that keeps me from telling Mia how proud I am of her for using her talents at the magazine to foster an audacity in our people to follow their creative dreams and rise above hindrances that seek to weigh them down? In her pursuit of a career I did not condone, she succeeded in accomplishing the very thing I thought she could not. She has inspired a whole new generation of creatives and thinkers, and she did it without the support of the one person who should have always believed in her brilliance. This I will forever regret.*

I was sure that the unfamiliar pang in my stomach was a result of finally learning that my mother did in fact see the value in what I did. The tears that now marked my face had a will of their own. My mother was proud of me; it was confirmed. She was proud of me yet I would never be able to hear her say those words. I would never be able to share a tender moment with her, letting her know that it didn't matter how long it took her to come around. The fact that I now knew she believed in me meant absolutely everything to me.

However, the turmoil expressed in her journal kept me from enjoying this newfound knowledge. I stood up abruptly and tossed the book down on the couch as if holding on to it would somehow infect me with her tragic aversion to her own life. Her journal was an escape for her. Just like Tyrese's poor mother, my own mother suffered from a pain that she felt no one could help. But unlike Tyrese's mom, my mother used her journal as an outlet for her pain. Were her entries desperate words written to free her from all those feelings that she thought she could not otherwise express? I couldn't take it any longer. I wished that my selfishness hadn't prevented me from being there for her for at least one moment before she passed. I could have done that, whether or not I understood or forgave. I could have just *done* it. I wished I had known about the torment she put herself through. But more importantly I wished I had let the love that was still so strong rule me, instead of the anger I had nursed for so many years.

The room was spinning—or was it my mind that caused the illusion? I reached for the wall to steady myself. Suddenly feeling my stomach churn, I ran into the bathroom across the hall and reached for the toilet bowl. I flipped the lid and seat up together just as the churning inside me released the contents of my stomach. My throat burned with intensity. I wasn't sure whether my wailing cry was a result of the stinging pain in my throat or the result of all that I had just learned. The sound coming from my mouth was completely foreign to me, yet I was very aware that it was coming from me, nonetheless.

My mind buzzed with so many questions, and I couldn't hold onto any of them for too long. Did I want to know all of those things about my mother? What would Nancy's reaction be to the haunting words on those pages?

Why did those words affect me so deeply? My poor mother suffered, and I wasn't there for her. What kind of daughter was I?

I sat on the floor, leaning my chest against the bowl, my eyes looking at the disgusting slop inside it. I felt heavy, unable to move, as if lead had replaced all of the fluid in my body and forced me to remain still. In my weighted state, a numbness grew from the pit of my stomach and traveled to my chest, staying there, and in all of its discomfort, admonishing me for my mother's pain. Even when my mother was dying, I failed to see her weakness. All while growing up, her attitude towards her family and the respect she received from her colleagues deceived me into thinking that my mother was strong. The pain that she revealed through her wretched words in that journal devastated me. I didn't know what to do with the knowledge of her pain. Perhaps I had been paying for my role in contributing to my mother's distress. My mother. She had been the one person I regarded with absolute respect. My mother was the rock and cornerstone on which our family was built. The leader both in her professional world as well as in her family life. The thought of this woman in pain felt like a blade twisting in my heart, ensuring its agony.

I knew now that it was guilt that prevented me from being able to move. All these years, I made it all about me and never considered what my mother was possibly going through. I was such a cold person, a selfish, self-centered bitch who made everything about *her*. With all the strength I had within me, I reached my hand to flush the revolting bile, desperately wishing I could flush away the hurt, the heaviness, the self-centered part of me as well. I took a deep breath. Finally feeling the normal sensations throughout my body and regaining command over my limbs, I slowly rose to my feet. Finding a bottle of mouthwash in the medicine cabinet, I rinsed my mouth out and splashed water across my face. In utter despair, I sluggishly walked back to my mother's office and retrieved my cell phone from my purse to call myself a cab that would be willing to drive me to my apartment in Manhattan.

I felt completely depleted as I waited in the August heat on the sidewalk directly in front of the large house. The minutes seemed like hours. I stood motionless like a lifeless zombie, unable to understand any of the feelings inside of me. I needed to talk about it; I needed some form of a release. A sudden impulse came over me to call Nancy. Again, questions raced through my mind about why I didn't wait to connect with her before reading the journal's contents, about whether she'd be angry with me for that. I needed to know how she would have handled the information.

The automated voice picked up, informing me that the number I had dialed was not available and to please leave a message after the beep. "Nancy, this is Mia. I was at the house today. Nancy. I found the box. I found the fucking wooden box. It's on the couch in mom's office. Can you call me please? I need to talk about this."

Gradually, I began pacing the sidewalk. I now felt desperate for her to call, as if my sanity hinged on it. I needed to know what her reaction would be when she read it. I wanted to know what she would think and what she would do to prevent herself from going crazy upon learning our mother's secrets.

A car finally arrived. I clutched my cell phone in my hand on the ride home as if that would make Nancy call me quicker. I dialed her number again, and again the voice message came through. Where was she? Why wasn't she picking up? I needed to talk to her. Frustrated, I hung up. The endless ride home forced the thoughts inside my head to fill me with anxiety.

When the car finally turned onto 73rd street, I exhaled. Home. Relief. It no longer mattered how long it took to get to the safety of my home. All that mattered was that I was there. And there I stayed for the next few days in the deepest depression I had ever experienced.

Part 5

Falling into Darkness

Chapter 33

Wednesday Night, August 21 - Sunday, August 25, 2002

Since the first night I learned of the existence of my mother's wooden box, I thought I wanted to know more about my mother and why she treated Nancy and me the way she did. I was entirely unprepared for my image of her as a strong Black woman to dissipate so quickly and so completely. Knowing what she went through emotionally somehow humanized her for me, and I started to feel for her the way I never did when she was alive. Or rather, the way I never did *as an adult* when she was alive. It was too late to harbor that kind of love and sympathy. I refused to be reminded of the fact that when she died, I continued to resent her and everything about her. After reading her journal, the guilt of never allowing myself to feel compassion for a woman who was in pain haunted me deeply.

My thoughts turned to Tyrese, and I immediately felt a wave of complete relaxation throughout my body. Every time the phone rang, I thought it would be him. I suddenly realized that I wanted to share with him what I learned about the reason behind my mother's rigid authority over Nancy and me. Instead, I found myself becoming annoyed as I screened all my calls, before deciding to let the answering machine deal with the rest of them.

A knot in my stomach prevented me from sleeping and eating. Surprisingly, I spent many hours thinking about my time with Tyrese and how I had betrayed Derek. The gnawing feeling in my stomach and tightness in my chest developed each time I thought about my infidelity. And I stayed that way for days, going back and forth between thoughts of my mother's personal hardships and thoughts about how wrong I was for my transgressions against Derek. When I wasn't thinking about either one, my thoughts painfully rested on the fact that I had been overlooked for a position that I felt would have propelled me forward so completely in my profession. I told no one about what I was going through; I stayed in because the thought of facing the world outside was simply too difficult.

I reached over and pulled open the drawer of the end table, finding my own wooden box that contained stories and poems and novellas that I had written when I was in college—the same work I had given up in order to please my mother. In it, there was a bright, yellow notebook with a cartoon image of a black woman with an afro on it; she held a notebook in one hand and a pen in the other. The gift had confirmed my father's support of my writing. The pages in the notebook were empty, save for about four or five. I took a pen from my purse and thought about what Tyrese had once said: *"Okay, so you were an unexpected surprise. Turn that around and make that something millions of people will celebrate for years to come. You were put here in this world to do something wonderful, Mia. Stop thinking the negative and finally do what you were meant to do."*

So I started to write. My story began with the day I placed the pink petunias and yellow marigolds on my mother's gravestone; the same day I attempted to break up with Derek earlier in the month. So much had happened since then that my hand started to cramp as I wrote about it all. But I ignored the pain because I had a story to tell, and I was going to tell it. My story continued when I found my mother's note, to the serendipitous moment I met Tyrese and how he made me feel, to my sessions with Dr. Flare and my lunches with Glory. I filled the pages with the details and my thoughts about my discussions with my father and then my sister's unexpected phone call, and how that led us to finally speaking and confiding in each other. It included my arguments with Derek and the solace I found in Tyrese; the days at the office and Morgan's email acknowledging Bill Anderson's promotion. My hand used the pen to write about my affair with Tyrese and my suspicion about Glory and Derek. I could not recall the last time I had written so much, and it felt wonderful to be using the pen again as my instrument of art. But it didn't matter how much I wrote. The sadness overpowered the joy that writing gave me. I was suddenly snapped back into present-day reality.

Morgan called several times, at first leaving messages of concern, which frankly baffled me. But on the third day, he asked me to come in so that we could have a conversation. I was still too angry and disappointed to even listen to anything the man had to say. If he was not going to acknowledge all the hard work I put in for the magazine, then I didn't want to have anything to do with him or the job. I knew my worth as an industry professional.

With a determination my tired, aching body had no choice but to obey, I left my room and marched into the kitchen. Opening cupboard doors and slamming them shut, I frantically searched for something that would help numb the pain I was feeling. I found nothing. I opened the refrigerator and was so excited to find two bottles of white wine. It was the brand Derek always bought me, which made me think he must have brought them with him the last time he was there, intending to cook me dinner but making out with Glory instead. It didn't take me long to open one of them and when I did, I chugged it straight from the bottle. I brought it back to my room with me and climbed back onto my bed, cross-legged.

My mother loved white wine. My mother. Her depression, the babies she aborted, and how she sacrificed her career to bring me into the world. Although she loved me, I was not a pleasure for her. I was a curse, her daily reminder that her life did not turn out exactly the way she had thought it would. Yes, she had the career, the husband, and the babies. The problem was in her inability to enjoy it all because of her guilt. She wrote it down herself: the fetuses that were never allowed to exist haunted her, taking away her ability to love. Being human, she had to place the blame for this loss on someone. Either she secretly blamed me and Nancy for that or she blamed herself, never allowing herself the pleasure of giving or receiving love from the family she had always wanted.

I took another gulp of the wine as my thoughts turned to Nancy. Her reaching out to me was probably the bravest thing she had done in her entire life and I felt a sort of guilt for never reaching out to her in our younger years. Once she started misbehaving in high school, I didn't try very hard to reel her back in. I suddenly felt that, as an older sister, it was my responsibility to help guide her away from the negative influences that bore their clutches into her. I looked at Nancy now—rather, thought of her—in a new light. She was the precious one who had gone out of control due to neglect. Almost instantly, and without conscious effort, I found a special place for her in my heart. I loved Nancy as I did my father. To tell them so felt like a next to impossible task.

It hurt. Everything from the recent revelations about my mother's struggles, to the pain of her passing, to Derek ending our relationship. It hurt so much way deep down inside, in a place I could not reach, let alone comfort. Embracing my stomach tightly, I rocked back and forth, sitting cross-legged on my bed. I felt it in my stomach, a tightening ball that threatened to squeeze itself up through my chest and into my throat. The tears flowed like water from a spout and it was not my will to stop them.

What I felt was much more than sorrow. It was a deep fury directed at myself. I betrayed Derek; he didn't deserve that. At the time, I felt no shame or guilt about my deception but now I was finally able to see the indecency of my actions. We both had the right idea during that last meeting at Alimento—it was the healthier choice for the both of us. Fond memories of our times together—getting to know each other at the beginning, the dinner where he told me he'd continue to be patient—those and other experiences we shared flooded my mind and I felt my heart skip with a new appreciation for them. And although knowing that he would not be in my life in any capacity hurt, it finally felt okay. I was no longer afraid of it. Nevertheless, the longing for a vice that one has become accustomed to is still a longing that leaves one feeling empty when lost.

Taking two more gulps from my wine bottle, I thought about Tyrese and his hard, beautiful body, his sweet face and his ability to make me open up and talk about the things that bothered me until I understood more about myself. It was my fear of entering a real relationship with him that made me break up with him. Each time I thought about my last conversation with him, it made me sick to my stomach. So I pushed those thoughts away as I drank the last of what the bottle had to offer me. However, the thoughts kept coming back like hungry animals and therefore consumed me, sinking me further into my depression.

Although I knew these feelings would eventually subside, that knowledge was too far away; the present was unbearable. I felt incredibly lonely. I was so lonely that I couldn't imagine being around another person. Depression had hit me hard in the past, but this time it seemed so intense, so inescapable. Curling myself into a ball on my bed, I cried new tears for nothing in particular, but everything in general. I felt as though I was trapped in a deep, dark hole, with no escape from the lonely agony of bitter, angry feelings. I wanted the feelings to go away. I wanted it all to be over.

Chapter 34

Monday, August 26, 2002

I finally checked my messages. Tyrese had called to see how I was doing and left a message asking to see me again. Derek left a message saying he would return his key to my apartment on his way out of town. Glory surprised me by calling as well, but she didn't leave a message; I saw her number on my caller ID.

Morgan reached out to me, leaving a preposterous message about possibly sharing the position of editor in chief with Bill Anderson. Apparently, Morgan didn't know me at all if he made such a laughable suggestion that, were I to agree to it, would undermine the integrity I had as a professional. Then my assistant Cynthia left a rather sweet message, letting me know that I could call her if I needed to.

I was especially surprised to hear Dr. Flare's voice on the answering machine requesting one final session as some kind of closure. She also had suggestions for other treatment options she felt I would be open to.

My father called to tell me that he spoke to Nancy and that they wanted me to come by the house. Nancy herself finally called me back and expressed her interest in talking to me because she had read the journal. I couldn't do it. I didn't have the energy to talk about what I learned from reading my mother's journal. I just couldn't do it.

The phone calls annoyed me, so I turned off my machine and completely silenced my phone.

Chapter 35.

Tuesday, August 27, 2002

Tyrese stopped by my apartment, saying through the door that he was worried about me and that he knew I was home. I didn't answer the door.

Chapter 36.

Wednesday, August 28, 2002

My father sat at the edge of my couch as Nancy stood directly in front of Tyrese's painting, intently studying it as if to discover a hidden message within it. Together, they had come to my apartment door early in the morning because I had not answered any of their calls or returned their messages. My father had been worried about me after learning that I found my mother's journal and insisted that Nancy come with him to check up on me.

"I never knew this book existed," my father said, his eyes locked on the journal in his hands. He turned the book around and backwards and every which way, almost determined not to open its pages as if he were afraid of the secrets spilling out and hurting us all. But that was too late, wasn't it? If it weren't for the pain that escaped from the book's pages, my sister and father would not have been there in my apartment.

"Was it you?" I asked my father in such a small voice. I didn't have the energy to even speak, let alone amplify my voice. Feeling numb, I didn't even have the drive to get up and sit next to him. Instead, I stayed at the other end of the couch, wrapped in a blanket that kept me safe.

"Was it me, what?" my father asked, looking at me.

Nancy turned away from the painting and gazed at my father, her arms wrapped around her chest, waiting for his response.

"Were you the father of the babies that she aborted?" I asked, a fraction louder than before.

My father inhaled and then heaved a loud sigh. "No, I wasn't. According to the details of the journal, I met your mom shortly after—" he hesitated. Then, in a voice that resembled the same heartbreak as my own, he said, "the twins." He raised his right hand to his eyes, suppressing the tears that threatened to fall. Nancy walked to him, took the journal from his left hand and gently placed it on the couch beside him. She knelt in front of him and hugged him in a gesture that was so sweet and tender. They spoke not a word. He allowed himself to be held.

I wasn't the only one suffering with the revelations from my mother's journal yet I still didn't know how to process the information. I couldn't imagine what the knowledge of my mother's unveiled secret would do to my father. He never understood the source of her discontent yet he continued to love her anyway. That was a special kind of strength that I didn't think I would ever know.

Watching my father and sister together, I willed myself to get up, almost tripping off the couch, which startled Nancy. Once I gained my footing, I secured the blanket around me once more as I placed myself next to my dad and leaned my head on his shoulder. He put his right arm around me, and we sat in silence. Nancy remained kneeling on the floor, holding onto my father's free hand.

"It wasn't her fault," Nancy said. "She did the best she could for herself and also for her family. Just like you said once, Dad. She had her demons and they kept her from seeking the help she needed. She's just another example of the pressure we as black women place on ourselves to remain strong despite the things that threaten to dismantle us. She was ambitious and catered to her ambition to the point where it ravaged her and took the love she had for her family as a source of payment. I don't know why she didn't confide in you, Dad. All I know is that she was lost and didn't know how to find her way and the only way to keep herself sane was to release her demons in a diary that promised not to judge her. Like so many black women of her generation trying to make it in a world where she was still invisible, she was forced to figure it out on her own and in doing that, she lost herself." Nancy looked at the two of us and smiled. "I don't know about you, but I know that it gives me comfort that she found *something* to help her through her despair." She looked at Tyrese's painting on the wall and then to me. "The paintings helped her, Mia. I believe they did, not just her diary. That's why she needed to share *both* with us."

A wave of goose pimples came over me. "Wow, Nancy," I said with a deep sense of pride and admiration for my sister. "It makes so much sense the way you just explained it. How did you do that?"

Nancy smiled. "The psychology classes are helping. But I feel I would have never understood her without this diary." She picked up the journal and leafed through the pages.

"Tell her what else you're doing, Nancy," my dad said, seeming proud.

Nancy exhaled and then said, "I finally started seeing a therapist and I'm only a few sessions in but *my god* does it help to just get the stuff out of my head and start unpacking them."

My father slowly stood up to address us as Nancy took his place on the couch, right next to me.

"Your mother was a troubled woman and I didn't know how to help her—just like I didn't know how to help both of you girls. There were so many things we could have all done differently. Your mother never told me about her past and as far as I know, she didn't share that information with the doctors who were trying to help us have a baby. She carried that burden alone. There was no way for me to know she went through what she did. When we first started seeing each other, she seemed happy and free. She never seemed weighed down by her past. Every day with her was a joy until we started having trouble getting pregnant."

He looked at me then and said, "When she was pregnant with you, Mia, I could feel her slipping away from me. I tried to get her to open up to me but I think you now understand your mother's resolve to remain silent about her trauma. There were times when she seemed like the woman I fell in love with and those days were great. And that's how you came into existence, Nancy." He turned to Nancy and smiled very briefly before continuing his story, focusing his eyes now on both of us. "But she slipped away from me again and never came back. Emotionally, she was just...gone. We were like two strangers keeping it together for the sake of the kids and I never understood why. She pushed me away every time I tried to get her to open up but I also wanted to respect her feelings. I just didn't know how to help her. Now looking back, I simply didn't do enough. And for that, I will always have guilt. I just let her be, thinking she would talk to me when the time was right for her. That moment never happened."

He trailed off and Nancy and I kept our eyes down to the floor.

My father continued. "During her last days in hospice, I helped to take care of your mother and I knew there was nowhere else I wanted to be. I knew that this would be the last thing I could do for her to show her that my feelings for her were not gone like I thought they were. And she understood that too. There was no confession about her procedures. But she did tell me that she never stopped loving me." He pursed his lips together. "And that gave me peace."

"But Dad," I said. "If that gave you peace, then why are you still carrying so much sadness over it? You don't seem to be at peace."

He sat down next to Nancy, his body facing our direction. "It pains me to see the way your relationship with each other has disintegrated, knowing that your mother and I are to blame for that. Your mother's death left us all with a heaviness that we never took the time to resolve." He paused. "But what I see happening between the two of you and finding and reading her journal is making me understand that I could never be at complete peace until I see the two of you girls loving each other again. That's why I knew it was important that you come here with me today, Nancy."

"Dad," Nancy said. "Did she say anything about us before she died?"

"Yes," he smiled. "She told me that you two would find your way back to each other. She made me promise me that I would be there for you when you do. And that's why I'm here today with you girls."

Then, Nancy did something completely unexpected. She stood up, stepped over to my father on the couch and sat on his lap, placing one arm around his neck as she used to do when we were children. A warm chuckle escaped my father's mouth as he held Nancy in his arms.

"I love you girls," my father said. And there was so much warmth and hope in the way that he said it that I felt a wave of serenity flood over my entire body.

I moved closer to them on the couch in order to join in and found myself feeling like I wanted the moment to last forever and if it did, then depression, melancholy and desolation would no longer have a place in my mind and in my life. But the moment couldn't last forever. And soon, after they had gone, the wretchedness I had felt before my family's visit consumed me once again like a monster that fed on the pain and suffering of the doomed.

Part 6

A Way Out of the Box

Chapter 37.

Friday, August 30, 2002

It had been two days since I'd spoken to anyone. My father and Nancy's visit really helped me to finally understand just how trauma can damage so many more people than the ones suffering with it. My mother's trauma affected the way she and my father communicated to each other and the way they raised Nancy and me. That, in turn, marred my relationship with Nancy and our relationship with our parents. Our toxic family dynamic informed the questionable decisions I made at work, with my friends, and with men. The more I thought about the endless cycle, the more I felt defeated.

I hadn't set a foot outside my apartment or eaten properly for an entire week. Hunger left me feeling frail and lethargic, causing me to fall into a semi-dream state. I lay in bed thinking about Tyrese. My mind quickly wandered to the very moment he broke up with me. With that thought, a strange sensation in my stomach compelled me to roll out of bed and onto the floor. On my hands and knees, I regurgitated all the wine and whatever else was in my stomach. God only knew what I could have possibly thrown up for I hardly had anything to eat in days. I sat against the bed in my own yellow, slimy vomit, too weak and too sad to lift myself from the mushy stink. My throat burned, my nausea remained, and I felt so disgusted with myself. I sat on the floor against the bed a few minutes longer before experiencing a sudden case of hot flashes. I took my top off because it suddenly felt like too much clothing. Then in an instant, the room was filled with a brilliant glow and everything seemed so perfectly vibrant and clear. A cold sweat overwhelmed me. My vision blurred and distorted everything I looked at. Finding it extremely difficult to see, I tightly shut my eyes for a few seconds of relief, to no avail.

A migraine was coming on. I remembered the medication I had recently refilled. I tried to carefully stand up so that I would not slip and fall in my own vomit. But what I had tried to prevent happened anyway. I banged my right knee on my night table as I slipped. The pain was so unbearable that I grabbed my knee as a strange moaning sound escaped my mouth. Standing up proved to be almost impossible. The room was spinning. I was delirious with fever and feeling quite feeble. Positioning myself onto my hands and knees, I limped my way to the bathroom. It took me several minutes, but I finally made it. Using the toilet as a crutch, I pushed myself up and managed to get the medicine cabinet door open. I knocked everything into the sink and onto the floor, finally retrieving my migraine medication.

I swallowed one pill, drinking directly from the faucet. Fully aware of the fact that my stomach was completely empty and would probably reject the pill, I took it anyway. I had to try something to prevent the pain from coming. It at first felt like a dull ache but was slowly turning into a pounding headache; I was desperate to avoid experiencing it again. I carefully sat back down on the floor to catch my breath. I thought about my mother and the personal torment she went through. I was just like her, wasn't I? Haunted by the choices I made in my own life. What kind of life was I living? No matter what I did and no matter what I tried, I would always be the same old miserable Mia Hill. I wasn't satisfied with just Derek but I had to have Tyrese too and then let go of him to be with Derek who didn't even respect me enough to stay away from my best friend. I no longer even recognized myself.

Breathing heavily, I thought about my father who was rendered emotionally paralyzed by the secret I asked him to keep from my mother. I caused that rift between us. I thought about Nancy and how she was finally doing something with her natural talent and insight. I was so proud of her. She had finally reached out to me and I was so grateful to her for that. Unfortunately, that moment in her bedroom as we discussed the paintings and the notes would be the best, most honest and anger-free moment we would experience together as adult sisters.

I prayed for Derek and the future of Jones Press. In the end I felt that Derek was not always there for me but I loved him for the support he tried to give me throughout the years. He was too wrapped up in himself and his business to ever really be there for me but I genuinely believe he did the best he thought he could to help me through my own issues. I was starting to understand that just because I kept him around did not mean I did it out of love. Derek wasn't always good to me, and I wasn't always good to him.

And just as I found myself feeling angry for the way I treated him, I heard the words come weakly from my mouth, "No regrets."

Tyrese was never far from my thoughts. His voice, the way he listened, those light brown eyes. I ended things with him so badly. I *was* meant to have a life with him; I finally understood that. But there were so many things keeping me from loving him. It was my fear of heartbreak that prevented me from pursuing a life with him. It was the guilt of having cheated on Derek that made me back down. Would I even have been happy in a relationship with Tyrese? I would still be me—unhappy, depressed, bitter and miserable. Being with Tyrese would not have magically fixed that. Nevertheless, I was thankful that he had come into my life when he did. Through his paintings, he helped me open up to discover so many feelings and emotions I had locked deep inside of myself. It was obvious that he had done the same thing for both my mother and my sister without even knowing it. His paintings truly did impress upon us the kind of sensibility he admitted he strove to spark within his supporters. And it wasn't just *The Box* that spoke to me. No! His painting *Solitary Agony* was not just for Nancy; it was a grim reflection of my own little agonies. It was also his painting, *Comfort in Pain* that resonated with not just my mother but with me as well.

I finally understood the meaning behind it. I finally understood that I essentially did not want to rid my life of depression. I tried to deny that fact when Dr. Flare said it to me during our very last session. And I thought about it briefly when I saw the *Comfort in Pain* postcard in my mother's office, standing against the books stacked on her desk. The fact was my depression was something I didn't want to lose. My depression had always been with me; it was my comfort blanket. It was not only a part of me; it *defined* me. As bizarre as it seemed, I actually took comfort in the pain of being depressed.

Suddenly, everything made sense. I had that same profound feeling of clarity as I did the day when I tried killing myself in college. For the first time since then, I felt connected to my emotions. It was as if I finally knew that my depression and my acceptance of it was the answer. I had found comfort in my pain my entire life. I knew what I had to do. I needed to finally accept, and succumb to, my comfort blanket. I resolved to let it smother my pain. I resolved to let it smother *me*.

Taking in a deep breath, I grabbed the bottle of pills and crawled back into my bedroom, avoiding the watery vomit on the floor. After climbing into bed, I shifted my body several times before finding a comfortable position. I closed my eyes, took another deep breath, concentrating on the air that filled my lungs and finally exhaled. My hands shook uncontrollably. Deciding that I was finally doing the right thing, I nervously uncapped the bottle and emptied its contents into my mouth. The second bottle of wine I had found inside the fridge was on my night stand. I stretched my body to grab the bottle, pouring all of the wine inside my mouth and swallowing all of the pills.

There. It was done. There was no turning back. As scared as I was, I knew that I had no choice but to deal with the consequences of my actions.

The pills I swallowed quickly took effect. With blurred vision, I looked at the phone. I had wanted to use it but didn't know why. I might have even reached for it. Either I actually dialed someone's number, or the pills distorted my perception of reality.

It didn't take me long after that to fall into a deep and restful sleep. And during that sleep, I dreamed of a beautiful smiling woman who looked just like my mother. Her dark brown hair was neatly matted down, and her chocolate-colored skin glowed radiantly as if she had her own spotlight. I remembered feeling glad to see her; a feeling of comfort and love enveloped me. The smiling woman told me that my life of pain was about to end. But I already knew that because that was what I had intended by taking the pills. She then told me that I would eventually make the right decisions. To imply that I would be making more than one decision was to suggest that my current attempt would once again fail. I assured her that it was too late, that the pills were already in my system and that I intended to end my life. I wished her away and she suddenly disappeared.

I slowly opened my eyes. From where I was by the bed, I could see Derek at my bedroom doorway looking at me. His eyes were glassy as if he were deliberately preventing himself from crying. I noticed that people in dark uniforms, who seemed to take good care in moving my body, surrounded me. Who were they? Extremely disoriented, I could not figure out what was going on. I looked at Derek again. Although he was standing several feet away from me, I knew that the hand holding mine was his. It was comforting to have him there with me during my final moments. I knew I was dying; nothing they could do for me would save me. That was the way I wanted it.

My eyelids were heavy, so I closed them. Somewhere in the far distance I heard someone calling my name. One of the men in uniform looked into my eyes as I slowly opened them again.

"Can you do something for me, Mia?" he said. "Can you keep your eyes open and look at me? Keep them open, Mia. We don't want to lose you."

But I felt so sleepy. All I wanted to do was rest and close my eyes. I looked again at Derek across the room, and I squeezed his hand. Just as I opened my mouth to tell him that everything would be okay, I fell asleep again. My mind told me that I was dreaming.

I saw the smiling woman and she filled me with so much comfort and warmth. She showed me someone's wedding, but I couldn't make out who was getting married. She next showed me a man holding a baby, but I didn't know who the man was because his face was blurred. Finally, the smiling woman showed me a woman in a business suit shaking another woman's hand. She was beginning to annoy me. Why was she trying to disturb my plans? Why did she make me feel like I had so much to live for?

Tyrese's painting suddenly came to mind, the painting that I secretly loved the most. I was the woman in that painting; Tyrese had even recognized that. Throughout my entire life I had perfected a box for myself so that no one could ever reach me emotionally as I turned my back on all who loved me. Now I would be placed in a real box. People would have no choice but to give up trying to reach out to me. They could finally see how well my box suited me.

But I didn't want them to give up trying to reach out to me. And I did. I wanted to remain hiding inside my box and at the same time I wanted to break down its walls to free myself. The smiling woman in my dreams confused me. I wanted to welcome my eternal sleep, but for some reason I couldn't. Why did I feel like I had something to live for, something to go back to? I turned my focus to my original plan. Two thoughts kept me from wanting to go back to life. One was that I was actually looking forward to meeting my mother again and sharing with her all that I learned in the past few weeks. I wanted to tell her, without any fear of doing so, that I loved her and that I missed her and that I finally understood her and her pain. And my second wish was to meet the siblings who were never given a chance.

But the smiling woman told me that there would be plenty of time for all of that. At first, I didn't understand what she meant by that statement. She told me that the fact that I could see her meant that death was not really what I wanted. *See* her? She didn't exist; I *dreamed* this woman. I was too heavily sedated by the migraine medication to think clearly. Could it be? There was no way an angel *actually* came to see me. No, she was a dream that my subconscious mind worked up just to save me from doing something I did not know at the time that I didn't want to do. Did I really have a guardian angel after all? She told me there was so much I had to live for and that I needed to believe in that. I felt my lips slowly start to smile.

"We got a stronger pulse!" a woman in uniform said. "Mia? Mia, can you hear me?"

The angel told me that I knew all along what I wanted to live for. There was only one thing, she told me, that I'd be willing to risk. And it wasn't even difficult realizing what that was. Tyrese. I was tired of being afraid, sick of feeling vulnerable. But with that one thought of Tyrese, I suddenly woke up coughing and throwing up. There was clapping and cheering. My body shivered in the cold air and someone placed a blanket over me. Disoriented and confused, it sounded to me like at least two or three more people were in my apartment, other than the two paramedics and Derek.

"We got her back, boys!" the female paramedic said. Then to me: "For a moment there, we thought you'd given up."

What had happened? What did she mean by that? Was my plan sabotaged? I inhaled deeply in order to calm myself, trying to understand what was going on. And then it hit me: I wasn't going to die. I had been given another chance. I exhaled in relief. At that moment, I realized that I really *didn't* want to die. I never really wanted to die. It was just that learning about my mother and the thought of never seeing Derek again and losing that promotion and breaking up with Tyrese all pushed me into a state of temporary psychosis where I just wanted to end the intense pain I had felt so deep within my soul. My chosen solution would have been permanent, but something more powerful than anything else in this world had other plans for me. For the first time since I could remember, I felt hopeful. The feeling made me smile. I was ecstatic inside. There was so much I wanted to do and accomplish that I decided that I could no longer allow my depression to keep me back. I had things to do.

I looked at Derek, and he heaved deeply as he closed his eyes.

"Thank you for calling them," I whispered to him, using what little breath I had inside of me.

"I didn't," he answered, moving closer to me. "They were already on their way when I came to drop your keys off."

I was confused. "Then, who?"

I suddenly became aware that the hand that was holding mine throughout the entire ordeal, and that was still holding on, did not belong to Derek. I looked beside me to find Tyrese smiling down at me. And as he did so, he squeezed my hand.

"Oh my God, Tyrese," I said, unable to control the flood of emotions that caused tears to fall from my eyes. After the way I had treated him and the mean things I said to him, I couldn't believe he was there with me. I was touched. I felt loved and cared for. I was overcome with emotion. He cared about me enough to help me in a way I would have never asked him to.

"You were here the whole time?" I whispered to him.

He nodded his head and smiled, taking my hand to his mouth and kissing it.

"If it weren't for you," I said, "I would have died."

My voice cracked, and I cried so hard that my head hurt. I cried tears of relief. I had finally allowed myself to open up and risk a love and a life I was so afraid would emotionally destroy me.

"Ssh," Tyrese said, quieting my tears. He kissed my forehead and then hugged me, placing my head against his chest.

I wiped the tears from my face and cleared my throat. "How did you know to come for me?" I asked him.

"Don't you remember?" he asked. "You called me."

What was he talking about?

"No, I didn't," I said, pushing myself away to look at him. "I never called you."

"Yea," he assured me. "You did. Right after you swallowed the pills. You called and told me you took the whole bottle and you wanted me to come right over."

Oh, my goodness! Yes, I did remember looking at the phone, but I didn't recall dialing his number, much less actually speaking with him.

We stared at each other and then he kissed me again on my forehead.

"You did it all on your own, girl. You pulled yourself through. You were gone for a while, but you brought yourself back."

Part 7

Life outside the Box

Chapter 38

10 Months Later

After I came home from the hospital the previous year, I had taken some time off from work to focus on starting group as well as one-on-one therapy with another therapist, Dr. Tracy Lyon-Brown, who also happened to be African American. The therapy sessions were long and quite difficult to handle, but my weekly acupuncture sessions and morning meditations helped smooth out my journey to emotional and mental health. It was a long road to recovery, and it could have been dark too, but I had Tyrese and my father and sister supporting me through it all.

My former boss, Morgan Riley, for some reason thought I would jump at the idea to share the editor in chief position with Bill Anderson. When I refused the offer and politely resigned my tenure at *Fresh Voices*, I didn't worry about my next steps because I felt so empowered by standing up for what I believed in. Not too long after that, I received a call from Tiana Brown, Tyrese's cousin, the woman I had met at his gallery the day I was there to interview him. She had been following my career and wanted to know if I were interested in taking on the position of Managing Editor of her newly launched literary magazine *Black Prose Literary*. The position didn't provide a higher salary than what I had received at *Fresh Voices,* but the potential to grow with a company created by a black woman that celebrated the achievements of black women was something that was incredibly exciting to me.

I shared my personal story in the pages of *Black Prose Literary,* using that opportunity to explain what depression is and the different ways it can affect people and their loved ones. My article was so well-received that it even interested Midnight Muse Publishing House, one of the oldest black-owned book publishers based in New York City. They approached me with a deal to write a book about my experience. I used what I had started writing during my dark days that last week of August the previous year. The yellow notebook my father had gifted me had become a tool I was able to use to share my message about trauma and depression. It opened the way for me to develop a platform on which to reach a larger audience. I was the subject of feature stories in magazines and local newspapers and I was invited to speak on some local television and a few radio talk shows. I accepted this attention as a blessing and understood it as something bigger than me. Though I was able to snag a book deal for my fiction work as well, my personal story of triumph over my battle with depression was the story I was meant to tell the world.

Derek's decision to sell Jones Press to Words-in-Rhythm, Inc. proved to be an extremely smart move. He called me once while I was still at the hospital but never called me again. I was surprisingly okay with that. He sounded excited about his new venture when I spoke with him so if I never heard from him again, I at least knew that he was doing well, and that he was happy. It would have saddened me to never have contact with him again, but I think that being with Tyrese truly helped ease me into that transition. I didn't miss Derek as much as I thought I would. Perhaps it was because I knew we had both made the right decision for ourselves. I finally made the choice to be with Tyrese. And I felt it in my bones: it was the smartest decision I had ever made.

As much as it surprised me, I was actually very disappointed to never hear from Glory again. Though I expected to see her every now and then at different publishing functions, I didn't. I never learned what became of her, and I mourned her friendship more than I probably should have. Having a girlfriend to talk to about things I couldn't share with my man was something I definitely missed. But most of all, I did miss her. After getting over the initial shock of realizing the kind of crude person she was when I first met her in college, I had grown to accept her the way she was, and I loved her for it. I was deeply sorry she was no longer in my life, despite what she had done to me. She said some cruel and hurtful things to me at the end, but I felt like I knew where it all was coming from. I'm not going to say she didn't mean it because I think she did. But I was able to look past that and focus on when our friendship seemed genuine, and that really helped me through it all.

I also finally came to the realization that I made a mistake in thinking most people would view my depression the same way Glory did. She showed me support, yes, but she never grasped the understanding that depression is a serious illness. In fact, my thought that I could *just get over it* was a result of what Glory always told me to do whenever I did mention anything about my melancholy. Unfortunately, her lack of empathy made me believe that others would respond to my vulnerabilities the same way. Thankfully, sharing my story with the public proved that belief wrong.

Things were better with Nancy; we weren't the best of friends but we were communicating. We talked often about our mother's journal, and our interpretations of what she wrote. It bonded us together in a sad, but powerful way. We were slowly putting the pieces of our relationship back together again.

And my dad came to see me every day. When he couldn't come to see me, he'd call. Though I found it to be a bit overbearing, I knew he was making a concerted effort to strengthen our relationship. So I talked to him. I told him how I was doing; I asked about his day. It was a challenge, but what I saw building between us was important to me. It wasn't a happy ending—he would never be a perfect father, nor would I be a perfect daughter—but it wasn't a tragic ending either. And, life didn't always have happy endings.

As for Tyrese, he helped me open up to the potential heartbreak only vulnerable hearts can suffer. I was more than happy to let him in. We didn't live happily ever after. There were times when life became too much, and my depression would come crawling back from limbo to haunt me, but Tyrese was always there for me. And I was there for him after the issue of *Fresh Voices* with my feature article about him hit the stands. Tyrese's new-found attention was a bit stressful for him at first. Yes, I finally saw a side of Tyrese that I had never seen before. He was very busy at the gallery, but the extreme amount of stress and pressure he was under gave us the opportunity to seek ways in which we could help each other de-stress.

I kept thinking about the inner turmoil I felt leading up to the second time I tried to end it all. I was in such a dark place. Now, it was strangely difficult for me to understand how hopeless and lonely I had felt, especially during a time when I knew that people all around me were trying to help. I had indeed been inside of a box, and I will never forget that pain. To forget the pain would be to forget where I came from and that would be like denying the person I am today. But as Tyrese had once wisely said, with my box finally gone and my walls forever down, there was no need for me to look back as long as I understood the hardship I went through in finally becoming a person I could deeply love despite my many flaws.

Chapter 39

August 1, 2003

My father, Nancy and I decided to visit my mother's grave together on the anniversary of her burial. It was a warm summer day; the sky was a bright blue with patches of clouds interspersed throughout. There was a slight breeze that kept us cool despite the sun's strength. We walked towards the gravestone in silence. Nancy had a bouquet of pink petunias and yellow marigolds that she positioned on the ground against my mother's gravestone. We learned through reading her journal that those were her favorite flowers. The irony that they represented anger, resentment and grief was not lost to her. So my father made sure he brought tulips and roses, happy flowers that counterbalanced the gloom of her favored floral arrangement. He set them on the ground next to Nancy's. He placed his right hand on the stone, letting it rest there for about ten seconds.

My sister took my hand in hers and flashed me a warm smile. I returned her smile. My father stepped back from the stone and looked at us with an unmistakable expression of contentment on his face.

"You girls will be all right," he said. "We will all be all right."

· · · ·

THE END

Overcoming Depression

THANK YOU FOR TAKING the time to read this story that is so very close and dear to my heart. I'm no stranger to depression and I talk about my struggles with it openly. I've been in therapy off and on for a number of years. I've taken medications (what I liked to refer to as "my happy pills") such as Zoloft to combat my depression. While I felt that medication worked, the serious drawback was that I had to consistently replenish. Below are several different things you or someone you know can do to overcome depression. There is no one formula because everyone is so different. But it's worth trying a few or all until you find one or a combination that works for you. But remember that one can only combat this thing if one has the mindset to do so.

Talk therapy. I've been in therapy for years and I feel it works because there is only so much complaining you can do with your friends. You need a sounding board, someone who is skilled in objectively listening as well as providing guidance and tools needed to handle situations that seem too overwhelming. Again, you have to want to get better in order for this to work for you.

Acupuncture. I've tried this many years ago and didn't really feel it was working until I stopped! The acupuncturist will know which pressure points in your body to use to help combat depression. This is something that may work in combination with any of the other suggestions on this list.

Meditation. I've been meditating every morning for a few years now and I find that it truly does help to focus my mind, calm me down, and fill me with positive thoughts and energy. A skeptic or someone with the belief that meditation is silly or can never work to empty one's mind of thoughts cannot be successful with this. You have to keep an open mind for this to help you. I didn't start feeling its affects until weeks after I first began meditating.

Exercise. I made a New Year's Resolution about ten years ago to work out every day because I knew that I needed consistency to see the results I wanted in my body. It took me months to realize that my consistent depressive state had disappeared when I maintained a strict exercise routine. If you've never exercised before or just don't like to, start off with something easy and enjoyable. I started with working out only ten minutes a day until I gradually got myself to where I am now. For those of you who hate going to the gym, you can do this right in your home like I do. It does take discipline and patience to start seeing and feeling the results.

Eating right. If you eat right, you'll have no negative feelings about the foods you put into your mouth. The idea is to avoid any negativity. If you like sweets, as I do, indulge in them—but don't beat yourself up for it. Leave the sugar and carbs alone if you know you'll feel bad about them later. Eat foods that maintain a healthy brain. Eat foods that promote happy moods and positive thoughts. You have to do the research to find out what they are. But the information is out there, and it is possible.

Your passion. Immerse yourself in the things that bring you passion. Is it drawing? Writing? Photography? Your kids? Reading? Helping others? What is that one thing you feel you cannot live without? Find a way to do that thing on a regular basis and you will find yourself happier, looking forward to spending all your free moments doing it and loving yourself for filling your soul with it.

All of these require work on your part. But if you truly want to overcome your depression, you have to put in the work and effort. *Disclaimer*: The suggestions on the list above are not necessarily approved by any medical board. These are techniques that I myself have tried and I offer them to you here as a starting point. There really is no easy way out of this. Therefore, I would like to strongly suggest that suicide is ***not*** an option.

~*Cathelina Duvert, 2024*

If you or someone you know is battling depression, please contact the National Depression Hotline at 866-629-4564.

Acknowledgments

This book has been with me for over twenty years, and in that time, there have been so many people who expressed interest in reading it and for that, I am very grateful. The first person to ever provide constructive criticism, which I didn't always take so constructively, was my own twin sister. Thanks for always being so honest, sis!

The very first editor to ever read the earliest draft of this novel was Tina Pohlman who told me that what I had was "a very good skeleton". I always remembered the time she took to discuss my novel with me without seeking anything in return. Thank you, Tina. Your honesty and kindness helped me push through. I'm thankful to Margaret Diehl, the first editor to look at my work after I put some "meat" on my skeleton. I was thoroughly impressed with your insights and suggestions and they took me so much further than I thought I could go with my story. And then there was Ms. Marita Golden, who I was so fortunate to work with on my final edits. Thank you for your wise words and insights, for helping me realize the holes in my story and for helping me believe that this was truly a worthy story to tell.

And finally I'd like to thank the Women's Fiction Writers Association, without whom I would have never been paired with my publishing mentor, Edy Hackett. Edy, your patience, kindness and guidance were truly a god-send because I was so overwhelmed before we were paired together that I was just frozen; unable to do anything. You allowed me to see that there really is a light at the end of the self-publishing tunnel.

Many thanks to those family members who obliged this future author and read and discussed the work with me while always believing in me. You know who you are! To all my good friends and the rest of my beloved family who have heard me go on and on about this book. It's finally done, you guys! I finally did it!

About the Author

Cathelina Duvert, a graduate of Hofstra University with a degree in Creative Writing and Literature, is known for her insightful blogging. She spent six years working in the book publishing industry before becoming a teacher. Her latest project, *Cathy's Cross: A Depressive's Positive Perspective*, chronicles her personal journey battling depression. Based in New York City, Cathelina's writing resonates with readers seeking understanding and inspiration.

Don't miss out!

Visit the website below and you can sign up to receive emails whenever Cathelina Duvert publishes a new book. There's no charge and no obligation.

https://books2read.com/r/B-A-CCQMB-ZPSLD

BOOKS2READ

Connecting independent readers to independent writers.